The Darkness of Light:
The Creation Catastrophe

B. P. Evans

authorHOUSE®

AuthorHouse™ UK Ltd.
500 Avebury Boulevard
Central Milton Keynes, MK9 2BE
www.authorhouse.co.uk
Phone: 08001974150

First published by AuthorHouse 6/29/2011

ISBN: 978-1-4567-8162-0 (sc)
ISBN: 978-1-4567-8163-7 (e)

Table of Contents

Chapter 1 –
The Perfect Universe

Every universe is a tiny speck compared to the realm inhabited by the Faaz, an intelligent race who created universes and watched them grow and develop. They could create universes exactly like their own, or completely unlike their own. It was a craft that was key to their culture and identity and made the Faaz the most developed of all the many types of beings who dwelled in that realm. A few Faaz were especially famous for their abilities to fashion extraordinary universes and nurture them well. They had been doing this for many generations, passing on techniques on how to create the best universe possible. One Faaz, however, didn't think the whisperings of the ancients would assist in creating the perfect universe. This Faaz, of the name Assa, hoped to break the mould and revolutionise the art and science of creating universes by making a universe so beautiful, strange and controversial, yet entirely new and somewhat risky.

*

'I have told you time and time again, Shenn, that you are not seeing my latest project.'
'Why not?'

'It's top-secret. I'm allowing no one to know anything about it.'

'Not even me and Hyuul?'

'Not even you and Hyuul. I'm sorry, but no.'

'Are you sure? Me and Hyuul won't tell anyone about it. You know you can trust us, Assa.'

'I'm sure. I just need to keep this project to myself that's all.'

'Is there anything so special about it? Is that why you're guarding it so defensively all the time?'

'Yes, there is. You will find out what it is soon enough. As for the time being, a little privacy wouldn't go unappreciated.'

'OK, then. Well, I guess just let me know if you change your mind.'

*

The Faaz had a long and colourful history; their universe-making history was equally as colourful, as they had been honing their technologies for generations, as well as sharing secrets and tips with one another. A multitude of created universes existed for all to see and wonder at. Some, of course, had died, but that was only a fraction of the total number – the ones that had perished were only a small amount of the very earliest that had been created. Assa's universe was going to astound generation after generation forever, something others had been unable to do, seeing as so many universes had been created it was now increasingly difficult to be original. It was going to fascinate and inspire every single Faaz to create new, dazzling and exciting worlds, something previous creations hadn't quite managed as well as they could have. Assa was going to take the science and art of universe making to a whole new level.

*

'I have told you, Hyuul, no. I will not allow you to see it or know anything about it.'

'Why not? Give me a valid reason, Assa.'

'No one must know about it. I can't trust anyone with information regarding my creation.'

'You can trust me and Shenn, Assa, we're your friends. Come on.'

'I can't even trust my friends.'

'Why not? If you can't trust your friends, who can you trust?'

'I just can't trust anyone. I'm afraid in case someone leaks details of it to others – I simply can't tell anyone.'

'Friends, *true* friends, wouldn't do that. *I* wouldn't do that.'

'Wouldn't you? I don't think you'd be able to keep it to yourself if I told you. You wouldn't want to keep it to yourself, believe me. You'd want to claim my brilliant idea as your own, and I can't afford to run that risk.'

'Well, then, you can no longer call me a friend, Assa, if you can't trust me. Just stay here and work on your world, but I won't be at the creation ceremony! You can count me out until you treat me as a friend and stop behaving so ridiculously!"

'You'll be there. I know it, everyone will.'

*

The building blocks of a universe were designed and then set into motion at a creation ceremony, where Faaz would gather to see the new world come into existence. Each universe was contained in an expandable orb, into which the universe could expand and grow. The creators simply stood back and observed as their universes grew and grew. A crea-

3

tor could speed up the universe, fast-forward it so as to get to the point of first life more quickly. It was extremely rare for a universe not to harbour intelligent life of some degree.

*

'I want to find out what's so special about Assa's new universe, Shenn.'

'Assa won't tell us, Hyuul.'

'I know, but why is Assa being so defensive? Assa has never been so reluctant to show us the plans before. This time, something must be different, since Assa usually can't wait to show us the plans. Why would Assa be so secretive and protective?'

'I have no idea. I think we need to respect Assa's wishes, though, and not inquire into this any further.'

'But Assa can't and won't trust us! Assa has deemed me and you untrustworthy. How long have we both known Assa for?'

'Pretty much our whole lives.'

'Exactly, and now Assa is throwing all that away.'

'But you can't begrudge Assa a little bit of privacy. Anyway, we ought really not to be too nosy.'

'If Assa wanted some privacy or wanted not to confide in us, I'd be okay with that, but what is vexing me is that Assa openly admitted to being unable to trust us, and unwilling to do so.'

'Assa is still our friend.'

'A lousy one.'

'Well I think you're just as bad as Assa. You're making such a big fuss and are prepared to throw away so much friendship without even giving Assa a chance to explain or apologise.'

'What are you saying, Shenn? I'm not as bad as Assa!'

'The way you're behaving right now, yes you are, Hyuul. We need to find out what is the matter with Assa, not storm around demanding to see the new universe plans.'

'I want to do both. Even if Assa's universe does happen to be ground-breaking, we should still be informed. Assa should be able to trust us with anything. We are friends.'

'You're making a big mistake, Hyuul.'

'Assa's the one who making the mistake.'

*

Universe creating was an art form. Some could make a living from it, but others tried and failed. For some it was a nice hobby. Some of the more learned Faaz studied creation and sought to learn exactly how they, beings of non-physical entity, could make *physical* universes. Faaz couldn't actually interact with their creations; once the universe was born and contained inside an orb there was nothing any Faaz could do until it eventually died and popped back out of existence. A group of scientists called the Elders were the highest authority on creation. To create a universe, one needed an amount of substance called Panmatter, which the Elders only gave to trustworthy universe creators – novices needed a qualification to show a high amount of education - for any misuse of the substance was a punishable offence, and it was a very complex substance to control and use. The Panmatter was physical, contained inside orbs so it could be conveyed, and was essentially a building block for the whole universe, as creators would draw up their plans and then crack the orb open and then apply the plans to the Panmatter inside, which was so-called because it allowed the creators to make practically anything possible. The crack was then sealed before the universe began with the big bang; occasionally the random inept creator forgot to rectify the orb in time and the universe ended up expanding out of the orb and creating a whole lot of mess. That particular creator didn't make any universes for quite some time afterwards. Assa's Panmatter had gone unused for quite some time now, as the new universe plans kept becoming more and more elaborate. Someday the orb would be cracked open, the plans would be applied to the Panmatter within, the crack in the orb would be sealed and Assa would watch as the long-planned universe would be born and grow.

*

Assa had told no one else the exact feature of the universe which set it apart from all others, a feature Assa was sure would revolutionise the art of creation forever; but this secret was not going to be spilled yet. Every creator had a ceremony for the unveiling of their latest universe, which was attended by at least a few of the Elders and some other Faaz. Today there were so many creators vying for glory and so many similar universes being created that it was rare for an unveiling ceremony to have a large attendance; it was rare in these times for one single creator to be held above the rest for their designs, as it had got to the stage now when there were so many creators that originality was very hard to come by, and that's why Assa was certain this universe was going to be exceptionally original and fiercely discussed. Assa had been promoting the unveiling ceremony for ages, ensuring all knew that this event was one not to be missed, though it would take a lot to impress.

*

Nothing would ever destroy this most perfect creation, nothing at all. It was logically impossible for this creation to be wiped out of existence as, unlike other creations, which eventually died, this one had been designed in such a way that it could last forever and ever and ever, continuing to amaze and inspire. Nothing would ever come to close to replicating the success this universe was, Assa hoped, going to achieve.

*

'I've got a plan, Shenn. I've come up with a way of finding out about Assa's universe-to-be.'

'What? Hyuul, you can't be serious!'

'We have to find out!'

'You mean *you want* to find out.'

'Aren't we in this together?'

'I want to be friends with Assa. Doing something like this would wreck any chance of friendship. Don't you realise that, Hyuul?'

'Assa destroyed our friendship long ago, Shenn. For absolutely ages we have tried and tired and tried but to no avail!'

'Even if Assa hasn't been as sociable recently, doesn't mean we should do this. Maybe Assa just wants to concentrate on the creation for a while.'

'Stop defending Assa! Are you in or aren't you? Assa needs a slap back to reality.'

'I'm not in, of course. Count me out. Don't come to me expecting sympathy or advice. You're on your own.'

*

'Assa! Assa! It's Shenn. I've something really important to tell you.'

'What? I'm very busy.'

'It's Hyuul. Hyuul wants to find out about your creation and has some sort of plan.'

'I don't care. Hyuul is not going to find out about my creation.'

'Hyuul sounds very serious and determined to find out what you're up to whether you like it or not.'

'Hyuul won't find out. Nor will you. Now leave me alone, please.'

'Aren't you listening to me? I'm telling you Hyuul is deadly serious! Your reluctance to tell Hyuul about your creation is only fuelling Hyuul's impatience and determination.'

'I'm busy, Shenn. Extremely busy. I haven't time to listen to Hyuul's empty threats.'

'But I'm telling you Hyuul is serious! These aren't empty threats!'

'Is this all you have to tell me?'

'Well, yes, but it's important. I'm telling you so you can protect your project.'

'Hyuul won't find out about it till everyone else does, which will be very soon. Hyuul can be patient, and you can stop wasting your time.'

'Fine! You can spend your time here cut off from everyone else working yourself to death on your creation. I'm willing to help you, but the way you're going on, treating everyone despicably, you're going to alienate everyone to the extent that no one will care about your creation.'

'They'll be impressed. Just you wait and see.'

'This is your last chance, Assa. Do you intend to remain friends, or would you rather spend all your time working on your creation?'

'The latter.'

'Goodbye, Assa. You've ruined everything.'

*

'I've tried and tried, Hyuul, but Assa has just become completely absorbed in that darn creation!'

'Surprise, surprise. Assa is not going to budge.'

'I know that now.'

'So, do you want to help me in finding out what Assa's up to?'

'I'm not stooping that low, Hyuul.'

'Who knows what Assa's creating! Assa could be making some sort of weapon or maybe something else. No one gets this worked up over a project! No one secludes themselves and rejects friendship when creating, it simply just doesn't happen! Assa's creating something abnormal, if you ask me. Whatever Assa's up to, we have to find out.'

'I...I think you are speaking *some* sense.'

'You want to find out as much as I do.'

'I...guess I do. But only for Assa's sake. We still ought to help Assa. Even if we do find out what Assa's creation is going to be, we shouldn't tell anyone about it.'

'I'm glad to see you've seen sense. Now, this is how we find out about Assa's creation...'

*

Shenn and Hyuul were disgusted to learn of Assa's plans. They were shocked and confused both by Assa's daring and by Assa's determination. Yes, this universe of Assa's would be a prototype, but a prototype, which, Shenn and Hyuul especially thought, would outrage the creator community. Assa seemed to ignore their reactions, and carried on with the plans nonetheless, despite even fiercer protests from both Shenn and Hyuul, fired by a determination to make Assa see sense and scrap the plans.

*

'I knew Assa was up to no good! Didn't I tell you?'

'Yes, you did, Hyuul.'

'Aren't you revolted? I mean, a universe with no free will? Assa has the nerve to pre-decide and pre-determine every single thought, feeling and action of every life form in that universe! And pre-decide every single thing that happens in that same universe! A universe full of slaves to Assa's decisions! It's absolutely disgusting! Creating a universe that runs according to one's wishes, its life forms ignorant of the fact that they don't have free will! That universe, if it goes ahead, will indeed be the first of its kind, but for all the wrong reasons! No one will accept it; the Elders will never condone such a creation, nor will the community.'

'Are you quite sure of that, Hyuul?'

'What? Of course Assa's universe will be rejected! How could anyone be insane enough to laud it? Pf! No one will accept this disgusting insult to creation!'

'It might be accepted.'

'Please tell me you think Assa's universe is a cruel, un-ethical creation?'

'Who is to decide that? Are we to decide what's right and wrong?'

'We create universes; we owe it to the life we create.'

'You didn't answer my question. Who is to decide what Assa's doing is ultimately wrong?'

'No one can ever truly know what is right and wrong, Shenn, you know that. We, as a community, decide what we *think* is right and wrong. We have free reign to create entire worlds, but we create worlds that aren't governed by our wishes and have always done so.'

'Just because we've always created universes with free will, that doesn't mean a universe without free will is wrong.'

'I can't prove to you that Assa's universe is wrong – I

never can. Right and wrong are opinions. I hope you share my opinion on this matter.'

'I can see where you're going with this. I'm not going to listen – no argument will persuade me.'

'But think of how much planning Assa has done.'

'So?'

'Assa will have achieved a monumental amount by the time the universe is finished.'

'Are you on my side or Assa's?'

'You can't make me choose! All I'm saying is you shouldn't shoot Assa down. Think about the positive points about Assa's creation.'

'I was going to see if you wanted to help me; obviously you won't want to.'

'Help you do what?'

'Stop Assa's universe from coming into existence.'

'You can't be serious!'

'Deadly serious. I'm saving countless life forms from a false existence.'

'By preventing them from being born?'

'It's better for them not to be born rather than be born and have no free will.'

'Assa will hate you if you succeed. Do you realise that?'

'Yes, but Assa already hates me, and you, it seems. The only thing Assa's concerned about is *that* creation.'

'Even still, you can't ruin Assa's project! You'll be in seri-ous trouble if you do – the Elders might even deny you the right to more Panmatter!'

'I'm willing to risk all that, Shenn. This universe must not come into existence. I shall see to that.'

'Count me out.'

'Fine.'

*

'If Shenn won't help, then I'll just have to do this on my own - but how? I could destroy the plans – oh, but plans can't actually be destroyed. Hmmm. I could steal the plans and hide them somewhere, but Assa might have numerous copies hidden away somewhere. Trying to persuade Assa not to go through with creating this universe is a pointless course of action. What can I do? Ah! I could tell the Elders who could then disallow Assa the right to Panmatter, but would they believe me and what proof could I show them? Argh! The creation ceremony is soon, so I haven't much time. Right, Assa's universe shouldn't come into being, but I can't do anything at all to prevent that from happening. I'll have to think of something to do. It's the creation ceremony, Assa smugly has the orb, cracks it open, then – that's it! That's what I'll do! Hah! It'll be risky, but it's my only option.'

*

The plan Hyuul devised was simple, but very risky indeed. It would ensure free will existed in Assa's universe, despite anything Assa could possibly do to try to stop this. Hyuul was certain the sabotage would have no chance of failure. The creation ceremony would still go ahead and Assa would still announce what was so special about the controversial universe, and then Hyuul would enact the sabotage, which would have to happen after Assa's announcement in order to justify it. Hyuul was certain this would work and wasn't afraid of any consequences.

*

'Fellow Faaz! I, Assa, invite you all to the unveiling of my latest project. The universe I have planned will be a groundbreaking, revolutionary prototype, which will astound and inspire you all. Much, much time and effort have gone into this design, as well as a heap of my own creativity and imagination. No other creator in all of history has made a universe quite like mine, I can assure you that! Once you have witnessed the marvels and sheer beauty of my design, you will take a brand new approach to universe creation! The perfect universe is almost ready. Very, very soon indeed the ceremony shall take place, to which each and every Faaz is invited, and there you will witness the birth of the first universe of its kind. I'm not going to reveal just yet what it is that makes this creation stand out from the rest; for that I shall wait till the ceremony, where I will amaze you all!'

*

'Assa, I really think you ought to be extra cautious during the creation ceremony. I think Hyuul might be up to something.'

'I can assure you, Shenn, that nothing whatsoever is going to go wrong. You both will be there, but nothing Hyuul does or tries to do will prevent me from creating my universe. Even if Hyuul dares to do anything, which is very unlikely, my security guards will stop him.'

'You'll have security guards there?'

'So many Faaz are coming; it'd be crazy not to have security. Once I reveal the details of this universe to the public, I shall become unbelievably famous and from then on I shall need the highest security.'

'If you say so.'

'It'll be one of the most memorable times ever, if not *the* most memorable.'

'If you insist.'

'Finally I can share with the world what I've been working on for such a long time! So much effort and time…and now all that awaits me are eternal praise and commendation! My hard work will have truly paid off when everyone remembers my name forever and every generation knows of me and of my great achievement. Assa, the creator of the perfect universe!'

*

'Assa's universe is going to be a creation catastrophe! Shenn, you know as well as I do that everyone will abhor it.'

'The thing is, I don't know. The ceremony's very soon, Hyuul; I really think Assa's universe will be admired. Can't you just give Assa's creation a chance?'

'I can't and I won't.'

'Are you coming to the ceremony?'

'Of course I'll be there.'

'You do know Assa's got security and everything? Anything you do will not go unnoticed and unpunished.'

'I'm aware of that, Shenn. I've recently come to the realisation that there's really nothing at all I can do. I tried thinking of plans, but none would work. I still won't accept Assa's universe for what it is though.'

*

Creation ceremonies were commonplace, given the large number of creators, and were often very similar to one another. So far, a vast, vast number of Faaz had turned up for the ceremony – a number many times greater than the number of attendees for a run-of-the-mill creation ceremony. Assa was delighted with the turnout. More and more kept coming, including Shenn and Hyuul. Soon it was full and Assa decided to have the ceremony out in the open, so many more could be witness. Assa rejoiced at the sheer volume of Faaz that had come totally unaware of how much they were about to be amazed.

'My fellow Faaz! It is with the greatest pride that I have invited you all to witness the birth of my new universe. I promised you all a revolutionary prototype guaranteed to astound you all, and that is exactly what you are going to get. I shall tell you all now exactly what it is that makes my universe stand out, then I shall apply my plans to the Panmatter, with you all as witnesses to this most important day in the history of creation. Now, as you all well know, all universes are created when plans, consisting of the laws of nature and science the universe obeys, are applied to them and the creator watches as the universe then takes its own path. Some universes produce copious amounts of civilisations, rich and prosperous, whilst others produce weak civilisations which soon die out. Each universe is different. Some of the more noted creators of our generation have created beautiful universes with thriving civilisations, but I do not think that's enough. I wanted to start a revolution because the art of creation has remained unchanged since it began. The way a universe is produced is fast growing stale. It is difficult for anyone to gain recognition in these times, seeing as there are so many universes and so many creators. However, I am making a change to all that. My universe will differ from all others in that I have not only planned the laws of science, which will govern the universe. I have pre-decided every single thought and feeling every living thing will have and every movement it will make. Furthermore every single action, reaction, occurrence, happening – every single thing that happens in my universe will have been pre-decided by myself. For ages I have been deciding every single thing that will happen in my universe, and I will continue to do so, to ensure the universe always remains governed by me. This universe is also a display of my imagination and vision: I have thus had licence to make whatever I want, and I have chosen to make a universe of real beauty, awesome wonders and astoundingly developed civilisations. All this you will be able to see once I apply the plans, my delicate plans, to the Panmatter. So, there you have it: the perfect universe. Now are there any questions?'

'Assa!'

'Yes?'

'It's Hyuul. All I want to say is that your creation *catastrophe* isn't a triumph; it's a disgusting piece of work whose inhabitants you wish to cruelly control, robbing them of free will and a chance to think, feel, decide for themselves. Elders, you have to stop this monstrosity of a universe from being born, please!'

'We approve of Assa's originality and we all commend Assa to the highest degree for this feat of breathtaking daring, unmatched determination, ingenuity and highly laudable devotion. We are eager to see this universe born. Security!'

Hyuul was removed from the bustling crowd of Faaz, who were excited, motivated and stunned, listening to Assa's every word and disregarding Hyuul.

'Sorry about that! I can assure you all that nothing else shall ruin this day for you all. And now for the creation!'

All the Faaz watched in awe as Assa held the orb full of Panmatter high above for them all to behold.

Hyuul had calmed down and the security let go.

'I've calmed down. There's nothing else I can do,'

Hyuul moved back through the crowd as Assa made another self-appraising speech. Hyuul soon found Shenn.

'How dare you, Hyuul!'

'It's all part of the plan, Shenn.'

Assa cracked the orb and everyone watched as Assa applied the plans to the Panmatter then sealed the crack in the orb.

'Now the plans have been applied! Yes!'

Chapter 2 –
The Creation Catastrophe

Inside the orb Panmatter was rapidly stirring. It shrank and shrank further and further inside the orb until it was infinitely small. But, there was something else there. Inside the Panmatter, which was now starting to change into the atoms Assa had decided upon, were tiny, tiny anomalies, instruments placed in the Panmatter by Hyuul to thwart the plans. The Panmatter formed the atoms Assa had designed, but they started acting of their own accord, due to this alien matter. The swirling mass of atoms reacted around the tiny anomalous specks. Everything collapsed together into a single dot, the atoms Assa had designed and the anomalies which, few as they were, would have a devastating effect on the atoms around them. The dot gradually grew smaller and smaller and the atoms were packed together as tightly as they could be. The ball kept shrinking until -

'Now the big bang is about to happen!' Assa cried out with glee.

Orbs were designed to house universes, but they were also designed to show certain parts of the universe at the creator's will, as if the orb had some sort of screen wrapped around it. It was also as if there was some sort of camera inside the orb itself as well, as one could show what has going on a large screen if the correct actions were carried out. This was how a creator could show off particular parts of the universe. There was now a large screen behind Assa and many others were placed around the area, on which the shrinking Panmatter was being shown for all to see. Assa couldn't detect the anomalies just yet, but soon, Hyuul realised, Assa would notice the slightest change, the slightest deviation from the meticulous plan, at which point Assa would realise all the plans made had been thwarted. Hyuul also knew that if Assa realised this after the universe's big bang had taken place, it would take so much longer to rectify than if the anomalies had been noticed before the big bang happened. Now that the big bang was happening, Hyuul watched rejoicefully as Assa confidently simply observed the crowd's reactions as opposed to the developing universe. The orb's edges were showing what the screens were showing. By now there was a very tight, compact ball of atoms packed so densely together it was glowing white and could be easily mistaken for one single speck of light. The longer Assa watched the audience, the longer Assa would go without realising.

Then the infinitesimal ball exploded, and everyone watched transfixed as the massive explosion sent super-hot atoms in all directions. It was all too awesome to take in for Assa, having spent so long and having devoted such amounts of time to this universe. Although pretty much all of the audience had witnessed the birth of a universe before, there was a feeling that this one was special, and they watched in awe as the universe expanded into the nothingness of the orb at an amazing rate. They were mesmerised and some found it hard to take in that this reaction had actually been designed and was all part of some large-scale plan. Some Faaz couldn't comprehend how anyone could plan something of such a grand scale.

'The start of the perfect universe.'

'Don't you mean the creation catastrophe, Assa?'

'Security! No more of this, Hyuul!'

'Don't bother, Assa. Watch your precious universe. Notice anything…*different*?'

'Stop talking nonsense.'

'I'm not talking nonsense, though. Look at what you've created and see what's happened?'

'What do you…?'

Although the universe was continuing to expand and nothing appeared to be wrong, Assa inspected the universe and then noticed something was wrong.

'HYUUL! SECURITY, BRING HYUUL HERE NOW! Everyone, I apologise, but…Hyuul has just…has just destroyed…the plans for my universe. No, this cannot be happening. The amount of *time* I have spent on this plan, and Hyuul has *selfishly* wrecked it. THIS CANNOT BE HAPPENING.'

The crowd was stirring and all had turned their attention to the deflated Assa; some started leaving, let down by the easiness with which this seemingly revolutionary universe had been corrupted. Others were stunned and upset; some were simply confused.

'Hyuul, I want to speak to you. NOW!'

Hyuul gladly broke away from the security and headed up to Assa.

'How DARE YOU, HYUUL! HOW DARE YOU! Not only have you wrecked my universe, you have also very selfishly prevented the start of a new age of universe creating. Fortunately, I noticed early on and can repair the damage, but what you have done is unforgivable.'

'I told you to think twice about this universe. This universe is cruel and disgusting, well, *was* cruel and disgusting. *I* saw to that.'

'You insolent, vile and pathetic little –'

Shenn appeared from the mumbling audience to say, 'Assa! Let it go, okay? Surely you have copies of your plans? Can't you just request more Panmatter and apply the plans to that?'

'I didn't make any copies. Making copies would have taken an extremely long time, time which I don't have. You don't appreciate how much *time* I have spent on this universe, none of you do. I could make other plans, but that would take almost as much time as the original plan took! You are very lucky I can repair the damage done, otherwise my anger would have been limitless.'

'This universe should *never* have been brought into existence, Assa,' Hyuul exclaimed, making this sentiment particularly emphatic to the audience.

'Free will is morally mandatory for every universe, Assa. We should have drilled that notion into you before you wasted so much time concocting this travesty of a universe.'

'There are no rules when it comes to creating universes. I checked and double-checked. What I'm doing is not only perfectly legal, but it is also the only way in which the art of universe creating can move forward. My universe is the first of many of a new age, a new age which will not stop at this universe. I will rectify the damage you did and assure you all that this universe will go ahead exactly as planned. In order to do that, I will do something which has never been done before: I will make myself half-physical in order to be able to fully interact with the universe and rid it off the anomalies.'

*

Creators were non-physical, that is to say that they weren't made of the atoms which their universes were made of. They could apply plans to Panmatter, which was physical, but couldn't fully interact with it. Creators could enter orbs and see universes for themselves, but they were unable to affect it in any way whatsoever. Therefore, once a universe was created, there was nothing its creator could do to change it. Assa has discovered the answer to one of the most heavily debated questions among Faaz: whether or not it was possible for creators to physically interact with universes. Assa had discovered how to become half-physical whilst doing research and tests for the universe and had intended to give this discovery more importance, yet Hyuul's sabotage had lessened its impact. Everyone was talking about the first universe that lacked free will and how it had been corrupted just as it came into being.

Yet despite the sabotage, Assa's universe received universal praise once it was confirmed by the Elders that the plans were genuine and Assa showed them how the plans could be applied to Panmatter and that the universe could be constantly sustained by continuously applying newer plans to it, thereby guaranteeing it longevity. It was said that this was one of the greatest travesties of recent times and Hyuul was therefore disrespected by the creator community. It was generally agreed that Assa would be remembered thence onwards for the ingenuity, originality and daring shown in creating such a universe, despite its relatively short life. Thus, Assa was revered, but not as much as Assa would have liked.

*

Time works in a very funny way, in that time in created universes runs as fast the creator wishes it to run, so a billion years in a created universe could pass by in a Faaz second. Assa currently had the universe on pause just a few moments after the Big Bang: what had once been a miniscule speck had now exploded in all directions and atoms had shot off in every direction at an unfathomable speed with such unthinkable force. All this was paused, yet once it was resumed, it would simply continue to expand as if there had been no pause at all. Pausing a universe for however long a time simply had no effect on it whatsoever.

Assa now had the challenge of finding the anomalies and destroying them entirely then adjusting the universe, so that it was exactly as it had been planned, so it would then continue as if nothing had happened. This was a great challenge and a rather tricky one.

Firstly, Assa entered the orb normally, that is to say as a non-physical being and was very soon in the frozen universe: the sight of this paused big bang left Assa dumbfounded and inspired. The atoms were halted in their rush to zoom across into nothingness, their automatic rush to give the universe size. This mass of atoms would eventually continue to expand in all directions, stretching the universe as far as it would go. The heat in that one tiny speck that started it all was infinitely hot, yet had cooled significantly with the big bang, although it was still unbelievably hot. Fortunately, Assa was immune to this. On and on Assa searched, looking everywhere for the rogue particles.

*

'What you did was disgusting, Hyuul.'

'I had to do it, Shenn. And it succeeded! Now Assa's in the universe trying to find what I put in there.'

'What *did* you put in there?'

'I found notes Assa had made on how to become half-physical when I was looking for the orb. I was initially going to steal the plans so Assa couldn't apply them to the universe, but once I saw I could become half-physical I decided that introducing alien particles to the universe, thereby spoiling those precious plans, would teach Assa a lesson. So right before Assa came to the creation ceremony, I became half-physical and put some atoms from one of my own universes in the Panmatter Assa was going to use. I couldn't resist telling Assa in front of everyone.'

'And that's all you did?'

'Yes. Assa had to be taught that there must be free will in all universes.'

'I agree that free will ought to be prevalent, but surely it makes no difference to the inhabitants of the universes? Those living in Assa's universe would have no idea whether or not they had free will. They'd be unable to tell whether or not it was all planned. In fact, inhabitants of every single universe will question free will and whether or not everything in their universe was pre-decided.'

'The difference is that in normal universes, inhabitants can think *freely* and are able to come up with ideas all by themselves yet in Assa's universe, sure inhabitants might consider free will and debate about it, but all that would have been pre-decided by Assa. The ideas and thoughts would not be their own; they'd be Assa's. Yes, they'd not know their whole lives have been pre-determined, but they'd be living empty lives.'

'But if they don't know they don't have free will, then what's the problem?'

'The problem is that we know they don't have free will and we ought to be concerned. We ought to be rallying round as a community, denigrating this creation of Assa's because of its lack of free will. I'm stunned it's being lauded so much. We should be thinking about the poor inhabitants-to-be of Assa's universe.'

'Why do you sound so concerned, Hyuul? You've already

sabotaged Assa's universe – you've given the future inhabitants free will!'

'I think Assa could very easily find and remove the particles I placed in the universe then set everything right so it's going according to plan. The universe is incredibly young and therefore the atoms have just started moving, so it should be easy for Assa to set them right.'

'So you knew all along that this could happen? Why didn't you simply just put many more particles into the universe?'

'It's all part of the plan.'

'Hyuul! Are you saying you plan to do this again?'

'I wasn't going to tell anyone, but I think I will because I owe it to the future inhabitants of Assa's universe. Yes, I plan to sabotage that universe again, once it's unpaused. I'll admit it proudly. *I* should be the one who's lauded for setting right a universe that is morally wrong.'

'You shouldn't be doing this. Assa has come up with this idea and should have the right to follow that idea through.'

'Not while I'm around.'

'How do you plan on sabotaging it again?'

'You should be able to work it out.'

'You're going to place something more than a few atoms in it, aren't you?'

'A few things, actually. Actually, I think I'll put many things in the universe and hide them very well so Assa can't ever find them!'

'I'm going to let Assa know.'

'Even if Assa knows, I can still get into the universe and sabotage it.'

*

24

'Look, Assa, just listen to me. Hyuul is going to sabotage your universe again.'

'The nerve!'

'I'm sorry about all the stuff Hyuul's done. I tried getting the idea into Hyuul that you should be allowed to follow your idea through, your *great* idea. However, Hyuul just won't accept the fact that there can be universes that don't have free will. I personally think it makes no difference whether there's free will or not – it certainly makes no difference to the inhabitants in question. Hyuul is determined to give free will to your universe. I should warn you that I think even if you repair the damage done by this second sabotage, Hyuul will keep introducing foreign atoms to your universe so as to disrupt your plans.'

'I too can tell Hyuul's passion is not going to burn out anytime soon.'

'What are you going to do then?'

'I can keep pausing the universe and repairing the damage done by Hyuul – but why should I have to spend so long looking for anomalies and rectifying damage done? What I'm going to do is ensure that Hyuul never does anything to my universe again.'

'Assa...what do you mean?'

'I have potentially the most unique and important universe that's ever been created. I was too short-sighted to see that Hyuul might read my notes on how to become half-physical and would then succeed in polluting the Panmatter. What I have to do is destroy my notes on how to become half-physical.'

'Why? That's a massive breakthrough in its own right! That would have received just as much attention and praise as your universe had Hyuul not ruined it. Why?'

'Hyuul now knows how to become half-physical; there-fore, the only threat to my universe at the minute is Hyuul.

But, so long as I have the notes, someone could steal them or find out from Hyuul how to become half-physical.'

'But Hyuul's the only one who feels this way! Everyone loves your universe and is appalled at Hyuul's actions.'

'I will destroy the notes. I've memorised them. Once I'm sure the universe is safe, then I'll make them public. As for the plans, they're safe because I'm the only one who can apply them, because of their complexity.'

'What about Hyuul then?'

'I can't have anyone destroy my universe, I simply can't!'

'Assa, what about Hyuul?'

'I will have the orb guarded perpetually. Security around it will have to be the best possible security. All threats will have to be nullified.'

'Assa, you can't!'

'I am very lucky I can repair the damage, very lucky indeed because my universe is so very young and relatively simple. If it happened that I couldn't fully repair the damage, there would be no way whatsoever to alleviate my anger. It is also a very difficult and time-consuming task because I have to account for my half-physical self being there. So I have to retrace my path and make sure everything is right.'

'What about Hyuul, Assa? You said all threats had to be nullified.'

'I'm not going to kill Hyuul. I am known as a great creator, one of the best and most important ever and once I finish rectifying my universe, I'll then be able to resume it and show everyone the wonders I've created. I will not be so silly as to tarnish my reputation by committing murder!'

*

At the same time, Hyuul was already in Assa's paused universe, paused because Assa hadn't yet fully repaired it.

Hyuul had tricked Shenn into thinking the next sabotage would only happen once the universe was unpaused, whereas the next sabotage was actually happening right now. Hyuul reckoned Assa would greatly amplify the security around the universe so now was the time to act. This time, however, Hyuul wouldn't be placing extra-universal particles into the frozen mass of hurtling particles; instead Hyuul intended to place the new particles, the many trillions upon trillions of new particles, into the nothingness that the universe would gradually expand into. Assa's rectified universe would then meet these particles when it expanded. And so Hyuul travelled to well beyond the current limits of Assa's universe, so far that Assa's universe wasn't visible. Hyuul was still inside the orb, which on the inside was almost infinitely massive: each orb's inside was big enough to easily hold a universe that expanded for its whole life.

There, in a random place, Hyuul scattered a few million atoms into the nothingness. After travelling for a while, Hyuul left behind an object, a complex configuration of atoms. And so Hyuul went on and on, eventually encompassing the entire universe, sometimes leaving behind a random collection of atoms which would be scattered into nothingness, sometimes leaving behind a whole object. However, the last few objects and collections of random atoms Hyuul saved, deciding to use them at a later point.

*

'Now you are all here to witness the resuming of my universe. Unfortunately, due to a particular narrow-minded individual, the last time I started the universe off, there was a hitch and my universe couldn't go ahead as I'd planned it. This time, I have painstakingly corrected the universe and it is exactly as it should be. There are no anomalies whatsoever to cause chaos this time round. Once I have resumed the universe, I have a further announcement to make which I touched upon last time I was here but couldn't elaborate on due to the unforeseen circumstances. However, I will make that announcement very soon! After the blip last time, I have striven to ensure that my universe has but the best security around. Now on to my big announcement: whilst developing the plans and ideas for this universe, I solved one of the most hotly disputed questions we ask: how can we physically interact with our universes? I found out how to make myself half-physical so I could interact with the physical universes whilst still being able to interact with this world. I was lucky I made this discovery, for if I hadn't, I would not have been able to correct the damage Hyuul done.

Seeing as my universe is safe from any hostile Faaz, I will share with you all exactly how I discovered this, but I will refrain from telling you until I've resumed the universe and have finished talking with you about it.

Now, the current set of plans covers the birth of the universe and the beginning and development of the first galaxies and stars. Once the time comes, I will apply the second set of plans, which will herald the first planets and the earliest forms of life. Each set of plans develops the universe more and more. So far, I have fifty sets of plans and will continue making plans so long as I live.'

Assa then resumed the universe as the audience looked on in awe. Atoms continued to stretch in all directions, just exactly as Assa had planned. Every single atom moved in the exact same way Assa had decided. Everything was back to how it was destined to be. This universe was now going according to plan. Assa rejoiced and began giving a detailed commentary to the audience, reciting how this was the first ever controlled big bang and how this had been the hardest thing of all to plan, given its complexity and sheer importance. The audience were lapping it all up, mesmerised by the fact that this marvellous event had in fact been artificially reproduced and so meticulously planned. Assa beheld the audience's reaction and delighted in the reception being received.

Shenn was there among the audience, watching the first few moments of this universe and was hoping that, for Assa's sake, it would all go off without a hitch. The only thing that was different to the last ceremony was that Hyuul was not present. Come to think of it, Shenn hadn't since Hyuul since they'd last argued just after the first ceremony. Shenn assumed Hyuul had just gone off somewhere to hide away from the public scorn. No one knew where Hyuul was, least of all Assa.

*

'I'm exulting in the reception my universe and my discovery have received, Shenn!'

'I'm glad to hear it, Assa, and I'm relieved that Hyuul didn't manage to do anything this time round.'

'Hyuul will never dare to do anything to my universe ever again.'

'Have you seen Hyuul recently, Assa?'

'Not since the creation ceremony. Why? Does it matter?'

'I haven't seen Hyuul since shortly after, when Hyuul was expressing intentions to sabotage your universe again.'

'Well, clearly Hyuul has finally seen sense and has desisted from attempting another malicious sabotage.'

'I'm worried about Hyuul. This is not the sort of thing Hyuul would do, to simply vanish like this.'

'Maybe Hyuul has finally realised that attempting to sabotage the greatest and most innovative universe ever created was a stupid mistake to make and has gone into hiding to avoid shame and embarrassment.'

'Perhaps. But still that's not something Hyuul would do. Hyuul was so intent on going ahead with another sabotage, and as much as I didn't want Hyuul to do that, I'm surprised nothing was attempted.'

'I couldn't care less, Shenn.'

'Assa…you didn't…did you?'

'Didn't what?'

'You didn't see to Hyuul did you? You said you were certain nothing would ever happen to your universe again.'

'Yes, because the security has been increased ten-fold. Anyone wishing to enter the orb and see the universe first-hand has to undergo lengthy, regulated security checks and now that the universe is in motion, I check it very often for any anomalies anyone might have put in, although the chances of that happening are now nothing.'

*

Much, much time later, Assa's universe had continued to expand as according to the plans. Galaxies were forming and stars and planets were being formed within the massive, swirling nebulae. It was all going like clockwork. However, at one of the furthest edges of the universe, there was a solar system, beyond which lay nothing, a vast emptiness the universe would expand into. Half the time, the sole planet of this solar system was the last thing before the universe hit total nothingness, half the time its sun was. Of course, there were millions and millions of bodies lining the perimeter of the edge of the universe, but this particular planet was special because it was the first to happen to meet with something extra-universal.

The planet was a lifeless melting pot of superheated

gases, a gas giant. It was a rusty red colour with streaks of amber and salmon across its surface. The planet was a fuming inferno, seemingly without purpose. It was almost akin to its sun in vivacity and ire. There came a time, a very important and unprecedented time in the universe, when something was pulled into the planet's atmosphere by its gravitational pull. This object hurtled through space at an awesome speed and was quickly met by the atmosphere; the penetration along with the sheer heat of the planet caused the object to roast and explode into flames upon impact with the atmosphere and within a second it was now smithereens. Hyuul witnessed this from beyond the universe just after Assa had paused the universe, checked it and applied the seventh set of plans to it. Now Hyuul's aim was to ensure all the other objects and clusters of atoms made their way into the universe and stayed there for as long as possible before Assa checked the universe again. Because the universe now had many civilisations all across it, a much higher number of beings could have free will restored to them than if it were thwarted at an earlier stage.

*

The seventh set of plans applied, Assa confidently resumed the round of talks about universe creation and continued receiving universal praise and commendation. Seeing as Hyuul hadn't been seen for quite some time now, Assa was confident no sabotages would again be made on the universe. As such, Assa was checking the universe less and less regularly. However, when flying through the universe non-physically one time, Assa noticed something which caused instant fury: there was a rocky planet, most of which was covered in dark-blue ocean and whose few landmasses were sparse yet luscious. As such, the overall population of the planet was not too high; there were just over a hundred million of the highest and most advanced life form on the planet: large, imposing quadrupeds of faint purple skin with pug like faces and long, slender tails. These creatures dwelt in the rivers and rivulets and along side them in the grassy knolls and marshy swamps. This species was relatively young and had only been around for a short amount of time vis-à-vis the planet's history. Their evolution over the years was astonishingly fast and they soon dethroned another species as the most dominant of the planet: this other species soon fell prey to the quadrupeds and was almost wiped out. What infuriated, shocked and perplexed Assa was that this other species was never meant to be almost wiped out. According to the plans, the species that was dominated was meant to be dominant for much time to come and was destined for inter-planetary travel and eventually was meant to come into contact with a species from a planet orbiting the closest star. Instead, another species had become masters of the planet.

Assa instantly paused the universe and calmed down in order to work out what was going on. Sometime between applying the seventh set of plans and now, someone must have placed something in the universe to cause disruption and a chain of events that would eventually lead to the collapse of a species and the uprising of one meant not to be dominant.

Yet nothing had got past security. Nothing had entered the universe. Assa therefore concluded that any anomalies must have been placed in the universe before…but then again the last time Assa was in the universe, everything was fine. If there weren't any anomalies in the universe itself and no one had been able to place anyone, then where did the anomalies come from?

Assa pondered this for a while and tired to work it all out. The only way this was possible was if… - if the anomalies had been placed beyond the universe then the universe met them whilst expanding! That was it! Assa had worked it out: Hyuul had most likely done this and had likely placed many more anomalies in the empty space the universe would expand into. Assa then flew into the empty space beyond the universe and after spending ages searching, finally found a tiny cluster of atoms a few thousand light-years outside of the universe. The atoms had no meaning to them: they formed no object, instead they were just a meagre group of atoms that had no purpose other than potentially corrupting the precious plans. Assa wondered how many more groups of destructive atoms had been placed in the universe. Only one thing now mattered to Assa: to find the culprit to ensure this would never happen again. Hyuul must have become half-physical in order to accomplish this, so therefore Assa would have to entirely remove Hyuul altogether from the universe as Hyuul's mere presence in the universe was also affecting the plans. Assa would search the whole universe for Hyuul and even the space beyond the universe. As soon as Hyuul was found, Assa would ask Hyuul to leave the universe for good and be tried for criminal deeds and if Hyuul refused, Hyuul would be killed.

Chapter 3 –
Symmetry Peak

The knock at the door was getting louder and louder as Maude made her way downstairs. It was half past two in the morning on the 16th January, 2010, and the call she'd got half an hour ago had woken her up. Now her ride was here. Now was the time that she'd been dreading for years.

'So this is really happening then?' she said to the visitor outside her door, a large, brawny man of an imposing stature named Harold.

'Yes, it seems so. I can't actually believe this day has finally come. I've been waiting so impatiently for this – every day, whilst doing the most mundane, boring things, this has always been at the back of my mind. My patience is about to pay off.'

'I must admit, this is all a bit unnerving, don't you think?'

'How can it be unnerving? Aren't you excited? We're part of something massive, don't you realise that?'

'I do, but I'm not really sure whether I'm ready or not. I mean, it's all a bit sudden. When we were asked to do this all those years ago and then it never came to be, I thought that would be it. I thought it was just forgotten and we'd just carry on with our lives as usual. But now it's happening all of a sudden, the plans are being put back into action and it's got me a bit worried.'

'But our safety has been guaranteed. Our *lives* are going to be protected, Maude, don't you forget that. You wouldn't want Assa to hear you talking like this, would you?'

'You can't expect me not to feel a bit apprehensive,' Maude retaliated.

'You can back out if you want, but you know what will happen if you do.'

Maude stood on her threshold and stared into Harold's eager eyes, which seemed to be aglow despite the darkness.

'I'm ready,' she said after a moment's contemplation, though she didn't mean it.

The two got into Harold's car and he drove them out of the little village and on across Helmia, the crescent-shaped island.

'So where are we going again?' Maude asked as she zipped up her coat.

'To Symmetry Peak. It should only take us about half an hour to get there.'

'OK. What do you think our instructions will be?'

'Well, given the result on the Counter, hopefully this'll be it and there'll be nothing that gets in the way of Assa's plan.'

'I hope it will be the real deal this time as well,' Maude lied with the faintest hint of reluctance in her voice. She was horrified to find herself saying this.

'I should hope so too. We've been waiting for fifteen years!'

'Yeah,' Maude replied and took to looking out of the window at the nothingness that was rolling hills and fields. She lost herself in thought as time went on. This was the beginning of the end, she told herself, but it might not have to be. Something could go wrong. Something should go wrong – yet the plan was infallible, as was the mastermind behind it. She wondered briefly whether what was promised to her and Harold was just an empty promise, or whether those promises would actually be fulfilled.

'Aren't you nervous at all?' she asked Harold.

'Of course not! I'm too excited about the good that is yet to come for us.'

'But what if it doesn't?'

'It will and we will both play our parts very well, I'm sure.'

'Look, what if this doesn't go according to plan and we end up getting found out? What then?'

'That's not going to happen. The plan is fool proof: we both know its failure is an impossibility. Like we've been told, it's happened many times before and has always been successful. Anyway, who cares if we get found out? Assa will see to whoever gets in our way. Just concentrate on our *reward* once this is all over.'

'I must admit, the reward does sound very promising.'

'So stop worrying then. Nothing's going to happen to us.'

Maude wasn't reassured, however, and resumed looking out into the night. She reminded herself of the reward and how great it'd be, despite how fantastical it was.

'Plus, they'll get you if you quit,' Harold said rather menacingly, his eyes fixed on the road ahead.

'I'm not thinking of quitting!' Maude snapped.

'Good, because I can see you're becoming reluctant.'

'I want this as much as you do, OK? I'm just tired and have other things on my mind.'

'Well, like you've been told several times now, this has never failed and is not going to now. I won't tell Assa you've been hesitant this time, but you'd better hold your tongue in future.'

Maude didn't bother replying, choosing instead to consider things peacefully in her mind. The drive was getting rather bumpy here and there as they approached the mountain. Nevertheless, Maude fell asleep and was woken once they'd got there.

'Are we there now?' she said, surveying her surroundings, forgetting it was night.

'Yeah. Symmetry Peak.'

'That's the cave there,' she said after they'd got out of the car, pointing to a cave in the mountain a few metres away from them. Symmetry Peak was a flat part of land that jutted out from the mountain about two thousand and three hundred feet up and was home to a few souvenir shops, a café and a small car park; people would normally drive up here then walk the rest of the way to the top. The cave, too, was open to tourists but it was only about a hundred metres long before it ended.

'Right, here's your torch,' Harold said, handing it to Maude.

Once the car was locked, they passed the shops and café and entered the cave.

'I'll go first,' Harold decided.

'That's fine by me.'

And so they ventured forth, both of them gradually got swallowed by the darkness, the only light coming from their torches. Harold edged forward slowly, carefully scanning the view before him as he advanced. Maude did the same and occasionally turned and shone the torch behind her just in case. The air seemed to grow colder the further they progressed.

'Wait,' Maude instructed.

'What? We're nearly there!'

'Nearly where? The cave ends soon. I've been here before

– there must have been a mistake because it doesn't go on for much further.'

'No. We were told to come to this cave and keep going.'

'But it ends soon and there's nothing there. The ceiling's getting lower – after another minute or so it ends.'

Harold ran ahead a bit, the torch still aglow, and shouted back, 'there's no end to this cave!'

'What do you mean?'

'There's no wall. At least as far as I can see…'

'That can't be so. I was only here last October and the cave ended after about a hundred metres or so,' Maude was now running to catch up with Harold.

They stood next to each other, both torches shining the way ahead.

'Look, the cave turns to the left!' Maude said, not believing what she was saying.

'Keep coming,' a voice came from further down the cave, a voice that shocked both of them and steadied their resolve.

'See, we're doing it right,' Harold gloated to Maude, who was feeling more and more nervous by the second. The closer they got, the closer she was to making what could be the biggest mistake of her life. Harold didn't really care about the consequences or the aftermath, whereas they were all Maude was thinking about.

'Let's go on then,' he suggested, and they continued on, going further into the cave than perhaps anyone had gone before.

'What's going on here?' Maude mumbled, her nerves getting the better of her.

'You are well aware of what's going on.'

'I mean the cave! It was a solid wall and now it's just gone!'

'I don't think that's important. What's important is waiting for us at the end of this tunnel.'

On they went, eventually curving to the left only to hit a dead end.

Harold touched the cold stone wall and felt it a bit before disappointingly concluding that there was nothing there waiting for them.

'You didn't need to touch it to verify that it was there,' Maude derided him, but before the man could reply, something tapped both of them on the shoulders; they dropped their torches and spun on the spot. The cave was suddenly illuminated.

'Don't worry, the cave still looks dark from outside,' the voice came; what was standing in front of the two and what had tapped them on the shoulder was now visible: a really tall human being, but a naked, androgynous human being. It had no nose, hair, nipples, bellybutton or genitalia. It was a body devoid of gender and distinction. It looked oddly ethereal yet slightly eerie at the same time.

'Sorry, did my appearance startle you?' the human said, its voice low yet croaky.

Neither Harold nor Maude replied but merely stared at the blank body before them, but before they could take it in any longer, the body had morphed into a more typical human: a tall woman with long, wavy brown hair and casual attire. The being now spoke with a lowly feminine voice:

'Now, I am very glad you both have come. As you know, when I last visited Earth fifteen years ago, I would have checked the result on the Counter but Hyuul stole the orb from me. I eventually managed to find Hyuul after some time searching and gave chase. Tonight Hyuul flew down to Earth with the orb with me in hot pursuit, but therein lies the hitch: Hyuul has hidden the orb somewhere in Moistree or Leafdew, I am certain of it. What I need you both to do is to scour the *whole* of Helmia and find the orb in case it is somewhere else.'

'You finally found Hyuul then?' inquired Harold, knowing how long Assa had been conducting the search.

'Yes, although Hyuul is a lot more powerful than I'd envisaged. I still don't know why Hyuul is in this universe when so much damage has been done. Since I first realised what had happened, I calculated how much of the universe has been affected by Hyuul's disruption: roughly a quarter of the universe still goes vaguely according to plan, whilst the rest has been affected, be it planets sprouting new civilisations or stars forming where they shouldn't have. The damage will take me longer to rectify than it took to make all my current plans for the universe. I remember fifteen years ago when I saw Hyuul in the Helmian sky and I was immediately struck down then awoke to find my orb gone and Hyuul flying away with it. I would have come to you two to give you further instructions but I had to follow Hyuul. Tonight my chase ended: we fell through the sky locked in combat, then Hyuul zoomed off towards Helmia and flew to Moistree; I flew throughout the whole town looking for Hyuul, but to no avail. Then I saw Hyuul was flying back into the sky from Leafdew without the orb. I summoned all my strength and shot a destruction beam at Hyuul, powerful enough to maim, which sent Hyuul falling to the ground on the mainland; then I came here.'

'But what if Hyuul's dead?'

'Hyuul won't be dead. I still don't know what exactly Hyuul is. I've started to realise that Hyuul might actually be fully physical, in which case it's likely that I've succeeded in mortally wounding the piece of filth.'

'Why would...'

'Hyuul became half-physical to introduce atoms to the universe after the seventh set of plans were put into place. What I fear is that Hyuul went one step further: if Hyuul is fully physical, then as long as Hyuul exists in this universe, it can't go according to plan. Any anomaly, no matter how small, can trigger a chain reaction that can have devastating effects.'

'So if Hyuul's dead, then that's good?'

'Hyuul's last words to me will be the location of the orb.'

'So how should we go about scouring Helmia?' Harold asked quivering a little, though this went unnoticed.

'Be very discreet. Recruit helpers but only people who you trust entirely and who will not fail to give you the orb should they find it. Also, you must not tell anyone exactly what it is you're looking for. I myself will go looking, of course, but you two must still help me and scour Helmia, understood?'

'Yes,' Harold and Maude responded simultaneously, a slight hesitation in both their voices.

'Of course, once the orb is back in my possession, I will be able to continue perfecting my universe, and you two will remain in the shadows until the time comes. If you do exactly as you're told, I will reward you as promised. You must understand your roles are very important and I selected you two for a reason. What I need you to do in addition to attempting to find the orb is to find out whether there are large, blonde aliens in Helmia. They call themselves the Keelot. They once tried to sabotage my attempt to rectify a planet and I *almost* had to punish them. The Lormai have informed me that these aliens have been sighted in Helmia recently. Speak to people, search online, do whatever, because these aliens should not be visiting Helmia, let alone Earth.'

'Why?' Harold asked.

'I will *not* have them try to stop me again. I believe they came through with the Lormai the last time I visited Earth fifteen Earth years ago. I don't want them killed, because they are part of my original plan for the universe, but I don't want them here either. Let me know if you find out if any are on

Earth. I will *not* have them attempt to thwart my plans this time round – I won't have it!'

'Can't you stop them?' Harold asked, seeming concerned.

'Of course. I could wipe them all out if I so wished and I have been really tempted to, but I won't. There are two more matters: firstly you must maintain your covers and not discuss anything unless it is just the two of you, understood?'

'Yes,' both said.

'And most importantly, the Counter. What is the number on it?'

Maude felt her strength collapsing; she felt her knees growing weak.

'The last time I checked, which was last week, it was three-hundred and seven,' Harold said proudly.

Maude couldn't believe Harold's pride. She was looking at the floor, lost in the hope that this was all unreal.

'Three-hundred and seven? I had suspicions that the number would be high, but not that high. My mind is made up: the plan will go ahead. This planet will be transformed!'

Maude was bursting to escape the moment, Harold was delighting in Assa's glee.

'I will go to Hyuul and attempt to find out the orb's location, then I will look at the Counter, just to double-check.'

'Yes.'

'What about the test subjects?' Harold asked eagerly.

'If you happen to know any of them, leave them be. I insist you treat them as normal, which was the whole point of it after all. They have all served their purpose and don't deserve to find out what they really are. You are not to divulge information about the test subjects to anyone, understood? They could be used as weapons if in the wrong hands.'

'Yes.'

'I've changed my mind: I will quickly check the Counter

then will search for the orb myself; I doubt Hyuul will tell me the location of the orb anyway. Remember: finding the orb is of the utmost importance as is safeguarding the Counter - I am fully confident that no one can find it – anyway, Hyuul doesn't know it exists so its safety is all the more guaranteed. Once the orb's been found, then you will focus your attention on the search for the Keelot. Now find that orb!'

'Yes,' both replied, one with pride and eagerness, the other with slight hesitation and reluctance.

The woman before them morphed into the grotesque genderless human body and vanished before their eyes, as did the light in the cave.

'What now?' a panicking Maude asked after a few moments during which she attempted to take everything in.

'We go back to our homes and start searching for the orb; that is what we have to do, after all.'

'So this is it then?'

'Yeah, this is it. Well, let's go then! No point standing around here. There's an orb to be found.'

And so they both turned their torches back on and made their way back through the cave, the trip back less unsettling than the trip into the cave. They were out of the cave and back on Symmetry Peak before they knew it. The gentle breeze shook Maude and made her shiver. She looked out at the town far below in the distance, its night lights glowing incessantly.

'It's so beautiful,' she commented.

'What are you looking at?'

'Moistree.'

'Oh. Well, come on then. We have work to do.'

Maude hesitated for a second, captivated by this rare view of the town; in the distance, shining just as brightly was her hometown, Puddlepond.

'Alright, I'm coming!' she moaned when Harold started coughing.

The two were soon in the car and were heading back down the side of the mountain, the only noise being the sound of the car.

'I can't believe that just happened. I mean, Assa – there! Right before us again! It just seemed so unreal.'

'What's wrong with you? You knew Assa was going to come back one day, so why are you acting all worked-up and stressed about it? Deal with it: it's happening!' Harold was clearly getting quite flustered now.

'You do realise exactly what we got ourselves into fifteen years ago, don't you? It's perfectly acceptable for someone to have second thoughts and be anxious when they're caught up in something like this. Yes, I am worried. I'm worried for everyone out there. For once, stop thinking about yourself and think about other people!'

'There's no point worrying about other people, you know that.'

With that, conversation between the two ceased and Maude once again lost herself in her thoughts until the car came to a stop.

'Thanks for the lift,' she said to Harold as she got out.

'Remember, we have to do this. Let me know how you get on,' he said, before driving away, leaving Maude alone in the starry night outside her cottage. She watched as he drove off and wondered whether he was being sincere or not. Taken aback by the suddenness of Assa's arrival back to Earth and the night's events, she went into her dainty cottage and collapsed in tears on the sofa.

All the different possibilities and outcomes were being unwillingly played out in her head. She knew that they were all disastrous and that she should never have got involved in this, but deep down part of her knew this all was inevitable and was always going to happen sooner or later. She was lying down on the settee sobbing hysterically, letting all the pent-up fear and anxiety out. She knew she'd got herself in a hole with slippery slopes and that there was no way out.

'Time is running out,' she mumbled to herself through her outpourings of tears.

She grabbed a cup from the coffee table and threw it against the wall, smashing it into pieces. Another cup she threw, and another until the wall was partially bespattered with splashes of coffee and the carpet was strewn with shards of china.

'You're wasting an awful lot of china,' came a voice. Maude jumped up and stopped sobbing.

'Who said that? Get out of my house!' she shouted, spinning round on the spot too fast to notice the person standing beside her dining room table.

'I'm here,' the voice came again.

'Oh, it's you. You startled me!' Maude said, going over to the visitor and hugging her.

'I'm so glad you're here, Susie!' she added once consoled a little, letting go of her visitor.

'I take it you've just got back from meeting with Assa?'

'Yes. I'm just completely overwhelmed and don't know what to do. It's so out of the blue.'

'So this is it then: Assa knows the number on the Counter has passed two hundred?'

'Yes…I'm horrified, Susie, absolutely horrified.'

'Did Assa say anything more?'

'We have to find the orb, that's the most important thing and something about finding the Keelot and leaving the test subjects alone, but the orb – Assa was really concerned about the orb because Hyuul hid it and is searching Helmia now to find it, specifically Leafdew and Moistree.'

'Which is why I need you to have a look at your dining-room table,' Susie said, indicating with a turn of the head the dining-room table, on which was the orb.

'That's it! Get it out of here, Susie! Do you realise how dangerous it is having the orb *here*?'

'It's okay, Maude. Calm down. It'll only be here for a couple of days.'

'A couple of days! A couple of *days*!!'

'Yes. Then it will be moved.'

Maude took a few moments to recover, looking into Susie's stern face, then asked,

'Is there any way to destroy it?'

'Sadly, no. This orb is indestructible. Therefore, the only thing we can do with it is to hide it somewhere good so as to delay Assa's plan being put into action. What's the deal with the Counter?'

'Harold told Assa the number and Assa's gone to double-check before starting the search for the orb. Susie, this cannot be happening! The day the number passed two-hundred was the day we knew this would definitely happen! Assa told me and Harold that if the number on the Counter surpassed two-hundred within five years that proved the human race was unfit to live on this planet, and after four years and one month, it passed two-hundred. I've been dreading this day for years. I feel guilty for saying this, but I hoped that Assa would return to Earth after my own death so that I wouldn't have to live this through,'

'We are still alive, Maude, therefore we have a chance. We can delay this happening and we are going to!'

'What good's a delay? The orb could be hidden for five years or five minutes and either way, Assa's going to do what Assa set out to do. We are all doomed: we were the day the test condemned us to our fate. Why not just get it all over with now?'

'How dare you! You are not just talking about yourself, do you realise that? You have everyone else to consider.'

'I'm sorry. I'm just tired and snappy and overwhelmed.'

'You're doing well. This is the worst news possible, I see that, but the only good that can come from it is that it urges us on,' Susie paused for a moment before saying, 'we need you to keep the orb in your possession for a short while, by the way.'

'Why me?'

'It has to be you. Hyuul suggested a place to hide it and I think it's a very good hiding place, but you are only to hide the orb there in a couple of days' time, understood? It is very likely that Assa will check Leafdew first then move on to the rest of the island so the orb will remain in Puddlepond until Assa starts checking Puddlepond, then it will get moved again.'

'Why not just hide it on the mainland or drop it in the middle of the sea?'

'Hyuul's instructions were clear.'

'Why can't it be moved now? Assa could very easily find the orb in *my* possession.'

'Yes, that is a possibility, but the hiding-place won't be suitable for a few days just yet, like I told you. I will let you know when you should go there. In the meantime, you will keep the orb here in your house.'

'Why are you doing this to me?!'

'I know it's not ideal, but trust us. We have this all thought out.'

'Assa is going to search the whole of Helmia for this orb and it will probably only take a few days. Chances are, Assa will search my house and find it.'

'If we find that Assa is searching nearby, we'll have the orb moved straight away, otherwise it's to remain here for a couple of days.'

'If Assa finds the orb in my house, do you know what will happen to me?'

'I'm sorry, but it's what we've got to do. I promise you the hiding-place will be ready in a few days and I promise we'll have the orb moved elsewhere if Assa's been searching in the vicinity. The longer the orb remains hidden the longer we'll have to prepare ourselves. By the way, we need you to find out from Assa how to get into the mountain.'

'When Harold and I went there just now, the cave was somehow extended beyond normal. I've been there several times but this time it was longer before. It was all Assa's doing of course.'

'Did you actually get inside the mountain?'

'We were just in the extended cave.'

'Well, find out if there's any other way at all to get into the mountain itself. It may be our only hope when the time comes.'

Maude looked pensive and disturbed. Susie looked at her sympathetically. Then there came a buzzing noise.

'It's my phone,' Maude jumped and gasped a bit before getting her phone out of her pocket

'Oh no.'

'Maude, calm down.'

Maude was holding the phone but hadn't looked at it.

'Is it Assa?'

'Yes.'

'Well?'

'Assa's just verified the number on the Counter and is now going to search Helmia for the orb. This is why the orb needs to be taken somewhere as far away from here as possible, Susie! How reckless of you to even think of keeping it here.'

'The decision has been made, Maude.'

Maude didn't reply. Instead she put her hand over her

mouth and gasped, then started panting and panting, slightly swaying back and forth until Susie came over and grasped her by the shoulders to steady her.

'Look, we're prepared for this. I reaffirm everything that I said before: we will look after you and will strive to keep the orb away from Assa for as long as possible so as to delay this all from happening. Look at me, Maude. Look at me.'

'This is the day I've been dreading for ages, Susie, ever since the number on the Counter passed two-hundred. I want to go to sleep and wake up from this nightmare.'

'This is as real as the stars up above, Maude.'

'Promise me Assa won't get the orb.'

'We can't promise that. It's inevitable that Assa will get the orb back one day. I'd be deluded if I thought that we'd be able to keep it from Assa forever. One day Assa will find the orb, and what we've been fearing will happen. Hopefully, it will not be in our lifetime, but that we can't guarantee. Cooperate and we'll be able to delay it. Calm yourself down and you'll see things in a much more positive light.'

'How can any of this be seen as positive?'

'What's the date today?'

'Friday 15th January, well now it's the 16th really.'

'To everyone who doesn't now how to live properly, every day is just another day, but to those who do know how to live properly, how to lead an adventurous life, every day is not unimportant; those who know how to live properly can do more in six months than most people do in their whole lives. This is awful, we all know that, but try to see it as a blessing in disguise, because once it hits you that we may not have long left, and it will hit you soon, you'll live life properly.'

Maude looked down, her brows furrowed. It had sunk in, but she didn't feel that energy and vivacity Susie had been describing. All she wanted to do was to go back to a few hours ago and flee Helmia before she could get involved in this again.

Chapter 4 –
The White Pyramid

It was just after six in the morning. Most people in Helmia were sleeping, unaware of the two alien visitors the island had received that night, whilst somewhere on the British mainland there was a large crater in a farmer's field. The injured creature in the heart of the crater was semi-conscious and close to death. Hyuul was motionless and could just about make out the morning sky, a warm amber with hints of rose and faint streaks of a fiery red breaking the sky. The moon was barely visible, almost like a dim imprint. The country was soon bathed in the light from the rising sun and a gentle breeze rustled the low-cut grass here and there. The air was chilly and harsh. A few sheep were still asleep. In the distance was a farmer's house and inside the farmer and his family were still fast asleep, soon to awake to get to work. Hyuul was still not moving. All of the farmer's family had slept through the upheaval caused by Hyuul crashing to the ground. Only a few of the farmer's animals were killed by the impact.

Hyuul lapsed into unconsciousness as a few sheep in the field started waking up and bleating. They started chewing on grass and commenced their daily wandering of the fields, a somewhat robotic way of life. All these lowly sheep did was eat, sleep and reproduce. They were one of the less inspiring forms of life that was never meant to be.

A few timid sheep approached the mouth of the crater, which was about fifteen feet deep and twenty feet in diameter. Hyuul lay right at the bottom of it. The sheep were too intimidated by this hole in the ground to go down into it, so they went back to grazing, ignorant of the importance of the crater and the being inside it.

*

Sometime later back on Helmia, on the outskirts of the city Puddlepond, a man called Demzel Harmelo was deep in sleep. He was a teacher at Puddlepond High School and had been looking forward to a relaxing weekend given he'd already got all of his marking done. However, when he awoke that Saturday, he scrapped his plans for a lazy weekend and dedicated his weekend to researching a dream he'd had, one which he remembered every detail of.

He was in his classroom teaching one of his favourite classes: Year 9 Mythology. Only nine students in the whole year had opted for this class, but that didn't bother Demzel. His love for mythology and all things unknown would always be flourishing despite the subjects' lack of mainstream appeal. In this dream class, however, there were a few extra students: Demzel looked round the class to see his boss Mr. Dazzle sitting in the back row, his friend Angela in the front row, his parents sitting next to each other somewhere in the middle and the famous actress Mary Morton also sitting the front row.

'Now class, I trust you have all done your homework on the Wandering Widow? And you have all revised for your test on Helmian mythology?'

'Yes, sir,' the class mumbled in one voice.

Before Demzel knew it, he'd collected all the homework and was sat at his desk marking it while the class did their tests. They were all writing away, the scratching of pencils a pleasant noise blissfully filling the room.

A second later, or so it seemed, Demzel was putting a mark on the final piece of homework then looked up to see that everyone had finished their tests and were all eagerly eyeing the clock above him.

'You can all put your pens and pencils down,' he told the class, a wide smile across his face.

'And you are all dismissed, except you, Miss Morton.'

'Have I done something wrong, sir?'

'No, I'd just like a word that's all.'

And so the class departed one by one. The last one to leave was a girl with dirty-blonde hair, a round face and eager eyes, always kinetic and alive.

'Lola, is there something I can help you with?'

'I was just wondering if I could have Mary Morton's autograph?'

'Of course,' Mary replied, getting out her pencil from her pencil case.

'There you go.'

'Thank you so much. I'm a massive fan and hope you don't get together with Demzel, here.'

'Excuse me?' a startled Mary replied.

'I'm not stupid. Demzel has a crush on you, we all do. You're gorgeous and incredibly successful yet you remain down to earth and humble.'

'Lola, don't you have another class now?' Demzel asked.

'You know once I leave this classroom and you can't see me any more I'll cease to exist until your mind conjures me up again.'

Mary looked at Demzel with a raised brow. What Lola

said was entirely true; Demzel had admired Mary ever since he saw her first film and followed her career intently. Here she was, tall and slender with long, flowing brown hair and deep, blue eyes. Her appearance and beauty were both enticing.

'Lola, off to your next class now, please.'

Lola, looking calm and fully aware of what was going to happen, left the room and closed the door with a cheeky wink at Demzel.

'Good luck, Demzel! My voice is disembodied now,' she uttered from beyond the room.

'Now, Mary, I think you know why I asked you to stay behind.'

'I think you have a crush on me, is that right, sir?'

'What can I say?'

'You can say you'll take me to dinner tonight. I know this great Italian place just off the High Street.'

'That sounds like a great idea.'

'Will you pick me up at my house then?'

'Where do you live?' asked Demzel keenly.

'You don't know, therefore I don't know. I think I should meet you at yours.'

'Sounds like a plan.'

Demzel blinked and she was gone. He was alone in his classroom, whose walls were adorned with newspapers clippings and posters pertaining to various things mythological, supernatural and paranormal. His classroom was his second home, a place where he often spent numerous hours outside the school day reading and researching myths and things unknown.

He left the room to find himself not in the corridor whose walls were punctuated by classroom doors and rows of lockers, but back at home, sitting in his living room all dressed up for his date with the celebrity.

There was a knock at the door.

Demzel opened the door to find Mary on his doorstep, dressed very elegantly in a sparkling black dress. He had chosen his finest suit and had spent ages getting ready, at least it seemed that way. He invited her in and they had a glass of wine each.

'You look stunning,' he complimented his date

'Why thank you. I must say you look very handsome indeed, sir.'

'Call me Demzel.'

'Okay…Demzel.'

'So how did you get here?'

'I don't know. Last thing I remember I was talking to you in your class.'

'Guess you don't have a car here then?'

'*You* should drive us there,' Mary suggested.

And so they were in Demzel's small car and were driving around the island's biggest city, Puddlepond. Occasionally they saw a monorail glide by, illuminated in the night and streaking across the city, which was surprisingly quiet.

'I can't find this Italian restaurant,' Demzel told Mary as they drove past a groups of faceless buildings and people.

'Where is everyone?' Demzel asked after pulling over. They were in one of the streets that branched off from the High Street and were looking down at the High Street, which would usually be full of people: it was the busiest street in Puddlepond and consisted of fancy shops, bars, restaurants and the odd gallery and a few normal shops.

'We're here alright, but where is everyone?' Demzel asked again.

'Mary?' he turned to look at her but she was gone. He got out of the car briskly and looked all about the darkened street but saw no one, nor did he see any restaurant or any shop or anything whatsoever. They were just blank buildings.

He spun around, looking from building to building and the High Street, which soon became blank buildings too.

Then Demzel found himself in a white room. Everything everywhere was just white, a dazzling, glittering and somewhat hypnotising white.

Demzel was perplexed by yet attracted to his surroundings. He started walking and walked for ages; it seemed to him this place he was in just kept going on and on. He couldn't understand where he was or why his dream had changed so rapidly.

Then he noticed something that had appeared in the distance: a black dot. He couldn't tell exactly how far away it was, but that didn't stop him walking towards it. He wondered what this darkness was.

A thought came to his head, though he didn't know why it had, nor did it seem to have any relevance. Another one pervaded his mind, this one even more nonsensical.

'What is going on?' asked out loud, hoping somewhere there'd be something or someone that could reply; yet no reply came.

The black dot in the distance was getting larger, expanding into the shining white. He continued walking towards it, but it seemed to him that he was actually getting no closer to it.

*

Back in what some call the real world, Demzel was sound asleep in his room in his house in the very east of Puddlepond as he continued dreaming on. His room, much like his classroom at Puddlepond High, was a nest of newspaper trimmings and books on mythology and the supernatural and paranormal. It was organised chaos: it appeared to be messy, but Demzel could locate anything within a minute. The only thing majorly different was that his bedroom had a few posters of Mary Morton up on the walls, with a few more stashed in his cupboard. This room was his private sanctuary; he was tetchy about even his closest friends seeing it.

He slept on, still dreaming of the white room and the growing darkness in it, unaware of the something else in his room.

Then everything stopped: the darkness stopped growing and Demzel found that he had come to a halt. He noticed the darkness was no longer simply just a ball: it had sprouted arms which were branching off in all directions. He also noticed that he was immobile. The arms kept sprouting more and more arms, which continued to pollute the perfect white which gradually began to lose its sparkle. Something felt wrong.

Then the two thoughts again came to the forefront of his thoughts, one of them making sense, the other not making sense. He felt as if he were looking for something here, but couldn't find it, nor did he know exactly what he thought he was looking for.

He wondered and tried to wander but still couldn't. He felt frustration at whatever was restricting him and struggled, hoping to break free, but to no effect.

The thoughts wouldn't escape his mind. They were fighting to stay there and were overwhelming him; he couldn't get rid of these thoughts as hard as he tried. He felt as if his head were going to explode.

Then the thoughts were gone and he was in a new place: he was staring up at a massive white pyramid, glistening and gleaming just like the white from the other place. All that wasn't the pyramid was the deepest shade of black. At the first glance, Demzel thought the pyramid ascended forever, but then he realised it had an apex. He didn't know why, but he felt an impulse to climb the pyramid all the way to the top, and so he began to ascend it.

Despite being in not the best shape in the 'real' world, here in this dream world, Demzel never grew tired on the climb. On and on he went, higher and higher, without tiring at all. His energy and strength seemed limitless. Not once did he look back, not even when he heard a great whooshing behind him. He had a feeling that he should get to the very top of the pyramid and not stop for anything. A little later on, the whooshing noise came again, this time a lot closer to him. He didn't care to look behind him to see what it was.

The pyramid was glistening in the dark but Demzel couldn't work out what it was made from. It certainly didn't look like it had been made from any kind of stone. He carried on running, faster and faster, getting ever close to the top when he noticed up above a being of sorts looking down at him. It was a winged creature bigger than Demzel with a slender, white body which sparkled just like the pyramid. It had beady eyes like a fly that were just about discernible and seemed to be very observant of Demzel.

Nevertheless, Demzel kept going as he was almost at the apex. He upped his speed and dislodged all concerns about the waiting creature from his mind.

In an instant he was at the very top of the pyramid standing on the small, flat apex. The creature, dazzling and brilliant, was opposite him, its head bent down to behold him. Its wings were flapping fast yet there was no sound from them.

'What do you want?' asked Demzel, thinking the creature would understand him.

All that happened then was that the creature flapped its wings again and in a flash there was an orb suspended in midair between the creature and Demzel. The orb was perfectly spherical and about the size of Demzel's head. It exuded a hypnotic attraction and captivated Demzel. The creature opposite, however, merely continued flapping its wings to stay where it was.

The orb had Demzel transfixed. Something about it made him not want to divert his gaze. The longer he beheld the orb, the more beautiful it appeared to him and the less he wanted to stop looking at it. The thing was, he didn't quite know what exactly was inside the orb: it was some sort of substance that was moving about inside and seemed to sparkle a bit. The substance was halfway between solid and liquid. It seemed to be suspended in the orb, not quite touching the edges of its container.

Demzel blinked and the orb was gone; he was standing face-to-face with the creature, its wings flapping strangely slowly. It looked at Demzel with a look of menace, agitation and fury. Demzel didn't know whether to turn and run back down the pyramid or stay here and see what was going to happen; he opted for the latter, emboldened by his newfound courage and strength.

'Why are you so angry?' he asked of the creature.

The creature gave no reply; it simply vanished right in front of Demzel's eyes, along with the orb. He was left by himself atop this great, gleaming pyramid, a sole beacon of light in the darkness. He looked around but all he could see was darkness. There was no sign of anything else anywhere. He started to wonder what exactly that orb was; something about it made him quiver.

Demzel was now at the foot of the massive pyramid, craning his neck up to see the top. He didn't know what had become of that creature. He wondered what this pyramid was doing here in the darkness. For the rest of the dream, all did was stand and stare.

*

'I'm telling you, Angela, it was the weirdest dream I've ever had,' Demzel admitted later on as he sipped his coffee.

'It certainly sounds very strange. And you say you can remember it all perfectly well?'

'Well the first bit's a bit hazy. Everything from the white room onwards I remember perfectly well and I can recall every single detail.'

'Hmmm. It's very odd, I must admit.'

'I'm starting to wonder if it has something to do with what went on last night.'

'How could aliens *supposedly* flying down to Helmia affect *your* dreams?'

'I really don't know but I just feel there's some connection. Plus, I think that creature I saw in my dream could possibly be one of those aliens.'

Angela stifled a laugh.

'What?' Demzel asked.

'Demzel, you'll never change. Every time there's some mention of aliens somewhere, you try to involve yourself with them.'

'Maybe I do, but this time I genuinely think I saw one of those aliens in my dream. I'll describe it to you now then once a photo of that one that crashed on the mainland gets released, I'll prove to you I was right all along.'

'How could you have seen them though? You were asleep and didn't know about the aliens till you woke up this morning and saw it on the news.'

'I still think I saw one.'

'It's a coincidence, Demzel.'

'Thanks for your optimism!'

'I'm being realistic. When you have a dream, what you see is either what your mind has conjured up, or reflections of what you've seen in life. You have never seen aliens before, therefore this *alien*, as you call it, was merely a figment of your imagination.'

'Are you scared, Angela?'

'Scared of what?'

'Aliens.'

'I'm only going to bother being scared of them if they become a threat to my loved ones and the chances of that happening are miniscule. As far as I'm concerned right now, they're just another silly news item.'

'Won't you *believe?*'

Angela laughed and rolled her eyes, 'look, I'll only believe when I see them for myself. Until then, they're just *make believe.*'

'But they've come here! Of all places, they've come here, to Helmia! You might not believe right now, but you will very soon when this story blows up. Mark my words, when you go home and turn on the news, this will be the number one story and it will dominate the headlines for months. Those two aliens were caught on several cameras flying down to Helmia fighting with each other. This is concrete evidence that aliens exist! For years now the existence of aliens has been hotly disputed and questioned. After last night, there need no longer be any uncertainty.'

'I'm not going to listen to any more of this, Demzel. I'm sorry, but it's just nonsense.'

'But this is it! We now know aliens *do* exist!'

Angela was now standing up, about to leave the quaint coffee shop hidden between two department stores on the High Street. She wasn't going to take any more of this.

'Look, Demzel, I don't believe in all this and I have my reasons for not wanting to believe as you know very well!' she said before turning and leaving; Demzel decided it best to give her some space and was thus was left to finish his coffee by himself, unaware that Angela was walking down the High Street crying.

He couldn't understand why Angela was being so narrow-minded and was refusing to believe. He wondered if perhaps he'd touched a nerve or been too pressing on the matter.

For the next half an hour or so, Demzel sat in the coffee shop, taking his time over his drink, staring out of the window and watching all the people go by. He wondered how many of them believed in aliens before and how many had been now convinced of their existence. He himself was overly thrilled that their existence was now entirely undeniable, though he couldn't help but wonder exactly why the aliens had come to Earth. Given the circumstances, most of the reasons he could come up with were implausible. For most of his life he'd been a firm believer and had tried to convince his friends on many occasions that aliens existed. Whenever there was some new story of someone somewhere being abducted or the night or someone somewhere seeing strange lights in the sky, he'd research it thoroughly and would usually conclude that it was indeed more proof of aliens' existence. He had struggled to see why some of his friends would refuse to believe, especially now after being shown incontrovertible evidence. Now, he thought to himself, they were starting to perhaps grow a bit sick of his insistence.

According to the news reports, the two aliens hadn't yet been seen to leave Earth. This didn't cause any concern for Demzel, however, if anything, he was rejoiceful. He'd been waiting for this day for ages, the day when alien existence was finally confirmed. He listened in on conversations people nearby were having, yet none of them were talking about aliens. He looked round and saw a young couple holding hands over the table, an elderly lady sipping her drink while reading the paper, a group of friends having a giggle and a man in a top hat and suit looking rather out of place and tired. Demzel wondered to himself whether any of these had heard about the aliens. The elderly lady caught his eye as she looked round the room, then buried her head back in the paper.

About half an hour later, Demzel was on his third cup. He looked round and saw it was a little busier now. He watched as the man in the top hat yawned, received a phone call then left hurriedly, talking in a low voice and stifling another yawn. Two young girls came into the shop, loudly discussing aliens. Demzel was just about to listen in on their conversation when his phone rang.

'Hello?' he answered.

'Demzel, it's Ivan. Don't suppose you've seen the news? Looks like you've finally got your proof.'

'I can't believe it's finally happening! And in Helmia too! Haven't I been telling you for ages that this was going to happen one day? And look who was right.'

'Bet you're dead excited, eh?'

'Excited is an understatement,' Demzel admitted, but then he felt a pang of guilt.

'I've just been with Angela and I think I've irked her a bit.'

'What happened?'

'I was shoving this alien stuff down her throat.'

'Not again...'

'I was insisting that aliens exist and was being quite annoying. I'm just too damn excited about these aliens! Although I guess I can be a bit too excited at times.'

'You don't say! Do you know how many alien stories me and Ange have had to listen to? I think you know as well as we do that you are completely obsessed with aliens. Don't you think Ange has had enough of all this?'

'Maybe, but this time it's the most reliable piece of evidence yet!'

'So how long have you spent researching this latest story online?'

Demzel blushed a little whilst saying, 'only half an hour this morning, actually.'

'Demzel, I'm sorry but I've gotta go now. I'll ring you later.'

Ivan hung up and put his phone in his pocket. He was at home, a swish flat in the heart of Puddlepond, which was decorated modern and trendy. He had lived here for a good few years and had worked in the same place, Puddlepond High School, for roughly the same amount of time as a sports teacher. As for the aliens, he didn't quite know whether he truly believed or not. He liked winding Demzel up about his devotion to them, yet sometimes he was inclined to believe some of the stuff he said. On the other hand, he completely understood why Angela was so reluctant to believe; he often found himself unsure of what to think and occasionally ended up caught in the middle: Demzel would insist aliens exist given the evidence, Angela would refute it all and both would have to be stopped from arguing by a usually neutral Ivan. He didn't want to get caught in yet another dispute. He went and opened his door.

'How did you get in this building? I don't recall buzzing you in.'

'Never mind that,' said the main standing in his doorway, 'I need you to do something for me. Can I come in?'

'Sure.'

Ivan and his guest were soon sat at his dining room table, sitting opposite each other, each with a cup of tea.

'I'm not certain when exactly I'll be needing your help, but it will be soon. I will let you know nearer the time; and by the way…'

Ivan saw his guest produce something from his inside jacket pocket: a gun, which he pointed directly at Ivan.

'Whoah! What the hell have are you pointing that thing at me for?'

'I'm not going to shoot you. I'm just going to tell you that no one must know about this, understood? You are to tell no one of me being here, or about what I'm about to ask you to do. The day you tell anyone whatsoever will be the day you die, I assure you of that.'

Ivan stared at the gun before him; he was a little intimidated though he knew the man opposite him could never pull the trigger. This was simply a desperate act to buy his silence. Ivan decided to feign fear and cooperation.

'No one will know, OK? Stop pointing that damn thing at me. Why would I tell anyone anyway?'

'I'm not afraid to kill you, Ivan. I repeat, tell anyone and I will kill you regardless of any excuses. Understood?'

'I'm not stupid enough to tell anyone. Now will you put that thing down? There's no need for it and frankly you're being ridiculous and out of order.'

'This is not an empty threat, Ivan.'

'Sure,' Ivan thought to himself.

'So what exactly am I doing for you then?'

Ivan's unwelcome guest explained the task, then Ivan asked, 'have you lost your mind?'

'I assure you I am perfectly sane.'

'And you seriously expect me to believe all that?'

'It's all true.'

'What if I said I don't believe you?' Ivan asked in a slow voice, though he wasn't entirely certain; he looked at his visitor as he lowered the gun.

'I don't care whether you believe or not. I just need you to do this for me. Anyway, you will believe for certain once you've done this for me.'

'And what if I don't?'

'This is quite an expensive flat you have here. I wonder how you can afford such a place on your wages?'

'That's none of your business.'

'I knew you'd say that. Anyway, I know all about your gambling problem. You may have been lucky so far, but the amount I can promise you will ensure you never have to go to that rotten casino again.'

'How much?'

'Given it's only one night's work, I think this much should be enough?'

Ivan looked at the amount scrawled down on a piece of paper tossed to him; the amount stunned him: he never knew his visitor was so wealthy and generous.

'That…is definitely enough.'

Ivan looked up to see the gun now aimed at him again, his visitor stony-faced.

'I'll do it,' Ivan acquiesced.

'Good,'

'But why me?'

'You're the right man for the job. It'll be challenging, but I trust you to do it and not tell anyone.'

*

Meanwhile, on the mainland, a farmer was standing at the edge of a crater in one of his fields, a massive crater that definitely wasn't there the previous night. He'd woken up and had gone out into the fields just as usual when he noticed the steaming chasm. Immediately he made for the gaping hole, and now he was peering down into the hole, wondering what on Earth could have crashed and made such a hole as this. He hoped to find whatever had crashed in the crater, yet after circumambulating it, he saw that there was nothing whatsoever there.

Chapter 5 –
Lola Spears

It was the following Monday morning and it was destined to be just another typical day in Helmia. Except now, Helmia was abuzz with gossip, discussion, rumour and fabrication. The story about the aliens flying down from the sky on Friday night had become the number one news story in the world, thanks to numerous eyewitness accounts and incontrovertible video evidence from CCTV, as well as individual phones and cameras. Every news channel across the world was eagerly following the story of the two aliens.

The first one was seen by people in Moistree, a small town of a few thousand inhabitants in the middle of the crescent-shaped island. It was overlooked by a large mountain, which divided Helmia in half. The alien had flown down into the town itself then flew over to Puddlepond, which was to the east of the mountain, but was later seen flying back up into the sky from Leafdew, to the west of the mountain.

The second alien had also flown down to Moistree and flew through the town, frantically searching for the other. About twenty or so minutes later, according to the witnesses, the first alien flew up into the sky from Leafdew. The second caught sight of the first and chased it ferociously up into the night sky. Then there was a massive explosion.

'I bet you anything this alien business will be all Demzel talks about today. He must be so excited,' said Lola Spears, a girl of fifteen who was sitting in her form class talking with her friends and waiting for the school day to officially start. She was fiddling with the ends of her hair and staring eagerly at the clock.

'I'll be surprised if he even turns up! Do you remember the last time there was some big story about aliens and he was "sick"? He'll never change. He's probably at home right now poring over documents on the Internet,' said Hannah Dawson, a girl notable for her dark grey eyes and her somewhat odd, yet alluring face.

'I hope he doesn't come in today – I still haven't finished my homework!' said Thomas Sinclair, a boy of wispy brown hair whose face was laden with freckles.

'The essay? But we've had weeks to do it,' Hannah said.

'Well, I've had other things on my mind,' Thomas replied, blushing a little.

'Let me guess: instead of doing your essay, you've been spending your time with Edward Scott,' suggested Lola, a cheeky smile across her face.

'There are more important things in my life than some essay on the East Coast Beasts,' replied Thomas.

'Did anything happen then?' asked Hannah; the girls were sitting either side of Thomas and were both looking keenly at him.

'No, we've just been talking, that's all. We're just friends, you know.'

'Is anything going to happen?' Lola asked keenly.

'Well, I really don't know. If something happens, it happens; if it doesn't, it doesn't! Anyway, we have Paranormal and Supernatural Studies after lunch; that gives me morning break and lunchtime to finish this essay off.'

'Do you think you'll get it done? It took me a couple of hours,' asked Hannah. Thomas shot Hannah a furtive look.

'I'll just grab a quick lunch and I'll put it in a big font and I'll just lie about the word count.'

'Do you think teachers will ever realise the tricks we use?' Lola asked the two of them.

'Of course not. Teachers will never sit there and count all the words. As long as the word count is realistic, it shouldn't be a problem. Plus, a bigger font makes it look like there's less of it. I wouldn't like to read an essay in a tiny font,' Hannah replied.

'I'm just glad we don't have to do them by hand, otherwise my essay would have very rushed and messy handwriting indeed.'

'Imagine having no computers or Internet,' Lola wondered.

'We'd have nothing to do! The world would be a much duller place,' Hannah replied.

'I hardly go on the Internet any more,' Thomas told the other two proudly. Lola looked stunned:

'What have you done with the boy who used to be surfing the net during *classes*? The boy who'd spend hours and hours every day trawling the most pointless of sites?'

'I've cut back a lot, yeah. I only go on every couple of days now; are you proud? What about you two?'

'I have Internet on my phone. I think that answers your question, Thomas,' Hannah said, eagerly checking her phone for any updates.

'I'm not on as much as I used to be. Though I did spend a long time on this weekend reading news reports about those two aliens.'

The bell went and their form teacher, Mrs. Elaine Dazzle, came into the room and sat down at her desk. She was a voluptuous woman with dark, puffy red hair and a pale heart-shaped face. She had an air of radiance about her. Lola noticed she looked a bit tired.

'Good morning, class. I trust you all had a good weekend despite the obvious. Let's just try to make this week as normal as possible. Routine is good for the soul, after all.'

She then proceeded to do a register; everyone was present.

'Mr Dazzle won't be doing the assembly as he's away on business yet again, so Miss Bay will take assembly this morning. Make sure you all go because there is a very important and serious announcement and you know what Miss Bay's like. I'll see you all in English later on this morning.'

She then got up from her desk, her register in one hand, an apple in the other.

'What do we have after assembly?' asked Thomas as they shuffled out of the room.

'We have Maths then me and Lola have Geography and you have Modern Technology. After break it's double English then in the afternoon we have Paranormal and Supernatural Studies then French and double Chemistry.'

'Double English *and* double Chemistry? I forgot Mondays were so bad.'

'Thomas, are you ever gonna learn your timetable?' asked Lola.

'I don't see the need to, really, when I can rely on you to know it for me.'

The three of them went to the assembly hall and sat in their usual place: near the back row of benches on the very end so they could make their escape as quickly as possible.

'Do you think she'll mention the aliens?' Lola pondered out loud.

'Doubt it. Remember what Dazzle said about keeping this week normal?'

'I wonder what this big announcement will be then,' Thomas wondered with sarcastic excitement.

They speculated and wondered until Miss Bay took to the stand. She was a small, skinny woman with a croaky voice who looked somewhat out of place conducting the assembly for over a thousand pupils.

After the usual deluge of announcements and notifications, she said, 'now, some of you may be aware that your headmaster's office was broken into and vandalised on Friday night. Mr Dazzle has conducted a thorough search of his office and he assured us that all that was taken was a couple of ten-pound notes from his safe. The police have of course been alerted and have a few suspects in mind. However, I urge any one of you who might know anything to come forward and tell us immediately. Anything you might know that might help us and the police will be greatly appreciated. Anyone who knows something but deliberately withholds their information will be punished.'

'Blimey! What a weekend it's been! First the aliens and now this,' Lola whispered to Hannah and Thomas.

'Maybe someone saw the aliens in the sky, panicked and decided to turn into a vandal? It happens all the time in films,' Thomas theorised.

The assembly soon finished and everyone scattered off to their first lesson of the day. The three sat through maths; Thomas was eagerly concentrating, whereas the two girls' minds were elsewhere. Lola looked round the room when the teacher was busy writing some equation on the board and, judging by everyone else's faces, they too were all bored.

'This lesson is so dull,' she whispered to Hannah.

'You've just realised that?'

'There's still fifteen minutes left!'

'Time goes by so slowly when we're sat here supposedly listening to the teacher.'

'I agree. I actually wish she'd get us to do some group work or something so then we could talk properly.'

'Sh, guys!' Thomas whispered.

'I don't see how he can like maths so much. What use is maths to me when calculators exist?' Hannah said.

'While I find it tedious, it's probably a lot more relevant and worthwhile than Mythology and Supernatural and Paranormal studies. Would employers want someone who can think a problem through and solve it or someone who spends all their time watching the skies for aliens and hunting for ghosts?'

'I'd employ the latter; they sound much cooler.'

'Now class, your homework. I'd like you to do all the exercises on page 34 for next lesson, please.'

The class noted down their homework perfunctorily and before they knew it, it was the end of the lesson. Thomas remembered that he'd forgotten his Modern Technology textbook so they hurried back across the hall to their lockers. Whilst Thomas hurriedly rummaged through his locker, which was in a perpetual state of disarray, Lola looked about the main hall and saw the reception area beyond the many rows of pews. There was a man in a top hat yawning as he waited to be seen by the head. Next to him a long-haired woman with overly large sunglasses, a large bag by her feet and beret on was getting up and was going into the head's office.

Modern Technology was one of the more popular optional subjects at Puddlepond High School. Pupils were taught all about gadgets and gizmos, how they worked and how future objects could be produced based on current designs. Some just took the subject because they liked fancy hi-tech objects and others because they thought the subject was easy marks.

'Why not just read the instruction manual?' Hannah had said to Thomas when they chose their subjects the previous year.

'It's interesting to learn how these things actually work. I mean, look at a TV. How on Earth did they manage to make that? Or a computer? I find it fascinating.'

The morning flew by and it was now the lunch break. Thomas retreated to the library after a hurried lunch, moaning and muttering something about him not being a good student, while Hannah and Lola wandered through the school, killing time.

'Do you think all this alien stuff is just another case that will be forgotten about quickly?' Lola asked Hannah as they walked through the assembly hall and sat down on one of the pews.

'It all seems pretty genuine. It said on the news that loads of people caught them on camera and stuff.'

'Hmmm. I don't know. It all seems rather odd. I mean, these two aliens fly down to Earth, to Helmia, and then one of them gets blasted and lands on the mainland and they both just vanish. It's all a bit odd.'

'Lola, you're turning into Demzel, do you realise that?'

'I'm not turning into Demzel. For starters, I haven't been researching this at all; I lie, I've researched it a bit, but not as much as Demzel will have done.'

'Well I'm not really buying into all this alien hoohah. For starters, none of these two *aliens* have been caught so we don't actually know they're alien. I know Demzel will no doubt be convinced that they are indeed aliens and will shove it down our throats this afternoon.'

'What do you expect when you take Paranormal and Supernatural Studies?'

'I am interested in it all, but I'm not ecstatic about it like Demzel is. I guess for me it's just another subject at school, not a genuine interest.'

'Fair enough. To be honest, I want to know what Demzel has found out about this. I'm kind of excited actually.'

'You have turned into Demzel,' Hannah remarked, a disapproving look on her face.

'Aliens fly down from space and come to Helmia. One of them eventually vanishes. The other crash-lands on the mainland and it too vanishes. There is no explanation as to what they are or why they came here. I certainly want to find out more.'

'Do you think you will though? If both of these aliens have vanished, then how could anyone find out why they came here in the first place?'

'Good point. I hadn't thought of that before!'

'That's why you should be happy to have me.'

Lola looked at Hannah and knew what she'd just said was right.

'At least they're not invading us!' Hannah quipped.

'What?' Lola replied a few moments later.

'The aliens. You know, the ones we were just talking about?'

'Oh yeah. Sorry, I was miles away. What were you saying?'

'At least they're not invading us.'

'I really don't think we've anything to worry about. Like Demzel said, all aliens that come to Earth are probably here to learn.'

'How can anyone be sure that's their intention though? Like you said, they may be learning now, but later on once they've learnt enough, they might then decide to invade. We can never know their true intentions. Sure, there's no panic and they have supposedly vanished…for now, but who knows what they have in mind? They could come back with some massive alien army and try to wipe us out for all we know.'

'Sounds like you've been watching too much TV,' Lola remarked.

'For me, when aliens are spotted such as the two last Friday, it makes for a great story. Everyone's experiencing different feelings: some are excited, some are terrified, some are curious whilst others are doubtful. The reason why I don't really buy into it all is that these things never turn out to be much. Aliens and UFOs are sighted, someone might get abducted and returned, but that's all that ever happens. Call me pessimistic, but this will all blow over in a couple of weeks. As far as I see it, it's another sighting, albeit a decent one, but it will soon be forgotten about. I just don't have the patience and enthusiasm Demzel has.'

'You do have a good point. I guess all Demzel does is wait for new sightings, research them thoroughly, then wait for the next one to see if that's any better.'

'I'd be more interested if there was some advancement.'

'What do you mean?'

'I mean something more than just sightings, such as communication with them, which, realistically, probably won't happen in our lifetime.'

'I think it could. Aliens have been visiting our planet for decades now, so surely they'd want to start communicating with us soon enough?'

'I guess so. When that happens, I'll take more notice, but for now it's just another sighting to me and all sightings are pretty much the same.'

'But this one is so much different from all the others, Hannah! They were sighted by hundreds of people in Moistree, Puddlepond and Leafdew and one of them started flying through Moistree and was caught on CCTV and tons of cameras before blasting the other one to bits, which was also caught on camera. So many people saw them arrive and fight. There's so much mystery surrounding this.'

'Maybe *you* should teach Supernatural and Paranormal Studies?'

'I don't think so. Well…guess what time it is?'

'I can't wait to see how overly excited Demzel's gonna be,' Hannah said.

And so the two walked over to a nearby classroom for their Paranormal and Supernatural Studies class. The room's walls were covered in posters and newspaper clippings of aliens, monsters, ghosts and all other things supernatural and paranormal. The desks were arranged in a U shape and Thomas was sitting at one of the ends.

'Did you get the essay done?' Lola asked, sitting next to him.

'I printed it off two minutes ago. Phew! It's a hundred or so words less than what Demzel asked for but he doesn't have to know that.'

'You'll never change, Thomas,' Hannah commented, having sat down next to Lola.

'I can do maths homework in hardly any time, but when we're given long essays to write, I just always seem to put it off.'

'You and the rest of the world,' said Lola.

They were the only three in the room until the door opened and a few people walked in: a tall girl with wavy blonde hair, a small mousy boy with too many books in his hands and a well-to-do boy with dark hair cut short very neat and proper.

'Hello, Edward,' said Thomas, Lola and Hannah simultaneously.

'Hi, guys. How are you?'

Lola and Hannah let Thomas answer: 'I just spent lunchtime finishing this damn essay so, I'm quite tired. How about you?'

'I'm fine. I was up till three last night finishing the same essay,' Edward confessed before sitting down opposite Thomas as he yawned.

'The joys of procrastination!' Hannah whispered to Lola.

'Are you going to the theme park this weekend?' asked Thomas.

'Probably. Are you all going?' Edward asked.

'Of course! It's already nearly February and I haven't even used my annual pass yet,' Lola said.

'Lola, what's wrong with you? You usually open the envelope, find the pass inside then off you dart to the theme park leaving the rest of the presents unopened,' Hannah said.

'As far as I'm concerned, an annual pass to Puddlepond Theme Park is the best present anyone can get. I'm so lucky to live near it!'

'Did you know that they're tearing down that old wooden coaster this summer?' asked Edward.

'I couldn't believe it when I read it online,' replied Lola, 'that roller coaster is over forty years old! It's one of the oldest in the country and it's running perfectly fine – no breakdowns or anything, so it escapes me why they want to get rid of it. They're probably going to put some ridiculously expensive tall steel coaster in its place.'

'I thought you loved tall steel coasters?' asked Edward.

'I do, but not when a classic woodie is *killed* to make room for it.'

Lola was a massive roller coaster fan and visited the local theme park about once or twice a month and received an annual pass every Christmas, much like most of the other kids her age. She'd been visiting the park every single year since she was two and was now dismayed that its oldest roller coaster was being demolished.

'I guess they have no choice. They haven't built a new coaster in five years and so they want a new one to attract guests and they're running out of room so it's their only option,' Thomas said, his eyes darting from person to person.

'It's a shame really,' Lola replied, looking downbeat.

'Lola, it's only a roller coaster. Don't get depressed or anything,' Hannah said.

The class was now starting to fill up. Before they knew it, everyone in the class was there, all except the teacher, Demzel.

'What did I tell you?' Hannah said.

'If he doesn't turn up, I'll kill him; all that rushing about and finishing my essay for nothing!'

'Well then you should have finished it the night before like the rest of us,' Hannah said.

'Next time I will, I promise.'

'You said that the last time and the time before that.'

Just then a harried Demzel entered the class and dropped a load of newspapers on to his desk.

'Good afternoon, class. I bet you have all heard what happened here, right here, over the weekend! I hope you all realise we are at the heart of the biggest and most important event in the hunt for aliens the world has ever seen,' Demzel said in a hushed voice for effect. Some of the class seem entranced; Hannah didn't.

'I've decided,' Demzel continued on, 'that instead of going on to international sightings of the East Coast Beasts, we're going to spend the next few weeks studying last Friday and any developments that should, dare I say *will*, arise.'

Lola could detect a bubbling enthusiasm in Demzel. He was standing over his desk with his hands on it, talking rather slowly, carefully pronouncing each word. He often did this when excited.

'I spent all weekend researching this. I have been in many online forums and have scoured regional, national and international papers for information. I have also watched as many videos as I could find online. Yes, that is why I've switched to coffee and have massive bags under my eyes. I'm going to get another cup from the staff room then when I get back I'm going to tell you all exactly what I've read then we'll discuss and theorise!'

Demzel then hurriedly left the room in search of his next fix. Most of the class didn't know what to say, except Hannah, who said, 'he's actually outdone himself this time.'

'He looks like he hasn't slept for ages!' someone in the class commented.

'I wouldn't be surprised if he hasn't,' replied Hannah.

Soon enough, Demzel came back, a fresh cup of coffee in hand.

'Before I begin, I'd like any of you who have theories about what happened last Friday to tell them to the class.'

Only two people put up their hands: a meek, thin boy and Lola.

'Yes, Andrew.'

'From what I've read, the alien that was being chased had an orb with it, and so it's likely the other alien was chasing the first alien to try and get the orb.'

'Exactly, Andrew. It seems this orb is the heart of it all. Any ideas on why they're so far away from home?'

'It doesn't seem like they've come to Earth to learn about us. Rather, it seems like they're here by accident.'

'Lola, anything to add?'

'I agree with everything Andrew said. I don't think they both could have vanished though. Maybe the one that crashed on the mainland recovered then just flew off somewhere and the other one is off somewhere chasing it.'

'Hmm interesting...that's definitely plausible. What is certain is that the farmer who called the police said there was nothing in the crater at half-seven on Saturday morning. Now, I've gathered all the evidence and have an account of exactly what happened.'

Demzel coughed then started his recitation: 'at 11.57pm, last Friday night, Gene Peterson and his wife Harriet Summers were walking along the beach at Moistree when they saw a beam of light coming down to them from the sky. Harriet got her phone out and took a video, which shows one being rush by heading straight for Moistree. The other soon rushes by then the video ends because her phone ran out of power. According to other witnesses, the first one flew right on to Puddlepond whilst the other flew about Moistree looking for the other. Witnesses in Puddlepond saw the first one flying about for a bit then at 12.20am it was seen flying up into the sky from Leafdew. A few moments later, the second flew up from Moistree and blasted the first as it was flying away. This too was caught on video – it's like something from a film! We'll watch it a few times so I can point out all the details I've noted. The alien was blasted on to the mainland, whilst the other was last sighted flying about Puddlepond at roughly one in the morning. Both have not been seen since, nor have there been any sightings of this orb they appear to have been fighting over.'

'Sir? People said they saw lights in the sky, but surely the lights wouldn't have been the aliens themselves? Were the lights possibly UFOs?' a girl in one corner asked.

'Video evidence has shown that the lights people saw were actually the two aliens themselves. Evidence has shown that these aliens radiate light, hence their stark appearance in the night sky; furthermore, they are seen to be elongated humanoids, with no nose, hair or distinguishing features. They seem to be blank human bodies. This is the first time such aliens have been sighted on Earth, I think. I searched for ages and no one on Earth has reported seeing them before, so it seems this is their first visit to our planet. So, we can assume this orb had something to do with why one was chasing the other, but what we don't know is why they were here on Earth, more specifically, Helmia. We all know Helmia is a bit odd and I am being bold in proposing that the reason why the aliens were in Helmia of all places may have something to do with Helmia's history. Now, I have seven different videos to show you all and we'll watch the one taken by Gene Patterson on the shores of Moistree beach!'

Demzel bumbled about as he pulled down the screen and fiddled about on his computer. Then, the whole class had their eyes fixed on the large screen as he played the recording. Demzel paused it just as the first alien flew by Gene; the freeze-frame showed the face of the first alien, the one with the orb; its face was a dazzling white and its features were contorted to show a look of haughtiness and determination. It didn't have a nose.

Lola looked intently at the alien face and instantly became fascinated: now this was very real indeed. She instantly began to wonder where in the universe it was from, why it was fleeing from the other with that orb and why they were on Earth.

'The story is starting to explode,' commented Demzel, 'it dominated the front page of all the big papers and is being reported all over the world. This image of the alien, along with the video footage and the witness reports, is being relayed all across the world. This is the number one global news story right now – and we are right where it happened! In case you haven't noticed already, I am very excited and happy!' and with that, Demzel took a large sip of coffee.

Lola couldn't stop looking at the alien. She felt an impulse of curiosity she'd never felt before. She wanted to find answers to all the questions being asked.

Demzel proceeded to show the class the rest of the videos and pictures he'd gathered, each of which transfixed Lola even more. There was one freeze-frame which showed a shower of electrical beams firing across the sky towards the alien that had had the orb. Before she knew it, it was the end of the class and Demzel was telling them all their homework.

'Your homework this week is easy: all I ask is that you follow this number-one story and be prepared to discuss new developments in our next time. That's all.'

'What a class! Did you see all those photos he printed out! I didn't realise his printer had so much ink!' Hannah said as they gathered up their stuff. Demzel was leaving the room, an empty cup in hand.

'Oh man!' cried Thomas, 'he forgot to collect in our damn essays! Great!'

'Haha! I think he has a lot more important things on his mind at the minute, don't you? This is the number one story in the world after all,' Hannah said.

'I should have known he'd be too preoccupied to remember our essays which we spent so long on.'

'You didn't spend long on it Thomas, come off it,' replied Hannah.

'Maybe I didn't spend as long as you, but I spent a solid lunchtime slaving away, racing against a deadline.'

'This will teach you a lesson.'

'Yeah right, Hannah. What lesson will that be? When a news item attracts your teacher's attention, don't bother with essays?'

'That's the one.'

They left the room and went to their final lesson of the day. Afterwards, they went to the locker room. Lola was sorting out her books in her locker when someone tapped her on the shoulder.

'Oh, hi Natella!'

'Hello, Lola. How's it going?' Natella was a very beautiful girl with fiery red hair and deep blue eyes.

'I'm…not bad thank you. I'm just a bit overwhelmed by all this alien stuff, I guess.'

'Likewise. It's all terribly out of the blue, don't you think, and so random?'

'That's one very precise way of looking at it.'

'And here in Helmia of all places!'

'We were discussing it in Supernatural and Paranormal Studies and Demzel thinks Helmia's history may have something to do with why they came here.'

'That's certainly a very interesting idea. So, what are you doing this weekend?'

'I'm finally going to the theme park on Saturday for the first time this year. You should come along.'

'Who's going?'

'Me, Hannah, Thomas, Edward and his sister Erica, and probably a few others.'

'Well I'm definitely up for it. Text me later.'

'Will do,' Lola looked as Natella left the room. Thomas then came over to her, looking shifty.

'Lola, can I have a word?'

'Of course. What about?'

'I think we should go to a classroom.'

'OK.' Lola packed her stuff up in her bag then followed Thomas into an empty maths classroom.

'I just wanted to say sorry.'

'For what? You haven't done anything.'

'I have. I was rattling on about Edward earlier on and I didn't want to.'

'You weren't rattling on. We were just having a normal everyday conversation. Secondly, why did you not want to?'

'I felt like I was rubbing it in. I mean, me and Edward are getting really close well kinda, and I feel guilty talking about it because…'

'Because of me and Hannah?'

'Yeah,' Thomas said quietly.

'Listen, just because I fancy Hannah and I know she'll never reciprocate that, doesn't mean you can't enjoy being with Edward.'

'I'm not *with* him.'

'I know, but it's heading that way.'

'Yeah, very slowly.'

'I know it's just a silly schoolgirl crush and I'm blowing this way out of proportion, but still…'

'You can't help how you feel.'

'Look, I'm really happy you have Edward, OK? Whenever you talk about him, it definitely doesn't make me feel bad; I feel good because one of my best friends is happy. Now, let's go and do that French homework because you need to stop doing homework the day it's due.'

'I can't really be bothered to.'

'Would you rather do it now or rush it on Wednesday afternoon?'

'Rush it. Apparently your brain works better when it's under pressure. Therefore, I work better when I'm pushed for time.'

'I knew you'd have some excuse.'

Chapter 6 –
Puddlepond Theme Park

'One thing I should also mention which I think deserves attention is a rather peculiar dream I had the night the aliens came,' was the first thing Demzel said to his first period Wednesday class.

'It slipped my mind last time but now I will give it the attention it deserves. Now listen carefully everyone. On Friday night I was having a normal dream when I found myself in a black space with a massive, glistening white pyramid. I climbed it and found some being with an orb at the top. I am adamant that this has some connection to the aliens – it's just too much of a coincidence. What makes this dream so remarkable is that I can recall every exact detail and I remember it all perfectly. It was like no other dream I've ever had. It was almost like I was living it. This is all one big puzzle and I am certain my dream is another piece of it. And what use is a puzzle unsolved?'

Lola sat and wondered as Demzel droned on. She looked round the class and saw an unimpressed looking Hannah, a quizzical Thomas and a few other friends who looked interested.

Once Demzel had theorised about his dream and had

shown them some more news articles about the on-going alien story, he gave the class their homework.

'For next time, I'd like you to write a few paragraphs on what you think it means to be alien. Next lesson, we're going to discuss what it would be like to set foot on and experience an alien world, so I'd like you to do some thinking beforehand.'

Then before she knew it, it was Friday lunch break and they were sitting in the assembly hall.

'That maths homework looks interesting,' said Thomas.

'Interesting? Confusing more like!' Hannah replied.

'I can't believe she's given us another Mythology essay to do!'

'You might as well stop worrying about it now; you know as well as we do that you're going to do it the night before.'

'That's true, sadly,' replied Thomas.

They sat and continued talking then two people came and sat down with them.

'Hello, Erica and Kelly,' said Lola.

'Hello, guys,' the two girls replied; Erica was a tall lightly-tanned girl with long hair, and ocean-blue eyes whilst Kelly was dark-skinned with black hair and large eyes which were turquoise in colour; both girls were always smiling and giggling.

'What are you up to?' Kelly asked, sitting down next to Thomas.

'Just talking about homework, of all things, how about you?'

'We've just been to running and we are both really tired so we're just off to the Mythology building to go to that lovely vending machine. Do you guys wanna come?'

'Yeah sure,' Lola replied; the five of them set off.

'What are you all doing this weekend?'

'We're going to the theme park on Saturday. Are you two coming?' Hannah asked.

'I can't, I'm afraid,' Kelly replied, 'I'm going away for the weekend to visit my grandparents.'

'I'm still going and Edward is too,' Erica said nonchalantly. Lola and Hannah looked across to Thomas, who smiled a little.

'Sorry you can't make it, Kelly,' Lola said.

'Me too. If only my grandparents lived in Puddlepond then it wouldn't take a full weekend to visit them.'

'Where do they live?' Thomas asked.

'In Blackpool. Dad insists on driving, so we leave on Saturday morning and come back late Sunday evening. I'm going to have massive bags under my eyes on Monday morning.'

'I've had bags under my eyes since I was five,' Hannah quipped.

They each got a snack from the vending machine in the quiet Mythology building and went to the spare classroom to sit down and eat. The classroom was hardly ever used and was home to no form class so it became the perfect place for a quiet sit-down with friends when the hustle and bustle of the busier parts of the school became too much.

Before long, the bell sounded and Lola, Hannah and Thomas went downstairs to Demzel's classroom.

'Have you done the homework, Thomas?' Lola asked.

'I have actually. I did it this morning before leaving home. It was hard though trying to put myself in an alien's shoes.'

'I wonder if aliens do wear shoes?' Lola replied.

'Do they even have feet?' Hannah asked.

'That's why I found the homework hard,' Thomas said, satisfied.

They were soon in the classroom awaiting Demzel's arrival. He came in a few minutes after the second bell rang, looking harried. He sat down at the desk, took a sip from his cup of coffee, then got back up and wrote on the board:

'What is an alien? What does *alien* mean?'

He then sat down at his desk and a smile came across his face.

'Good morning, class. Today I thought we'd try to understand our alien friends a little better.'

His announcement was met with looks of confusion and disbelief.

'What do you mean exactly?' someone asked.

'Next lesson, I'm going to teach you about the alien's supposed biology and some other general information we have gleaned from visits over the years, but what I want to concentrate on today is how it *feels* to be alien. This is what I mean when I said we're going to understand them a bit better. Today, we'll not need books or pens and paper, instead all you need is yourselves.'

'Now the main objective of today is to understand how one feels when setting foot on a new world for the first time in history. Imagine you are an astronaut and you're on the first ever flight to a planet that is known to house life intelligent enough to communicate with you. How would you feel when you leave Earth knowing your destination is an unknown alien world? Consider it for a few minutes and read what you've already prepared while I go and get a drink then we'll discuss it when I return.'

'That man has no self-control,' Hannah mumbled once Demzel had left the classroom; Lola and Thomas nodded assent.

The teacher soon returned and asked the class for contributions to set off the discussion.

'Yes, Andrew.'

'If I were an alien, I would feel exactly the same as I feel now, that is to say, I'd feel comfortable in my body and would have some sense of the world around me. I would only begin to question how it could be different once I'd become aware of other life forms existing. So if I were landing on an alien planet, I'd mostly be curious.'

'So what would you say an alien is?'

'An alien is whatever we are, only slightly different. We all share a common trait: life. We may appear and act differently, but underneath it all, we're all the same.'

'Very interesting. What does anyone else have to say?'

'I'd be really scared if I was on an alien planet,' a short, fidgety girl with bright red hair replied, 'wouldn't aliens be hostile to visitors? How would anyone know it's safe to visit an alien planet?'

'That is another good point too, Alice. One of the most terrifying things in the universe is that which is unknown. You can learn a certain amount about a planet from a distance, that is to say, through the use of telescopes, but actually being on the planet itself and exploring it as it really is teaches you a lot more about it than any telescope can. You can know a few things before arriving on a planet, but so many things remain unknown – anything could happen. It would be foolish not to feel some apprehension.'

There seemed to be a sense of tension in the classroom: silence ensued for a few moments while Demzel looked from student to student with eager eyes.

'Who knows what secrets the planets up there have?' he exclaimed looking at the ceiling, perhaps a little too dramatically.

'Now, another question to be discussed is this: what would an alien visiting Earth feel like? How would we appear to extra-terrestrials? What would we seem like? What would the planet seem like?'

A few hands went up.

'Yes, Darren.'

'I think we'd seem really weird because we come in all shapes and sizes. This planet, I think, would appear quite overwhelming because there's so much diversity. I don't just mean in humans, but also in animals, plants and even the land.'

'Another very interesting point! Aliens visiting this planet would have to stay for an awfully long time to sample even a fraction of the wide range of wonders this planet has to offer. They could visit the Sahara Desert, the Amazon Rainforest, the Great Barrier Reef, the Himalayas, the Grand Canyon, see the Northern Lights…there are so many marvels it's impossible to name them all. And that's just a selection of the natural wonders. No matter where aliens land on Earth, they'd undoubtedly find so many things to admire. Now, does anyone have any ideas as to what Earth would feel like to an alien?'

Edward Scott raised his hand.

'Yes, Edward.'

'If aliens are visiting Earth now, then they must be more advanced than us because we can't fly to other planets yet. So we must seem a bit behind because we haven't advanced as much as them.'

'I agree. Whilst the aliens are very probably masters of more advanced technology, and we will seem less developed than they, perhaps this will incite the urge to help us advance even more. Our technology can only improve and as it does, it will be able to do more and more. While we may seem behind, we may seem ahead in terms of other areas of development. What we conclude is that any alien coming to Earth will have many, many questions about it. They might not have come to Earth to admire it, but they won't be able to help doing so once they behold it for the first time.'

Lola spent the rest of the lesson thinking and taking notes. She hadn't really considered much of this before and found it really interesting.

The school day ended and everyone set about heading home.

'I fear this will soon become an epidemic,' Hannah said to Lola as they walked home from school later on, 'first Demzel, then you, then the whole of Helmia!'

'Come on, I'm not as bad as Demzel. I'm only doing the homework we were set, which was to keep up with the story as it develops.'

'But Demzel does it for us! Every class this week he's just summarised the developments, shown us a few videos then asked us for our theories. I haven't been doing the homework and I survived. I thought about the questions he set us but didn't write anything down. And he still hasn't asked us for our essays on the East Coast Beasts.'

'He does tend to get engrossed in anything to do with aliens.'

'Yeah. I kinda see where he's coming from though. Aren't you desperate to know why they came here?'

'Not particularly.'

'Are you desperate to go to Puddlepond Theme Park tomorrow?' Lola said with a smile.

'Of course! We haven't been since the week before Christmas. That seems like ages ago now.'

'It's only been about a month.'

'Time flies too quickly,' Hannah said.

Lola stayed quiet and thought to herself for a few moments. Time always seemed to fly by for some reason. It seemed like two minutes ago she was holding her brand new annual pass in her hand on Christmas Day and now it was almost a month old.

'It won't fly by on Saturday though!'

'I should hope not,' replied Hannah.

'We should head to Woodwinder first; we should really get as many rides on that as possible cos they're stupidly closing it down later this season.'

'Then we should head to that really massive one, you know, the big blue one. That ride is so scary!'

'I love the views you get. I wish it would break down right at the top of the lift hill so we could be able to appreciate the views a bit more.'

'If that happens, you can stay there admiring the view; I'll be running down the lift hill!'

'Haha!'

'So it's us three and who else?'

'Edward and Erica, Natella and Darren too. We're all meeting there outside the front gates at nine. Are you alright with Darren going?'

'Of course. I've got to it always being awkward between us two. It will be fine.'

'It might be different this time.'

'It won't though. It's so annoying. I like him and I can tell he likes me. It's just so damn awkward all the time.'

'I think he is a bit shy,' Lola remarked.

'A bit?'

'OK, maybe very shy.'

'That's more like it.'

The girls both lived on the same street, Sunnyside Lane, a long winding road with houses dotted about on either side. The street was on the very edge of Puddlepond, such that the houses on one side of the road were sandwiched between the road and fields and forests that stretched for miles.

'Do you want to do the maths homework tonight?' asked Lola.

'Yeah let's. I wouldn't be able to do it by myself. Where's Thomas when you need him?'

'He's gone to Edward's, remember?'

'I have a feeling he'll be getting a call from us when we get stuck on the maths homework.'

'We should probably do the English and the Paranormal and Supernatural Studies homework too.'

'I am not doing that piece of homework.'

'Why not?'

'Come on, Lola. Our 'homework' is to formulate theories about why the aliens are here. How are we meant to work that one out? What will happen on Monday's class is that he'll tell us his theories on why two aliens have come to Earth then there'll be a discussion and a few people will put their hands up then he'll spend the rest of the lesson going off on some tangent.'

Lola realised that was indeed very probable.

'I guess you're right.'

'I still cannot believe he forgot to collect our essays. Haha! Thomas must be up the wall!' Hannah laughed.

'If Thomas had known this was going to happen, he still wouldn't have it done.'

'I agree. I am so excited for tomorrow. Let's stay all day.'

'Of course! We'll stay for the fireworks like last time.'

They carried on walking and talking. There was that wintry chill in the air that seemed to constantly cling to their cheeks and hands. Lola found the weather very odd, particularly seasonal weather; she'd grow acclimatised to wintry weather then before she knew it, it was starting to get warm again, and then just like that it was summer. Change would often happen when she least expected it; gradual, subtle changes were the ones that affected her the most. She shivered a bit though she didn't know whether it was due to the cold or whether due to the notion that change came too fast and was inevitable. She knew deep down that this year would fly by. Time seemed very odd to her: sometimes days would drag on and on, whereas sometimes a whole week would have passed by in what seemed like mere minutes. Sometimes Lola thought it was just her, but she often heard complete strangers talking about the same thing.

They arrived at Lola's house; her front garden was quaint whereas the back one was quite large and beyond it lay fields and hillocks and eventually a dense forest a couple hundred metres away. Her bedroom window looked out on to the back garden and all that lay beyond it; at night when she couldn't sleep, she'd stare out of her window at the forest which frightened her a little. She often had nightmares which involved her being trapped in the forest running about looking for an escape. What she was most scared of was entrapment, especially in small spaces. As a kid, she'd been shopping with her parents when all three of them got stuck in a lift with a happy young couple and an old man. At first, all was relatively calm. After about twenty minutes, the old man started freaking out and the couple started arguing and Lola was confused and scared: how could such nice, friendly-looking people suddenly turn this way?

The shouting got louder and louder until it stopped when everyone realised the old man was having an asthma attack, clutching his chest and falling to the ground. Chaos followed as Lola's mother frantically checked the old man's pockets for an inhaler whilst her dad did the same. The small lift was full of noise corruptive to the young Lola.

She turned towards the corner of the lift and sank down, shut her eyes tight and imagined she was somewhere far away. She was in a hot desert riding a camel and sweltering under the baking sun. However, she could still hear the raucous noise from the lift. She was further away now, standing on the edge of a lone iceberg wrapped up in too many layers of clothes. All she could see was the briny sea going on forever, calm and serene. She started to relax and feel fine but then she heard in her mind the choking sound of the old man and the bickering couple. Suddenly the sea wasn't so calm. She needed someone further away, somewhere where nothing at all could disturb her. The place was outer space: she was floating and could see nothing but stars in all directions. She felt herself permanently away from all the horrible things in the world: the poor health of the old man, something she feared would one day happen to her parents and the disputing couple, and something she also feared her parents would one day become. Here in outer space, she had nothing to worry about. As long as she was here, the stars would keep on shining and there was nothing that could stop them. That experience in the lift was a turning point in Lola's life. Thenceforth, she realised that everything in life wasn't as she'd previously imagined it: safe, secure and steady. Instead, what was a solid bond between two people could almost be severed by arguments and people got ill. The world to Lola was now a scary place. Suddenly she realised her parents could any day have an argument and any day one of them could have some health problem or fall ill like the poor old man. That was the day she first understood what it meant to be truly afraid of something.

Ever since that day, Lola saw the stars in a new way and more often had her window open whenever she was in her room. Whenever she was feeling down, she'd imagine floating in space with the twinkling stars in the background. As she grew older and her fantasy of floating among the stars became more and more important to her, she started learning about space and became fascinated with everything to do with it: the supposed creation of the universe, stars and planets, astronomy, the hunt for extraterrestrial life. Whenever she imagined space, she was instantly miles away from the scary things in life and was back to her regular life safe of worries which she had before that day they got stuck in the lift. She was only seven when her outlook of the world changed forever. She entered the lift as a little girl and left it as something else.

It was now late at night. Lola was staring outside of her window at the stars, deep in thought and concentration. She couldn't get those aliens out of her head and it was annoying her immensely. Just a week ago Helmia had supposedly been visited by aliens that had since vanished. It all seemed surreal to Lola. Life in Helmia hadn't changed at all since; sure, there was excitement and commotion right afterwards, but because of the lack of news in the past few days, it all seemed to be calming down. She thought it would eventually, given that the aliens were no longer around and it therefore couldn't be verified that they were actually aliens, despite it being obvious they were aliens. Earlier she'd been on the computer talking to some of her friends and many of them thought it was some elaborate hoax pulled off in an attempt to boost tourism to Helmia and to increase its popularity. Once or twice in the past week, Lola had passed people in the street talking about how excited they were to be in Helmia and to be going to where the aliens were sighted.

She went to sleep soon after and had a dream in which she was flying higher and higher above the Earth in a massive rocket. Time flew by and she was stepping out on to the moon in a spacesuit. She saw the Earth in all its splendour and realised just how small it really was. All those people so far away on that tiny, seemingly insignificant planet were miniscule in the grand scale of things. This was all that there was for humanity at the present, this planet. Sure, humans had landed on the moon and would no doubt eventually travel to other parts of the solar system, making giant leaps across the cosmos, but Lola couldn't help but think that it was all pointless. What if something came along and wiped out the human race as well as all other life on Earth? Then it would be just another empty planet. She was quite divided in her opinion: on the one hand, humanity was lonely and somewhat isolated, yet on the other, Earth was bustling with life and technological development and humans were ambitious enough to want to explore the rest of the universe as much as they could. In all, Earth was really quite strange, but humans were full of fire that would never die down.

She woke up the next morning thinking it was one of the weirdest dreams she'd ever had. It was wonderful, but odd. Within half an hour, she'd had breakfast, had showered and was ready to go. Before she knew it, she was with her friends outside the gates of the theme park waiting for one more person, Hannah. So far Lola, Thomas, Erica, Edward, Natella and Darren were there. The theme park was the island's main tourist attraction; last year it welcomed over four million guests.

It was a chilly day, which was also slightly dank owing to the dull grey rain clouds up ahead. The path was slightly coloured by the little amount of rain that had poured so far. All in all, it was a typical January day. Looking at the gates, a few of the taller attractions were visible: the observation tower, the drop tower, the odd thrill ride and a few roller coasters. It was a view that Lola loved, as it always seemed to invite her in.

Hannah arrived in about ten minutes then the excited group went in, flashing their annual passes to the attendants at the ticket booths, something that they did every year ritualistically.

The theme park was split into eight different sections, each one of which was elaborately and lavishly themed, as were all rides and attractions housed in that particular section. The park boasted a wide selection of thrill rides, family and children's rides, water rides, roller coasters and shows, as well as the park's own monorail. It was open year-round and had seen its attendance increase year-on-year for the past decade. It was Lola's favourite place: here she was always guaranteed a good time and the atmosphere was generally one of blissful enjoyment, carefree and lax. She'd never had a bad day here.

After a few rides, they decided to head to the park's tallest and fastest coaster: Arch Enemy. The queue, however, was already over an hour long, though no one was reluctant to queue because they thought the coaster was by far the best attraction in the park. The queue consisted of a cattle-pen system of lines inside an air-conditioned building of futuristic design.

'That breeze is lovely,' Hannah said, leaning against the railings.

'It's actually warmer outside,' replied Thomas, his hands in his pockets.

There were four people per row, so it was decided that the four girls would go in one row and the three boys in another. They passed the time talking and gossiping about people and teachers at school. Before long, they were at the station, their party waiting for the train currently at the station to fill up. Once the gates to the individual rows on the train closed, they were let on to the platform to stand for a row by the attendant. The boys opted for the back row because that offered the most intense ride, whereas the girls had to settle for the penultimate row.

'Just a few more minutes to go,' said Hannah.

The four of them watched as the ride operators came round and ensured everyone's restraints were in place, one on each side of the platform, each checking one side of the train. Once the all-clear was given, the operator in the booth at the far end of the station pushed a button and the train started slowly edging its way out of the station, some riders cheering, others looking a bit scared. As the train went by,

Lola noticed a girl sat in the side closest to her, a girl who looked exactly like her. Lola was transfixed: her gaze told her this girl had the same face, same hair colour, skin tone; the girl's part of the train had soon left the station and was inching up the cranky lift hill.

'Lola?' said Hannah.

'I've just seen her.'

'Who?'

'That girl. The one who looks exactly like me. I just saw her on that train.'

'Really? Are you sure it was her?'

Lola looked at Hannah as if he'd just asked her what two add two was.

'Of course you're sure! What am I saying!'

'I swear it was her.'

'How many times have you seen her now?' asked Hannah.

'This is the fourth or fifth time I think.'

'What girl, sorry?' asked Natella.

'I've seen a girl who looks the exact double of me a few times now. She really freaks me out.'

'And she looks exactly like you?' Natella enquired.

'Same hair, same everything,' Lola said, sounding a bit spooked out.

'Maybe she's a long lost twin or something,' Erica joked.

'She could be, but I'm certain I'm an only child, absolutely certain.'

The next train had pulled into the station and the gates were opened.

'Hopefully we'll be able to find her once we've got off the ride: she won't have got that far. Imagine what that would be like, I mean, you've said a few times you'd be interested to meet her,' Hannah suggested.

'I'd rather not. I just want to forget about her and enjoy Arch Enemy,' Lola replied.

The four of them got on and eagerly put their restraints in place, all of them desperate to be climbing the lift hill.

The train soon left the station and started its slow ascent up the lift hill. Suspense was building as the altitude was increasing.

'I can't believe you haven't been on this before, Natella,' called Darren from behind, 'you will love it; it's one of the best here.'

'It's always had really long queues whenever I've been here.'

'You're about to see why,' Lola said; they were over halfway up the lift hill, whose apex reached just over a two hundred and forty feet. Higher and higher they got until the train crested the apex and plummeted down the steep first drop, gracefully soaring back into the sky to crest another hill.

'Woohoo!' Lola cried as each of them floated off their seats for a brief second or less before plummeting back down to Earth. There were a few more airtime hills followed by an overbanked turn, during which Natella screamed loudly and closed her eyes, then there were a few more steep drops and a few twists and turns before the train smoothly came to a halt on the brake run.

'Wow!' was all Natella could say.

'This is definitely my favourite coaster,' Lola told her.

'I can see why. My eyes are watering.'

'I'm dreading the photo,' said Hannah.

Once off the ride, they followed the exit path and came to the little futuristic-looking booth painted in a silvery metallic paint and with a few chirpy attendants behind the silver counter. The screens above showed all the pictures taken for the last few trains.

'There we are,' Thomas pointed out the photo of the boys' row; the photo of the girls' row was the next one along. It showed Natella almost in hysterics, Hannah with her hands up, flailing wildly, Erica cheering and Lola with a massive smile on her face.

'Let's buy it,' Lola suggested, but Hannah was already standing a few feet away, taking a picture of it on her phone.

'Can we have this emailed home?' Lola asked an attendant, a cheery young woman with braided hair and large glasses.

'Sure, but it will cost you, I'm afraid. Just write down your email address here in block capitals and it will only cost you five pounds to have it emailed to that address.'

Feeling slightly swindled that she'd just been charge for an email; Lola paid the attendant after giving her a slip on which her email address was written. Erica, Hannah and Natella each give her some money towards it.

'It's much better getting it digitally; now we can all have a copy,' Erica said.

The boys didn't bother buying their photo. It was nearing lunchtime so they decided to take a break from the rides and head for the nearest restaurant. The queue was rather long; the wait seemed twice as long as it actually it was owing to their hunger. Time crawled by as they waited and the queue gradually whittled down; they split up into smaller groups to go to different counters. Lola had completely forgotten about the girl she'd seen before.

Eventually they were seated round a large table eating their food. The restaurant was still exceedingly busy.

'Just nipping to the loo,' Lola said after getting up; she walked by many people, some carrying loads of food, on her way to the toilets. Once she was done, she was washing her hands when she looked up in the mirror and, after hearing a toilet flush, saw someone leave a cubicle: the girl she'd seen earlier.

'Oh my,' the girl said, looking at Lola earnestly.

Lola herself was lost for words.

'Who are you?' the girl asked.

'I'm Lola Spears. Who are you?'

'I'm Abi Wren.'

'You look exactly like me.'

'I was just about to say the same thing. Are we not… related somehow?'

'I'm sure I have no relation my age, absolutely positive.'

'Me too,' Abi said, sounding a little nervous.

Lola was perplexed: the more she looked at Abi, the more she realised that they were identical down to every last detail.

'This is too weird for me,' Abi said as she left the re-stroom.

'Wait!' Lola rushed to follow Abi but bumped into an old woman coming into the restroom. Lola hastily apologised then entered the restaurant, by which time Abi was walking out of the doors with a friend running after her asking her what the matter was.

Chapter 7 –
The Snowy City

Lola spent the rest of the day with her eyes alert in case she saw Abi again. Sometimes she thought she'd seen her, but then in the blink of an eye it turned out to be someone else. After realising the chances of seeing her again that day were very slim, Lola started to relax and enjoy herself more. Once she went on another ride, she'd practically forgotten all about Abi, until she found herself in the queue for a ride where she'd last seen her a few years previously.

'I didn't even find out where she lives,' she said to Hannah later on while the seven of them were queuing for the log flume.

'You know her full name so you can find her online. She's bound to have a profile; everyone does these days. Even my five-year-old cousin has one.'

'I'll have a look when I get back home.'

'Do you think this girl is actually related to you?'

'I don't see how she can be. I know everyone in my family and am certain there are no secret people lurking about.'

'You don't think she's a twin that got separated at birth or something?'

'That's probably the most likely solution, but I'm an only

child. The first time I saw Abi was ages ago and I was only little then. I panicked and asked mum and she was just as puzzled as I was.'

They looked at each other, and then Lola decided to change the subject, though she was still thinking about it.

After the log flume, they hit a few a few more rides before calling it a day. They all got the monorail back to the front of the park then got the other monorail back home; Darren left a few stops in so there were only Lola, Hannah, Thomas, Natella, Erica and Edward remaining.

Hannah gave a sigh of relief.

'It wasn't that bad,' Lola said to her.

'I just wish he would talk to me. He's too shy.'

It was getting dark and there was a chill in the air. The sky was a dark purple.

The six of them ended up going back to Lola's. She'd opened her window to let in some of the crisp air.

'Are you sure I should find her online?' Lola asked.

'What harm could it do? You don't have to add her or anything. You want to know who she is, and now you can find out. She's probably doing the same thing right now.'

'Hannah's right, Lola, what's the harm in finding her?' Edward said.

'OK. I'll look for her,' Lola went over to her computer desk and turned the computer on.

'That's her!' Hannah said from over Lola's shoulder a few minutes later.

'She lives on the mainland. She's the same age as me!'

'Go through her pictures,' Hannah said, 'this is so weird…it's like I'm looking at pictures of you.'

'I know what you mean,' Thomas said, at Lola's other side.

'If you think about, we all must have look-alikes,' Erica mentioned, sitting on the edge of Lola's bed, 'I mean, there are billions and billions of us, so it's only natural that every-one would have a few look-alikes out there.'

'That's probably true, sis. Remember our auntie Sharon? The last time she visited she told us about seeing a look-alike.'

'That poor woman; I'm sure she's lost it.'

'Send her a message, Lola,' Hannah suggested,

'Why?'

'Come on, you want to find out *exactly* who she is, don't you?'

'But do you really think she's someone though, Hannah?' asked Thomas, 'Erica's right; this Abi is probably just some-one who just happens to look a lot like Lola.'

'I think she's dodgy,' Hannah admitted, 'the way she ran off like that. I think she knows something but she's not letting on.'

'Our auntie Sharon started acting very weird indeed after she saw her look-alike,' Erica explained, 'she gradually became convinced that her family were lying to her and there were all sorts of arguments, silly, pointless quarrels, all rooted in her insecurity, or at least that's what mother told us.'

'Lola's not going to end up like that though,' replied Hannah, 'because she's going to write that message, aren't you, Lola?'

'I don't know what to write.'

'Let me do it...there, done! Short, sweet, and to the point.'

'What did you write?' asked Natella, who was sat on Lola's bed looking pensive whilst everyone else was crowded around Lola.

'I just asked her when she was born,' replied Hannah, sounding proud of herself.

Lola felt a bit nervous. What if it turned out that she and Abi were long-lost relations or something? She knew for certain that couldn't be the case, but when she pictured Abi in her mind, she wondered how they both looked identical. She then realised she hadn't been listening for the past few minutes.

'Apparently she's coming to Helmia in a month's time to promote her new film,' Erica was saying.

'Who are you talking about, sorry?' Lola asked.

'Mary Morton, of course,' Erica replied, 'her new film's coming out in March and she's got a book coming out. Have you seen the poster for the film? She looks so different in it – her hair's much longer than before.'

'She's already in Helmia; I read in the paper that she'd pulled out of a TV series and was having a break from acting for a while. According to the paper, once she's done the promotion for this film and her book, she's going away for a while,' Edward told them all.

'Sounds like she's going the same way as Auntie Sharon,' Erica joked to her brother, who looked unimpressed.

'Look! You've got a reply from her already,' Hannah stated with glee.

'What has she said?' asked Natella.

'She says she was born in early December, 1994 and that she doesn't know the exact date.'

'Early December?' Thomas asked, 'but Lola, you were born on the 3rd? That is weird.'

'I don't have a twin, Thomas.'

'How could she not know the day she was born?'

'She says she's an orphan. She was left on the steps of an orphanage in Old Merrington when she was only a few days old and her parents have never been found. That's why she thinks you're her twin, Lola.'

Old Merrington was a seaside town on the east coast of Britain, which was the closest mainland town to Helmia, and subsequently had a large harbour from where ferries took people to and from Helmia every day.

Lola didn't say anything. She sat there and sank deep into thought. She felt sorry that Abi had never known her parents. Part of her saw Abi's way of thinking, but the other part knew fine well that she did not have a twin at all. She was baffled; she thought Abi must be anxious to find out the answer seeing as she was so willing to divulge such personal information to someone she barely knew.

'Write back to her, please, Hannah. Tell her I'm sorry but I can't help her; I don't know why we look the same but I know we're not in any way related.'

Hannah spent a few moments typing then sent the message; after waiting for a while no reply came, however.

'Oh well,' Hannah sighed.

'Like I said, Lola,' started Erica, 'I wouldn't worry too much if I were you. Yes, she looks a lot like you, but is that really something to get worked up over? Our auntie Sharon reacted a bit oddly, but she was always a bit kooky.'

'No she wasn't!'

'Edward, she was, you can't deny it. Our mother always said there was something slightly weird about her sister, that she was always deliberately uncouth to us all just because we all wouldn't believe her when she was going doolally.'

'It's not fair to say this about Auntie Sharon, Erica. Yes, she couldn't cope quite as well as expected, but it wasn't her fault and the family certainly didn't help her by constantly ignoring her.'

'I'm only telling the truth.'

'Now, now, you two,' Hannah said.

Erica stared at her brother for a second, and then returned her attention to the computer. Lola looked and saw that Edward was looking at Thomas, mouthing something to him.

'What happened to Sharon?' Lola asked Edward.

'The last time we saw her was about three years ago. About six months later she snapped and moved to America. Quit her job and everything. She used to work as a stylist and worked with quite a few big names.'

'Really? Who?'

'Ray Mungo, David Sears, Betty Logan, even Mary Morton in fact. She had a job she loved and was paid really well, but then she gradually became more and more insecure and filled with anxiety until she decided to wipe the slate clean. She now works at a salon in Seattle.'

'But is she happy?'

'Yeah. She still keeps in touch.'

Lola smiled. She could never do what Sharon did and move all that way to start a new life. Helmia was her home and always had been: she couldn't imagine leaving it to live somewhere else one day, no matter what problems should arise, if any. She'd planned to live here her whole life, most likely still with her family. When her brother went away to uni, Lola was gutted to see him leave everything behind, but he reassured her he'd always come home and that it wasn't goodbye, because in seven weeks or so they'd see each other again. At first, Lola missed him dearly, and then she decided she should get on with her own life and carried on, looking forward for his return. She knew he was enjoying living a life up there, making new friends and living in a new town, and that he always loved coming up and seeing everyone there, but she knew one day she'd have to do the very same. She wanted to go to university and Andrew had told her on his first visit home that he made the right decision in leaving Helmia, because he no longer felt tied down to one place.

'I know it's ages away for you, Lola, but when you go to uni, move away. There's a world out there and you're not going to see it if you're tethered to one place your whole life,' were his words to her when she asked him whether she should do the same as him.

But for now, Lola was happy in Helmia. She was still only in Year 10 and had plenty of time before she had to even start thinking about uni. Deep down, a clock was ticking, slowly but surely.

Her friends gradually left then Lola was alone in her room, having seen Thomas off. Her parents were out. She was sitting on her bed contemplating Abi Wren, unable to come to a worthwhile conclusion as to who exactly she was and why she looked identical to her. She vacillated for what seemed like ages, going over all possibilities; eventually she concluded that she had no idea whatsoever what was right. For the mean time, Abi would just be a girl who looked exactly like her.

She read for a bit then rolled over and went to sleep, unaware of what time it was. She wondered what Abi was doing right now and whether she was fretting just as much she was.

On Sunday, she didn't do much apart from get all her homework up-to-date. She did a bit of research on the Internet but found no more news items about the aliens other than a few more witnesses who'd come forward merely repeating what others before them had already iterated. Everyone was hungry for more news about that famous Friday night, maybe even more actual developments, yet nothing had happened and it seemed as if nothing was going to happen. Nevertheless, Lola kept up her regular search for more updates.

That evening, she was watching telly with her mum in the cosy living room reclining on a sofa while her mum had her feet up on the coffee table. The film they were watching was only a few minutes in when Lola's dad came in from the dining room where he'd been on the computer and said: 'have you seen the snow out there?'

'Snow? Come on, dad, we never get snow here.'

'I'm serious, look outside.'

Lola and her mum got up and went over to the living room window, opened the curtains and looked outside: there was a thin blanket of snow on the garden, which completely covered the lawn and had buried the soil of some of the pot plants. Snow was falling from the dull, grey clouds up above, and it was falling fast. Wind was blowing vehemently with a distinctive howl.

Lola could only ever remember it snowing in Helmia once before, and that had been when she was five years old and there was a brief flurry of snow the day after Boxing Day.

'Wow!' she exclaimed, 'look at it out there! I can't believe it.'

She instantly forgot about the film and hurriedly got suitably dressed then went outside, the fine snow softly crunching beneath her feet as she crossed the drive to the front lawn, which looked so odd glittering white. The wind was buffeting her cheeks, as were tiny snowflakes being wildly blown about. It was freezing out here, the coldest it had been for ages. Just half an hour ago the weather had been normal, and now this. Lola saw the houses nearby were barely visible owing to the heavy snowfall. She shivered a little and felt the cold clinging to her face, which felt taut and sensitive to the severe change of weather it wasn't yet acclimatised to. It was quite gloomy outside and visibility was low, yet the glittering of the snow everywhere could still be seen.

The wind started getting a little harder and the snowfall started getting heavier. Lola was constantly being pelted with tiny snowflakes that, coupled with the wind, made her face in a constant state of mild pain. She braved the weather, her resolve being to experience it.

She picked up a heap of light, powdery snow in her hand

and, with open palm, watched as the wind soon blew it all off her hand in an instant. Her face was starting to tingle.

She looked inside and saw her mum snuggling up on the sofa watching the film. There was a healthy fire glowing vividly. Lola's dad went over to his wife with a cup of tea then went back to the dining room to continue his work.

The snowfall seemed incessant, as did the wind. Lola ran round the house to the back garden and saw the trees in the forest in the distance were starting to get covered in white. The forest looked thicker and more impenetrable than ever. The air filling Lola's lungs was crisp and fresh. She took a deep breath and continued to endure the battering from the weather. There was snow everywhere.

Once back inside, the warmth flooding her as she entered, she decided not to watch the film but to go upstairs on her computer. She checked the news and saw that the weather was one of the main items of news. It appeared that this sudden downpour of snow was unforeseen and had thus rendered weathermen and –women baffled. They'd expected the evening to be bleak and cloudy then for there to be a few bursts of welcome sunshine the following day.

'Well, the snow has certainly taken us all by surprise. Hopefully it should have stopped by before midnight,' one weatherman said excitedly, as if the drastic change in weather was the most interesting thing that had happened to him of late.

However, when Lola awoke the next morning, not really ready for another week of school, it was to find the snow still rapidly falling, if not a bit heavier than the last time she'd seen it, and the wind still viciously blowing across the land. She managed to pull open her window against the gust of wind and looked outside to see that at least two feet or so of snow had fallen and that it was almost completely white: only the fronts of houses and parts of cars were visible: everything that was flat or angled had been buried in a mass of snow. The houses' roofs were all snow-capped and the tops and windscreens of cars were now all white, as were the road and paths either side of it. It seemed, given that it was still plummeting to the ground, that there was a limitless amount of it up there waiting to descend in a flurry to the ground.

Lola could see mounds of snow packed against the side of buildings. Looking down, she saw a mound of snow about two feet high stretched along the entire front of the house, and, she guessed, all around the house's perimeter too.

That moment, her phone started ringing: it was Hannah.

'Have you seen the snow?'

'How could I not see the snow? It's everywhere,' Lola replied.

'Luckily, the snow's hit the school too, because school's cancelled today!' Hannah said triumphantly.

'Brilliant.'

'I can't get over this weather. I know weather's always boring, but this is fun!'

'We should get everyone together and have a massive snowball fight,' Lola suggested; she heard Hannah tell her mother she'd be going out and didn't know when she'd be back.

'Yes, mum, I'll take my phone and I'll be careful to make sure it doesn't get damaged in the snow. Shall we say the park where Sunnyside and Malvern roads meet at ten?'

'Sounds perfect. Get texting.'

Lola said goodbye then hung up and started fervently texting everyone, excitement in her fired up by the fact that she'd be having her first ever snowball fight. She finished typing her message then sent it to everyone, hoping everyone would be there.

The abrupt change in weather seemed to bring nothing

but cold, heaps of snow, a wild wind yet there were many advantages to this: no school, snowball fights and lovely never-before seen, picturesque wintry views. Helmia seemed to have transformed completely. All of the island had seen and felt the effects of this atmospheric aberration and everyone seemed to be rejoicing: as Lola walked to the park, a mere ten minutes away, wrapped up warm, there were little kids playing in the snow with their parents, youngsters mucking about having snowball fights; the streets were noisy and full of laughter, despite the ongoing wind. It was a blustery wintry day, but one that got people out of their houses and playing together.

Before long, Lola arrived at the park, hampered somewhat by the treacherous way of getting there: twice she had to muster her strength and press on against the powerful wind. Nevertheless, she was one of the first at the park, the others being Thomas, Hannah, Edward, Darren and Natella, who were all huddled together by a few aged, bare trees now besprinkled with snow in the middle of the large park.

Lola went over to them and saw them all looking at her, and then before she knew it she was being pelted with snowballs by all of them. She just managed to protect herself with her hands just in time to stop the last one, which crumpled when it came into contact with her hand.

'Guys, you'd all better run.'

Lola picked up a clump of snow and ran at whoever was nearest and threw it at them hitting them square in the back. It turned out to be Natella, who got an even bigger amount of snow and dumped it over Lola's head as she bent down to pick up more snow. Her hair was quickly wet, cold and dripping.

After a few more people arrived, the chaos escalated. Soon there were twenty people throwing snowballs at one another, some tiny, wispy balls of snow, others great, solid ones bound to hurt whoever they hit a little. The merriment continued for many hours; the wind and snowfall both started waning in strength. Nevertheless, Lola was soaked through by the time she took to standing by the trees for a rest after three hours' running about.

She felt a snowball crash into her back then she abandoned her rest and ran after the attacker, temporarily stopping to gather as much snow as she could before carrying on her pursuit and eventually pummelling snow into their back as they ran on. Snow was flying everywhere and every few seconds, someone was hit. Everyone was laughing whilst running about, with the result that a few ended up swallowing snow.

Lola seemed to be running on an endless supply of energy given the amount of running about she was doing. The second time she stopped to rest, the wind had abated even more. She noticed a group of children playing nearby, laughing merrily. Then she got hit right in the side of the face by a snowball and she scooped up a ball of snow then darted after Natella.

'I'm gonna get you!'

She ran after her and luckily threw the snowball just as Natella turned and hit her right in the face.

'Ha! Serves you right.'

Feeling victorious, Lola stood still and surveyed her surroundings: Natella was running away for cover by the trees, whilst everyone else was still running amok, snowballs flying everywhere. The children nearby were also having their own little snowball fight, at least that's what Lola first thought she'd seen; on closer inspection, she saw that most of the children were ganging up on two of the smaller kids, pelting them with snowballs. The two victims were covering their faces with their arms and wailing, whilst the children pelting snowballs at them were laughing derisively. One of the little ones fell over; the other went to help him but found himself getting kicked to the ground.

'Oy!' Lola shouted to them, but the snowfall had started getting heavier all of a sudden and the wind was growing stronger; her voice failed to rend the air, however, as the wind's might was too great. She shouted even louder, but she again went unheard and the two kids carried on being hit with snowballs as she started to walk over to them.

She stood in between the littler ones and the bigger ones, who immediately stopped slinging snowballs.

'I saw you kick him to the ground, now you are not to do that again, understood? If you do, you'll have me to answer to. Where are your parents?'

The group of six kids couldn't have been more than ten, Lola thought to herself. None of them spoke, however.

'Come on, where are your parents?' she asked fervently.

'None of your business,' spoke the little boy who'd done the kicking; he was wrapped up in many layers of clothes and had a raspy voice.

Before Lola could reply, he pelted her with a snowball right in the face.

'You lot had better run. All my friends are over there; there are nineteen of us. Unless you want nineteen older kids to have a snowball fight with you, stay away from these two here.'

The little gang started running away.

'Are you two okay?' Lola asked the two kids on the floor.

'Yeah, thank you, Miss,' one of them said.

'Do you know them?' Lola inquired.

'Yeah. They go to our school. We don't like them though.'

Lola turned round and saw the gang run up to a gaggle of

parents sitting down on a white, glistening hill, all wrapped up in many layers.

'Are your parents up there?' Lola asked, pointing to the throng. She noticed the snow was now getting considerably lighter and the wind was practically non-existent.

'Yeah,' one of them said. Lola helped them up and took them over, hand in hand, to the group of parents. A mother came over and took the two kids from Lola, thanked her warmly for her intervention, asked whether they were okay and told her that her back had only been turned for a few moments.

'Ooh look, Ben, did you build that snowman?' she asked, pointing to behind Lola; Lola saw her friends, the trees where Natella was and a little distance from the trees was a large snowman, about the same size as Lola.

'No,' Ben muttered,

'Did you build it, Liam?'

'No,' Liam mumbled.

'Can you take us to it?' Ben asked Lola.

'If that's okay with your mum,' Lola said smiling.

'Of course. As long as you're quick, because we have to be going soon.'

'I'll be back in a few minutes with them.'

Lola walked back the way she'd come with the two kids either side of her, both holding on to one of her hands.

Lola couldn't remember the snowman being there before and reckoned one of her friends must have built whilst on a break from the snowball fight. They were a few metres away from it when Natella came over to Lola and said: 'do you know where that snowman came from?'

'Didn't one of you build it?'

'I've been here watching them all. It was probably some-one else.'

'Yeah,' Lola said. She looked at the snowman and thought it quite a nice pleasant: it had a lopsided top hat, a long scarf wrapped round its neck, two shiny pebbles for eyes, a long carrot nose, a beaming smile made out of smaller glassy pebbles and thin prickly twigs for arms, one of which was holding a long thick tree branch, one end of which was planted firmly in the snow.

Natella had gone back to join in. Lola looked at the snowman and couldn't believe someone had built this so fast. She was sure she hadn't seen it earlier. There were no footprints in the snow anywhere near it. Lola walked right round it with the kids, but the only footprints she saw were the ones they'd just formed. They were only a metre away from it and Lola was just about to tell the kids to go and look at it more closely when their mother shouted them and Lola took them back.

The snowball fight soon died down, with people drifting at now and then to go and get lunch. They all went to a nearby café to get a quick bite to eat. As they trundled there, the snowstorm gathered pace once more.

'I wish this blizzard would just stop altogether instead of coming back all the time,' Hannah whined.

'I love the snow,' replied Darren, 'and I love the way the wind whips your face.'

'If it gets any worse, we'll all get blown over,' replied Hannah, looking down after she spoke.

'Come on, Hannah, would you rather be here being blown about or in school?'

'Here.'

'You must love it a little bit then, surely?' Darren said.

'It'll take a lot of getting used to before I ever love *this* weather,' she replied, looking directly at Darren.

'We Brits always talk about the weather, but then when it does get exciting, we act adversely to it, have you noticed?'

'I guess that's true. We just love to complain!' Hannah replied; Lola saw she was fretting a little.

Once they left the café, it had turned into a proper blizzard, such that they couldn't even see the park and could barely make out the few cars on the road. The storm carried on all night and was still raging on Tuesday morning; school was cancelled again and they all had another snowball fight in the park.

'I'm enjoying this bout of weather,' Lola told her parents at breakfast.

'I'm glad you are, honey. Make the most of it because tomorrow you could find yourself back in school,' Lola's mum advised her, before moaning that she was still expected at work.

'I'll have to brave the storm and get the monorail,' she sighed.

'Will the monorail still be running in this weather?' Lola asked.

'It should be, unfortunately.'

Lola's mum wrapped up warm and soon left for work, as did her dad, who only worked a short distance away by foot.

Before long, Lola was back in the park with her friends, and, inspired by her mother's words, decided to make the most of it and stayed there until she and Edward were the only ones left, Hannah and Natella having gone off at about quarter past two to get some late lunch.

They walked through the park together and sat down on a bench after wiping off as much snow as they could.

'I am freezing,' he said, rubbing his gloved hands together.

'Me too. It's worth it though.'

'Definitely. That was so much fun. I hope it snows tomorrow too.'

'If it does, I'm getting you back for throwing that massive snowball right at the back of my head.'

'I was aiming for your back, by the way.'

'Excuses, excuses.'

They sat and talked about the snow for a bit longer then decided to call it a day, seeing as they were both shivering and their insides seemed to freeze every time they inhaled some of the bitingly cold air.

Lola got back home at around three, turned the fire on and sat down with the news channel on. The main news item was the weather, namely last night's blizzard.

'We simply don't know how long this spate of extreme weather will last. However, it does seem to be getting worse so we would suggest that you don't make long journeys, especially in cars, just in case. What has baffled meteorologists is that this snowfall has come right out of the blue and defied all their predictions. Furthermore, the snowstorm is directly over Helmia and has barely moved at all in the past two days. Yesterday, the snowfall's intensity kept wavering, however today it has got progressively worse, so we expect it to worse throughout this evening and perhaps tomorrow as well, although we cannot be certain.

'It pains me to say that the number of people who have died during the snowstorms has now risen to thirty-six, most of which have been collisions on iced-over roads. The most recent people to perish were two teenagers who were skating on Summerstone Lake in Moistree when the ice gave way and they fell in. Passers-by were unable to save them and the lake has been cordoned off. All are advised to stay away from any frozen-over body of water and to take caution.'

Lola looked solemn; while she'd been having fun with her friends, she'd been unaware that so many people had died because of this treacherous weather. She had just assumed that this was a free few days off school where she could have fun with her friends and hadn't really thought of any possible downsides to it. Feeling rather guilty, she turned the TV off and stared out of the window, hoping her parents and friends, and everyone else, was okay and out of harm's way.

Chapter 8 –
Snowman Battery

Lola awoke on Wednesday to find it still heavily snowing; the blizzard seemed relentless. Assuming school would be cancelled again, she rolled over in bed and went back to sleep for a bit.

When she eventually woke, it was to an empty house. Her parents had left her a note on the fridge telling her school had indeed been cancelled and that they'd be back just after four. Lola looked outside to see the monstrous blizzard still raging outside, just as strongly as yesterday.

She was in the kitchen making herself some toast when she looked out of the window and could barely make out the back garden. Everything was buried in feet of snow. She ate her toast slowly while she watched the tumultuous blizzard outside. Yawning, she went to the living room, lay down on the settee and turned on the telly. Flicking to the weather channel, she learned that it was still unknown when this weather would stop. She went back to the kitchen to get a drink of orange juice and looked out of the window as she drank. She noticed something that hadn't been there the last time she looked: a snowman in her garden.

'What the?' she said to herself in disbelief. She blinked

and squinted, pressing her face up to the glass to allow for a better view, and there it was, the snowman, smiling at her; she thought it looked exactly like the one she'd seen in the park the day before but then told herself she was just seeing things and that it just looked a bit similar to the one from the day before.

Lola didn't know what to do. Reason told her she should just stay inside and ignore it, but her inquisitive side told her she should venture outside and see the snowman closer up. Her reasoning quelled in an instant, Lola went upstairs to get changed into suitable clothes and when she got back downstairs and looked at out the kitchen window, saw that the snowman was a bit closer to the house than it had been previously: it had been right next to a row of bushes but was now closer to the middle of the garden. Lola could just about see the imprint in the snow of where it had been.

'Eh?' Lola said to herself.

She thought it was one of her friends playing some sort of trick on her: they'd built a snowman out of something, had placed it in her garden and were now hiding somewhere nearby.

She opened the kitchen door a little bit, felt the force of the blizzard outside bursting to get in and slid outside and shut the door behind her.

It was even colder and harsher than the previous few days. Lola was constantly battered by the feral winds and the snow seemed to almost scratch her face. Wishing she could somehow negate the effects of this hostile weather, she endured the weather and staggered over to the snowman.

'Come on guys, the joke's over,' she shouted so she could be heard amidst the howling wind.

'Now how did you move?' she whispered to herself as she surveyed the snowman.

After a few more moments, Lola did a double take: she

thought the snowman's head had twitched. She rubbed her eyes and told herself she was just seeing things. She took a step back then saw the snowman's pebble smile somehow turn into a frown.

She told herself again she was seeing things: this was merely a hallucination of some sort. Freaked out, she turned round and started running towards the kitchen door when something very hard hit her on the right side of her head and she fell into the snow. There was an aching where she'd been hit; the right side of her face felt searing hot with pain, despite being submerged in the snow. She could just about make out a low humming noise coming from somewhere. She got up out of the snow and turned round to see the snowman a few feet from her; it had a look of contempt on its face and was holding the long branch above its head with its twig arms, which seemed to have somehow extended to the length of normal arms.

The snowman brought down the branch with such speed that Lola couldn't avoid the attack, and with such force that she instantly cried out in anguish the moment it brutally hit her sides. Instead of lying there and taking another beating, she managed to roll over just in time to avoid another attack from the frenzied snowman and clambered to her knees, struggling with the intensifying pain in her side and her head, the whole of which felt hot from the pain, especially her forehead.

She turned round and ducked just in time as the snowman swung the branch round with might. Still being buffeted by the storm, her visibility was still low and running was a great difficulty, owing to the wind.

She was flummoxed to see that the snowman was swinging the branch around its entire body with the same arm revolving in circles. It stopped swinging the branch, jumped up in the air a little bit and landed even closer to Lola without its body being affected in any way whatsoever.

Lola acted on instinct: she lunged forward and grabbed on to the branch with both hands and tried desperately to yank it out of the snowman's scraggy hands but the snowman had too tight a grip, despite its arms and hands being flimsy twigs; nevertheless, she held on, grasping tightly, then she kicked the snowman's massive belly for a reason she didn't know and flinched and yelled when her foot pervaded the snow easily yet hit something solid in the middle of the snowman's belly. She let go of the branch and fell over on to her back, her foot in the snowman's belly. Its face was looking down at her, irate in expression. She rolled over again as the branch crashed to the ground with a thud, narrowly missing her. Her foot was now out of the snowy belly, which, due to her kick, had lost some mass and now caused the snowman to be a little lopsided, and even angrier. Lola got up and ducked again as the snowman slammed the branch down. She kicked it again and again; each time puffs of snow flew out.

Now free and with the snowman having let go of the branch due to its crumbling, Lola grabbed the branch and threw it with all her might into the wind, which blew it and sent it crashing into the garden fence. Lola turned and saw the snowman significantly smaller than it was previously. She decided only one thing would destroy the snowman, and she quickly battled the blizzard to get back inside the kitchen. She stood there in disbelief, thinking it extremely absurd that she'd just been attacked by a snowman. Her head and side were hurting still. Telling herself to block out the pain, she grabbed a bucket from underneath the sink and started to fill it with warm water. She looked out of the window and saw the snowman standing in the garden with the branch back in its hand; she would have to be very agile if she was to avoid getting hit again. She took a few deep breaths then turned the tap off, grabbed the bucket in one hand, forced the door open with the other, and slipped outside into the fray.

Once again she steeled herself to endure the blizzard and felt her body's temperature instantly plummet. The snowman was slowly jumping towards her. The bucket was poised and ready: Lola threw the water at the snowman as it began to swing the branch once more. Not wanting to risk another attack, she stumbled back inside, arms over her head, and slammed the kitchen door shut, locking it for good measure. She dampened a tea towel and put it over her warm forehead to cool it down a bit.

'Ouch,' she said as she touched her side. She noticed there were droplets of blood on the kitchen counter; she felt the side of her face and saw there was more blood on her hand. A look in the mirror told her there was a series of small cuts on her cheek, all fortunately quite shallow.

'That damn snowman,' Lola mumbled as she got a box of plasters out from one of the cupboards.

Once she'd attended to her modest injuries, she had a few biscuits and a drink then felt as if she'd convalesced a bit. She looked outside but saw no trace of the snowman: all that was there was the garden, covered in snow.

'Eh?' she said to herself.

She continued to look outside for a while in case she saw the snowman again, but there was nothing to see apart from the seemingly unstoppable blizzard. She texted her parents, Hannah, Thomas and Demzel as well as a few others, telling them all what had happened; within a minute she was getting a phone call from Demzel.

'Lola, what on Earth happened? Are you okay?'

'I'm fine, Demzel, absolutely fine. I'm just shell-shocked and freaked out.'

'You say a snowman *attacked* you?'

'One minute there wasn't anything in the garden, the next

minute there was a snowman there. I went out to investigate and it started whacking me with a branch it was holding.'

'How odd.'

'I know. At first I thought it was someone playing a trick of some sort, but it was very real.'

'Was it actually made of snow?'

'Well, part of it was. I kicked it in the stomach and hit something solid in its middle.'

'I wonder...'

'I know it sounds crazy, but that's what happened.'

'Don't worry, I believe you. Where is the snowman now?'

'It's been gone for at least half an hour.'

'Were there any footprints leading up to it?'

'None at all. It jumped a few times so I guess it just jumped into my garden.'

'Hmmm. This has to have something to do with the aliens,' Demzel said; Lola knew he'd bring the aliens up sooner or later.

'Think of it Lola,' Demzel went on, 'a snowman that attacks people?'

'I guess it could be alien. But why would aliens make a snowman that attacks people?'

'If this is alien technology, we *will* find out why,' Demzel affirmed confidently.

Later on, Lola got replies from Hannah and Thomas and phoned each of them to tell them what had happened. Both were perplexed by Lola's tale; they both offered to come round and make sure she was okay, but Lola told them what she really needed was a lie down and some sleep. She went up to her room, put her pyjamas on, got into bed and turned her TV on.

She flicked through many channels, alarmed at the lack of quality TV there was given the sheer number of channels they had. She turned it off and got her laptop out instead and decided to do some research.

Her phone then started ringing: it was her mum.

'Lola, I've just checked my phone - what on Earth was that text about?'

'I know it sounds crazy, mum, but it's true. A snowman in our garden attacked me with a large branch.'

'What? Lola, you know I don't like nonsense.'

'I know it sounds totally absurd, but I'm telling you it happened. I have scratches on my face and my side still hurts.'

'Lola, how could a snowman attack you?'

'I don't know but it did.'

'Are you hurt?'

'A little. I'm getting better though.'

'Was it someone from school who hurt you?'

'No, mum, I'm telling you it was a snowman,' Lola realised the ludicrousness of what she'd just said and understood why her mum was having trouble believing her.

'I'll speak to you when I get home. Make sure you take care, OK?'

'I will, mum, bye.'

Lola hung up. She suspected her mother would be reluctant to believe her, but then again anyone would have difficulty believing a snowman had seemingly come to life and attacked her with a branch. She herself kept replaying it in her mind; every time it seemed more and more surreal. The biggest shock wasn't the attack, but what had been attacking her.

She scanned the news website for any more updates on the alien story; unfortunately, there weren't any. The story seemed to be drying up. However news item did catch her eye and she began reading it immediately. The snowman attack suddenly started seeming less and less weird – because it had happened to other people, too.

Lola watched a video, filmed only a few hours ago, of a middle-aged woman who was being interviewed in her kitchen, snow falling furiously outside the window behind her.

'I was coming home from the shops in the snowstorm just yesterday evening when I took a shortcut down an alleyway and saw a snowman at the end of it. I thought nothing of it first - it was just a snowman. So I walked down the alley, and was just approaching it when it started moving! Before I knew it, it tried to hit me with a branch it had in its hand but I'd started running before it could get me. I even dropped my shopping, that's how much it scared me. As I ran back down the alley, I looked over my shoulder and saw it jumping down the alley towards me. As I was nearing the end of the alley, I looked behind again and could barely see it for all the snow, but I could tell it was quite far away. I carried on running and didn't stop running till I was home.'

Lola paused the video, seeing no need to watch the interview the clearly traumatised woman, who, Lola found out, lived in Leafdew.

A news report accompanying the video told of snowmen appearing all throughout Helmia in the snow and attacking whoever approached them. All the snowmen eventually vanished. So far fifteen people had been beaten to death, most of whom were seen being beaten by a snowman, others were found beaten to death in the snow with no footprints or anything nearby. There was a warning not to approach any snowman. It hit Lola then that this was all real.

She was reeling; one of those fifteen poor people could very well have been her. She felt lucky to be alive and very grateful. She thought about all the people affected by this and their loved ones left behind. To be sure, she went round the house and locked all the doors and windows before going back to bed where she slept for hours.

'Lola? Lola, it's mum. Are you okay?' her mum said softly.

Lola slowly stirred awake and looked up to see her mum standing over her bed. She sat up.

'They said it's happening all across Helmia. I'm so sorry I didn't believe you straight away,' her mum said.

'It's okay.'

'Are you okay? Tell me everything that happened.'

Lola proceeded to recount her encounter with the snowman. Her mum looked on attentively.

'Lola...that *thing*...it could have *killed* you! And to think I didn't believe you! I'm so stupid. And you're stupid for going back out there after it had already hit you...'

Her mum was sobbing silently.

'I could have lost you,' she muttered.

Lola didn't know what to say. Instead of trying to think of something to say, she just sat there and let her mother cuddle her.

'We take it all for granted. We thought you'd be perfectly fine at home for the day. But then this thing came out of nowhere...this threat...this killer.'

Lola never thought she'd hear anyone refer to a snowman as a killer. She felt warm and secure as her mum muttered away, stifling her tears with a tissue.

As far as she could remember, she hadn't seen her mum like this at all. She felt a bit awkward, as if whatever she'd say would be the wrong thing to say.

'Any day of the week we could lose you just like that.'

Over the next five minutes or so, Lola remained silent while her mum hugged her and kept muttering such things.

'Lola, you must think I'm daft coming up here and being

all emotional and crying,' her mum said after a while, seeming to compose herself.

For the rest of the day, the atmosphere in the house was somewhat atypical. Lola's mum had taken to mollycoddling her a bit and seemed a bit emotional the whole night.

'She's out of danger now,' her husband told her in the kitchen while Lola was watching the telly in the living room, listening to them rather than the telly.

'They said on the news that all those snowman things had gone.'

'I can't believe we're having a conversation about hostile snowmen, Pete,' Lola's mum said to her dad.

'I thought it was some hoax at first, until one of my mates from work got a call from his daughter who was at home with one of the snowmen outside and didn't know what to do.'

'It's all so strange. I'm sure the police will get to the bottom of it soon.'

'I hope so. It'll be a hard task, mind, given that the snowmen seem to vanish once they're done trying to clobber people to death.'

Lola was listening attentively to her parents' discussion; the television programme appeared to make no sound, the people on it miming.

There was a knock at the door: Lola jumped a little. She went to the door, opened it and saw Natella standing there.

'Hi, Lola. Sorry for coming unannounced but I need to have a word with you,' Natella said, quite exasperatedly.

'Yeah, sure. Come on in,' Lola took Natella up to her room.

'I heard you were attacked by one of those snowmen,' Natella said, sitting on the end of Lola's bed.

'I got your text and would have come over earlier but I had to help my mum with the cleaning. Are you okay?'

'I'm absolutely fine. Are you okay?'

'I'm fine. A little out of breath though. I can see a few cuts on your face.'

'It got me with that branch it was brandishing.'

'You're lucky you weren't that grievously injured; people have been *killed*.'

'I saw it on the news. It's so weird. I can't believe so many have died. I guess my curiosity got the better of me. I'd be fine if I hadn't gone outside and investigated.'

'Lola, anyone's gonna do that when a snowman suddenly appears out of nowhere.'

Natella looked apprehensive.

'I just really hope nothing like this happens again. I just can't stop thinking about those poor people who died and their families.'

'It will happen again,' Natella said impulsively, instantly regretting it.

'What do you mean?'

'Well, it's safe to assume, isn't it, that as long as this snow continues, they will probably appear again,' Natella uttered.

'*Is* it going to happen again?' Lola asked.

'How am I meant to know? It might, it might not; I definitely hope it doesn't.'

Lola was listening very carefully to what Natella was saying; she could tell Natella wasn't meant to be saying this.

'Are you sure you're okay?' Natella asked.

'I'm fine, honestly,' Lola saw Natella had worry written all across her face.

Natella left after about half an hour, Lola wishing her a safe walk home in the blustery blizzard. Lola decided to have an early night.

She awoke the next morning to find the snow just as bad as the previous day. In disbelief, she watched as the snow continued to fall from the sky and be blown vehemently by the incessant wind. The view was practically identical to the one from yesterday, except, when she looked out of her window and looked down; she saw the snow was deeper than ever, at least three feet deep.

Her phone started ringing: it was a call from Thomas.

'Hello, Thomas. How are you?'

'I'm sick of this weather. I wake up every morning only to find out school's still not on. I could have had four lie-ins! How are you? Are you feeling better?'

'I'm fine. If school's cancelled again, I might just stay in bed all day with some DVDs.'

'Do you think they're cancelling it? I mean, school being closed for three days due to bad weather is bad enough, but if it's closed today, we've practically missed a week!'

'Are you complaining, Thomas?'

'No…I mean obviously I like being at school, but I miss it a little.'

'Please don't tell me you miss Maths.'

'Well, kind of, but I miss everyone. You know, being there and seeing loads of people and going to lunch with them and hanging out during breaks. You don't get that when you're in the house all day because of the weather.'

'You've got a good point,' Lola said, realising that she too missed it all, deep down. The first two days off had been a welcome change, mainly because of the snowball fights, but now with the chances of missing a fourth consecutive very high, she found herself longing to be at school, then reason came and she said:

'But, there's no point missing it too much, Thomas, we'll be back soon, and we've got years left.'

'Just ignore me, Lola, I'm just being silly. Do you really think they'd cancel it for a fourth day in a row?'

'I guess they've got no choice. Most of the teachers drive

to school and the roads look dangerous to drive on. I think some take the monorail as well though.'

Whilst they talked, Lola checked the school's website on her computer to see school was indeed cancelled yet again.

On Friday, the snowfall was still persisting and was still causing chaos and depression across Helmia: after a few days, everyone had been hoping it would stop so they could get back to their regular snow-free lives and not have to trundle through the freezing cold. The whole island had been at a standstill: Lola stared out of her window for an hour before she had lunch and saw not a single car or person go by.

She checked the news online to learn that there had been another spate of snowman attacks yesterday evening: the number of people injured was significantly smaller than the first time round, as was the death toll. Still, it was disturbing to Lola to think that these things were still attacking and managing to kill. The snowmen were still vanishing after carrying out their gruesome attacks, and the police, flooded with calls, were at a loss to explain what was going on. Lola read how someone saw a snowman in their front garden, realised it hadn't been there a few minutes ago, then called the police. By the time she'd hung up, the snowman had gone. All the police could do was to issue an edict telling everyone to stay away from all snowmen. There was one report of a policeman managing to pulverise a snowman that had suddenly appeared when he'd turned his back for a second, till it was just more flat snow on the ground; this left everyone baffled. No one could provide an explanation for this or the freak blizzard.

The weather abated on Saturday and it was back to grey skies, resulting in a region-wide sigh of relief. All was back to normal. The streets were full of an unpleasant looking slush, which clogged the sides of the roads. The snow was starting to melt and the buried island was starting to gradually be uncovered.

The following Monday, Lola found herself in her form class with everyone, waiting for their form teacher to come in.

'Good morning, class,' she said, suppressing a yawn.

'Well, what a week it's been. I hope you are all well and that none of you or any of your loved ones were affected by this terrible weather or those damn snowmen. Please come to me if someone you know was taken and you need to talk; I'm always here,' she smiled to the class, something she hadn't done recently.

'As you can imagine, we're all in a sticky situation, what with school being closed for a week. The next two weeks will progress as usual, as will your February half term. The only thing that will change is that your classes will be a bit harder for the next two weeks as all the teachers will naturally want to catch up with the stuff everyone's missed. We're all in the same boat, so let's get back on track together. I hope you all checked the school website and email and found any homework your teachers might have sent you; I'm sure they'll be lenient if for some reason you haven't had access to a computer recently. I'll stop talking and get the register done then you can go off happily to assembly and I look forward to English with you later on.'

The first day back was a solemn one: there was a special assembly in honour of the three students and one teacher who'd died in the past week. Lola felt awful as Mr. Dazzle spoke about all of the deceased. She was glad she didn't know any of them, but felt very sorry for those who did. She felt very lucky to be there, with her friends by her side and her family waiting for her when she'd get home later on. A few days later she was sat in assembly again. A few heads were turned when the main door to the school could be heard opening and closing; a few people, including Lola, turned and watched as a man a top hat with a large briefcase went into the reception area. Lola recognised him from somewhere. She watched as the receptionist let him into the head's office. Assembly ended a few minutes later and Lola watched as Mr. Dazzle went to see his guest.

It was break time. Lola went to the form room and found who she was looking for. She asked them if she could have a word with them in private. She took them outside, where hardly anyone was.

'You know something,' she told Natella sternly.

'What?' Natella replied, her marine-blue eyes gleaming.

'That's what I want to know. What do you know about this?'

'Lola, I don't know anything.'

'You let it slip the other day. You said this was going to happen again.'

'That was just a guess!'

'People have died, Natella. If you know something, tell me.'

'How could I possibly know anything?'

Lola realised she was grilling Natella over nothing and apologised, realising she'd come across as impulsively desperate and paranoid for no good reason. Natella's phone started ringing; she answered it and a few moments later told Lola she had to go, heading down the corridor, texting someone on her phone. Feeling curious, Lola decided to follow her.

A few minutes later, she was in the Mythology building watching as Natella slipped into the spare room. Lola passed by quickly and caught a glimpse of Natella sitting next to a long-haired woman with massive sunglasses, who had her face in her hands on the desk. Lola listened in.

'Did you check on the orb, Maude?' Natella said.

'Yes I have been doing that and it's still there,' the other replied.

'Good.'

'I'm freaking out with worry every second of the day. I'll be so glad once this orb is away from Helmia, where it should be. I can only begin to wonder why it has to be hidden and why I have to keep checking up on it.'

'I'm sure Susie asked you for a reason.'

'But why *me*? It was bad enough when she told me to keep the orb at my house. I was out of my mind with worry. Assa could very easily have found the orb then and I would be dead right now. I'm sure it's what Susie wants.'

'Why would she want you dead?'

'For getting taken in by Assa's promises.'

'When Assa recruited you fifteen years ago? Surely Susie would not be concerned about something that happened so long ago?'

'I'm sure she is though. We were promised eternal life elsewhere in the universe, a life free from anguish and pain. I admit I was gullible enough to be charmed by that offer. And now look where it's got me!'

'Do you really think Assa would have seen that promise through given what the plans are?'

'Of course not. I'm not stupid enough to believe what Assa tells us. And I don't believe for one second that Hyuul would have wanted the orb hidden in Helmia. This is such a mess!'

'Then why did Hyuul suggest it then?'

'I have a feeling Susie is working with Assa.'

'What? How can you even think that?'

'I'm convinced she is. She gets the orb then is supposedly told to hide it in Helmia, the one place in the world Assa is searching thoroughly? I don't believe it. I think she asked for me to hide the orb in Helmia so Assa could find it easily enough and I'd get punished.'

'Why on Earth would Susie be in allegiance with Assa?'

'I don't know. Something's not right. The night Assa and Hyuul came to Earth, the one person Hyuul came to was Susie, obviously, but we only have her version of what was said. I think Hyuul told her to hide it somewhere far away while Assa was distracted searching Helmia.'

'But she's the head of the Wrinkles Club! She's in allegiance with the Blondies and all of humanity! How could she even think of being on Assa's side given what Assa plans to do?'

'I really don't know. But what if Assa has found out about Susie and her connections to the Blondies and Hyuul, recruited her and convinced her to pretend Hyuul had told her to hide the orb in Helmia so Assa could find it easily and quickly?'

'I really don't think that's what's happened. Is there any word on Hyuul, by the way?'

'No. We have no idea where Hyuul is, nor do we even know if Hyuul is alive.'

'Susie would never want all this to happen.'

'You have admit, Natella, that hiding the orb in Puddlepond is a ludicrous idea. This orb should be hidden on the other side of the world not right under Assa's nose!' Maude was getting worked up, her speech getting faster.

'Assa's non-existent nose,' Natella joked, making the other laugh a little.

Chapter 9 –
Lola's First Encounter

The next few weeks passed by rather quickly for Lola. Her parents took her to the hospital to have her injuries checked out just as a precaution, but she was fine and was told she'd soon recuperate. The workload at school increased a little, but this didn't bother her much. Thomas, on the other hand, was getting stressed about the amount of work they were getting. He spent many nights staying up till the early hours of the morning finishing off work owing to his procrastination habit, whereas Lola spent her time wondering about the conversation between Maude and Natella; she'd tried to approach Natella at school, but she always denied everything.

Before long, it was the Monday of half term. Lola's lie in was disrupted when her phone went off: it was a text message from Demzel.

'Eh?' Lola said to herself. She read the text again and didn't quite know what to make of it. She decided to phone Thomas to see what he'd make of it. Still lying about in bed, she rang him.

'Thomas? It's just me. I haven't woken you, have I?'

'No, no, I was awake. What's up?'

'I just got a text from Demzel. He said there's gonna be something happening at the school tonight and he wants to know if I'd go along with him and find out what it is.'

'I thought the school was closed during the holidays?'

'It is but apparently Demzel overheard Mr. Stone on the phone to someone saying that he would be on guard at the school tonight. That's all Demzel knows.'

'It sounds a bit...dodgy.'

'I know but it I'm curious. You know what I'm like when I'm curious.'

'You're going, aren't you?'

'Of course.'

'Are you not worried?'

'I'll have Demzel there and if anything happens, we'll just leave.'

'I have a feeling you won't.'

'We'll be fine. What are you doing today?'

'I'm going over to the mainland with my parents. We're visiting my cousins and staying there overnight. We should get together tomorrow and do the English homework.'

'That sounds like a good plan. What's with not leaving it till the last minute?'

'As ironic as this sounds, I can't be bothered!'

'Haha! Ooh, I'll have to go. I've got another call coming through. Have a good time at your cousins' and I'll speak to you soon.'

'Be careful tonight.'

'We will,' Lola hung up and saw it was Demzel who was ringing her. She accepted the call.

'Lola, it's me, Demzel. Did you get my text?'

'Yeah, I was just about to reply to it actually.'

'So are you coming?'

'Yeah definitely! What exactly is going on though?'

'Basically, I overheard Mr. Stone on the phone clarifying

140

that he was going to be at the school at ten tonight and would be on guard. I have no idea what's going to happen so that's why I'm going.'

'Will it be safe?'

'Of course. I've got it all planned out: on Friday I left one of the windows in my classroom slightly ajar; we'll be able to open it from the outside, climb into the classroom and unlock it from the inside. If we meet there at ten, Ivan will already be inside so we won't set the alarms off. As you can tell, I'm dying to know what's going on.'

'I can tell, Demzel. So shall I meet you outside the school then?'

'Yes, but be discreet. If you happen to see Mr. Stone, just say you're walking back home from a friend's.'

'Sure.'

Lola hung up and thought about what Demzel had said. She wondered why Mr. Stone, her P.E. teacher, would be guarding the school and what he could be guarding it against. With Thomas and Hannah both away, she decided to busy herself by going downstairs and getting some breakfast then getting washed and burying her head in a book.

She was in the living room reading when her parents came in and told her they were heading out to the shops. Lola declined the invitation to come, instead preferring to get on with her book and dream up many possibilities of what was going to happen that night. She let her mind wander and wonder.

The day passed unusually quickly for her. Before she knew it, her parents were coming home and she found herself at the table having tea talking with them.

'Andrew's coming home a week on Saturday for a visit,' her mam told her.

'Brilliant! I'm looking forward to seeing him again.'

'He gets back from his holiday on Friday and is getting

a flight straight to uni. I persuaded him to come down for a weekend because we haven't seen him since New Year and he was meant to be spending his break here,' said Lola's mum.

'He's growing up, Ange. You've got to let him go on holiday with his friends,' replied Lola's dad.

'I know. I just miss him when he's so far away.'

Lola saw something in her mother's face she hadn't seen for a while: sorrow.

'Mum, you'll see him soon.'

'I know. Just ignore me, I'm being daft.'

There was silence for a few minutes. Then Lola realised she hadn't told them she was going out.

'Can I go round to Demzel's tonight?'

'Of course. What time?'

'I'll leave at half nine and get back for half eleven.'

'OK. Make sure you have your phone with you.'

'I will.'

'And say hello from us.'

'I will.'

Lola then offered to clear up the dishes and suggested her parents relax in front of the telly. She never lied to them and felt ashamed of herself for not telling them the truth, yet she knew she'd get away with it because Demzel would vouch for her should that be necessary. She'd go to the school with him, get back in time and no one would know anything.

As she did the dishes she looked out of the window and saw there was light snowfall. Beyond the back garden were the sprawling fields and the large forest which Lola and some of her friends took walks through during the summer.

The snow was starting to get heavier as she made her way to the school to meet Demzel but that wouldn't stop her: she was far too intrigued to let anything get in the way. Even if her parents hadn't allowed her to go out, she probably would have rebelled just this one time. She got to the front gates of the school by quarter to ten, her journey somewhat hampered by the carpet of snow on the paths. She looked at the school and saw that there were no lights on. The building was over fifty years old yet it didn't look half its age. The main building which stood before Lola housed the assembly hall, staff room, reception and head's office as well as a few classrooms.

'Ah, Lola!' came Demzel's voice; Lola turned and saw him approaching wrapped up in a thick coat, a torch in one hand.

'It's freezing out here!' Lola said.

'We'll be inside soon,' Demzel replied, 'thanks for coming by the way. What did you tell your parents?'

'That I'm visiting you.'

'I'll vouch for you if I have to.'

'What do you think is gonna happen?'

'I have no idea, and that's why I'm so excited!'

'And you're sure it'll be safe?'

'Of course. I am your teacher and a family friend and will not let anything happen to you. If something should happen, we'll leave.'

'OK.'

They made their way round to the back entrance of the school where the staff car park was.

'We should get in pretty easily,' he explained, 'because I drove down here earlier and hid a ladder in the bushes over there. We'll be able to get over the gate but we'll have to be careful when climbing down it.'

'How would we get back out?'

'Oh. I hadn't thought of that,' Demzel sounded slightly embarrassed.

'There must be some ladders in the school,' Lola reassured him.

And so Demzel got the ladder, Lola looked out at the

B. P. EVANS

school's several buildings and wondered what Ivan could be doing inside. She looked up and saw many stars then shivered a little.

'Right, I'll go over first, and then I'll help you down,' Demzel instructed; Lola acquiesced.

Demzel put the ladder up parallel to the gates then climbed it and made his way down the gates on the other side. Lola then did the same and they both headed alongside the field towards the building on the far right which Demzel's classroom was in. The building was the Supernatural and Paranormal Studies and Mythology building. Both subjects were relatively unpopular such that three teachers shared the teaching for both, given they were quite similar, and the building simply consisted of three classrooms, an office, a restroom and a spare classroom where random classes were taught. It was the smallest and quietest building given that it was right at one of the far ends of the school; only at break and lunch did it get some people in it who weren't heading to lessons as there was the vending machine on the top floor which always had a queue every lunch. However, Demzel deeply loved this building and always thought that this building was perfect for the subjects taught within: as far as he was concerned, the subjects would lose their appeal and edge if they became mainstream and were seen as popular.

They were outside the ground floor classroom Demzel taught in. Lola looked all around her in case anyone else was there while Demzel opened the window to his classroom. She looked at all the school buildings and the sports field in the dark, worrying in case she saw the slightest anything. She felt slightly unnerved and jumped when Demzel spoke to her.

'Are you okay? I've been in here for a minute watching you just staring about.'

'Oh. Yeah I'm fine. Was just looking about,' Lola then

proceeded to clamber through the open window and found herself in Demzel's unlit classroom.

'I've never seen it like this before; it looks so strange,' she commented.

'The school looks completely different at night. When I was little, I was once so curious to see what my school was like at night that I phoned my parents, told them I was staying at a friend's house and hid in one of the classrooms. I managed to avoid the cleaners and eventually I was the only one there. I left the classroom then set the alarm off and got quite a big punishment for doing that,' Demzel recalled rather proudly.

'Well let's just hope that doesn't happen to us.'

'It won't. The alarm's not on. Ivan's already here somewhere. Did you notice any lights on in any of the buildings when you were outside?'

'No, I didn't,' replied Lola, wishing there had been an illuminated room at least so they'd know where to go.

'So where should we go?' she asked.

'Let me think. We're in the far east of the school so we'll just keep moving west and no doubt we'll find him. Maybe we should go up to the first floor.'

'OK,' replied Lola. She was glad to leave the eerie room which she'd always remembered as being cosy, unique and friendly.

Outside in the corridor, they listened for any signs of movement but heard none, so they went over to the stairs and ascended them. Once on the first floor, they stopped again but heard nothing so they turned right and slowly made their way across the walkway which connected the first floor of the Mythology building to the Arts building, always alert.

'Demzel,' Lola whispered, 'if Ivan said he was gonna be on guard, doesn't that mean he's likely to be at one of the entrances to the school?'

'That is an excellent idea, Lola, a very sensible one indeed. We should head to the main building in that case.'

'I could be wrong of course. I guess he could be anywhere really,' Lola acknowledged.

'I think you're on to something though.'

And so they slowly and quietly made their way through the top floor of the Arts building, which was where the art department was. They were just about to turn the corner and head long the next walkway when Demzel stopped, clung to the wall and told Lola to do the same. There was no window nearby so they were engulfed in almost complete darkness. The only sound came from their own deep breathing, nervous and erratic.

'Why don't you phone or text Ivan? That way if he's nearby, we should hear his phone go off,' Lola suggested in a hushed whisper.

'Another excellent idea, Lola.'

Demzel then got out his phone and proceeded to ring Ivan.

'His phone's off,' Demzel said a minute later, 'it was worth a try.'

'So should we go on?'

'Wait - I think I heard something,' Demzel whispered.

They both crouched down and looked at each other nervously and silently. Both were listening intently for a sound, but none came.

'False alarm.'

'What did you think you heard?'

'Footsteps. Shh.'

They listened carefully once again but heard nothing.

'I think we should move on,' Demzel whispered into Lola's ear; Lola acquiesced and they carried on slowly edging their way across the walkway to the main building, the school's biggest building. Slowly and carefully they went, ensuring as little noise as possible was made. Moonlight allowed for some visibility as they crossed the walkway, but still that wasn't much; they could see the hall in the distance and some faint moonlight lighting part of it for them. Once in the next building, they stopped again, slouched against a locker rack outside a classroom and listened in once more.

'I'm sure I just heard someone walking,' Demzel said.

Lola listened carefully and could just make out footsteps in the distance.

'They sound like they're coming from the hall; everywhere else nearby is carpeted,' she theorised.

'I think you're right. Let's go then.'

Once they passed the two classrooms on either side of them, they were on the balcony that overlooked the main hall. The footsteps were getting louder so they ducked down and peeked through the railings. They couldn't see anyone down there.

'He might still be there though,' Demzel mentioned.

'I can't hear any more footsteps. Oh no! He's coming up the stairs!'

Lola had seen Ivan proceeding up the stairs, which were just to the right of where they were now situated. The stairs twisted halfway between the two floors and it was as Ivan was nearly halfway up that Lola had seen him.

'Get into that classroom over there,' Lola was told; she sneaked off into a nearby English classroom and kept the door ajar peeking out to see Demzel not coming towards her, but staying on the spot, facing the way they came, presumably looking at something down the walkway.

'Demzel!' Lola hissed, but to no avail. The look on Demzel's face was one of unexpected horror and shock. He looked genuinely frightened beyond anything, such that he was rooted to the spot.

'Demzel!' Lola hissed louder, yet he still crouched there,

staring at something. Lola saw Ivan get higher and higher up the stairs.

'Demzel? What on Earth are you doing here?' she heard Ivan say; he had a tone of surprise and a hint of anger in his voice.

'L-look over th-there!' Demzel replied in a stammer, pointing at whatever it was had scared him so much. Ivan merely looked that way without so much as a reaction.

'Are you alone?' he asked.

'Y-yes. It's coming towards me!'

Ivan put out his hand at whatever was coming down the corridor. It seemed to have stopped, judging by Demzel's calming down.

'You have to leave Demzel. Just come down with me and I'll let you out the front way. I'll explain it all tomorrow, OK? And don't tell anyone, understood?'

'Ivan how on Earth –'

'Look, I'll explain it all later. I'll let you out like I said.'

Lola watched as Ivan led Demzel down the stairs and out of sight. Knowing that Demzel had bought her some more time to investigate, Lola decided this was the time to do it. She was just about to leave the classroom when her phone vibrated – a text from Hannah. She quickly switched it to silent without reading the text.

She opened the door slowly, unnerved by a few inevitable creaks it made. Once out on the balcony, she considered her options: she could head back to the Arts building and find out what had scared Demzel so much, or she could go down the corridor past the English classrooms for no apparent reason whatsoever. She decided to be adventurous and find out what else was in the school with them. She heard footsteps down below in the hall and ducked behind one of the pillars before Ivan could see her. He soon disappeared from view. Taking the opportunity, Lola quickly crept along to the small corridor with classrooms either side of it that led to the walkway. She was standing in the corridor looking down but couldn't see anything, though she heard a door being shut somewhere in the Arts building. She then heard another door creak open. She knew it wasn't Ivan, so assumed it must be whatever had scared Demzel. She inched along the walkway a bit but then froze when in the shadows beyond she saw something. A gut feeling told her she should run; something told her what she had just seen but she couldn't be entirely sure.

'Come out of the darkness, scaredy cat,' she whispered to herself, lurching forward an inch or two, 'I won't hurt you. Just wanna see what you are.'

Despite being confrontational, Lola felt her bravery had peaked. She watched cautiously as the something moved about in the shadows. She couldn't tell whether it was getting closer or not.

'Come on,' she piped up.

She watched closely, trying her hardest not to blink, but then she heard a few faint footsteps and no longer saw any movement in the shadows.

'Come back,' she whispered.

After a few moments, there was still no sign. Lola felt as if she'd scared it off.

'I'm not gonna hurt you, I just wanna see you,' she whispered once more into the darkness. She felt annoyed that it had gone away like that and curious to find out what exactly it was. Fear in her was dissipating, overridden by a thirst for knowledge. She edged forward a few steps. She listened carefully and heard a few footsteps. She heard a few whispers, thought she couldn't make out what was being said. She then heard a few more footsteps and concluded that there was more than one. A few doors opened and shut. Lola could hear her own breathing get quicker and slightly louder.

There was the sound of talking, a faint, incomprehensible murmur. Following that was the sound of footsteps, several footsteps, several different things walking at the same time. Lola could just make out that the footsteps were getting louder. She saw something in the darkness but couldn't make out what it was. In an instant there appeared a laser coming from the darkness which luckily missed Lola. Another one appeared, this time a bit closer to her. Both started moving around a bit. When a third came, Lola finally decided to scarper and she darted back into the English classroom she'd been hiding in previously and peered out of one of the door's panel windows. She saw about five laser beams.

Lola felt more and more afraid by the second. She wanted desperately to find out what was there, but on the other hand she thought the right thing to do would be to find Ivan and get out of the school. In an instant she knew that she'd stay and find out whatever it was that was now pointing lasers down corridor. She knew it was dangerous, but was willing to take that risk. This was the first truly dangerous thing she'd done in ages. She felt excited, cautious, scared, nervous and curious all at once. The adrenalin pumping through her was more intense than when she was on the rides at Puddlepond Theme Park.

She jumped a little when she saw something come round the corner. She decided she'd hide and hoped they'd bypass this room. In a moment she was cowering under a desk, hoping they'd walk by so she could get out, catch a glimpse of them, then charge down the stairs. She sat crouched down, her face against her knees, her breathing heavy.

The door creaked open and Lola automatically shut her eyes. She heard footsteps mere inches away from her. The desk's drawers were all opened and shut, as were all the cupboards, then whatever was in the room with her gasped. It said something incomprehensible in a deep, croaky voice.

Lola thought it was trying to speak to her, but she didn't know what to do so she stayed exactly where she was. The voice came again, this time sounding a little more harried and agitated.

Lola's heart was beating faster and faster. She couldn't think of what to do. The voice came again. She crawled out from under the desk and got up, her eyes still closed. She had a feeling whatever was in the room with her wasn't friendly.

The voice came again, this time sounding authoritative, though there was a slight tremble in it. It was speaking in some weird language. Lola was shaking slightly. She could feel her head getting a little warm. It was sweating a little. She wiped it with her hand and the voice came again, barking some sort of order, or so it seemed. Lola took a deep breath and opened her eyes. What she saw standing a few feet away, a few desks between them, rigged her to the spot.

An alien was standing in the classroom. It was a bit taller than Lola and had dark grey saggy skin and a bald head with large shiny black eyes, slits for nostrils and a thin lipless mouth. Its arms and legs were thin in comparison to its massive head. It was wearing a tight metallic silver suit, almost like a space suit, that seemed to cling to its skin. It was also wearing thick grey shoes that looked like they were made of foam. Lola was rooted to the spot; in a second she thought she should run, but instantly decided against it in case the alien came after her. She thought it looked oddly humanoid. Its eyes were what caught her attention the most, its large oval glasslike eyes. They were over half the size of its head.

Both were frozen there, alien staring at human and human staring at alien, both aliens to each other, both from entirely different worlds. Both were eyeing each other eagerly, Lola thinking this was the only thing she should and could do. She was horrified: anything could happen. She wondered whether it would attack her or do anything. Then she remembered she was the closest one to the door. She heard a few footsteps outside then acted on impulse and ran to the door and locked it, sealing herself in with the alien.

'No more are getting in,' she said, even though the alien couldn't understand her. It looked confused, but hadn't moved, to Lola's surprise. She put both her hands up and looked at it, hoping to communicate some sort of sign of peace. The alien merely continued looking at her. It then spoke.

'Yaw neemh,' it said, its voice still croaky, a slight tinge of authority in it. Lola thought the alien was a bit nervous.

'I-I don't understand,' Lola replied a little shakily, waving her hands about.

'Yaw neemh!' the alien said, this time a bit louder.

'I don't speak your language,' Lola replied, holding on to a nearby desk. She was shaking a bit and was starting to regret locking herself in. Tears were forming in her eyes.

'P-please don't hurt m-me. I don't know who y-you are but I-I am not g-going to hurt you.'

'Yaw neemh!' the alien shouted, taking Lola aback. It looked quite angry now.

'I don't understand you!' Lola shouted back, surprised at herself.

By the moonlight pouring into the room, Lola could see that the alien looked quite menacing now. It repeated what it had said then after a non-reaction from Lola, it withdrew some sort of gun from its back pocket. Lola froze on the spot and started panicking. Her head grew warmer and sweat formed in little beads everywhere on her. She thought this was going to be the end of her life. All she could do was stand there and stare at the alien as tears trickled down her face, trying to make some sort of gesture that would translate as meaning that she meant no harm and didn't need to be shot. Then in a flash it came to her: this was one of those key moments in her life, a major turning point like when she got trapped in the lift all those years ago. She had changed into a person scared of the world and all its horrors, open and hidden. Now the biggest horror was in front of her; it wasn't the alien, but the gun, the weird-looking gun from somewhere in outer space - Lola didn't want to imagine what that gun could do. She could either submit to the horrors and all the things she didn't like or she could fight back and prove to herself that the world wasn't such a scary place, that lifts could be broken out of and that something capable of being overpowered could actually be overpowered. Now it was time for her to be brave.

A few seconds after the alien had pointed the gun at her, a red laser dot appeared on Lola's chest. The laser beam was thin but surely deadly. All the while, Lola was rapidly formulating a plan of action.

She shouted, 'I don't understand you,' to the alien and just as it began to reply, she ran forward and smacked the alien's left hand, which the gun was in, causing it to fly across the room and land on the floor by the teacher's desk, its laser still strong. The alien grabbed Lola by the throat and snarled, 'yaw neemh,' yet again to her, its breath cold and frigid. Lola spat in its face and it let go. She turned and ran towards the door, zigzagging among the desks but froze once more when there was a loud bang and the sound of breaking glass; the alien had shot at the window. Lola turned round to see the gun pointing at her once more and the alien running over to her. It pressed Lola against the door, put its hand across her mouth and put the gun to her neck. She could see some of her spit glistening on its face. She stared into those huge eyes then kneed it in its groin; the alien fell back and grabbed its crotch. The gun had been dropped. Lola picked it up and pointed it at the alien, which was still bent double.

'Jaz yaw neem,' it wheezed.

Then the penny dropped and Lola understood what it was saying.

'My name? You want to know my name?' she felt more powerful and alive than she had in years. She felt as if she could take on anything.

'My name is Lola Spears. *Never* point a gun at me again,' she told the alien, though she was still unaware of whether it would understand her or not. She wondered how it knew English. The gun was still fixed at the alien's chest. Lola felt relieved now that she was in control. All the fear was flooding out of her.

'I don't know if you understood that, but I'm saying this anyway: I'm going to leave now and I'm taking this with me so you can't get me. Sorry if I hurt you,' Lola eyed the gun and unlocked the door whilst still facing the alien. She kept the gun pointing at the alien as she left the room and closed the door. She turned round and took a few breaths and wiped her forehead. She still felt a little warm. There were footsteps. Lola looked to her left to see several grey aliens running towards her, and more leaving classrooms and joining the run, all of them keeping guns pointed at her. She acted on instinct and ran straight for the stairs and sped down them, jumping a few at a time. She ducked as she heard a few gunshots and was very lucky not to get hit. Once on the ground floor, she ran panting and sweating to the staff room on the left and found it was locked. The footsteps were coming thick and fast. Lola didn't want to run through the hall and to the building's main exit because the aliens would have the perfect opportunity and would surely shoot her without missing. She didn't know how many were running down the stairs.

Within half a minute she'd run across to the nearest classroom, had locked the door and was opening one of the windows, her hands unsteady and shaking. Tears were pouring down her face and her breathing was irregular. She jumped back from the window when she heard a sonorous thud on the door followed by the sound of guns being fired and the door panels shattering. Realising she had mere seconds, Lola found something in her to overcome the fear and she hoisted the window and climbed out into the night. She could either run to the entrance she and Demzel had used, or she could try to get to the main entrance on the other side of the buildings. Realising the aliens would probably come after her, she decided what she'd do.

She ran round the corner of the building then watched the aliens run on to the field. Very quickly, she opened one of the side windows of the classroom and clambered back in. To her horror there were two of the aliens standing by the windows looking out; when she got in the room, they instantaneously turned round, saw her and whipped their guns out and fired just as she darted out of the room and down the main hall. The aliens were in hot pursuit of her. Lola ran across the moonlit hall as fast as she could and made it to the main entrance, only the door was locked. She tried banging on the door and violently shaking the doorknob but it remained as it was. She gave up and held on to the doorknob and sank down, knowing the aliens would come and shoot. In a few seconds they were there, both of them bearing a gun, both of them in metallic-looking clothing, one a dark purple, the other a light blue. They looked quite different to the one Lola had encountered in the classroom: the one in the dark purple had slightly smaller eyes which were more of a circular shape, was slightly shorter and had thick grey skin whilst the other was skinnier and had very light grey skin and a few cuts on its face. Both looked riled and baleful.

'P-please, what do you want from m-me?' Lola cried, cowering against the door.

The aliens moved closer to her and Lola tried sinking into the door in vain. She knew this was going to be the end. Eyes closed and breathing uncontrollable, she felt defeated. After a few tense moments that seemed to go on forever, seeing as they hadn't shot her yet, she felt it safe to assume that that wasn't their main intention, for they surely would have done so by now. To her horror, however, she looked up and saw the two still pointing their guns down at her, muttering something in their language. Even though she felt a little brave, she didn't dare make a move when she was in this position and had two guns pointed at her. She realised she'd been too quick to judge: once more she closed her eyes, squeezed them tightly shut and then a voice came from one of the aliens.

'Shtee dair,' it said in a low, hoarse, raspy voice.

Lola looked up; the alien repeated what it had said but Lola, nonplussed, merely continued looking up at them shaking and teary-eyed.

'I'm sorry. I don't understand you.'

The alien that had spoken got out a small, thin device which it started tapping at with its thin fingers. It mumbled something to the other. To Lola's relief, they both lowered their guns.

'Thank you! Thank you so much!' Lola whispered to them through her tears. She fell back to the floor and lay there, feeling scared and alone. They'd lowered their weapons, she thought to herself, so they had no intention of harming her. However, she felt as if she should not get up unless they signalled for her to do so.

'Lola Spears,' she heard a familiar voice say.

'Mr. Stone? Is that you?' she looked up and, to her great relief, saw Ivan Stone walking up towards them. The aliens had their guns pointed at her again. Ivan said something in a strange language and repeated a few times until he'd said it correctly and the aliens lowered their weapons.

'I'm guessing you came here with Demzel. Come on, it's okay. I'm going to get you out of here safe and sound,' Ivan helped Lola up then got a key from his pocket and opened the main door. Lola went to leave, but turned round to see Ivan standing in the threshold and the two aliens skulking back into the school.

'Demzel's just around the corner.'

'We could have died,' Lola growled to Ivan, and with that she slapped him across the face, instantly regretting it. She watched Ivan's reaction but none of them said anything more.

'Normally if a student slapped me, they'd be suspended or expelled, but you've got good reason to.'

'Yes I have. Your aliens could have killed us! I can't count how many times I've had a gun pointed at me tonight!'

'I'm very sorry, Lola, very sorry indeed.'

'I don't know what to say. Letting aliens into the school! I feel like I'm having some crazy dream.'

'I can assure you, this is all very real. Once again, I can only say sorry. Once they let me know they'd found you, I instructed them not to harm you in any way. I was asked to do this and never expected anyone else to be here. I had a sneaking suspicion Demzel might turn up, though I didn't expect him to be so scared – I thought he'd be overjoyed when he saw them.'

'When someone sees an alien for the first time, they're stupid not to be scared,' Lola said, and with that she shut the door as Ivan looked at her apologetically and walked on with far too many questions in her head.

Chapter 10 –
Hoi Deinoi

'What the hell do you think you were playing at?' Lola shouted at Demzel, who simply looked taken aback.

'You left me in there with those aliens – anything could have happened!' she shouted again before Demzel could reply, unable to control herself.

'Exactly,' said a shocked Demzel, 'which is why I said I was the only one there so they wouldn't go looking for anyone else. Are you okay?'

Lola was panting and looking at Demzel. She thought she'd perhaps overreacted a bit and was starting to see his good intentions.

'I thought,' Demzel added, 'that they'd see to me then you'd be free to run.'

Lola stayed quiet for a moment then said: 'I'm sorry for lashing out. Really, I am.'

'It's understandable. I don't blame you. I left you in there with those Greys! I was completely senseless. Did they do anything to you?'

'Just pointed guns at me and tried to shoot me. The one I was in the classroom with hurt me a little bit I'm fine.'

'What did it do to you?'

'Nothing. Honestly, I'm fine. I was really scared at first - I could barely even speak! I just went for it and managed to escape.'

'Are you sure you're okay?'

'Yes. I'm just a little shocked by all this. How about you? You sounded pretty terrified to me!'

'I was. I never expected there to be Greys here in the school of all places. They certainly took me by surprise.'

They looked at each other for a few moments, then Demzel exhaled deeply and a smile grew across his face.

'Greys! Here in Helmia! First those two and the orb and now the Greys! I cannot believe we were witnesses to their being here. It's too much to take in. I've been waiting years and years to see aliens and now I have for the first of, hopefully, many times.'

'I'm surprised you didn't run up and hug them!'

Demzel laughed.

'This is all one big web. Those two aliens and the orb, the dream, those dreadful snowmen and these Greys. They simply must all be connected.'

'The first two that came weren't Greys, weren't they?'

'No, they were something completely different, definitely not Greys. As far as I know, their species, whatever it is, has never been sighted on Earth before. So there are two alien species involved. I can't believe Ivan didn't tell me about this; I can't believe he was asked to do this instead of me! I'd be perfect for the job. Although, realistically speaking, given my reaction tonight, I wouldn't have been right for it. I would have been too scared.'

Lola agreed, but didn't want to say that she did. She knew aliens had been Demzel's obsession and wanted to let him savour the moment.

'Who do you think asked him to guard the school?' she asked.

'I don't know but I'm going to find out. That, and what the Greys were doing there.'

'I think they were looking for something.'

'What gives you that impression?'

'The way that Grey came into the classroom I was in and looked in all the cupboards and drawers.'

'Hmm.'

'Maybe they were looking for the missing orb?'

'I think that could very well be a possibility. Yes, that orb certainly seems to be part of the reason why the first two came here, so it's sensible to assume that's why the Greys are here. Plus the first alien was seen flying around Puddlepond after it went to Moistree, so there's a chance it hid the orb somewhere in Puddlepond. Now these Greys are presumably after it for some reason.'

'It's hard to believe they're in there right now.'

'Part of me is tempted to go back in there and see them a bit more.'

'Only you would say that.'

'Well, how often is it that this happens? Aliens in the workplace?'

'They're dangerous, Demzel. They all had guns and were shooting at me even though I hadn't really done anything wrong. Plus, Ivan told me that once he found out I was there, he ordered them not to attack, so goodness knows what would have happened if he hadn't found out.'

'Again I'm sorry for leaving you there. Once I was outside I kept ringing and texting you because I know you keep your phone on vibrate, but you must have turned it off.'

'It was on silent.'

'I think we should go now. There's nothing more we can do here.'

'Should we go to the police?'

'The police? Why would we go to them?'

'There are aliens in the school,' Lola said, 'they could be a threat. They have guns. We don't know what their intentions are.'

'By the time we get the police, the Greys will most likely be gone. If that's not the case and the police do come in time, I'm sure whoever is behind this all has some plan. There's no point phoning the police. We're best leaving Ivan to it; he seems to know what he's doing so someone's probably been training him to deal with the Greys. The thing is, with aliens you have to be very cautious because you never know what they'll do or what they'll act like, remember when we discussed it in class? That's why I got so scared, because I had no idea what to do. I was afraid of the unknown. I must say you coped very well indeed. It's better if we just let them be.'

The two started walking away from the school.

'As soon as I see Ivan tomorrow, I'm going to ask him everything.'

'Good,' replied Lola.

'I'll let you know what he says. I'm very interested to see what he has to say and to find out who asked him to guard the school.'

'Greys in Helmia!' Demzel said, 'I still can't believe it. All the way from some planet in outer space to our little island.'

'It beggars belief.'

'It certainly does. The question to ask is how many there are and what their true purpose in being here is. Have they flown all the way here to get that orb? Are there more of them searching right now across the island? If they have come here for the orb, it must be pretty damn important. And where are those first two aliens? There have been no sightings of them at all. But as far as we know, they haven't yet left Earth.'

Lola contemplated all this as they carried on walking

away from the school and the aliens inside. She was still finding it hard to believe what had just happened.

They passed by rows of houses as Demzel did most of the talking. Lola nearly jumped when a ginger cat leapt down from a low wall and strode past them.

'The car!' Demzel exclaimed; they were ten minutes from the school.

'If you want, I'll walk you home and fetch the car afterwards,' Demzel said, but Lola agreed to go back and get the car. She was curious to see if anything else would happen at the school.

Once at the back gates, Demzel went over to his car and started it up.

'What should I do with these ladders?' Lola asked; the ladders were still set up parallel to the gates.

'Just put them back in the bush; I can't return them to the school now.'

Lola did just that, then got in the car and they set off. Before she knew it, they were approaching her house.

'Can you come in and tell my parents I was at yours the whole time, please?'

'Of course. I was assuming you'd want me to anyway.'

And so they got of the car, walked up the drive and Lola let them in. Both of her parents believed them, luckily. However, Lola did feel disappointed in herself about lying to them and getting Demzel to lie on her behalf.

All that feeling had dissipated by the following morning when she awoke. She felt as if she'd had some crazy, mind-bending dream. She felt euphoric and alive, still on a high from last night's adventure. She checked her phone to see it was half nine. She lounged about in bed for another couple of hours, thinking about last night, too immersed in thought, wonder and imagination to do anything productive.

Her phone buzzed: a text message from Thomas. She

read it then remembered they were meant to meet up to do the English homework. He'd said in his text that he was wondering when they could meet up; Lola replied that she was still in bed but she'd be at his by three. Whilst looking through her phone, she saw she had numerous missed calls and text messages from Demzel from last night. She read through the texts, all telling there were aliens there and that she should be very careful and ring him as soon as possible. Lola felt quite guilty and ashamed of herself even more for her harsh reaction to Demzel when she left the school. She texted him apologising once more for her uncalled-for over-reaction.

She had a bite to eat for lunch with her parents, who were still completely ignorant of last night's arrant chaos. All was normal in the Spears household, except the occasional conversation about aliens.

By the time three came round, Lola was outside Thomas' house knocking on the door, her bag dangling from her shoulder.

'Hello, Lola,' Thomas greeted her after opening the door and ushering her in.

'My parents are out,' he added.

They both sat down in the living room, which had plain peach walls, brown settees and a fancy coffee table, across which Thomas' English books were strewn. There were various paintings dotted about the walls. The room smelled of fresh pine.

'So did you have a good time visiting your cousins?' Lola asked.

'It was alright, I guess. Did you go with Demzel to the school last night?'

'Wait till you hear this! You're not going to believe what happened.'

'What happened? You didn't get hurt, did you?'

'Not at all,' Lola assured Thomas, before proceeding to tell him everything that had happened the previous night; Thomas looked aghast.

'Oh my,' was all he could say.

'And now it's just yet another day. Part of me wishes I could go back and relive last night.'

'Why would you want to do that?'

'I know it was dangerous and anything could have happened, but it was thrilling and was like nothing I ever do. I felt so different when I was there, like I was on some great adventure.'

'I can't believe Demzel left you there like that.'

'He had his reasons and they are good ones. Thanks to him, I wasn't found straight away and they could have done anything to us.'

'Did you go to the police?'

'I thought about it but then Demzel said there wasn't really much point.'

'Those aliens could still be here, Lola! What if we go back to school on Monday and they're still there? What if they get in the school again? I don't think Demzel should have gone to the school with you at all, to be honest.'

'Why not? We found out something really important.'

'How's it important?'

'We now know there are more aliens in Helmia and that this goes way beyond the first two aliens and the orb.'

'Are you sure you want to get involved in all this?'

'The past few weeks have made me want to know about it all. It's happened to everyone, you too. We're all curious to know why this is happening and what it all means. We're starting to see the bigger picture and that we're not alone in the universe. Until a few weeks ago, we were just plodding on as usual in our mundane lives and now we have been visited by aliens from faraway planets. I want to find out more and am willing to take risks and do whatever.'

'Wouldn't you rather be doing something worthwhile?'

'This *is* worthwhile.'

'Is it really? The only thing to come from it is that a few people now know there are other aliens running about. Until you tell the police, you might as well have not gone there yesterday.'

'Do you really think the police would believe us? We have no evidence.'

'They should still be told nonetheless. Lola, remember that these aliens had guns and shot at you several times. You are very lucky they didn't manage to shoot you. If you ever do anything like this again, I want you to promise me you'll be extremely careful. I don't want to lose you at all, especially not to some ruddy aliens.'

Lola was starting to see Thomas' reasoning. Perhaps she had been a bit too rash in her decision to accompany Demzel, who had perhaps been a bit overzealous, willing to go on such a trip without knowing what would happen.

'I'm sorry,' Thomas said.

'Why are you saying sorry? You haven't done anything.'

'I'm being too harsh on you. I've no right to say what you should do – it's you who should decide.'

'Thomas, you're just expressing an opinion. Stop worrying! I see sense in what you're saying. I need to be careful if something like this happens again. I need you to continue being my voice of reason.'

'OK. Are you sure you're fine?'

'I'm fine, honestly.'

'If it had been me, I would have been petrified and would never leave the house. It scares me to think that there were aliens in the school last night and now they could be anywhere.'

'I guess it's not an ideal situation.'

'That's an understatement.'

'Did you watch the news this morning?'

'Yeah why?'

'Has anything happened?'

'Not anything major. There was just some news item about how they're going to tear down Woodwinder. Apart from that it was just the usual bland stories. Why?'

'I was wondering if maybe there'd been any sightings of UFOs or anything like that.'

'You've turned into Demzel.'

'I know. I'm running on curiosity like he is constantly.'

The two then buckled down and got on with their homework. Lola noticed Thomas was quite keen to get it done.

'What's with the urge to get this done?'

'I'm just sick of always leaving things to the last minute and getting stressed.'

'Sick of procrastinating?'

'Yeah actually. Leaving everything to the last minute is actually start to drive me insane.'

They got the homework done and spent the rest of the afternoon talking about anything and everything. Thomas' parents came back and Lola stayed over for tea.

The half term flew by quickly: most of the days Lola spent relaxing and reading, not confined to any sort of timetable like she was at school. When Saturday came round, she was excited because Hannah was due back from her holiday and it was one week until her brother came home for the weekend. She went round to Hannah's with Thomas and was greeted at the door by a worn-out looking Hannah, who had bigger bags than usual under her eyes.

'Never let me go on holiday if there are night flights involved,' was the first thing she said to them, after which she told them to come in and they all went up to her room.

'I have the cold and my eyes hurt because of the two hours' sleep I got on that awful plane,' she continued once they were seated in her room; Hannah's room was quite big and was adorned with posters of various male celebrities, most of whom were topless. The walls which weren't covered in posters were a light blue and her double bed had an ocean-themed blanket on it. The three were sitting on her bed.

'So did you have a good time at least?' Thomas asked.

'It was brilliant. We spent most of the days by the pool sunbathing and reading. Have you seen my tan? We had a walk into the town one day and we bought a few nice things from these little stores. I got both of you some scented candles though they're somewhere in the suitcases; I'm not unpacking until I need to. I took quite a few pictures too, but I'm not uploading them till later. I'm knackered.'

'Were there any nice Italian boys?' Thomas asked suggestingly.

'They were all over the place! Nothing could drag me away from that pool with all those nice topless boys splashing about everywhere.'

'Sounds like you certainly enjoyed it,' Lola said; she always felt a bit odd when in Hannah's room.

'It was the best holiday ever, apart from the flights. I have no idea why mum booked a night flight there and one back as well. They really screw up your sleeping patterns.'

'You look exhausted,' Thomas remarked.

'Thanks!'

'Joking.'

'Anyway, no contact for forever, what have you two been up to?'

Lola and Thomas looked at each other, then Thomas answered,

'I just visited my cousins on the mainland and actually did some homework early.'

'What's happened to you, Thomas? I go away and you've become, well, me and Lola. Speaking of which, what about you, Lola?'

'Well, you're not going to believe this. Demzel got in touch with me saying that something was going to be happening at the school on Monday, that Mr. Stone was going to be guarding something at the school and that he wanted to know if I'd accompany him. I said yes and so we went to the school at night, and we bumped into some aliens.'

'Aliens?!' Hannah shouted.

'Shh!'

Just as she'd done with Thomas, Lola told Hannah the full story.

'Were you hurt in any way?'

'No, I was fine. Just a bit shocked.'

'I can't believe you slapped Mr. Stone.'

'Me neither,' Lola replied, blushing a little, 'I don't know what came over me. I just felt so angry that he'd let aliens into the school and that they were shooting guns and stuff. I apologised to him but still felt guilty when I got home so I sent him an email apologising again.'

'Do you know why this happened?' asked Thomas.

'Demzel says he hasn't heard from Mr. Stone and his phone's constantly off. We were talking about it the other day and we think the Greys were looking for that missing orb.'

'You are now officially Demzel,' Hannah said, 'we think... we were talking the other day...the Greys...'

'I admit we are both curious and eager to get to the bottom of this. Plus, no sightings of Greys or UFOs have been reported, which means that either the Greys managed to get in the school from wherever they came without anyone seeing them, which is very unlikely, or...'

'Or what?'

'I don't know.'

'If they were searching the school, then maybe they're searching other places as well?' Thomas pondered.

'We should keep an eye on the news in case there are any sightings. If Demzel manages to get in touch with Ivan, answers might soon come.'

They talked on and on and eventually the subject of conversation got back to Hannah's holiday. She told them all about the hotel, the boys, the sights they saw the few times they left the hotel grounds, and the sun.

'You have tanned really well,' Lola said.

'I'll be back to my usual self in a week or two; tans never last on me,' Hannah said regrettably. Lola always thought Hannah looked exotic and a little odd but still exuded beauty; she'd always been attractive but for a reason people couldn't quite put a finger on. Hannah was from Helmia – her mother had lived there her whole life, yet she looked like she came from somewhere far away.

The following Monday, it was back to the grind as they resumed school. Life seemed to be going back to normal. The news had died down and was now back to reporting mundane articles such as news on particular celebrities and stories that appealed to no one. Demzel told her when he saw her in the corridor that he hadn't heard from Ivan at all.

'And he's not here today either,' Demzel informed her, 'so I think he's done a runner for some reason.'

'I hope he's alright.'

'Me too. He was acting a bit odd before last Monday. He was kinda tetchy and edgy.'

'Probably cos he'd been asked to stay in here with aliens at night.'

'I don't like this, Lola, I don't like it one bit. I've known Ivan for years and he should have told me why he was asked to do this and who asked him.'

'Maybe he was threatened?'

'Maybe.'

They walked for a bit longer then the bell rang and they parted ways, Demzel muttering about how the bell was far too loud.

Lola found herself in her form room, in which they were also taught English, waiting for Mrs. Dazzle.

'Good morning, class, I hope you all had a good half term and didn't work too hard. I'll collect your homework in at the end of the lesson. I hope you all did your homework this time; sloth isn't good for the soul, after all, and too much slacking around means you only get half as much done, not even that sometimes.'

The lesson went by and Lola noticed that the teacher still looked a bit tired, if not a bit unwell.

'Please do your homework well this time, class. The last lot wasn't as good as usual. It makes me happy to be giving high marks.'

The bell went and the class gradually left the room, eager for their lunch break. Lola decided to arrange the next group trip to the theme park.

'Kelly! Do you fancy going to the theme park with us a week on Saturday?' Lola asked as Kelly was leaving the room.

'Of course! That will be brilliant.'

'It would be this weekend, but my brother's coming home from uni and Hannah's going shopping on the mainland with her mum.'

'A week on Saturday is perfect, Lola,' Kelly replied beaming.

Within a few minutes, Lola had also invited Thomas, Hannah, Natella, Erica, Edward and Darren, along with a few others.

'I can't wait. I'm dead excited,' Darren told Lola; he had long brown hair and always sat at the back of every class.

Hannah always said she hoped he spent classes staring at her.

'I had a good time last time,' Darren added.

'Did you have a good half term?' Lola asked.

'Yeah. Didn't do much. Just sat round playing video games and watching telly. Did you?'

'Yes it was alright. I basically did the same, minus the video games.'

'Sounds good. Oh that reminds me, I've got something to tell you. Not here though, come with me.'

Lola left the classroom and followed Darren; he led her all the way through the Arts building to the Mythology building and on to the spare classroom on the top floor; it was empty.

'I didn't want her hearing us.'

'Who?' Lola asked, cautious not to bring Hannah up.

'Natella. I was passing by here this morning on my way to the vending machine and I heard her in here on the phone to someone. I thought nothing of it and went to the vending machine but on my way back I looked in the classroom and saw her with her back to me and I listened in. She sounded quite worried. That's when she said it: "I suspect Lola Spears", then the bell rang and I made my way back to our form room.'

'Did you hear anything else that she said?'

'After she said she suspected you, she reiterated it then said she had a valid reason.'

'And before?'

'She just said she was still checking on it every day and that it was still there, though I never found out what she meant.'

Lola looked baffled.

'Lola? Are you okay? I'm sure it's nothing but I thought I'd tell you.'

'I'm fine. You're right, it's probably nothing. It'll turn out to be something silly. While we're here, do you wanna go to said vending machine?'

'Yeah. Lunch today looks awful.'

'You're vegetarian, aren't you?'

'Since I was ten. The mere thought of eating meat makes me cringe.'

'It's not the nicest feeling in the world, but it's still tasty!'

'Haha! I think I'll get some apple juice and a banana. I'm trying to eat more healthily.'

'Me too, though I always fail in the end.'

They went back to the spare classroom and chatted a bit more. Once the topic of conversation got round to Natella again, Lola reassured Darren that it was probably nothing and that she wasn't going to worry about it, even though she was formulating ideas in her mind and was starting to feel paranoid.

After lunch, which she went to with Darren and Thomas, she decided to confront Natella and ask what was up. She went back to her form class and found Natella chatting with Erica and Kelly.

'Natella, can you come here for a sec?' Lola asked. Natella came out of the classroom and said, smiling, 'what's up, Lola?'

'This will sound a bit odd, but Darren, well, he overheard you on the phone this morning saying that you suspected me of something?'

'That I suspect you of something?'

'Yes, well, that's what he told me.'

'I *was* on the phone, but he must have misheard me. I was talking to my mum.'

'He said you sounded quite worried?'

Natella looked down for a minute then said in a lower voice, 'my mum's had to go to hospital,' she said looking Lola directly in the eye.

'Oh gosh, I'm sorry. I didn't know,' Lola said, though something told her Natella's explanation was a fabrication.

'It's not serious, is it?'

'It could be,' Natella replied with watery eyes.

'I'm sorry Natella. I didn't know and wouldn't have brought it up if I'd known.'

She accompanied Natella to the restroom and she dried her eyes.

'She'll be fine, the doctor said so, but I can't help but worry a bit.'

'It's okay to be scared.'

'Thanks, Lola. You won't tell anyone about this, will you?'

'No,' Lola said, but a few minutes later, she was in the library telling Hannah and Thomas everything that had happened.

'I don't know whether to believe her, but Darren is sure of what he heard,' she told them.

'She said the snowman thing would be happening again and now she's suspecting you of something? It sounds fishy if you ask me,' said Hannah.

'And there was that weird conversation she had with that woman. Apparently that woman has the orb, but then what were the Greys doing in the school? It's not making sense.'

'I hope Natella's mum's okay,' said Thomas.

'I have a feeling there's nothing wrong with her mum,' Hannah said, 'that girl is definitely hiding something.'

Very soon they were in Demzel's classroom for Paranormal and Supernatural Studies; Demzel was beaming at his desk and there was a large picture of one of the Greys on the interactive whiteboard behind him. He was so excited he even forgot to do the register. Lola looked a bit worried and hoped Demzel wasn't about to do what she thought he was.

'This behind me is a Grey, arguably the most famous alien species. The Greys are very popular and have appeared in numerous TV shows, books and movies. The reason why we're gonna start focusing on them is because just this weekend, as you may have heard on the news, some of these Greys were sighted in Helmia. Jacob Wall, a security guard at the arena, was working late on Saturday night, when all of the CCTV cameras went off. He went to investigate and found all the exit doors of the arena had been locked shut. He eventually went outside to the seats and saw Greys everywhere, at least a hundred he said, some walking by the highest rows of seats, others right at the bottom. They all seemed to be looking for something, as they were inspecting every seat and looking under it. Before he was seen, he managed to escape, but by the time he'd alerted the police and they came, the Greys were all gone.

'A bit more about the Greys themselves, or as I like to call them: *hoi deinoi*. They have been visiting this planet on and off for over fifty years now and are the most frequently sighted aliens. They are known to have abducted people and seem to be quite an advanced race, given that they can travel across space. I have printed out an information booklet which has a few pictures of them as well as biological information. Although they are popularised as being grey, they can be dark grey, black and even sometimes white. One word which is often used to describe them is the ancient Greek adjective '*deinos*,' which means many things, including strange, terrible, clever, awesome, astounding, and shocking among other things. In my opinion, '*deinos*,' whose plural is '*deinoi*,' is the perfect word to describe these aliens, hence my nickname for them, for they are many things to us, yet we still know very little about them. They are different things to different people. Most people who've encountered them find them to be terrifying, cold creatures, whilst others are mystified by them and think they exude some exotic attraction. However, any and all aliens are extremely dangerous, despite what you may know about them already.'

Demzel then proceeded to talk them through their information booklets. Lola felt a chill as she beheld the various pictures of the Greys. The whole class was attentive and particularly earnest towards the end of the class when Demzel said he wouldn't be surprised if the Greys were sighted again and he stressed that aliens would always be dangerous, as their true intentions could never truly be known.

Lola stayed back after class to tell Demzel of the conversation she'd overheard between Natella and Maude. She'd been meaning to do it earlier, but the alien encounter had put it to the back of her mind. Demzel was perplexed yet delighted there was a development nonetheless.

'This Maude character knows the location of the orb... the plot thickens!' he pronounced with glee.

That week flew by for Lola. There were a few similar sightings of Greys, just as Demzel had theorised, and she was starting to grow worried. She noticed that most people she saw looked a little preoccupied as the number of sightings increased. By the Saturday they were due to go to the theme park, the Greys had been sighted six different times, seven if Lola and Demzel's encounter were included, and each time they'd eventually vanished without a trace.

There was still some of that wintry chill in the air, but it was generally getting warmer. The theme park was a bit busier than the last time Lola was here. She'd tried several times since overhearing Natella's conversation to find out what exactly was going on, but Natella kept on denying it, saying Lola had misheard them; Lola figured it best not to bring it up yet again at the park. They'd got there for the park gates opening and had headed straight over to Woodwinder. After a queue of only seven minutes, they got on the train.

The train left the station and started its slow journey up the long lift hill. Higher and higher it got. Lola looked straight ahead and saw the few cars up ahead and the heads of the people in front of her. The sky was clear and there was hardly a cloud anywhere to be seen.

That's when Lola saw it: something appeared in the distance, just like that. She blinked and there were a few more. Then a few more. By her rough estimation, they were a mile or so from Helmia.

The train then jerkily went down its first drop and followed the rest of its course, blocking whatever had appeared in the sky from Lola's view. Once off the ride, they had a look at the ride picture, decided it was awful then Lola looked up at the sky. A few moments later, a large craft flew right over their heads, making a very loud whooshing noise and temporarily casting a fleeting shadow over them and whatever was nearby. Everyone's attention was turned to it: Lola saw everyone nearby look up and watch the craft. A few more craft were flying near to it.

'Oh my,' cried Erica, 'what on Earth are they?'

But no one answered her; everyone was too transfixed by the craft, which were now flying fast in the direction of Mount Euscha. There was a fleet of about thirty of them all flying together. Lola wondered whether the pilots of these large craft were in fact Greys or something else, or actually human craft, though she didn't think there was much chance they were human craft, given their similarity to pictures of alien craft she'd seen. She started to panic.

Symmetry Peak was visible in the distance; it was a massive cliff top with the large lake below. Lola squinted as the craft grew smaller and smaller until they vanished one by one about halfway up the cliff face of Symmetry Peak. Then she realised what they probably were:

'*Hoi deinoi*,' she whispered to herself.

Chapter 11 –
The Lightshow

'The UFOs appeared in the sky a few miles out to sea then flew to Helmia, where they were seen vanishing near Symmetry Peak. People who were at Symmetry Peak at the time corroborated that the craft did indeed enter a large cave roughly halfway up the cliff face, which wasn't there previously. However, as of this morning, there is no large cave there. No craft have since been spotted. It had been confirmed by the military that these craft did not belong to them. What these craft are, therefore, remains a mystery. Everyone is asked to report any sighting of any kind to the police immediately.'

Lola was watching the news that evening. She was lying on the sofa eating some crisps, her mind buzzing with questions. She was waiting for her brother to arrive and he was due any minute now.

There came the sound of the door being opened and Lola turned to see her brother open the front door. She ran over to him and hugged him.

'Woah! I take it you've missed me?'

'Of course!' Lola said, letting go and looking at him; he

was tanned and looked exhausted, the bags under his eyes bigger than she'd ever seen them.

'Feels like I've never left!' Andrew said as he slung his bag down on the floor and collapsed on to the settee, stretching his arms.

'Mum, dad! Andrew's back!' Lola shouted up the stairs; within seconds her parents were coming downstairs.

'Good to see you, son!'

'I don't know why you didn't want us to pick you up from the harbour. We would have, you know,' their mum said.

'Let the boy have his independence,' their dad replied.

The family were soon settled in the living room and Andrew was showing them all photos from his holiday on his laptop.

'It looks like you had an amazing time,' Lola commented as she looked at a picture of Andrew and his friends standing on a golden beach with the sun blazing and a clear blue sky in the background.

'It was a blast!'

'How much did you spend?' their mum asked

'Not too much, don't worry, mum,' Andrew replied mechanically, as if he'd been expecting this question.

'We went out most nights,' he carried on, 'and never got in before five.'

'It sounds awesome,' Lola said; her parents looked aghast.

'Anyway, how are you all?'

'We're all a bit, well, anxious,' their dad replied.

'Anxious? Why?'

'Haven't you heard the news?'

'I told you when I phoned last week that I don't read the papers. It's not those snowmen again, is it?'

'It's UFOs this time,' Lola said, and proceeded to explain to Andrew what had recently happened.

'They can't really be aliens,' Andrew replied, his mother nodding assent.

'It's just too farfetched,' she added, 'and it's all absurd.'

'But it happened, mum, thousands saw the craft soar over Helmia then go into that cave that's disappeared,' Lola argued.

'It's a load of nonsense!' Lola's mum interjected rather snappily; Lola at that point wondered whether she should tell any of them about her encounter at school with Greys. So far she'd only told Thomas and Hannah, both of whom she knew would keep it secret. If she did tell them, she was sure her mother and brother wouldn't believe her. Her parents would be furious that she'd been in such grave danger by herself; Lola felt guilty for lying and guilty that Demzel was involved too. With Demzel being long-time friends with her parents, she didn't know how they'd react if they found out he'd taken her to the school at night and left her there with potentially dangerous aliens. Since there'd been a few reports about people seeing Greys, however, Lola and Demzel had mutually agreed not to tell anyone, given that their experience was just another encounter with aliens and, because a few had already been brought to the attention of the press, they felt they someone had already alerted everyone to the fact that there were Greys somewhere in Helmia, doing their job for them.

'Anyway, son, I think we'd rather hear more about your holiday.'

The change of subject was pleasantly welcomed. Andrew told them about a visit to a local village, which was more like a ghost town, and the day they spent playing sports on the beach and in the cool, clear sea.

'Are you glad to be home?' Lola asked him a while later; they were in his room.

'Of course I am. I'm always glad to see you all again,' he said as he looked round his room.

'It feels good to be back. Now tell me, Lola, are you sure you're okay? When you told me on the phone about that snowman attacking you I was so scared you'd been seriously hurt.'

'I'm fine, thanks. Just got a few scratches and bruises.'

'You were dead lucky though.'

'I know. Anything could have happened.'

'I want you to be careful, OK? Promise me you'll be alert and watch over mum and dad? There are some weird things going on on this island and I don't want any of you getting hurt. I know I'm not here all the time, but this will always be my home.'

He smiled at his sister; Lola was thrilled to hear him say this.

'So, did you meet any nice girls out there?'

'What happens on holiday, stays on holiday,' Andrew said grinning.

The two remained in Andrew's bedroom for some time, catching up and telling each other what they'd been up to recently.

That night, Lola was lying in her bed texting Thomas and Hannah. She stifled a yawn; checking her phone, she realised it was almost midnight and that she'd been lying there texting people for at least half an hour. She soon turned her phone to silent, turned her light off and went to sleep.

The next morning, she woke up and immediately went to her computer and within minutes was reading the news website. The disappearance of the craft and the cave they'd flown into were of course the top news item; it was reported a flight coming into Helmia from Denmark had at one point been a few hundred metres behind the fleet of craft; the pilot recalled how there was nothing detected on the radar until the fleet appeared, one by one, out of nowhere, all already in motion heading towards Helmia. Unfazed, he continued to fly the plane and landed it successfully.

Lola still assumed that the craft were of alien origin; she'd read many accounts of people seeing UFOs and always thought it safe to assume they were mostly alien, especially when abductions were involved. To her it seemed the most logical solution. There simply had to be life elsewhere in the universe, intelligent life, given the sheer number of planets out there. Sure, most planets would be inhabitable and life, if it did develop, could easily get killed off, but she remained convinced that there was at least one planet out there with reasonably intelligent life that would advance. Now she was even more convinced one planet had produced life that had developed interstellar travel, but for what reason, she wondered. Had the Greys come all this way, from whatever planet, simply to find the orb? If so, what purpose did the orb serve? Lola thought there must be some other reason for their being here, but every theory she came up with seemed as unlikely as the next. One thing she did know for certain was that they were looking for something, most likely the orb, but they could very well have been searching for something else, and if they were looking for the orb, that might have been a mere side quest and not their primary reason for visiting Earth.

She was lying there deep in thought that night, half an hour after midnight, when she heard a great whooshing noise outside her window. She clambered out of bed and looked out of her window just in time to see a sight that had her transfixed: the sky was aglow with numerous saucer-shaped spacecraft zooming through the sky. There were at least ten in total, Lola estimated, each one flashing different coloured lights. Lola thought it looked like some surreal light show.

There was a faint buzz in the air, the humming of the crafts' engines. She suddenly felt very small.

'Lola!' her mother cried from her bedroom next door, 'Andrew!'

The family were soon assembled on the landing, Lola's mother looking panic-stricken, her father looking exhausted, Lola and Andrew looking fascinated.

'Everyone to the basement, now! I'll get food and drink. Someone bring some blankets.'

'Mum, it's okay. There's no need to panic,' Lola said reassuringly.

'Have you *seen* them? There's so many out there! No, I'm not taking any chances. I want everyone in the basement in two minutes. Bring your laptop, Andrew.'

Lola saw that her mother looked genuinely horrified and thought it best to do as she was told. The sight of so many ships flying about, it seemed, had stunned her mother into believing that it was all real, happening, and truly terrifying.

Before Lola could have another look at what she considered to be a marvellous sight, they were all forced down into the basement, which, although relatively small and dark, was quite warm. Andrew was on his laptop, scouring the Internet for news. Lola's dad had fallen asleep on one of the blankets and Lola's mum was frantically pacing the room, biting her nails and mumbling to herself.

'Mum, are you okay?'

'I'm fine,' she replied, taking a deep breath after doing so. She started feeling her face with her hands.

'It says here,' said Andrew, 'that we might be getting evacuated.'

'What?'

'The ships are still all hovering above Helmia; they reckon there are about thirty-five. They're all over the island.

Each one is about the size of a small airplane,' Andrew was skimming the online article, which had only appeared online a few minutes ago and was written in very short, snappy sentences.

'The whole island has been ordered to remain indoors while they wait for something to happen,' Andrew carried on reading briskly, 'if the ships go, we're safe to come out, but only once an all-clear has been given. If, well, something else happens...' Andrew didn't want to finish the rest of the article; Lola looked from one parent to the other, then to her brother, who looked shocked more than anything, as if he were struggling to take this all in.

Lola, on the other hand, had embraced it all and was desperate to get out there and see the dazzling array of alien ships once more. She realised it would be potentially dangerous, but the pros outweighed the cons, she thought to herself. It wasn't every day that one had the opportunity to witness alien ships hovering above one's town. She was missing all that; they could fly away at any second. On the other hand, they could just as well attack; no one knew who they were or why they were here, after all.

She was starting to feel crammed in and claustrophobic in the basement, even though there was enough room for them all. She felt as if she should be out in the open streets at a time like this, not cowering away and eschewing such a rare and unique opportunity.

Her desire was at the forefront: she impulsively told her parents she was going to get some more food from the kitchen, ran up the stairs and shut the door as she heard her mum shouting after her, telling her to come down into the basement and running up the stairs. Lola ran through the house and soon heard her frantic mother yelling for her to come back, back to safety, away from the alien ships and the unknown.

She reached the front door and heard all of her family yelling protests for her to stay.

'Lola, where on Earth are you going?'

'Get back here, Lola, it could be dangerous out there! No one knows what's going to happen - we've been told to stay inside!'

'Lola, get back inside this house now!'

'Lola, please.'

'What's got into you?'

'Lola, you could get yourself killed!'

Once outside, she hastily locked the front door; her family would of course have their own keys, but this bought her time.

She'd done it. She was outside, where it was all happening, not inside watching it happen on a computer screen. She thought she'd been a little impulsive in rushing off from her family so fast without so much as an explanation, and she knew they'd doubtless be angry with her for leaving the house when they'd been instructed not to. She knew she was facing trouble, but the view was worth it.

She ran down the street the little and stopped a few houses away, crouching down behind a garden bush. Within a few moments, she heard the desperate cries of her name breaking the eerie silence, cries from her family, who were at a loss to explain why she had so recklessly ran off to meet danger.

Someone ran past calling out for her, running all the way down the street. Lola got up, looked up and around, then ran round to the back of the house down the small gap between the house and its neighbour. Once beyond the two gardens, she stopped and took time to rest. She could still hear faint cries of her name.

In the distance were the starry sky and the dead black forest. The sky was a dark navy blue; there were glittering stars dotted about all over the celestial dome. The two spaceships hovering above the forest, a few hundred metres apart and a hundred metres or so up, were emitting the most dazzling lights Lola had ever seen. One had dark red lights dancing all around it, the other amber lights. Lola was transfixed; she watched the motionless ships - there was a faint buzz in the sky - both of which were the same shape, large and saucer-like, an oversized spinner toy with a chunky, broad middle, a middle which seemed to have two storeys, as there were as many rows of windows gleaming with a dark yellow light. The windows themselves illuminated rows right across the central part of the ship. Lola was entranced by the beauty of the dancing lights; she thought it a graceful lightshow, a display of beauty and rhythm.

The ships, Lola noticed, were slowly spinning around on the spot. The lights around the rim of each ship were still randomly flashing on and off. Lola kept watching, wondering if anything would happen. She heard more faint cries of her name from her persistent and worried parents and brother. She turned her phone on then looked at it to see she had several missed calls from them. She quickly typed a text message telling them she was okay, that she was just watching the spaceships and would come home soon. Once the text had been sent to all three, Lola took a few pictures of the beautiful scene with the camera on her phone.

'Wow,' she said excitedly; as far as she was concerned, she was in no immediate danger at the present time. She was very glad she'd come out here to witness this once-in-a-lifetime event and knew she'd made the right decision.

Even though her feet were firmly on the ground, Lola felt as if she were flying up among the stars. Fear like she'd felt at the school wasn't present here; what she felt was ambition, curiosity and importance. She wanted to be in space, travel to a new planet so far away like these aliens so close to her had done; she wanted to find out what these aliens were and everything they had to tell; she felt emboldened and important to be here witnessing this, for she would be one of a handful of people who were looking at this.

She'd lived in this area her whole life and always looked to the forest when she was in the back garden. For fifteen years the view of the rolling fields and the densely populated forest had remained virtually unchanged. She found it hard to believe there were so many ships now hovering above Helmia. Her fascination overcame her fear; after the encounter with the Greys, she had quickly contemplated, when back in the basement, whether or not it was such a good idea to run out into the street, but this view was definitely worth the risk. She wondered how far these ships and their occupants had travelled. Most likely, she assumed, they had travelled several light-years across space to get here. But then, how long must they have been travelling for? Lola's mind was boggling. Was this the destination these ships had been travelling to for many, many Earth-years at extreme speeds? How fast could these ships actually travel? Or were they perhaps from somewhere closer to home, somewhere previously thought to be a body devoid of intelligent life? So many questions were flitting through Lola's mind, along with just as many answers, theories, ideas.

Then she remembered someone who she suspected would have some answers, even though she appeared reluctant to divulge the information she knew. In a few minutes, she found herself at Natella's front door, banging on it hardly, determined for her to answer, or at least to be in.

Natella opened the door, yawning a big yawn, dressed in her nightgown and looking forlorn.

'Lola!' she said, a tone of surprise in her voice.

'I want some answers, Natella, and I want them now.'

'Lola what are you on about? Have you seen the ships outside? You should be with your family.'

'They know I'm okay. Natella, please, I want some answers. You know about the snowmen, you suspect me of something and you know about the orb!'

Natella looked stunned.

'I heard you talking to that Maude woman at school, which you won't stop denying,' Lola iterated. Natella simply stared at Lola, mouth agape.

'Lola, I really don't know what you're -'

'Come on, Natella, is anyone going to kill you for telling me anything?'

'Well, no, but - '

'See, you do know something! And you can tell me, so go on then.'

Natella, still standing on her threshold, led Lola into her living room, telling her that her parents were still asleep upstairs.

'I thought it best not to wake them,' Natella said, 'they would freak out if they were awake now.'

'Does that Maude woman have the orb?'

Natella remained silent for a few moments then replied: 'the orb is safe. Maude's been asked to check on it every few days.'

Lola wondered for as few moments then a more pressing question came to mind:

'Are the aliens out there Greys?' she asked. Natella hesitated for a few moments before she replied.

'No, they're not. These ships are different – they're fatter round the middle and they're larger.'

Lola felt a pang of relief to hear this, yet she was eager to know whether these other aliens were more or less threatening than the hostile and impatient Greys.

'Who are these aliens then if they're not Greys?'

'We call them the Blondies,' Natella said with a serious face; Lola burst out laughing.

'The Blondies? Haha! Are you being serious?'

'You wanted answers, Lola, and that's what you're getting. I know it sounds daft, but we really do call them the Blondies, though their real name is the Keelot and the Greys are really called the Lormai.'

Lola imagined a spaceship full of blonde-haired aliens, each one with long hair; she thought it quite an odd image.

'So all those ships up ahead are Blondie ships?'

'Yes, all of them.'

'And they're here because...?'

Natella sighed, then said, 'it's quite complicated, Lola, and it goes back a long way. Basically, the Blondies, the Keelot, don't pose any threat whatsoever to us.'

'Why are they here then?'

Natella looked like she was spilling some secret she was longing to keep to herself.

'They are here to help and protect us.'

'From...?'

Natella hesitated again for a few moments then started talking again.

'From Assa. Look, Lola, it's complex and I'm not sure you really want to know. I think you're better off not knowing. Only a few of us know what's coming and we haven't announced it to the world because, firstly they'd think we were playing some sort of joke or that we were simply talking nonsense, and secondly, we're not sure it'd be a wise thing to do.'

'Why? Surely knowing is better than not knowing?'

'Sometimes people who know wish they didn't.'

'Well, I want to know. Come on, I'm not leaving till I have answers. Who or what is Assa?'

Natella took a few moments, then eyed Lola and eventually replied: 'what would you say if I told you this universe has a creator?'

'I'd say you're assuming quite a lot!'

'I'm being serious, Lola. Look, I know it's a lot to take in, but this universe has a very real creator, and that is Assa.'

'But what is this *Assa*?'

'Assa is a being from outside of this universe, a realm where other such beings live.'

'I can believe in aliens and ghosts and such things, but you're telling me the answer to one of the biggest questions there is and expecting me to believe it?'

'It's a lot to take in, I admit; it took ages for me to finally believe it. There is tangible evidence for the existence of aliens - look outside, but I understand there is no evidence for Assa being the creator of this universe other than what Assa and Hyuul have said and done.'

'Who's Hyuul?'

'Hyuul is...another being like Assa.'

'Are Assa and Hyuul those two aliens who flew down to Helmia ages ago?'

'Yes, that was them.'

Lola's head was swimming with questions.

'What if Assa's lying? What if Assa's just some random alien claiming to have created the universe? It sounds as if Assa's just a bit arrogant, if you ask me.'

'We all believe what they say and, given their actions, it all makes sense. Lola, you should go home and be with your family.'

'No, I'm staying. You said yourself that the Blondies pose no threat to us.'

'Is there anything else you want to know?'

'Of course there is! This Assa, if - wait, is Assa male or female?'

'Neither.'

'OK, then, so, assuming there are other universes then, what's Assa doing in this universe and why do we need protecting from Assa?'

'Well, basically…Lola, this is all a lot for you understand, and I won't be surprised if you disbelieve everything I say. Well, Assa created this universe with no free will, a universe where everything was pre-planned, pre-decided by Assa, it was the first of its kind, but Hyuul thought this was morally wrong, so Hyuul sabotaged the universe, so that it started to differ from the way Assa had planned it to be, and now Assa is going about rectifying it, getting rid of planets and civilisations that weren't meant to be and making sure the whole universe eventually gets back to how it was originally planned to be.'

'That is a lot to take in! Crikey, Natella,' Lola looked flabbergasted; she thought of something to say, but nothing came, for she was pondering so many questions.

'You may not believe it, Lola, but it is all real. It is real and imminent.'

Lola looked at Natella, who looked sombre and grim.

'All the Blondies can do is to help delay it. Stopping it is almost impossible; it has never been stopped before.'

'What do you mean by "it," Natella?'

'The Earth was planned to be inhabited by the dinosaurs for millions and millions of years; they weren't meant to be wiped out sixty-five million years ago. Assa came to this planet, saw a totally new race that had sprouted up, we humans, and is now…'

'Is now what?' Lola asked tenderly.

'What Assa wants is for everything to be as what it was in the plans. Humans were never meant to exist. We evolved by accident; the dinosaurs were wiped out and then we took their place, and now Assa…'

'Is wanting rid of us because we were never planned?' Lola said, looking aghast and appalled.

'Yes,' was Natella's simple reply. She looked stern and down. Lola got up, feeling fidgety, and she looked out of the window at the alien ships and their erratic lights. Now it all didn't seem like such a dazzling lightshow to Lola after all.

Chapter 12 –
Not So Alien

Lola was walking back home, having left Natella's wondering whether she should have gone there at all. The ships buzzing and whirring up ahead with their lights flashing on and off didn't distract her from concentrating on simply staring ahead as she ambled. What she had previously thought was beautiful and enticing was now a reminder of the horrors Natella had assured Lola of - what if it were all true? There were still some things she had forgotten to ask, but she reckoned what Natella had told her was more than enough for her to contemplate for now. Natella had seemed genuine, but Lola thought all she'd explained was too farfetched. The creator of the universe wanting to eradicate a species simply because it hadn't been in the plans? Lola had believed aliens existed for ages - those beliefs were backed up by mountains of evidence put forward in Paranormal and Supernatural Studies classes with Demzel, and by what had recently happened in Helmia, but she wasn't sure whether she could believe the universe had actually been created, as opposed to it having come into existence out of nothing. She had asked herself that question a few times over the years and had always decided that it was something that could never be truly answered. People could propose theories and ideas, but none could ever be proven. So now it seemed preposterous that someone was so confidently speaking of the solution to one of the biggest questions asked by humanity over the millennia. She realised once, a few years ago, that ultimately in the beginning there had to have been nothing before there had been something; that she was sure of, but what she was unsure of was whether it spontaneously came into existence of its own accord. She realised also that if there had been some creator, some cause of causes, then that too must surely have had a cause? It all boiled down to something coming from nothing. Lola's brain was hurting slightly, as it did whenever she pondered such huge questions. She couldn't quite accept what Natella had told her, as it seemed so ridiculous a concept, so grand an assumption. It was a mind-boggling idea to get her head around. The longer she thought about it, the more she realized she'd never be able to expel it form her mind. Before she knew it, she was approaching home; her brother was in the front garden, shouting out for her.

'Where on Earth have you been? What did you run off for? Mum was out of her mind with worry!' Andrew caught sight of her, looking angst-stricken.

'Calm down! Look, I'm sorry. I'm here now,' Lola paused and stared at her brother, his mouth agape; they were in the light of a streetlamp. Lola added:

'I had to come out here to see it all. Look up into the sky and tell me you think I did the right thing.'

Andrew looked up into the sky; ships were flying about, each one flashing different coloured lights into the late night sky. There was still the sound of the ships' soft humming and the great whooshing noises as they soared above. Andrew looked apprehensive.

'Lola, we should head back inside.'

'I have just realised that this, all this above us, is just a tiny glimpse of everything. We are so small.'

'Lola, come on, we have to go back inside, now!'

'I'm scared, I admit it. It's not just these aliens above us that scare me, but those two with the orb, the snowman, the reports of people seeing Greys, everything that's been happening recently,' Lola fired, luckily neglecting to tell him about the incident in the school.

'I can either remain scared and cower in the basement, or I can stand out here and watch it happen, because it might never happen again. This is history, this is something extraordinary. Nothing will keep me in that basement, Andrew, nothing,' Lola added defiantly, passion arising in her.

Andrew looked stunned, yet a bit disappointed.

'Lola, please. Mum's worried.'

'Tell her I'm fine, because I am. I'm just in the garden. I want to stay here and watch,' Lola said with determination.

'Anything could happen, Lola, this could be the start of an invasion or something. Please come and be with your family.'

'I'll come down if anything happens. Just let me stay up here and enjoy this, please.'

'Fine! I give up trying. You're making the wrong decision, Lola. Mum's not going to be happy.'

Andrew looked at Lola for a few moments then turned and ran inside. Lola thought she was absolutely doing the right thing. She was in no apparent danger, after all.

With no distractions, she sat down in the front garden, looking up at the ships flying all over the place up above, and tried to decide whether she believed what Natella had told her.

She got up and went round to her back garden and saw the two ships that had been hovering above the forest had now gone. For a few moments, she looked at the forest, though it was barely discernible, and imagined the ships were still there, then for a brief moment she wished she hadn't been so persistent in getting answers from Natella: she had been astounded by the ships before, but now she wasn't sure what to make of them, despite Natella's reassurance that they meant no harm. The lights might be enticing, but that could be a false representation of what was inside the ships.

Lola's thinking was interrupted when she noticed that one of the ships had now appeared in the distance and was flying over the forest, closer to her, and slowing down. Lola sat down and froze, only able to watch as the ship, larger than she'd thought it would be, began to slowly descend into the rolling fields separating the street from the forest. The humming gradually quietened down; the spinning middle of the ship gradually slowed down. Soon enough, the ship had landed on a flat plain atop one of the hills, its lights still flashing. Lola's eyes were wide, eager to take it all in despite facing the unknown.

'Lola! Lola!' Andrew cried, running from the kitchen.

'It showed us on the news they're starting to land!' he yelled, 'inside now!'

'Wait, look!' Lola said, pointing at the ship in the distance; she was still sitting down.

'Lola, come on, now! NOW!' Andrew shouted, yanking Lola by the shoulder, but she was refusing to budge.

Andrew gave up when he saw what was happening at the ship: he and Lola watched with a range of strong emotions fighting inside of them.

'Andrew, stay here,' Lola said.

A metal platform had descended from the ship, and walking down it, on to alien soil, was a tall, humanoid figure, eerily luminescent with striking platinum-blonde hair.

'W-what is that?' Andrew whispered to Lola.

'It's an alien - a Blondie,' Lola replied with a degree of calm.

'A *what?*'

'Never mind.'

'What do you mean, a *Blondie?*'

Lola realised she'd opened up a can of worms, but didn't want to elaborate on her slip-up any further.

'Lola!' Andrew whispered franticly to her, but Lola was unresponsive, merely staring at the aliens in the distance. What was now discernible was that the aliens were all carrying large helmets in their long hands. Their clothes were of a light metallic blue, which shone in the darkness. They could have been people in fancy dress, thought Lola.

'Lola, come with me now. You don't know what they're doing here! No one does!' Andrew grabbed Lola's arm and tried to pull her up.

'Andrew, get off me!' Lola cried.

'Lola, I'm being serious! Get up now,' Andrew shrieked.

'Andrew, please!' Lola was trying to wrest her arm from her brother's grip.

'Lola!' Andrew said with a shudder; his grip slackened. He was pointing in the direction of the aliens and their ship; Lola looked and saw the aliens were slowly advancing towards her and her brother: though they were quite far away, Lola still felt a pang of fear, despite her thought that they were rather humanlike in posture and stance, and therefore less intimidating.

There were five of them, all dressed identically, all in spacesuits.

Lola could feel herself being picked up and struggled to break free from her brother's grasp. He was holding on to her tight, trying with all his might to get her off the ground, but Lola was steadfast; she was standing up, her brother's arms around her, pulling her back, when she managed to break free. She ran forward a little before turning round and confronting her brother.

'I said I wanted to stay,' she said stubbornly.

Her brother finally seemed to acknowledge her wish: he looked solemn but didn't say anything.

Lola turned round and saw the aliens were still progressing towards them. One alien in particular was at the forefront: it was half a head taller than the others and seemed somewhat bulkier. They were walking down one of the hills and were briefly out of sight before they reappeared, walking up another hill towards them.

'If they wanted to kill us, they probably could have done that by now,' Lola told Andrew, who had come over to stand by her, holding her hand.

'Why do you want to see them so much?' he asked her.

'It's something new I've never seen before. Most people would be afraid and would runaway, but I don't want to runaway.'

'If they try anything, I'll kill them,' Andrew's grip tightened.

'I'm sure they don't want to do us any harm,' Lola said, although she wasn't entirely confident in this.

'Stand behind me, Lola, please,' Andrew said; Lola stood still, however.

'Lola, please.'

'I can defend myself should anything happen,' Lola retaliated.

The aliens were getting ever closer. Their movement seemed to be in slow motion. They were now mere metres away, having traversed a few more hills; Lola could feel Andrew's hand shaking vehemently.

The aliens came to a halt a few feet from the siblings. Lola felt tense and knew that anything could happen next.

'Can you understand me?' Lola asked, to which the main Blondie nodded.

'What do you want from us?' she spoke hurriedly.

She looked at a few of the alien faces, trying not to look them in the eye, and saw a few of them looked confused. Then to Lola and Andrew's surprise, the middle one spoke in a heavy, groggy and somewhat accented voice:

'We are here to help,' it said rather confidently, its vowels unusually long.

'To help us?' Lola said slowly.

'Yes. We want to help you and stop Assa.'

The last word of the alien's sentence had Lola thunder-struck. It was all falling into place. She realised then and there that there was truth in what Natella had told her. That this Blondie spoke English strengthened Lola's belief that they weren't so alien after all.

'Assa needs to die,' the alien added with an expression of anger.

'Why do we need help? What's going to happen?' Lola said slowly, yet she was excited.

'An alien Assa and other aliens called Lormai are here and they will kill all you humans when Assa has the orb.'

Incontrovertible proof was what this was. The words of these aliens matched with what Natella had said.

'Why have you come all this way to help us?'

'We have been waiting for this moment for some time. We have always been intent on helping you when the time came, and recently it did. We saw the Lormai flying towards the portal and we followed in their wake. Luckily, it remained open so we could get here.'

'But there have been Greys here for a while already. A few weeks ago there were some at my school one night looking for something.'

'We know some Lormai have already been here for a

while. We would have come here sooner, but the portal only opened recently because, we think, the final phases of the plan are to happen. The Lormai that arrived here just recently are only a small fraction of their total population.'

'What do you mean by 'the final phases of the plan'?'

'We have seen all this happen before. A planet near to ours was marked and we watched as it was purged and restored to how it was meant to be. We helped of course, but we couldn't do much. Luckily for us, our planet has advanced as it was meant to be: we are meant to be there. However, you are not meant to exist. Assa is now enacting the final phases of the plan: the remaining Lormai have been summoned and it will happen very soon.'

'What exactly do you mean?'

'Assa summoned the Lormai because Assa presumably now has the orb and is therefore ready to carry out the plans.'

'Which are?'

'To wipe out all humans,' the alien replied bluntly.

The reality of the predicament hit Lola. She remained silent as she thought things over in her warm head.

'But I heard a woman, Maude, tell my friend Natella that she'd checked the orb was still there, wherever that may be.'

'When did this happen?'

'A few weeks ago.'

'Assa could have found the orb since.'

'Do you know where the orb was hidden?'

'We were informed its hiding-place is in the office of Harold Dazzle.'

'What! Mr. Dazzle's office?'

'That is correct.'

'Mr. Dazzle as in the Headmaster of Puddlepond High School?'

'Yes, that is he.'

'Assa was flying round Helmia not so long ago. Why hide it there if it needs to kept away from Assa?' Lola was speaking more quickly as her eagerness for answers was rising.

'The orb was in a plant pot in the office on the orders of Hyuul.'

'Why not hide it somewhere better? If Assa needs this orb to kill humans, then why not hide the orb in some volcano or drop it into the ocean?'

'It was there on Hyuul's orders.'

Lola felt horrified; she forgot her brother was right beside her, his hand still trembling.

'So Assa's found it?!'

'Because the remaining Lormai have been summoned, it is safe to assume Assa now has the orb and will be soon putting into effect the final phases of the plan.'

'If Assa's found the orb, it's only because the hiding-place was rubbish.'

'Hyuul promised Assa will not find it. Hyuul is on our side and did all possible make sure the orb wouldn't be found.'

'Then why hide it right under Assa's nose!'

'That was Hyuul's decision.'

Lola was finding it difficult to take all this in.

'Can Assa…be stopped?' she asked with hope.

'We cannot stop Assa; we can only delay Assa.'

It was as if she were having the conversation with Natella over again, for Lola couldn't accept that these were aliens from a distant world. She'd always had ideas about what aliens would be like, and these Blondies defied all her expectations. What was most surprising was how human they were, having a conversation and coming all this way just to help. Apart from their appearance and the spaceship in the background, Lola couldn't note anything of alien origin about the Blondies. They could very well have been people merely dressed up.

'What are you going to do to help us?' Lola asked, accepting the reality of the situation.

'We are here to fight in your defence, once it comes to that. When the Lormai come out of the mountain and start killing you, we will help you.'

Lola wasn't sure if she liked the way this Blondie was putting things, even though it evidently meant well.

'We are going to fight the Lormai!' another Blondie exclaimed rather fervidly.

'They flew towards the mountain but no one's seen them since.'

'If they are in the mountain, we will only find them when they want to be found, which is why we have to wait until they want to be seen.'

'Why not target Assa?'

'We don't know how to kill Assa. Hyuul also does not know.'

Lola felt frustrated. She felt her brother's grip slacken; she turned and saw he was fainting to the ground. She snapped out of her frenzied state of curiosity.

'Andrew? Are you okay?' she was kneeling down beside him, feeling his forehead.

She started tapping his cheek gently and saw he was slowly waking up.

'Andrew? It's me, Lola,' she said, and to her amazement she saw the head Blondie was kneeling down at Andrew's other side.

'He will be okay. He is scared,' the alien said.

'Are you not scared of us?' another asked.

'No. I know you mean us no harm.'

'How can you be sure?'

'I can't be sure but I know I am. There's no point being scared any more.'

'Why not?'

'If I was scared, I would have run away from you and wouldn't have found out everything just now.'

'You are aliens to us. We are scared too, but we don't flee because we are also curious.'

'You wouldn't come all this way just let fear overcome you.'

'Your name is Lola?' the main Blondie asked after staring at Lola for a few moments.

'Yes. What's yours?' Lola asked, neglecting her brother a little.

'My name is Yeril. These are the some of the crew of the ship,' Yeril said, turning its head to the other Blondies, some of whom looked apprehensive.

'Lola!' Andrew yelled, scrambling to his feet instantly.

'What the hell are they!' he screamed.

'Andrew, calm down!' Lola said, a hand on each of Andrew's arms; she was looking into his eyes sternly.

'I promise you, Andrew, they aren't going to do anything to us. I know it's hard to believe, but I trust them.'

'They're aliens!' Andrew whispered harshly, trying to resist the temptation of actually looking at them.

'Yes I know they are, and they are good aliens. They are going to help us.'

Andrew was non-responsive for a few moments then he fainted again. Lola knelt down and tried waking him once more.

'We thought both of you would be that scared.'

'I'm more curious than scared,' Lola replied, tending to her brother.

'Most people let their fears overcome them.'

'What's going to happen now? When are the Greys going to leave the mountain?'

'We have to wait and see. Assuming Assa has the orb, then the final phase will start soon and we will rush to help you. Until then, there's nothing we can do because the Lormai remain hidden.'

'How do you know all that you know?' another Blondie asked Lola.

'A friend told me.'

'Who?'

'It was Natella, a friend from school' Lola was sure of what she was going to do next. She noticed some of them seemed to have recognised the name.

'You've heard of Natella?' she asked incredulously.

'Yes.'

'Well, thank you for answering my questions and, well, for being here and everything. I'm gonna take my brother and go,' and with that, she roused her brother, who was in a drowsy state.

'We were told to land all across Helmia, get some air, and then all gather together. We will occupy a space on this island but we promise you we will do nothing to you humans.'

'I believe you,' Lola replied, adrenaline coursing through her wildly.

'Goodbye,' she added. She helped support Andrew, who was half asleep yet capable of walking. Lola looked over her shoulder and saw the aliens regressing towards their ship. She couldn't believe she had just had a conversed with aliens - aliens that were fluent in English and happened to be able to answer her burning questions. She thought it a great coincidence at first but then realised this had to be a matter more complex than she'd previously thought. The Keelot seemed to know what was going to happen and seemed determined to protect humanity. So that was it: Assa must have the orb and have summoned the Greys to carry out the final phase. But what if, like the Blondies said, Assa didn't actually have the orb yet? Lola realised there was only one thing she could do, and she immediately started planning her course of action. Adrenaline was coursing through her as she helped Andrew back home.

Very soon, the ship was flying directly over the two of them: Lola looked up in awe and realised the full beauty of the dazzling lights and the aliens within the ship. She was very glad she hadn't let her fear get the better of her; sure, she was scared, but what kept her there talking to the aliens was her curiosity. She was amazed she'd had a full conversation with an alien from so far away, and their peaceful approach, coupled with the matching of their words with Natella's, reassured Lola that they were harmless aliens on humanity's side, aliens who would learn from other races rather than wipe them out. She wanted to find out more about the Blondies, yet there were more pressing matters at hand.

Andrew started waking up properly. He broke free from Lola.

'Lola, what's been going on? I think I had the craziest dream. And what are we doing out here?! We should be inside!'

'Inside's where we're going, Andrew, don't worry.'

'What are we doing out here anyway?' he asked; they were now walking down the gap between their house and their neighbours'.

'Never mind.'

To Lola's surprise, Andrew didn't inquire further; she suspected he was still a bit out of it. Once they got home, Lola made sure Andrew went in first, then, instead of following him in, she hastily shut the front door, locked it and deliberately left the key in, then she shouted through the letterbox, 'tell mum and dad I'll be back soon,' then she started running as fast as she could, for she had to know.

The lightshow had stopped; no longer were there ships flying about. Lola guessed they had all landed across Helmia and would soon fly to the meeting-place the Blondie had mentioned or they were already at that meeting-place, wherever that might be.

Every now and then she stopped to catch her breath. The streets were eerily deserted. It was still quite dark, yet a tad lighter than before.

She still had questions to ask; so many questions, yet there was one which she needed to know the answer to right now. It was the most important question of all, and she hoped others who were in the know were asking the same question.

On her way, she saw a few police cars and military tanks, yet managed to avoid being seen. The last thing she wanted now was to have some police tell her she should be indoors and take her home. Even if she told them all that she knew, she doubted they'd believe her.

On and on she went through the abandoned streets of Puddlepond. The streets were illuminated only by starlight and the patches of lamplight here and there. Lola could soon tell she was very close to her destination, as this was a route she was very familiar with.

Before she knew it, she was outside the back gates of Puddlepond High School. She knew she was acting on impulse and would undoubtedly get reprimanded by her parents, but she had to know.

The school looked just like it did the night she and Demzel met the Greys inside. She hoped the ladder was still in the bush and, to her amazement, it was. She did exactly what she did that night and was soon in the school grounds, yet she knew no one had left a downstairs window open in advance.

Nevertheless, she ran on, across the sports field till she was by the main building, wherein lay her destination. She had one plan of action, which she knew was reckless and would get her in serious trouble, so she reconsidered. There was no way to get inside the building and even if she did get in, she'd set the alarm off.

She was stuck. She'd acted on impulse but hadn't thought it all through. Checking her phone, she saw many missed calls and saw it was early in the morning. A new plan came to her: she'd wait till staff started to arrive, then she'd sneak in and get to where she wanted.

So she sat down against the building wall and waited, even more questions going through her mind. She told herself to stay awake, despite the fatigue and the cold. Very soon, however, she fell asleep.

She awoke about thirty minutes later. She checked her phone and saw more messages and missed calls from her parents and Andrew. She texted them telling them she was fine and was at an unspecified friend's house, then once that was dealt with, she set an alarm and put her phone on silent so any messages and calls would go unheard. Then she slept until the alarm woke her. She got up, yawned and stretched, then cautiously went to the nearest door and she pulled the handle – it was open! She quietly let herself in and looked from left to right: no one seemed to be about.

All she had to do now was to get to the headmaster's office and look in the plant pots. But how would she get into it? Would it be locked? It was then that she realised she was still in her pyjamas. Perhaps she shouldn't have acted so impulsively.

She managed to get to the reception area without anyone seeing her and soon found herself outside the headmaster's office door, unsure of whether there was anyone inside or not. She decided to act immediately lest she get caught, and opened the door slightly, expecting someone from within to say something. She was lucky the door was open. Slowly she pushed it more and more waiting for someone inside to speak, but no voice came.

She had a look inside to ensure no one was inside and went in, shutting the door behind her. There were two plant pots, either side of the Mr. Dazzle's desk. All she wanted to do was to check to see if the orb was still there. She thought it a ridiculous hiding-place for such an object.

The absurdity of the whole situation got to Lola: there were so many details she didn't know. She had a feeling that the more she knew, the more preposterous it would all become. She went over to the plant pot on the right and placed it on the desk. Then she stuck her hand in the dirt and plunged her arm down even further. She felt about quite a bit before concluding the orb wasn't there. Then again, she wasn't exactly sure how big or small this orb was.

Her mind started to race when she realised the orb *had* to be in this other plant pot. It simply had to be there – where else could it be? Something was stopping her checking the plant pot, yet something else was urging her to do so. She didn't know what to do. What would she do if the second plant pot was empty?

She knelt down beside the other plant pot and put her hand in the soil. She rammed it down further until – there was nothing. The layer of soil broke and crumbled to the bottom of the pot, sending the plant tumbling with it. There had been something there, Lola thought to herself, but now it was gone.

Chapter 13 –
Snatched

Lola was in her room asleep. After searching the plant pots, she'd managed to get out of the school without anyone seeing her. She'd gone straight home with a frenzied state of mind. She was frenetic with worry and panic; by the time she got home she was shaking and had to be put to bed by her parents.

As she started to come to, she kept her eyes closed to try to go back to sleep, which was what she wanted so much. A few minutes later, she heard her door being opened and people coming into the room: her parents.

'I can't believe they're letting everyone go back to school and work so quickly. It's ridiculous, absolutely insane. At least Anna's seen sense and has kept Hannah off!' Lola heard her mum say.

'I guess things have to be kept as normal as possible.'

'But no one knows what these aliens are here for! They could wipe us out or steal our kids!'

'Calm down, honey, nothing's happened so far and it's not going to either.'

'She's not going to school till those, *aliens*, are gone.'

'The Prime Minister says they are to be trusted, remember?'

'It's a load of nonsense. Does the Prime Minister seriously expect us to believe these aliens have spoken to him and assured him they pose no threat? It's codswallop! As long as those aliens are on that beach, they pose a threat to us. Who knows what they're hiding in those ships!'

'Would the Prime Minister announce it to the public if he wasn't 100% sure?'

'Well, no, but these aliens could very easily have fooled him. There could be hundreds of ships up there waiting to invade us or something.'

'Like the Prime Minister said, these aliens mean us no harm. I'm sure they could have killed us by now if they really wanted to. Plus, they speak English. Why bother learning a language if you're going to kill the people who speak it?'

No reply came from Lola's mum.

'You're coming round to the idea that these aliens are safe, aren't you, Ange?'

'She's off school today and tomorrow. If anything at all happens, she's not going back till we get an all clear. I can't believe she left us like that to go to her friend's house! She could have got killed!'

Lola could hear her mum sobbing and felt her hand gently stroke her cheek.

'She's here now and that's all that matters. Come, let's leave her. We'll have a word with her when she wakes up.'

Lola hated the phrase her dad had just used for it always meant she'd done something wrong, and this time she knew she'd have a lot of explaining to do. But what mattered most was that the orb wasn't there. She wondered what Assa was doing right now and how long it would be before what the Blondies said would happen would come true.

She remembered she needed to tell someone what she'd

seen; in haste she found her phone and started ringing some-one.

'Natella, it's Lola. The orb in Harold Dazzle's office is gone.'

'Lola, what are you talking about?'

'You know fine well, Natella. I know this is going to sound random, but I met some Blondies late last night and they told me the orb was in one of the plant pots in Dazzle's office. I went there myself and checked and it wasn't there.'

'Lola, this is not your business to be meddling in.'

'I don't care. Does this mean Assa definitely has the orb?' Lola pronounced her words with trepidation.

There were a few moments of silence before Natella replied:

'Lola, calm down, please.'

'Well someone must have stolen it because it's definitely not where the Blondies told me it was.'

'It's under control, Lola, trust me.'

And with that, Natella hung up. Lola had more to say: she texted Natella telling her to keep her informed. She felt restless and headstrong: she felt like she had to be doing something to make sure Assa wouldn't be able to follow the plans through. She was desperate to be as involved in all this as Natella was.

After a few minutes' thinking, Lola rang Natella again.

'What are you doing to find the orb and who else knows about it?'

'Look, Lola, I haven't got time to be answering all your questions. I understand you want answers, but the best thing you can do is to just let us get on with we're doing.'

'Us? How many people are in on this?'

'Lola, please just let me focus on what I should be focuss-ing on.'

'Do you have any idea where the orb is now?'

'What's more important, Lola? That I do what I have to do to help or answer a few questions of yours? One benefits everyone, one benefits only you.'

Lola was a little taken aback by this frank outburst.

'I'll let you go. Just promise me you will do everything to find the orb and prevent all this from happening.'

'Believe me, Lola, I'm just as worried as you are,' and with that, Natella hung up.

Lola sat in her room thinking: perhaps she'd best leave Natella and her people to their job and stop barraging her with such questions. She was starting to see Natella's side, yet the desire for answers and the frustration at not being able to do anything were overwhelming all the more. She'd expected Natella to supply information; the letdown only fuelled Lola's curiosity even more.

It was almost one. Lola stayed in her bed for a bit longer, frustrated and bound to a state of ignorance and anxiety.

Her phone started ringing: Lola hoped it would be Natella, but knew it wouldn't be.

'Hey, Lola!' it was Hannah; Lola smiled.

'Hi, how are you?'

'Off school for the day but I'm as bored as anything. I actually would prefer to be in school right now. I can't believe I've just said that. Are you in school?'

'No. It's a long story.'

'Wanna come over? My mum's not too keen on me leaving the house – she thinks I'm gonna be zapped by aliens. And guess what? *She's* gone to work!'

'But you're safe at home.'

'I don't like it. I know the aliens are all on the beach, but still it feels scary being in this house by myself when there are aliens only a few miles away.'

'I'll ask my parents if I can come over.'

'Ooh, upset them?'

'I might be in their bad books. I'll explain when I come over.'

'Nice to see you're optimistic.'

Lola laughed then said bye and hung up. She dreaded speaking to her parents when she was in the wrong, but she really wanted to see Hannah.

She got ready then went downstairs to find her parents in the living room watching the news.

'What's going on?' Lola asked, sitting on a nearby settee.

'The ships have been on the beach since early this morning and none of the aliens have come out. The Prime Minister has apparently spoken to them and has assured us that they pose no threat to us,' Lola's dad said rather monotonously, 'but enough of that,' and he switched off the telly.

'I think we should have a chat.'

'What about?' Lola asked, though fully aware of what was to come.

'We think what you did last night was reckless and silly, Lola. You could have got yourself killed. How dare you wander off like that! You could have been killed or abducted or who knows what else! Do you know how worried we were about you?' Lola's mum said rather slowly.

'I'm sorry, I really am, but I had to go.'

'But why? We were here and we were safe. Goodness knows what could have happened to you out there with those…those damn aliens flying about.'

'And what on Earth happened to Andrew? He said there were aliens in the fields!' Lola's dad asked.

'You'll not believe this,' Lola said directly to her mum, 'but it's true. They landed and they were coming towards us. I wanted to wait and see them but Andrew wanted to go back inside. I insisted on staying and seeing them, then I got a call from Hannah, who was really scared and wanted to see me.'

Lola hated lying to her parents, but knew that lie was more credible than her sneaking into school to search plant pots. She made a mental note to tell Hannah to back her story up. Her parents looked mortified. She knew they couldn't believe what she'd told them and knew if she was going to get to Hannah's today, she'd have to play the game very carefully.

'I'm sorry, really I am. It was stupid of me to do that and if anything had happened, it would have all been my fault. You would have had to suffer all because of me.'

'Yes and how we did suffer,' Lola's mum replied sternly.

'You're not to leave this house unless you have our permission.'

'What? Why?'

'What you did last night was stupid, Lola, and we're really disappointed in you. You'll go back to school tomorrow but other than that you're to be in the house.'

'That is so unfair!'

'Don't argue with us, Lola, you're already in enough trouble as it is'

Lola was annoyed, but understood her parents' reasoning. This was such a frustrating situation, she thought to herself. She knew she was in trouble but hadn't expected this.

'We love you Lola and are only doing this for your own good.'

Lola looked at her mum and saw a face of despair ridden with worry.

'Mum, everything's going to be okay,' Lola had to suppress a lot of her own worries to say this, 'I know you're worried about the aliens, but it looks like nothing bad's going to happen.'

Lola felt warm in the head and reckless. She wanted to

be out there looking for the orb, not stuck at home because of her own impulsive and somewhat rash behaviour. She knew what she had just said was also a lie, but she had to say it to console her mother, whom she could tell was very worried deep down.

'I'm sorry,' Lola said again.

'We were just so worried for you and you wouldn't reply to calls or texts.'

'I promise you I'll never do anything like that again,' Lola said with some degree of sincerity; she knew she was impulsive and did things without thinking, but sometimes that was a good thing.

'So if I'm not allowed to go out, can Hannah come here instead?'

Her parents looked at each other, then her dad replied:

'Yeah she can but you aren't to leave the house, is that understood?'

'Yes.'

Minutes later, Lola was up in her room lying on her bed, feeling trapped and frustrated. She felt she ought to be doing something, yet couldn't. She assumed her parents would let her out of the house once her mum realised everything was fine and there was no chance of the aliens attacking. Until then, she would just have to wait it out and saviour the walks to and from school.

She texted Hannah, asking her to come over and telling her to back up her story about the other night. Hannah replied saying she'd be over soon and that she was sorry to hear of Lola's punishment.

About forty-five minutes later, Hannah had come round and the two were in Lola's room chatting. Andrew had gone out with some friends and Lola's parents were out running errands.

'My mum's really worried. She doesn't believe in aliens

but she believes in threats and that's what the Blondies are to her. I can tell she's petrified,' Lola said.

'She has a right to be worried, we all do,' replied Hannah.

'How's your mum taking it?'

'She's got very protective of me all of a sudden; I had to spend about twenty minutes convincing her to let me come here.'

'I thought she was at work?'

'She phoned to check up on me as I was getting ready and I told her I was only coming to yours but then it started: she was going on and on trying to convince me to just talk to you over the computer and then she finally let me come but gave me a whole safety talk. Honestly, I've never seen her so paranoid.'

'I guess adults take this more seriously because they've got more to lose.'

'Yeah, I think you're right. I love my mum but she's driving me up the wall with all this safety talk. If I see an alien, I'm not going to run at it and hug it, am I?'

'She's worried for you. We're all worried for one another,' Lola said softly.

'Anyway, what's this about the Blondies being on the beach?' she asked

'Haven't you heard? They all landed there and then some almost transparent dome appeared, enclosing them. What's really freaky is that this dome is solid: even military tanks have tried getting in, but they've been unable to.'

'Crikey!'

Hannah looked pensive for a minute then uttered:

'You'll never guess where Thomas is? In school! He wanted to skip it but his mum and dad made him go. I was texting him over lunch rubbing it in how I was enjoying being at home so much with nothing to do.'

'I bet he's one of only a few.'

'He is; hardly anyone's there. Most of the teachers are there, though.'

'That reminds me. I've got to tell you about last night.'

Hannah listened attentively while Lola recounted her experience of last night.

'You went all the way to school and broke into Dazzle's office?'

'I felt I had to. I was so paranoid and just had to check.'

'But the orb wasn't there?'

'No. I phoned Natella and she told me her not to worry about it. I haven't heard anything from her and I'm really starting to panic.'

'If Assa did have the orb though, don't you think something would have happened by now?'

'What do you mean?'

'Well, Assa wants this orb so he can wipe out humanity, right? So if Assa really did have the orb, wouldn't we all be dead by now?'

'I guess.'

'Do you know what Assa is exactly?'

'Natella just told me she's a being from beyond this universe.'

'So Assa's a she?'

'I guess so. I don't even know if Assa has a gender.'

'I think Assa's a male. Only a guy would be so reckless with power. A girl wouldn't want to wipe out civilisations like that.'

Lola looked at Hannah, who was sitting cross-legged on the bed, deep in thought. Having Hannah round now was a good distraction from everything that was going on in Lola's head, but it also shoved something else to the forefront of Lola's mind: she wanted right now nothing more than to tell Hannah how she felt about her. The orb could very well be in Assa's possession and the human race could soon get wiped out, so why not tell her now? But then again, she wouldn't know how Hannah would react, and that was the worst part of it. Deep down, she knew her feelings wouldn't be reciprocated, yet she longed for them to be so much. She knew it was just a teenage crush and that it wasn't yet true love or anything as strong seeing as she was still young, yet it was still important to her. She really cared for Hannah and wanted her feelings to be appreciated. Most of all, though, she didn't want to lose Hannah, which was one of the reasons why she was so scared to tell her.

Finality was something that always feared Lola. She always tried to discard the notion, yet it was always there. She hated the prospect of something ending, be it something gradually changing or something briskly coming to an end forever. It seemed now that change was coming to everyone whether she was willing to embrace it or not. If Assa were to succeed, that would be the biggest change of them all, the greatest yet worst possible ending.

It was Monday 1st March. Lola realised that while this would ordinarily have been just another day of the year, it might turn out to be the single most important day for humanity. It might be the day humanity ceases to exist. Or that could happen tomorrow instead, or the day after, or even in a few weeks' time. Whenever it would happen, it was something that was looming, something that was in the distant future, yet it was uncertain how far away it was. Lola hoped with all her might that something was being done to ensure that if Assa had the orb, it was taken away from its master, and that if Assa didn't have the orb, measures were being taken to find it and hide it somewhere Assa would never be able to find it.

'Lola, are you okay? You look worried.'

'This could be the end.'

'Aren't you being a tad overdramatic?'

'Hannah, this is serious. What if Assa has the orb right now?'

Hannah had a deadpan expression on her face.

'Look outside your window,' she instructed, 'do you see death and destruction everywhere? Do you see people being killed? Do you see corpses?'

'No, of course not.'

'Well then, stop worrying. It's not happening yet.'

'I don't know how you can remain so calm.'

'I'll be running round screaming my head off if some alien comes and tries to kill us all, but that's not happening right now, so I'm not going to worry about it.'

'I wish I saw it the same way you do.'

'Try to.'

'I can't.'

'You worry too much, Lola. What you need to do is relax. Let me give you a back massage. I'm quite good at them, I think.'

Lola suddenly felt a bit tingly. It took a few minutes before she finally began to relax. She cleared her mind of all her worries and pressing matters. She found herself back in space flying amongst the stars. Everywhere she turned she saw stars in the distance and imposing planets close by. The sight was awe-inspiring. All things negative were so far away, an unimaginable distance away. They were no longer important. What was important was the here and now: the space Lola was in and what she was experiencing. She could do this forever, continuously being dumbstruck by the beauty and the sheer size of whatever she beheld. Nothing could bring her back to Earth once she'd sampled the delights of outer space. Nothing whatsoever.

'Lola?' Hannah's voice came echoing through space.

'Wake up.'

Lola slowly opened her eyes to see Hannah's face opposite hers.

'You fell asleep. Either I was so good at massages that you got relaxed and fell asleep or I was so bad you got bored and fell asleep. Was I good or bad?'

'You were very good, Hannah.'

'That's what I wanted to hear.'

They spent the rest of the afternoon talking before Hannah left because her mum wanted her back before five. Lola didn't quite know what to feel or what she should be feeling as her mind was rampant with so many different emotions and a plethora of questions. She needed to get away from it all like she did when she was being massaged on the back. The sense of onus, the need for it, was all becoming too much. She wanted more than anything to go to the theme park, yet she couldn't.

The rest of the day was spent passing the time by so tomorrow would come all the more quickly. Lola had an early night and woke up the next morning feeling refreshed and somewhat calmer than the previous day. She got out of her bed and turned on the computer. Once it booted up, she checked the news headlines and found there was nothing new about anything to do with the aliens, other than that the Blondies were still encamped on the beach and that none of them had thus far left their ships.

'It's a matter of waiting' Lola mumbled to herself after stifling a yawn. She took a deep breath and tried to clear her mind so she could focus on the day ahead. She would simply put her worries to the back of her mind. Thinking of Hannah, she assumed that Hannah didn't truly believe it all, given her calm reaction. She sensed Hannah believed her just because they were friends.

It turned out that school was cancelled that day as a safety measure imposed by the Headmaster. Lola couldn't really understand the reasoning behind it: the school was a few miles inland so the threat, if any, wasn't really far away enough to justify its closure. She thought fear of the unknown was the main reason behind the decision.

She spent the day keeping herself busy by reading and watching telly. The next day, school was reopened.

Mrs. Dazzle walked into the form room looking sullen.

'Good morning, class. I assume you all know why school was shut yesterday. Mr. Dazzle felt it appropriate to have you all at home as a precaution. If the...aliens....on the beach do become a threat to us, then appropriate measures will be taken, but for the time being, cleanse your minds and shift the focus to academia. Those aliens will hopefully be gone soon then all our minds can be put to rest.'

She then did the register and made a few announcements before suddenly putting her head in her hands and uttering: 'oh I wish those aliens would just bugger off!'

The class didn't know how to react.

'Sorry, class, I was just thinking out loud. Ignore me, I'm just cracking up. Where's a drink when I need one?' she said, 'a non-alcoholic one, of course.'

'Are you okay, Miss?'

'Yeah, Edward, thanks. I just had a late night...I was up till eleven. Believe me, that's very late for silly old me.'

'That's an early night for me,' someone else said. The teacher laughed then replied: 'the older you get, the earlier you go to bed. It's sad really. Now I hope you'll all have your English homework for me later on today. I need something to look forward to. Please don't disappoint me, class. Now go to assembly and try to have a good day.'

She then gathered her things up in haste and left the room.

'I hope she's okay,' Thomas said.

'I think she's just worried. I mean there are *aliens* on

the *beach* only a few miles from us. Anything could happen really,' Hannah replied.

'Correction: there are UFOs on the beach; whatever's inside hasn't made itself known yet.'

'True.'

Assembly was conducted by the Headmaster. Mr. Dazzle gave a few words about the current situation then proceeded to run through the mundane list of school announcements.

'And finally, the chess club's meeting this week will be cancelled,' he finished the last announcement in a monotonous tone.

As he dismissed the students, Lola couldn't help but wonder about him. She'd never really taken much notice of the Head before; to her, he was just someone who read out the announcements at assembly and was husband to her English teacher and form supervisor. Did he know the orb had been hidden in his office? Lola couldn't really tell and had other things to focus on, namely a Chemistry test.

'I hope none of you will blame your poor marks on stress or worry owing to the UFOs on the beach,' she said once the class were seated.

'But Miss, there are aliens inside them!'

'I don't care if there are nuclear bombs inside them, your test is more important.'

'Actual *aliens*.'

'Yes, I heard you the first time, unfortunately. The only thing you should be afraid of is failing this test. I assure you the consequences of that will be scarier than a few saucers on the beach.'

'She's an awful woman,' Hannah whispered to Lola, who nodded assent.

'You may begin,' the teacher said, having handed the papers around.

'Your homework for tonight is to read chapter thirteen

and answer all the questions in exercises one and two. That's due for Friday,' she told the class after the test had finished.

There was the sound of books being opened and pages being turned, followed by a collective groan once they realised how long chapter thirteen and the exercises were.

'Have you seen how long this is? This will take us ages,' Hannah moaned, not realising she'd spoken it instead of thinking it.

'Something wrong, Hannah?'

'Nothing,' she replied, sinking into her seat.

'Are you complaining at the homework I'm setting you?'

'No of course not. I'd be glad to do the homework,' she said with an enforced smile at the teacher.

'Your sarcasm isn't going to win me over, Hannah.'

'Sorry.'

'The homework has changed. In addition to exercises one and two, you will do three and four as well, thanks to Hannah.'

When the teacher's back was turned, Hannah made an angry face towards her.

'Remember, class, to thank Hannah for your long home-work,' Miss Bay said as the class left the room.

'She has a serious attitude problem!' Hannah fumed as they made their way to their next lesson.

'She is so cheeky and rude. She loves lording it over us. Did you see that old bat's grin when she reminded the whole class at the end? I cannot stand that woman.'

'Calm down, Hannah,' Lola advised.

'Oh come on now, Hannah, it wasn't that bad, was it?' Erica interjected, 'at least she didn't give you detention, which to be honest I thought you were going to get because you were speaking quite out of terms with her.'

'She deserved it!'

'Now, Hannah, please think before speaking next time. We don't want even more homework,' Erica said before striding down the corridor.

'I think she's a bit annoyed.'

'I don't care,' Hannah said.

After Supernatural and Paranormal Studies, Lola stayed behind to update Demzel with everything that had happened the night the Blondies had arrived.

'This is fascinating, but also seriously worrying,' he said with pursed lips and eyes staring at something behind Lola.

'Well, Lola, you know what to do. Simply try to find out whatever you can and please, please keep me updated. This is very interesting indeed.'

'Have you heard from Ivan yet?'

'Sadly, no. We've all tried but I guess he just doesn't want to be found. I wish he would just get in touch and let us know he's okay.'

'I'm sure he's fine, Demzel.'

'Anyway, let's focus on what I daresay I think is more important: these aliens! And the orb of course! Now you say it's missing?'

'It wasn't in any of the plant pots.'

'Well, that indeed is a mystery waiting to be solved. Does this Assa have the orb and why was it hidden where it was?' Demzel said looking inquisitive. Lola could tell he was enjoying all of this.

'But Demzel, this is real. This isn't just something that happens to someone else far away that you read about. This is real and this threat is looming. Don't you realise how scary this is?'

Once Lola said it, she knew fear was something she'd been trying to suppress.

'I find it better to treat it that way than to emphasise its true importance and be terrified by it.'

They talked for a bit more before parting. Lola spent the next few days on edge: she was desperate for any update but none came. She tried to busy herself with schoolwork but even when she was doing that she found herself being too easily distracted.

Saturday finally came around. She awoke mid-morning and lay in bed for a while before dragging herself out of bed and heading downstairs to make herself some breakfast. She felt tense and there was a pain in her stomach, which she told herself, would go away. Waiting without updates was slow torture to her.

Her mum had breakfast with her but was silent throughout.

'Are you okay, mum?'

'Yeah, I'm fine. I just didn't get much sleep last night. I guess I was worrying quite a lot.'

'Nothing's going to happen, mum. Hannah said she was only going to start worrying when she had to…I don't think you should because there's nothing to worry about really.'

'You're right. I'm just being scared.'

Lola spent the rest of breakfast trying to cheer her mum up. Her mum was also worried about Ivan and his disappearance. Lola reassured her that he'd turn up sooner or later and felt guilty in desisting from telling her what had happened at the school during half term. Later on she rang Thomas and Hannah, whose phone was switched off, hoping to meet up to go into town, having been given permission to do so by her mum.

'I'm surprised she has her phone switched off – it's always on,' Thomas said as he and Lola walked to Hannah's house.

'Oh no,' he exclaimed when he saw a police car parked outside the house.

'I hope nothing's gone wrong.'

They advanced and as they were approaching the front

door, a policeman came out and told them they'd have to wait.

'What's going on?' Lola asked.

'Are you friends of Hannah?'

'Yes, we're her best friends.'

'I'm really sorry to have to tell you this...perhaps you'd better come in.'

Once inside, they saw Hannah's mum in hysterics sat on the settee being comforted by a policewoman. The policeman led Lola and Thomas into the kitchen.

'I think it's best if Miss Dawson is left alone. Now, I'm really sorry to have to tell you this, but late last night, your friend Hannah was abducted.'

Chapter 14 –
The Rise of Helmia

'Abducted?' Lola and Thomas repeated simultaneously.
'I'm very sorry. I assure you we're doing everything we can to find her.'

'Well who took her?'

The policeman, a sturdy man with a muscular build yet a soft face and voice, replied,

'Her mother is claiming it was aliens. Now normally we wouldn't be inclined to believe it, but what with everything that's been happening, we now see it as a possibility.'

Lola and Thomas exchanged downcast looks. They heard Hannah's mum sobbing away in the living room.

'Is she okay?' Thomas asked the policeman.

'She's naturally upset, but we're reassuring her that we're doing everything possible.'

Lola didn't know what to do. Part of her felt like bursting into tears while part of her wanted nothing more than to barrage the policeman with questions. She stood there lost in thought, emotion welling up inside of her until it overcame her and she started crying.

'I promise you we'll find your friend,' the policeman said reassuringly.

'Lola, come on, it's going to be okay. They'll find her,' Thomas consoled her, his arm around her.

The policeman excused himself and went to check on Hannah's mum.

'I can't...believe this has happened,' Lola said.

'She will be found.'

'She *has* to be found!' Lola exclaimed hysterically. She felt something flowing out of her. The walls had crumbled.

'She has to be found! I want her back here right now,' she cried as she sank to the floor, her cheeks moist with tears.

'I need answers,' Lola said all of a sudden, wiping her tears away with her hands, 'come on.'

The two went into the living room to see Hannah's mum sipping on a cup of tea while the two police officers were going over some details with her.

'Are we allowed to be here?' Thomas asked somewhat nervously.

'Thomas...Lola...I'm so glad you're here. You've heard the news, haven't you?' Hannah's mum got up and came over to them.

'We have unfortunately. We're so sorry,' Thomas replied.

'Thanks...but...there's no need to be because she'll be back home soon, won't she?' Hannah's mum looked to the police officers.

'We're trying our best.'

'See? She'll be back home before we know it.'

'What exactly happened?' Lola asked careful not to seem too pushy.

'They didn't believe me,' Hannah's mum replied with a quick glance at the police officers, 'but I know you two will.'

'Of course.'

'Come and sit down.'

Once seated, Hannah's mum took a few deep breaths and tried to compose herself. Her face was strewn with tears.

'You don't have to tell us if you don't want to. We won't push you,' Thomas reassured her.

'It'll help to have people believe me. Anyway...I can't believe she's gone...why did they take her again?'

'Please calm down, Anna,' the policewoman came over and put her arm round her shoulder.

'Can I get you another cup of tea?' the policeman asked.

'No thank you.'

'Did you say Hannah was abducted before?' Lola questioned.

Hannah's mum sobbed a little and sipped her tea before saying,

'When she was only four. They've come back for her!'

'But she was returned, so that means she'll definitely be returned this time,' Thomas tried to sound optimistic. He looked at Lola; neither of them had any idea Hannah had been abducted as a child.

'She was returned two days later,' Hannah's mum added.

'See? Whoever's taken her will probably return her very soon as well.'

'I hope so,' Hannah's mum replied before taking another series of deep breaths.

Lola had many questions to ask but knew this wasn't the time to ask. She wanted Hannah back more than anything. No one knew where she was or whether she was okay, and that was the scariest thing. Again, it was fear of the unknown.

She suggested to Thomas that they go and leave Hannah's mum with the police officers. They bade them goodbye and told Hannah's mum if she needed anything to let them know.

'Thank you Thomas and Lola. I'm sorry for being so weepy, but I just really want her back. As soon as she's back I'll let you know.'

'Thank you, we really appreciate that.'

'Take care, I hope she's back very soon,' a teary-eyed Thomas said.

They were soon walking back. Neither of them had said anything. They hugged for a while before parting: Thomas walked away wiping tears from his eyes while Lola stood still and took a few deep breaths. She was trying to clarify stuff in her head.

She eventually got home and went straight up to her room where she flung herself on to her bed and buried her head in the pillows. She didn't know how long she cried for.

*

When she told her parents, they phoned Hannah's mum up straight away. Lola's mum then went round to see her. Lola decided on an early night.

She was lying in bed thinking too much, missing Hannah too much. What if she never came back? The thought of never seeing her again depressed Lola. She couldn't help but think the outcome of this would be the worst.

She was crying for Hannah's return. She was crying for a world where none of this would ever happen, a world where everything would stay the same and nothing would change, no one would go away. The tears were coming fast. Her pillow was damp.

'I want her back,' she sobbed into her pillow, 'I want her back now.'

*

Sunday went by in a blur. Lola spent most of the day sitting downstairs by the phone. Sadly, no news came.

It was during assembly on Monday morning when the Head spoke about the abduction that it hit Lola the most. In a monotonous voice he stated that he wished for her safe return and hoped all who knew her were coping well with the unfortunate incident. This was the last place Lola wanted to be. She wanted to help find Hannah, not sit around and carry on day-to-day life without her.

'I miss her,' she whispered to Thomas.

'Me too,' he whispered back.

The day seemed strange. Lola spent most lessons with her head down staring at her book. She forgot to note down several pieces of homework and had to ask Thomas over lunch what they were.

'What importance does homework have? I mean, really, it's pointless,' she mentioned to Thomas, who agreed.

'The most important thing right now,' he said, 'is that we hope for her safe return.'

'Which will happen any day now,' Lola said, not looking him in the eye; she hadn't looked anyone in the eye since hearing the news.

It was once they were in Supernatural and Paranormal Studies that something attracted Lola's attention away from Hannah.

'I have a special guest who is going to speak to you to-day about something you may be familiar with,' Demzel announced with glee.

Lola was glad he hadn't mentioned Hannah and guessed he wanted people to have a normal lesson without yet another reminder.

'This is Aaron Lineswell,' Demzel said proudly, at which

point an elderly man ambled into the room. He was quite a tall man with her hair neatly combed over to one side. His face had a fair few wrinkles and his attire was quite smart.

'Good afternoon,' he greeted the class with a gruff voice.

'Now, Mr. Lineswell, as some of you may know, is the one and only person who witnessed up close the rise of Helmia fifty-one years ago. So, Aaron, if you'd kindly tell the class what you saw...'

'Thank you, Demzel. I remember it like it was just yesterday. For me it was one of those events that stick in your mind and you can recall perfectly easily no matter how much time passes. That is how much it affected me.

'It was January 5th, 1959. Believe it or not, but back then I was just a bit older than all you. If only I'd stayed like that. You young people should make the most of it while you can. Anyway, back then I used to live in Old Merrington and I worked as a skipper ferrying people to and from Etolin Island. I was on the island, having brought some people there. Back then it was much more of a tourist attraction than what it is today. I went for a walk and when I got back to the dock a bit later than I said would, I found everyone from my boat had gone back in another boat. Mine was to be the last to leave the island but I double-checked anyway in case any of my group was still on the island. I ended up sailing back to the mainland by myself and that's when it happened.

'I was looking out to sea when I saw a large *creature* appear out of nowhere. I say creature, but I don't really know if that's the right word to use. Anyway, it wasn't human, although it did look vaguely like one, a really long one. It was flying although it didn't have wings. I stopped the boat so I could watch it better. It stopped mid-air about a few hundred metres away from where I was and was just floating there. I started the boat up again so I could get a better view.

'The creature was still hovering some distance above the sea. As I got closer to it, the sea started getting tumultuous and wavy. Before I knew it, the boat was being assaulted by waves on all sides. I tried to manoeuvre it to safety but the waves were too powerful for me to succeed. As it tried desperately not to be overcome by the waves, I saw something rising up out of the sea in the distance, roughly below where the creature was still hovering, yet I couldn't tell what exactly it was. The sea continued to batter the boat so I focused on getting out of there.

'That's when I saw what had been rising out of the sea more clearly: it looked like the peak of a mountain. I couldn't believe what I was seeing. It was rising further and further up. The waves started abating and before I knew it, I found myself on dry land. The mountain was rising up out of the sea and I was rising with it! The boat was on a small rocky plateau. I couldn't believe what was happening. I took a few minutes to catch my breath and try to work out what was going on. I looked up and saw the creature was holding on to the peak of the mountain as it continued rising.

'But it wasn't just a mountain that was rising out of the sea – it was a whole island. After about half an hour I was a few thousand feet up and could see forested land rising up out of the sea as well. I should have radioed the coast guard to tell him what was going on but I was too awe-struck by what was happening around me. I watched as more and more of this large mountain rose up out of the sea. The weird thing was that nothing around me, apart from parts of the boat, was wet. The plateau my boat was in was completely dry and parts of the rock nearby were covered in snow! Even the peak of the mountain was snow-capped! I was perplexed.

'But as the mountain kept rising, I was getting colder and colder and decided to remain in the boat trying to plan what to do. I finally got in touch with the coast guard and told him what was happening. Obviously he didn't believe me and thought I was playing some sort of joke on him, but then he looked out the window and saw something on the horizon that hadn't been there before: Helmia, rising from the depths of the sea.

'So once the island eventually stopped rising, I found myself several thousand feet up. I had never been so high up before and didn't know a thing about mountaineering so I was clueless about how to get down from the mountain safely.

'I got in touch with the coast guard again and he said he'd send a helicopter to pick me up, which I was very grateful for. While I waited for it to come, I saw the creature flying down from the mountain till it was so far away I couldn't see it because of the mist below. Then I noticed something in the distance approaching me: a fleet of about twenty UFOs flying towards the island. I told myself I should remain in the boat and stay safe just in case, but my curiosity got the better of me: I clambered out of the boat and carefully made my way over to a bit of higher land where I had a better view. I didn't dare look down though.

'They got closer and closer until they vanished just below what is now called Symmetry Peak. The helicopter soon came and I was taken back to the mainland. And that is the day I remember best of all the days I've lived.'

Demzel applauded wildly, as did a few of the students in the class. Lola had always known how Helmia had risen out of the sea so inexplicably all those years ago but hadn't believed the veracity of reports of aliens being somehow involved: now she did.

'That was an amazing account, Mr. Lineswell. Absolutely amazing. Would you mind answering some questions?' an enthusiastic Demzel asked.

'Of course not.'

'Does anyone have any questions?'

Lola's hand shot straight up.

'Yes, Lola.'

'Was the creature you saw the same alien that flew down to Helmia chasing another in January?'

'That's a very good question. After that day, I became interested in aliens and tried to find out what exactly it was I had seen. I read books and aliens and paid special attention to news items about them, but I never saw or heard of anyone else seeing that creature again until I saw it in someone's video flying through Moistree. I couldn't believe my eyes. I recalled the image of the creature and saw it was indeed the same.'

'And the UFOs, were they the same as the ones that recently vanished around Symmetry Peak?'

'Yes, I believe so. Once I realised the same alien had visited Helmia and the same type of UFOs had been spotted, I thought it was all going to happen again, that some other island would rise out of the sea like last time. Nothing's happened yet, but if an island rises out of the sea soon, I'll be gloating.'

Lola sat back and let her mind wander while Mr. Lineswell answered more questions. There had to be some connection between the rise of Helmia fifty-one years ago and the recent alien goings-on. She theorised over and over, quashing ideas that she realised were preposterous to eventually decide that at this stage, all she could do was to guess with the limited knowledge she had.

Yet again she found herself lost in theories and wonder. She was getting frustrated with all developments, for they only brought more and more questions with them.

'That was the day I realised we are not alone in the universe. That was the day my life changed forever and I never looked back,' she heard Aaron say.

Lola understood how he must have felt seeing aliens for the first time and realising the universe was not such a lonely place after all. Understanding that life was not unique to Earth was something great and difficult to do: it was simply impossible to imagine what alien life would look like, for most images thought up would have a human bias. Lola knew that sceptics often pointed out that most 'aliens' seen by people were humanoid in shape and theorised that the aliens' striking resemblance to humans meant that humans were dreaming them up, albeit with a human template.

To view humanity one day as a lonely race with no one for company but one another, and to view it the next day as one of possibly many other races could only be a great overhaul to one's belief system: the repercussions of such knowledge would but surely open one's mind to many more possibilities.

'How did your life change afterwards? What did you do after witnessing this?' a very curious Lola asked, eager to see where being privy to this marvellous event had led Aaron in his life.

'I amassed all the money I had, managed to get a little bit more from my parents, then I set off and travelled all over the world. I kept going, kept visiting new places, until my money started to run out, then I returned a few years after I'd set off. I no longer wanted to be tied down to one routine. I wanted my life to be constantly changing, full of surprises. I was ready to embrace anything the adventurous path I was travelling down led me to. I changed job, and sometimes location, twice a year. My favourite job was being an airline pilot. Every time I flew, I was closer to the rest of the universe. I'd love to be an astronaut, but health problems stand in the way of that dream. If I hadn't seen the rise of Helmia, I would have probably spent the rest of my years in Old Merrington doing the same thing again and again. Of course, there's nothing wrong with that lifestyle. That day, something awoke in me and ever since it's urged me on restlessly.'

Lola felt inspired by Aaron's energy and passion for life.

'I have a question, if you wouldn't mind,' she heard Demzel ask the guest.

'Sure, go ahead.'

'Why do you believe in aliens? Obviously you witnessed this extraordinary event, but none of the things you saw, the creature and the UFOs, might actually be alien; they could be of Earthly origin. What made you think they were alien and why does that still make you believe today?'

'Obviously people said it couldn't possibly have been aliens I saw, but my eyes told me otherwise. I just knew they were alien – my intuition told me so. I had never seen anything so awesome and weird in my life. I believed that day they were alien and no on has yet proved to me that they weren't alien, so I can therefore believe what I want to believe. Until someone gives me categorical proof they weren't alien, I can and will believe they were.'

The bell rang and Lola was very disappointed to see the lesson abruptly cut short. Demzel thanked Aaron enthusiastically before dismissing the class. Aaron thanked the class for their attention and questions and said before leaving, 'my outlook on life changed the day I saw Helmia rise out of the sea. What I've learnt over the years is that you don't need to have seen what I saw to change your outlook for the better. True change comes from within.'

The rest of that day, Lola thought of nothing but Aaron, his tale and his full life. She realised she admired him greatly and saw a few things in him that she saw in herself. It was only later on in the day once she was back at home that she remembered Hannah: her mind had been distracted ever since Demzel's class.

Waiting around for news, good or bad, was terrible; not

knowing whether Hannah was okay was much, much worse. But one thing that overpowered the negative feelings was Lola's hope and assurance that Hannah was perfectly okay. She knew Hannah would be fine, wherever she was. She knew she'd be home very soon safe and sound and everything would be back to normal soon. Once in her room and on her bed, the floodgates opened and the tears came thick and fast.

'Lola, you have to eat,' her mum's voice came at the door a few hours later.

'I'm really not hungry, mum,' she replied through stifled sobs.

Her mum came into her room, looking downcast and sullen; she had a tray in her hands with Lola's tea and a drink on it.

'I want you to have your tea, Lola. Please be strong. Be strong for Hannah.'

Lola looked at her tea, which her mum had placed on the bedside table. It was her favourite: a steaming bowl of pasta with sauce, a fruit cup for dessert and a glass of orange juice.

'I'm sure she's on her way back as we speak,' Lola's mum said with a smile, 'you'll be in the theme park together before you know it.'

Lola took a deep breath and looked into her mum's warm, comforting and reassuring face. She could tell her mum was also very upset about Hannah's abduction and whilst obviously worried about Hannah's well-being and whereabouts, she was also concerned with how much it was affecting her own daughter.

'I just want her back!'

'I know, honey. I am so sorry she's gone and I hope with all I have that she'll be back as soon as possible.'

She gave her daughter an especially tight hug, which

Lola sank into, dampening her mum's clothes with her tears and moist face.

'Why has this happened, mum? Why her?' Lola questioned, though she knew it was in vain.

'Believe me, if I knew I'd tell you everything and I'd tell you first. We don't know where she is, but what we do know is that she'll be back with us before long.'

They sat there for some time before Lola's mum offered to reheat her tea on the condition that she eat it. She spent the rest of the night indulging in newfound optimism. It was a matter of when, not if. Hannah's absence would make Lola's heart grow all the more stronger.

'Get yourself back here, we're missing you,' she texted to Hannah, speaking the words to thin air; she managed to silence the part of her mind that told her texting her absent friend was practically pointless.

The next day at school, Lola decided she wouldn't let Hannah's absence deter her from her daily life. Mrs. Dazzle was in a rather chirpy mood for once.

'Routine is good for the soul, so let's all embrace the day and what it has in store for us. I know one thing that will excite you all: today in English I've got a treat for you all. We're going to do something that's *not* on your syllabus for a change. While routine is good, too much of a good thing can suffocate. A regular break from routine is as healthy as the routine itself. You admire and appreciate the circle much more when you occasionally step outside it to behold it from another angle. Anyway, I've been rambling, much to your annoyance. Go off to your lessons and I look forward to our rebellious lesson later on,' she said with a wide grin on her face.

Lola went to assembly with Thomas and Darren.

'I'm surprised to see Mr. Dazzle up there,' Thomas whispered; the Head hadn't conducted an assembly, which he usually did twice a week, in over a month.

'Hadn't really noticed,' remarked Darren.

'Apparently, all this coming and going of his is putting strain on his marriage,' Thomas chattered.

'She's just...tired...so is he,' replied Lola, 'anyway, who says their marriage is on the rocks?'

'Quite a few people are speculating. I wasn't convinced at first, but Mrs. Dazzle's definitely not been herself recently – she's gone a bit, well, funny.'

'Thomas, you may have a point,' Lola said, slightly convinced. Up till now, she hadn't wanted to believe it because she'd always liked Mrs. Dazzle.

'Whenever there's a rumour, no matter how vague, there's always some truth to it, however distorted it may be. Now who's been drilling that notion into our heads for ages?' Thomas asked.

'Demzel.'

'Exactly. It's too much of a coincidence that Mr. Dazzle keeps being away for longer and more often that usual and soon after he first starts doing this, Mrs. Dazzle is constantly tired and in a funny mood. Something tells me all is not well in the Dazzle household.'

Lola began to wonder and speculate as she watched and listened to Mr. Dazzle lead the assembly.

'Before I let you all go to your classes, I'd like to assure you all that fear is only brought about by worrying. Yes, there have been unexplainable and potentially dangerous happenings recently, but, as my dear wife likes to remind me, a pleasant state of mind is achieved by routine and by focussing on your studies, you'll find you've nothing to worry about other than tests and homework. I implore you all to carry on as if each day were just another day of the year.'

Mr. Dazzle smiled a rather confident smile as he imparted what he obviously thought was great advice and strode off the stage beaming.

'It's natural to worry. We don't know what those aliens are here for so until we know for certain, we should worry,' Darren said as they got up, having been dismissed.

Lola was constantly worrying. She was worrying whether Assa had the orb and, if not, when Assa would regain possession of it. What she was most worried about, however, was Hannah, whose predicament was very real and directly affecting her, whereas whether Assa got the orb back and the ensuing consequences were all less real, somewhat fictional, seeing as the impending danger might simply be some great fabrication; from time to time, Lola actually dismissed it all as preposterous: the creator of the universe needing some orb to get rid of all humanity because it hadn't been planned? Whenever she doubted it, all recent events that had happened surged to the forefront of her mind as if to remind her it might be true after all, then she'd start worrying all over again. One matter was personal, the other was a matter that could potentially affect everyone. She didn't know which one it was right to be worried about more: was it selfish to worry about Hannah when Assa might be close to getting the orb?

'I hope Hannah's okay,' Darren said to Lola and Thomas sullenly.

'She'll be back soon, I'm sure of it,' Lola replied.

'I can't believe it's been so rubbish between us and now she's gone.'

'It hasn't been rubbish between the two of you.'

'Yes it has, Lola. I'm too shy around her and that's driving her away.'

'Darren, don't feel guilty. You've done nothing wrong.'

'I do like her. I miss her. If anything happens to her, I swear I'll get whoever's responsible.'

'Darren, calm down.'

'Why do we let such petty, silly things get in the way of good things?' he said with a sigh. Lola kept thinking on that for the rest of the day.

She got home and had a better night than the previous one at least. It was a normal night, which did her good: there was no mention of any aliens, orbs of UFOs, nor was Hannah's abduction referred to at all. It felt good to be able to find solace and peace at home.

Mrs. Dazzle's advice about breaking from routine had been good advice indeed: the English lesson they had spent watching a favourite film of Mrs. Dazzle's to cheer her up had in fact been a welcome change, even though the film, only half of which they actually managed to watch, was soppy and cheesy. Then Lola realised that that night, which should have been a normal night, was in fact a break from entirely new routine: coming home worried and spending most, if not all, of the night thinking too much about trifling matters had become Lola's routine of late. The break had been what Lola desperately needed, but she hadn't been aware of how badly she needed it. She vowed to return to her old routine, to once and for all stop worrying and going over things so much.

But then a question came to her that she hadn't considered before: what if Assa found the orb before Hannah returned? If that were the case, Lola would probably never see Hannah again. Hannah could return any moment now, yet Assa could lay hold on the orb any moment now as well. Lola wished the former would happen instead of the latter. She could feel panic and worry swelling up inside her, along with the tears that were welling up in her eyes, but she steeled herself, only because she had to.

Chapter 15 –
Meeting Mary Morton

That Saturday, Lola's outlook on everything was much more positive than it had been previously. She had something to look forward to today: the celebrity Mary Morton was in Puddlepond and would be signing copies of her book later on downtown.

'I thought she'd had a breakdown or something?' Thomas wondered. The two of them were on the monorail sitting opposite each other by the window.

'I think she's doing this and her film promotion then taking a rest.'

Outside, it was a dull grey everywhere. Weather like this really set the tone for the day.

'Are you okay, Lola?' Thomas asked.

'Yeah, I'm just a bit tired.'

'Come on, cheer up! We're going to meet *the* Mary Morton! How amazing is that!'

'I can't believe it. It doesn't seem real.'

'It's going to be a good day.'

Lola was silent for a while, then eventually replied: 'I hope she's better looking in person!'

The monorail came to a smooth halt at their station. It

was a sleek, seven-carriage vehicle painted in metallic silver that seemed to glitter in the sun. It glided by swiftly and almost silently up above on the beam. Lola loved the way it moved so gracefully and effortlessly.

As they got off, Lola had a quick look back at it, then went and caught up with Thomas, who was being absorbed into the crowd of strangers. They'd got off at one of the few Puddlepond stations, which were always the busiest by far, especially on weekends. Lola soon found herself lost in the crowd, looking for Thomas. She saw him a few metres ahead.

'Thomas, wait up!' she shouted through the crowd, to little effect.

Before long, they were out of the station, whose glass panelling made it resemble an overly large greenhouse, and were heading to a bookstore on the High Street. To their dismay, they saw a long queue of people emanating from the shop. It seemed to contain at a few hundred people.

'She'll be worth the wait,' Lola reassured Thomas, who seemed to be trying to count the number of people ahead of them. They joined the queue and began waiting.

The street around them was full of shoppers going about their business. Most of them looked harried and stressed.

'The shop's not actually open yet!' Thomas exclaimed to Lola, 'great.'

'It said on the radio the signing will start at four. What time is it now?'

'Oh...it's only half three.'

They stood in silence for a while. Lola was thinking of Hannah, though she had tried to tell herself not to dwell on the matter too much. Hannah should be here in the queue with them, she thought to herself. She stared at the strangers walking by, some in groups, some by themselves, and wanted desperately to see Hannah's face among them. She saw a girl who had the same colour hair and felt a pang of excitement, only to realise it wasn't Hannah at all.

'Are you okay, Lola?'

'I'm fine. I just thought I saw Hannah for a second.'

Thomas looked at her for a moment then did the one thing she wanted him to do: he gave her a hug.

'Thank you, Thomas' she whispered to him.

They broke apart after a short while and the mood changed drastically when they saw that the shop had been opened and they were letting the queue inside.

'About time!' Thomas said as they moved with the queue, 'she must be inside!'

'Hopefully.'

The queue stopped after a few moments; they were still quite a way from the bookshop.

'And the waiting recommences,' Thomas sighed.

Lola got lost in her thoughts as they queued. Every so often, they'd move a little bit closer to meeting the famed actress. Very soon, she felt as if she weren't there: it seemed like all the people going by were just one big blur and that the people ahead of her in the queue didn't really exist. She was thinking of Assa and the quest for the orb. She realised that she didn't truly believe it all; after all, she'd only told a few of her close friends about what she'd learnt. If she truly believed it, she would have told everyone. The reality of it hadn't yet hit her, for she wasn't sure if there was some element of reality to it all. The aliens she'd seen…what she'd been told…there was that final piece of the puzzle that was lacking. That final piece would be proof enough to convince Lola that every aspect of the matter was true. But what could convince her for certain? She knew nothing could ever convince her that the universe had been created, nor could this Assa being ever prove it was responsible for this universe, nor that it had planned for this universe to run like clockwork. Then Lola realised something: if Assa's intentions were so, then Assa wasn't omnipotent, as the orb was a necessary component to see the plans through, and Assa had the opportunity all those years ago when visiting Helmia. If the orb could have helped to wipe out humanity in an instant, it would have. But it didn't. There was therefore a limit to what Assa and the orb could collectively do. They didn't have the capability to eradicate a whole species in one go. That thought reassured Lola a little.

'Lola?' Thomas' voice brought her out of her trancelike state; he was a few feet away and Lola looked behind her to see the people behind her in the queue looking rather impatiently at her.

'Sorry,' she apologised, before joining Thomas.

'Are you sure you're okay?'

'I just realised that Assa isn't all that powerful. I'm going to stop worrying so much.'

'But what about everything you told me about Assa's plans?'

'All that's not real, at least not now.'

Thomas looked perplexed; Lola could understand why, but her newfound optimism and her new outlook had opened up a whole multitude of positive ways to see the situation. The one that Lola considered most was the possibility that this wasn't going to happen, that Assa would somehow be unable to obtain the orb and carry out the plans. Of course, Lola had thought about this before, but now, while she was appreciating everything and everyone around her, wishing for the world to slow down, she saw all the good things in her life and told herself she must concentrate on them, rather than fear possibilities and mourn any losses.

'I can't wait to meet Mary Morton,' she told Thomas with a smile on her face, a smile that, for the first time in a while, wasn't faked.

Before long, they were almost inside the shop. Lola tried to see inside the shop, but her view was blocked by the queue inside, which snaked round; it seemed Mary was right at the back of the shop.

'Great,' Thomas moaned on this realisation.

'We'll be there before you know it.'

'Oh no. I've just realised something else: I haven't started that essay that's in for Monday morning.'

'Don't worry about it.'

'I knew there was something I was meant to do this weekend. I know I'm going to end up doing it on Sunday night; let's face it.'

'It won't take that long.'

'I wonder what's made her want to take time off?'

'It could be anything, I guess.'

'I wish this queue would hurry up.'

They waited and waited, talking to pass the time. Eventually, they were only a few groups of people from the counter where they'd buy the book, then there'd be another short queue before they'd actually get it signed.

'Her book had better be good after we've queued so long just to buy it,' Thomas said.

'I'm sure it will be brilliant. Oh look, there she is!' Lola could see Mary clearly and without obstruction for the first time. She was sat at a desk signing someone's book whilst talking to them in a drawly voice. She looked nothing like she did in her films: the Mary at the desk was not the glamorous, well-presented woman Lola always saw in films and in photographs and publications, but instead she was almost like a shadow of her former self: there seemed to be no care for her outward appearance, as her hair was unkempt and her make-up-less face revealed signs of exhaustion. Mary yawned and Lola noticed massive bags under her eyes.

'Oh my...well, she looks different than I'd imagined,'

Thomas commented, sounding surprised, 'I guess they say you should never meet your heroes.'

'We've queued for over two hours; we're meeting her even if she turns out to be the Wandering Widow or something.'

'Haha.'

'I'm getting her to sign a photo as well so I can sell it online.'

'They only let each person have one thing signed to save time; sorry to burst your opportunistic bubble.'

'Damn! I've queued all this time I should be allowed to make some money out of her.'

They bought their books, which had a photo of a pensive Mary in a field on the cover.

'If this is a recent photo, it has to be airbrushed,' Thomas remarked.

'Obviously. It's a shame they edit photos so much and that so many of them do it. They're hiding their natural beauty more and more every time they do it.'

'I guess no one knows what they really look like any more.'

'Except their nearest and dearest.'

Before long, they were the next in line to meet the actress. Lola was overcome with excitement and anticipation. She had never met her favourite celebrity before and was trying not to hype this up so much so as not to be disappointed. She knew the meeting would be brief and would be over before it could properly begin, but she couldn't wait for it.

'Only a few minutes to go!' she whispered excitedly to Thomas.

'Hurry up, people,' Thomas whispered back to her, 'we've been waiting longer than you!'

One of Mary Morton's aides gave them the nod once the family ahead of them left, books signed, and Lola and Thomas eagerly approached the desk.

'It's very nice to meet you, Mary,' Lola said.

'Its' very good to meet you too. What are your names?' Mary replied, looking up to smile at the two, a lovely smile, thought Lola, which left her mute.

'Thomas and Lola,' Thomas stepped in, nudging Lola lightly in the side.

'We're both big fans of your work and are looking forward to reading your book,' Lola said automatically; she was overcome with nerves and was speaking without thinking.

'Thank you so much. I hope you enjoy it. It took far too long to write, owing to my laziness.'

Lola didn't know what to say except, 'can we have our photo taken with you, please?'

'Of course.'

They had their photo taken on their phones, having given them to the photographer, then bade Mary farewell. Lola thought Mary looked vaguely familiar from somewhere.

'Thank you so much,' Lola said as she clutched her newly signed book.

'Anytime,' Mary replied, her short, dark hair reminding Lola of Hannah's hair. Lola couldn't wait to see her friend again; Hannah's absence was really making Lola's heart grow fonder: she had something to look forward to. She smiled as she and Thomas left the store.

'Oh my...I completely fell apart,' Thomas remarked, sounding disappointed in himself.

'So did I. Why didn't I just compose myself!'

'I wish I could go back and do that again. I didn't realise how nervous I was till we walked over to her desk.'

'I wouldn't worry about it. She seemed friendly enough. What do you want to do now?'

'It's quite sunny still – we could go to the beach.'

'That sounds like a good idea. I know what would be even better: we could go and see where the Blondies landed.'

'What?!'

'I can't believe they've been here for two weeks and we haven't seen them yet!'

'But will we even be allowed there?'

'Of course. The police and army are stationed around that dome thing the Blondies put around themselves, but if we go to a higher place like one of the buildings facing the beach, we might get a better vantage point. Do you want to?'

'Oh my...do I want to go and see aliens? I'm really not sure.'

'It's just a few UFO's, that's all. Come on, you know you want to. Let your curiosity drive you.'

'Go on then,' Thomas acquiesced with a tinge of nerves in his voice.

Lola felt a rush of excitement course through her once again. She didn't know why she hadn't gone to see the aliens sooner.

'Are you sure you want to do this?' she asked Thomas again.

'I'm positive. Where abouts are they again?'

'They're on the smaller beach, near where the cliffs are.'

'Is there a monorail stop nearby?'

'Yeah there is. It should only be a ten minute walk.'

And so they set off, nervous and not knowing what exactly to expect. Lola was eager to see the ships, but she didn't know what Thomas would feel like seeing something alien for the first time in his life. In a way, Lola was desensitised to it all, whereas Thomas wasn't.

They were soon back on the monorail, heading out of the city centre to a quieter part of the city. They got off at the station, which was the shape of a small aircraft hangar but consisted of nothing but large glass panels, giving it a somewhat futuristic look. All the monorail stops in the city were of the same design; the ones outside the city were of a less grandiose design.

They were soon walking along the street which looked out on to the beach. In the near distance, they could see the thirty-five UFOs packed closely together on the beach, a perimeter of police cars and military vehicles surrounding them.

'Oh my,' Thomas exclaimed on seeing the scene on the beach; he stopped for a minute and held on to the railing separating the path from the beach below.

'Thomas, are you okay?'

'They're the alien ships, aren't they?'

'We can go back if you want.'

'What if something *happens*?'

'They've been here for two weeks and for two weeks nothing has happened. And if something does happen, there's all those military people surrounding them.'

'I don't know if I want to do this.'

'No one's making you.'

'I can't believe there are aliens a few hundred feet away from us.'

'You should consider yourself lucky you haven't experienced what I have.'

'I know; you're so brave, Lola.'

'Not really. I panicked when I was with the Greys, remember?'

'I still think you're very brave.'

'Thanks.'

They sat down on a nearby bench and were facing the row of shops facing the beach. Lola could tell Thomas wanted to proceed further to the beach, but hadn't gathered his strength yet.

'What did it feel like seeing aliens?' Thomas asked after a few minutes' silence. They'd discussed this in depth before but Lola realised Thomas was needing reassurance that he needn't be as scared as he was.

'To be perfectly honest, it doesn't feel like they're aliens. They look so different and act differently, but really, they are quite humanlike. I thought I would be so scared, well I was with the Greys because they were hostile and had lasers and whatnot but when I was with the Blondies, I didn't feel scared at all. I felt as if they were human. I mean, they were speaking fluent English with me! How weird is that! I realised that aliens aren't really that different after all, they're just humans but from another planet. We're all from the same universe, so I guess we all have some similarities.'

Thomas remained silent still. Lola then added, 'remember that lesson with Demzel where we discussed what it means to be alien?'

'Yeah.'

'Remember when Demzel said the most terrifying thing out there is the unknown? Well, those aliens over there may be unknown to everyone, but I've met them and I can assure you they are not hostile like the Greys. They are here to help us. I think they're put that dome around themselves so we don't attack them, which is a sensible thing to do.'

'Shall we go to the beach then?' Thomas said all of a sudden, much to Lola's delight.

They got up and went down the nearest set of steps leading to the beach. Then Lola realised that, despite it being a good day for going to the beach, it was empty. As quickly as she came up with an explanation, a tall, muscular police officer with a chiselled face and short, cropped hair, appeared at the foot of the steps. It was then Lola saw that the beach had been cordoned off.

'I'm afraid this beach is closed until further notice,' the policeman said in a gruff, authoritative voice.

'Oh, we're sorry. We didn't realise it was closed' Lola replied.

Another policeman joined the first.

'Are you okay, young man?' the second said to Thomas, who had been staring at the UFOs and had just taken a deep breath and sat down.

'He's just a bit spooked seeing the UFOs,' Lola replied on Thomas' behalf.

'Perhaps you'd best go home,' the first policeman suggested a little patronisingly.

'We've just come to see the UFOs,' Thomas replied sternly.

The second police officer, a less intimidating and smaller man with a more average build and a rounder face with sparkling blue eyes, smiled at Lola and Thomas then said: 'if you wish to see the UFOs, just walk along the path up there. We can't let anyone on the beach in case something happens.'

'Has anything happened so far?' Lola asked.

'Nothing has happened. They landed here about two weeks ago, then some sort of dome-shaped barrier appeared around them. People who tried to approach the craft before we got there told us they were met with an invisible wall, which we and the military have had surrounded ever since. Nothing has been seen leaving any of the crafts yet.'

'And none of the craft have moved since?'

'None of them has moved.'

'You see, our friend Hannah was abducted recently, by aliens, her mum says. I was just wondering whether it might have been one of these.'

'I am very sorry to hear that. I hope you notified the police already?'

'Of course,' replied Lola, 'they're doing all they can, but if she was taken by aliens, there's not much the police can do.'

'I can assure you that everything is being done to ensure her safe return.'

'Thank you,' Lola said, 'do you think these aliens will show themselves anytime soon?'

'It's impossible to say. We really don't know what's going on. All we can do is wait and see, but we can promise that whatever happens, we will do our best to protect the citizens of Helmia should it come to that.'

'I'm sure it won't,' Lola replied.

The kinder policeman bade them farewell and expressed the hope that Hannah would return soon safe and sound. Lola and Thomas walked back up the steps and started walking along the path, getting closer and closer to the landing site.

'Well, one of them seemed nice,' Lola said.

'He was gorgeous! I was lost for words.'

'I could tell.'

There was a brief pause before Thomas said, 'so if those aliens on the beach didn't take Hannah, who do you think did?'

It was a question Lola hadn't fully contemplated yet. Then the realisation came to her: it must have been the Greys.

'Oh no…I think it was the Greys.'

'The Greys?'

'What other aliens are there in Helmia? The Blondies have been here the whole time and the Greys…who else could it have been?' Lola was horrified at the conclusion she'd come to.

'There must be some other aliens who took Hannah. There might even be more Blondies out there.'

'Yeah.'

'She'll be okay,' Thomas said to Lola. They stopped walking; they were leaning against the railings looking out at the alien ships, the faint dome surrounding them and the numerous people and vehicles around the dome's perimeter.

'It's so surreal,' remarked Thomas, 'it's hard to understand that those ships are from somewhere so far away.'

Lola remembered when she saw these ships flying about the sky flashing lights of different colours. She remembered being entranced and enticed by the beauty of something so alien being so mesmerising.

She looked over at Thomas, who seemed to be just as entranced.

'They're *alien*,' he said, 'but it hasn't really sunk in yet.'

'I know it's hard to accept.'

'It's damn right difficult! I mean, they look like they could be made by humans, so really, what's to say they're alien?'

'How about the force field that's not letting anyone in? I'm not an expert, but I'm sure we haven't developed technology capable of making something like that yet.'

'True.'

They remained there for a while, staring at the landing site. Lola thought Thomas had a point, a point she herself had pondered over the past few weeks, that it was weird how much of anti-climax this all was. Thinking back to the class when they'd discussed what it meant to be alien, Lola realised that the aliens coming was no doubt terrifying for some, but for most people it hadn't had quite the effect she'd thought. She'd envisaged scenes of mass hysteria and civil disruption – on reflection, she realised she'd expected too much.

'Do you want to head back?' Thomas asked.

'OK.'

As they headed to the monorail station, Lola kept having one last look at the landing site. It looked surreal, out of place. She wondered how long they'd all have to wait.

She and Thomas went home and Lola spent the rest of that night and the whole of the next day taking things slowly and learning to enjoy the things she overlooked too often.

When Monday came round, Lola walked to school with Thomas and was looking forward to seeing people and having something to do.

During assembly, Lola tried to listen to what Dazzle was saying, but none of the notices affected or interested her in any way. She looked round and saw that most people were equally bored. She saw Mrs. Dazzle staring out to space, Miss Bay looking attentive, then she was shocked to see Mr. Stone on the balcony yawning.

She nudged Thomas.

'Look who it is, up there on the balcony,' she whispered to him hurriedly.

'Mr. Stone? I thought he left?'

'He did. I wonder what's brought him back…'

'I'm sure we'll find out soon enough.'

True to Thomas' words, they did find out that afternoon after their Paranormal and Supernatural Studies class with Demzel. They hung around after the lesson to ask him.

'It came as a shock to me too. I hadn't heard from him in ages then all of a sudden he turns up here out of the blue willing to go back to work. I tried talking to him but I can't get through to him. He's not the Ivan I thought I knew before though.'

'Who asked him to guard the school when the Greys came?'

'He won't tell. I can't understand why he's acting so oddly and, to be frank, I'm surprised Dazzle let him return. That poor replacement teacher who's been here for just a few weeks is being let go.'

'But he should stay! It's his job now,' said Thomas.

'Dazzle must want Ivan back,' Demzel suggested, only to

have Lola blurt out, 'you need to find out who asked him to guard the school. You know him best, Demzel.'

'I'll try my best. I don't want to drive him away again.'

'Again? You've never driven him away before.'

'Why did he go AWOL for a month then?'

'Maybe there was some family crisis or something?'

'He would have told me,' Demzel said, looking down. 'I think he needs a friend right now.'

'I've been trying to reach out to him for ages but he just won't listen to me. I tried to have a quiet word with him this morning when we both had a free period, but he just wasn't saying anything. It's like he's someone else.'

'Why do you think he left?'

'I really can't say,' Demzel replied disappointedly, 'he seemed perfectly fine and then he just left without telling anyone. Anyway, you two should be getting to your next lesson. It's a shame there can't be a fifteen minute break between every lesson,' he sighed. Lola and Thomas said goodbye and hurried to their next class, for which they were just on time.

Later on that day, it was the end of the school day and Lola was in the locker room getting the books she needed to take home that night. The room was crowded as people were in a hurry to get what they needed then go home.

'Lola, what was our English homework again?' Edward asked her from nearby.

'Wait a sec, I wrote it down in my planner.'

Lola fumbled about in her bad for her planner, which she extracted and opened.

'We didn't have any.'

'Great. Thanks.'

'What are you doing tonight?'

'I think I'm going to Thomas'. To be honest,' Edward looked round, scrutinising the people in the room, 'me and my sister had a bit of an argument over the weekend, and I need some space.'

'What did you argue about? I hope it was nothing serious.'

'She said I needed more of a backbone! I was just sticking up for someone she was criticising as usual, and then she turned on me.'

'Have you told your parents?'

'Yeah. They've had a word with her but I don't think she listened to them. Do you want to go to the theme park on Saturday? And let's not invite Erica.'

'What did you say, Edward?' Lola heard someone say; through the crowd of students packing stuff and milling in and out of the room she could see Erica just coming into the room

'Just exclude me from everything else, while you're at it,' she said before storming off.

'Erica, wait!' Lola watched as Edward left his open locker and ran after his sister. Lola closed Edward's locker door for him so people would assume it was locked. She left the locker room, having got all of her stuff sorted, and tried to find Edward to remind him his locker was still unlocked. She found him and Erica sitting next to each other on one of the pews in the main hall.

'Edward, your locker's still unlocked,' she told the silent Edward, who was looking enraged.

'Thanks, Lola. At least someone's nice to me!' he said to his sister, who crossed her arms and looked away.

'I'm going to go,' Lola said awkwardly, 'I hope you stop arguing. It's so silly.'

'I know,' Edward exclaimed. She'd never want to find herself arguing with her own brother for such petty reasons.

Lola couldn't take the atmosphere any longer, so she went. As she left, she could hear them arguing once more.

She walked home quite slowly as she was busy contemplating a number of things as usual. The mask she'd built up for herself recently by telling herself to view things positively crumbled to pieces and Lola ran to the nearest bench, sat down on it and started crying. She didn't know how long she was there for. She was sobbing hysterically, releasing everything she'd been hiding ever since Hannah had been taken away. Strangers passing by didn't stop to console her, which was what Lola wanted. She wanted no distractions or disruptions.

'Where are you?' she mouthed through her tears.

On the one hand, the release was cathartic and it felt good to get so much pent-up sorrow and frustration out; on the other hand, this seemed to only reaffirm how dire the situation was for Hannah. It was all very real.

'Where are you?' Lola mouthed again, her had in her lap.

She spent ages staring out into nothing. She was looking at the road, some houses and people going by, but she wasn't really looking at them. She was focussing on something that wasn't quite there.

It was getting late: she'd been there for well over an hour. She'd got it all out of her and was now just clearing her mind of everything bad. She watched as people went by and the world continued running to an unknown goal. What she wanted more than anything was for life to stop rushing all the time. People were always thinking about what would come next, what was going to happen in the future. Lola was guilty of that, too, and she knew it, but she wished everything would just slow down for once. She decided she'd text her parents, explaining why was late, and would tell them she'd be back eventually, that she was having a leisurely walk home for once. She hit the send button, then a few minutes later, her phone rang.

'Lola, it's mum. Where are you, honey?'

'I'm on my way home,' Lola replied, wiping her face of tears. She was surprised her mum didn't sound more worried.

'I've got some very good news for you: Hannah's back.'

Chapter 16 –
The Orb

Lola ran home as fast as she could. She got home before she knew it and, once inside, threw her bag down in the passageway and shouted for her parents.

'In the living room,' came her mother's voice.

Lola went in to find both of her parents sitting down. Her mother got up, came over to her and hugged her.

'She's back.'

Lola couldn't believe it. She didn't know if she should believe it.

'Is she okay?'

'She's absolutely fine. Go round and see her; she's at home and wants to see you.'

Her mother let go. She and her daughter were both crying. Lola looked at her father, who smiled back and said, 'she's waiting for you.'

Lola then thanked them both and told them she'd be back soon before she left, feeling more eager and happy than she'd ever felt in ages. Frustratingly, the run to Hannah's seemed to take much longer than it ought to have. She couldn't wait to see her again: seeing would be confirmation that she was alive and well. She couldn't wait to speak to her. Part of her was curious to know what exactly had happened to her.

Soon enough, she was approaching Hannah's house. She didn't bother ringing the doorbell and waiting to be admitted in; instead she opened the door and called out Hannah's name.

'Lola!' came Hannah's reply from upstairs. Lola ran upstairs and headed straight for Hannah's room.

'Hannah!' she cried on entering her room and seeing her lying in bed eating a yoghurt.

'Lola!'

Hannah clambered out of bed – she was in her pyjamas – and the two hugged so tightly for ages.

'I'm so glad you're back,' was all Lola could think of saying.

'I'm so glad to be back.'

'Are you okay?'

'I'm fine. I'm a little shaken up, but otherwise I'm good. I wouldn't let some stupid aliens affect me too much.'

'Are you sure you're okay? I've missed you so much. Not knowing whether you were...alive, that was the worst.'

'I'm fine, honestly. You don't know how much I've missed you and Thomas and everyone else. He should be here by now.'

Lola thought Hannah seemed rather unaffected by it all; she seemed her usual self, not traumatised as she'd expected her to be.

They let go of each other and Hannah invited Lola to sit on her bed.

'I'm dreading catching up with all the school work,' Hannah moaned.

'There won't be much; we haven't done much recently really.'

'Phew! Mum's keeping me off for a few days anyway till I *recover*,'

'When did you get back?'

'It's kind of odd really. I woke up in my bed this afternoon then ran downstairs and mum was there. She got the fright of her life when she saw me. I wish I'd taken a picture! It's weird because I was in the same pyjamas I was wearing when they took me. Mum's put them in the wash.

'Do you know what happened while you were…away?'

Lola knew Hannah wouldn't shy away from recalling as much detail as possible.

'I was in bed a few weeks ago. I was asleep and then this noise woke me up. There was light coming into my room from outside but it was the middle of the night. Then there were these two creatures in my room. I don't know how they got there. I was so scared. I screamed and could hear my mum coming, but before she got to my room, I guess they'd taken me because the next thing I remember is that I was in this spaceship and I was looking out the window. We were flying away from Helmia toward the mainland. I wasn't scared for some reason. I knew that I'd be returned soon, but I don't know why I felt so sure of that. I don't remember much of what else happened while I was away, though I do remember feeling tired often, so I guess I must have been awake a lot. The whole time I was gone just seems to have merged into one long day.'

'Who took you? Was it aliens?'

'It was yeah. They weren't Greys or Blondies, I don't think. They were tall, very tall, and they had massive triangular heads. They had a tail thing coming from the top of their head and they had two sets of arms and another tail round back. They were dark red, though some of them were a kind of dark purple colour. They looked dead weird and creepy.'

'Did they hurt you or do anything to you?'

'I don't think so, at least I don't remember it. I haven't got any bruises or anything like that.'

Lola wasn't liking what she was hearing. She'd read accounts of many people who'd been abducted by aliens and had a very patchy memory of everything they'd experienced.

'Were you in the spaceship the whole time?'

'I don't know. I remember it being pretty big. I was indoors the whole time, from what I remember, so I guess I must have been in the spaceship the whole time. There were other people there as well.'

'Who?'

'I can't remember them all. There was a little boy, a boy about our age, an elderly woman, a few middle-aged people and that's it I think. I don't think we ever talked to one another. I only saw them briefly though. I can't remember them all. There was a little boy, a boy about our age, an elderly woman, a few middle-aged people and that's it I think. I don't think we ever talked to one another. I only saw them briefly though. I can't remember...'

'Stop!'

'What?'

'You're repeating yourself. Are you sure you're okay?'

'I'm fine, honestly. Is Thomas coming over?' Hannah asked with a deadpan expression. Lola was starting to worry. Hannah's calm state and her behaviour were really starting to scare Lola.

'It's common for people who've been abducted by aliens to have memory loss.'

'I don't have memory loss, honestly. I can remember everything that happened.'

'Is Thomas coming over?'

'I don't know. Should I ring him?'

'You said before he was coming?'

'Did I?'

'Yes, you did, Hannah.'

There was silence for a few moments. As much as Lola wished this weren't happening to Hannah, she wasn't surprised there was something wrong with her.

'I'm relieved you're back,' Lola told Hannah.

'I'm glad to be back as well. Was I really gone for one week?'

'You were gone for two and it was the longest two weeks ever.'

'It felt like a lot less than that. Those stupid aliens: not only do they abduct me, but they make me miss a week of my life! I'm going to get them back if it's the last thing I do.'

'That might be hard to do seeing as no one knows what aliens took you.'

'That's a good point,' Hannah said, sounding disappointed, 'I tried to remember if I'd seen those aliens before, perhaps in one of Demzel's classes, but I couldn't recall ever having seen them.'

'I'm going to research them later on.'

'If you happen to find out where they are, let me know and I'll get my revenge. I'll get my revenge.'

Lola laughed a little to appease Hannah, but the laugh was put on.

'I mean,' Hannah went on, 'I know they didn't hurt me or anything but – well, I do have a bit of a strong headache but I'm guessing it's just nothing.'

'A headache? How long have you had it for?'

'I remember it came about when I was in the ship. I think I've had it for a few days. It's nothing serious.'

'It could be why you're forgetting things, have memory loss and keep repeating yourself!' Lola spat out, instantly regretting it.

'Do you think *they're* responsible?' Hannah said wide-eyed. Lola was feeling annoyed, not at Hannah, but at the state she was in and whoever had done this to her. There had to be some reason why she'd been abducted.

'I'm sure it's nothing,' Lola said, trying to sound reassuring.

Lola hugged Hannah again and they spent a while talking.

'Have I missed much?'

'We met Mary Morton at a book signing and we had a guest speaker in class the other day: Aaron Lineswell.'

'Who is he?'

'You know, that man who saw Helmia rise up out of the sea?'

'Oh yeah. Him. I think I remember hearing about him.'

'He was really interesting and inspirational actually. I really enjoyed that class.'

Hannah was going to reply when her phone went. She didn't seem to notice it.

'Hannah, your phone?'

'What? Oh yeah...it's Thomas! Thomas! It's so good to hear your voice. Where are you? Well get yourself round here, I've missed you! OK, we'll see you soon!'

'He just found out I'm back. Bless him. He's coming over right away.'

Before long, Thomas had arrived and rejoiced in seeing Hannah back home safe and sound. The three of them spent hours in Hannah's room talking and catching up. Every so often, one of them would ask Hannah if she was sure she was alright, to which she'd reply that she was absolutely fine and just needed a good night's sleep. She didn't mention the headache again, Lola noticed, although she did repeat herself a few more times and seemed to be regularly forgetting things.

'It's so good to have you back,' Thomas told Hannah for the umpteenth time as he and Lola left at half ten.

'You don't know how relieved I was when I got home. I would be jumping all about if I wasn't this tired.'

'Well, get some well-deserved rest and we'll see you tomorrow.'

'I probably won't be at school for a few days,' Hannah told them excitedly, 'my mum thinks I should stay off for a little bit. I'm dreading catching up on the work, but I really just cannot wait to lie around in bed all day!'

'Have fun then.'

'Say hello to everyone from me.'

'We will. Bye, Hannah,' Lola said, hugging Hannah tightly. She let go then Thomas did the same.

'Thank you for coming round, I really appreciate it. You guys are amazing. You guys are amazing.'

Lola and Thomas each hugged Hannah once more before finally leaving her to go to sleep.

They spoke with her mum before leaving.

'Sometimes she's fine, her normal self, then she'll forget something or she'll repeat exactly what she's just said,' Hannah's mum said slowly, not wanting to believe what she was saying.

'I can either come to an awful conclusion, or I can just deal with it as it comes and hope that once she's spent time in her usual routine, then she'll stop this,' she added, sounding a little relieved.

'Hopefully,' replied Thomas.

'If she's not fine by tomorrow, I'm taking her to see someone. I should really take her now but I want her to have some rest first.'

'That's perfectly understandable.'

Over the next few days, Lola found herself much happier than she had been recently. Hannah's safe return was a massive load off her mind. The friend she thought she was going to lose was back in her life, making everything just how it used to be. Hannah eventually showed up to school on Thursday, having been given the all-clear, and was bombarded with people expressing their joy that she was back safe and sound. A few people, however, persistently asked her questions, which she answered willingly, though Lola thought it was quite insensitive for someone who barely knew Hannah to suddenly be asking her about a seemingly traumatic experience.

Before long, everything was back to normal. The weekend came and Lola, Hannah, Thomas, Edward and Darren spent all of Saturday in the theme park.

'It feels like a million years since I was last here,' Hannah commented as they were in the queue for one of the park's roller coasters, Arch Enemy. It took them just a few minutes to get on the ride.

'I'm just going to let my hair down and have a fun day,' she added. They had arrived at the park just before it opened, and once they were admitted in, they had run straight to Arch Enemy, which they managed to three times in a row because the queue was so small.

'Three times in a row! Woohoo!' Hannah exclaimed as they left the station and went to look at the on-ride photos.

'I look horrific, as usual!' she cried on seeing her photo.

'No you don't,' replied Darren coolly; Lola looked at the photo and saw Darren grinning at the camera with his thumbs up, Hannah looking petrified, and everyone else looking like they'd been caught in a windstorm. Hannah was blushing a little at Darren.

'I can't believe I was forgetting stuff and repeating myself,' Hannah said.

'We were all worried, but are so glad it's stopped so fast.'

'I'm glad you're ok, too, Hannah.'

'Thanks, Darren.'

It was a lovely, warm day. The park was relatively quiet, much to everyone's delight. They didn't talk about aliens or anything like that until they went on the observation tower and, whilst the cabin was at the very top slowly rotating, they saw the beach and the Blondies' landing site in the distance.

'Wow!' exclaimed Hannah.

'Haven't you seen it before?' replied Darren, 'when I went there with my brother, there were so many people there. It was totally insane.'

'I'd never really thought about going to be honest.'

'You're not missing much. It's just a few ships and some rude police officers and tanks.'

'It sounds exciting though.'

'I haven't been either, Hannah,' Edward replied, 'and I don't think I'd want to go either. It would freak me out.'

'It's not as scary as it seems, is it Thomas?' Lola asked.

'Well, I was scared at first, but I guess it wasn't that bad.'

'I was expecting to see aliens running about,' Darren interjected, 'but it was lame really. You couldn't even see the aliens! Apparently since they got here, they haven't even left the ships. How pathetic is that? They must be frightened of us or something.'

'I guess they're like insects. You know how they say insects are more scared of us than we are of they?' replied Thomas conversationally as they started descending. The view was quite extraordinary: they could see the whole of Puddlepond as well as Etolin Island in the distance.

By the time they got off the ride, the sun was shining feverishly and almost blinding them with its rays. They headed to the log flume to cool off, but unfortunately did not get as soaked as they'd hoped.

Late in the afternoon, they opted for going to the beach to make the most of the good weather. None of them were really dressed for the beach, but that didn't deter them from going.

They all pitched in to buy a few towels and found a good spot about halfway down to the sea. The others were all engrossed in conversation, but Lola decided to rest. She stared at the sea for ages, admiring its simplicity and complexity. The sun began to set, producing a myriad of warm colours all across the sky. Lola fell in love with the view she was beholding. She looked to Hannah and hoped with everything she had that she was truly okay. The worrying thing was that there seemed to be no reason as to why she'd been abducted. The headache, memory loss and repetition seemed to be some side effect of something unknown. Lola kept a close eye on Hannah, just in case.

She told herself that, as long as Hannah seemed fine, she needn't worry, and, looking back towards the sunset, she started falling asleep.

She dreamt she was back in school and everyone was doing some sort of test, even all of the teachers – even the head teacher. They were in the exam hall, which was many times bigger than what it was in reality. Lola looked down at her paper and saw that it consisted of one-sentence questions with space to write an answer.

Question One: Who abducted Hannah?

Question Two: What did they do to her?

Question Three: Who asked Ivan to guard the school when the Greys searched it?

Question Four: When will Assa procure the orb?

Question Five: If not, what will happen?

Question Six: Can the orb actually be destroyed?

Question Seven: What is the Darkness of Light?

Question Eight: Is this all real?

On and on the questions went. There were two pages of them in total, but then Lola noticed more and more pages were appearing right in front of her, each with more and more questions. She didn't know the answers to any of them – she hadn't even heard of the phrase 'darkness of light' before either.

'Time's up,' a bodiless voice reverberated throughout the exam hall. Lola couldn't place the voice – it sounded artificial and robotic.

Then everything changed: Lola was now in the head teacher's office sitting at his desk, waiting for him to enter the room. He didn't come, however.

'You have failed your examination,' came the same robotic voice.

'How was I meant to know the answers?' Lola cried to no one.

'The answers are out there. You have failed to find them.'

'I didn't know where to look.'

'No more excuses. You failed the exam. You do not know anything.'

'Lola!'

'Who was that?' Lola asked, recognising the voice.

'Lola, wake up!'

Lola opened her eyes. She felt herself being pulled up.

'What's going on?'

'Look over there!' Hannah exclaimed, pointing out to the sea. Lola could see something hovering in the distance above the sea.

'It just flew up out of the sea a few seconds ago,' Hannah told her; all of them were watching this distant thing, curious to see what would happen next.

It seemed to be getting bigger and bigger.

'It's coming this way, whatever it is,' Darren said dully.

It looked to be some sort of elongated creature that was flying without wings, airborne through no apparent means. Lola could tell it had a long body, but other features were too difficult to make out. She watched the creature fly towards them and past the beach they were on – as it flew by, she noticed it seemed to be holding something: an orb. Lola froze on the spot, able to do nothing but continue to watch the being fly away into the distance. It soared magnificently easily. It was an amazing sight to behold. The wonder overcame her for a moment before she realised what exactly she was seeing.

She wanted to tell everyone it was Assa, but the words wouldn't come out of her mouth. Even though only Hannah and Thomas knew about Assa, Lola still felt the urge to proclaim this knowledge.

Did this then mean that the end was nigh? Assa appeared to have found the orb, but how long would it be before the final plan was put into action? Lola was starting to feel panicky.

'Was that…?' Thomas said.

'Yes!' snapped Lola, sitting down and putting her head in her hands. She needed to think, to assess the situation.

'Lola, are you okay?' Darren asked.

'I'm fine.'

'What on Earth was that thing?' Edward exclaimed.

Lola wanted to tell everyone the great predicament they all were in now that it seemed Assa had found the orb. Something was holding her back from doing this, however, and that something was her belief she lacked concrete proof. Then she realised that it didn't matter whether or not she had proof for other people, for she had believed it all without seeing absolute, concrete proof of Assa's plans and story. She still didn't know whether she truly believed all this, but she decided it wasn't right for her to not tell everyone.

'That thing is a being called Assa, who created this universe and wants to destroy humanity because we were not in the original plans; we came about by accident. That orb Assa has makes Assa able to wipe us all out.'

She'd blurted it out so quickly she wasn't sure everyone had heard it. She knew now was the time to tell people; she thought people wouldn't believe her unless there was proof, and now there was what was the closest thing to actually proof.

'It's all real,' she whispered to herself.

'Lola, are you okay?' Edward asked somewhat cautiously.

'Assa has the orb! This can't be happening!'

'Lola, calm down, please.'

'How can I be calm? Don't you realise what this now means? It was only a matter of time before Assa found the orb and now it's been found,' Lola uttered through hysterics.

'Lola, please calm down.'

'I'm not going to. Come on, this is the creator of the universe we're talking about here, a creator who needs that orb to get rid of us and now has that orb!'

'Lola, are you seriously asking us to believe that?' asked Darren.

'It's the truth!'

Darren looked stunned and confused.

'You don't believe me, do you?'

'Are you having us on, Lola?'

'What! Of course I'm not, Darren! I'm being serious.'

'That thing that just flew over our heads created this universe?'

'Yes and it's going to wipe humanity out because we were never meant to be here. Earth was meant to be inhabited by dinosaurs instead.'

'How are we meant to believe that? What proof is there?'

'I'm telling you, this is all real. I know it's a lot to believe but I assure you it is all true. Those other aliens that are in Helmia are here because of Assa; the Blondies are trying to help us stop Assa but the Greys are helping Assa.'

Lola looked from friend to friend: Hannah and Thomas looked worried, whereas Edward looked at a loss and Darren looked very sceptical.

'I haven't got time for this. I need to go. Please believe what I've told you,' she said before walking away from the four. She could tell from the looks on their faces that even Hannah and Thomas were slightly sceptical.

'Lola! Wait up!'

It was Hannah.

'Lola, what's got into you?'

'I'm so worried,' Lola said, bursting into tears. She slumped to the ground and continued crying profusely.

'Wouldn't it have happened by now though?' Hannah asked.

Lola stopped her chaotic thinking for a moment to consider Hannah's question.

'I guess it's going to happen soon, I mean, it could really happen any second.'

She looked at Hannah, behind whom there was the beautiful backdrop of the beach and the sea. Lola could hear the crashing waves coming into contact with the beaten land. She wanted this image to freeze so she could keep it forever: Hannah on the sunset beach, Hannah, lovely, perfect Hannah who would never like her in return.

'I don't want this to happen,' Lola sobbed.

'No one does. But people are reluctant to believe because, well, it's hard to accept. I mean, imagine being told that the universe was created and its creator has gone doolally and is intent on wiping out whole worlds? It's a lot to take in. I don't know if I believe it, although I'm trying because I know you wouldn't make something like this up.'

Lola was lost for words. All she wanted was for Assa and all the other aliens to have never come to Helmia, but she knew everything was now set in stone.

'Can't things be like they used to?' Lola cried.

'They are!'

'They're not!'

'I want things to be like they were before all this alien nonsense. It's changed our lives and we can never go back to how it was before.'

'Yes we can, Lola.'

'You've seen aliens. You know some of them are a threat to us. We don't know anything about them. Can you honestly say you don't worry about them? Can you honestly say you wished it were like it was before? The aliens have affected every single person who knows about them and we should all be petrified of them because we don't know what they're capable of, let alone Assa.'

'Lola, please calm down. Nothing's happened yet.'

'You were taken by them! You don't remember the better part of two weeks! Doesn't that *scare* you? What did they do to you to make you the way you were when you came back?' Lola was shouting louder and louder, trying to get her point across.

'I don't remember them doing anything to me. If they did do something, then isn't it a good thing that I can't remember it?'

'They could have done anything to you! For all we know they could have done surgery on you or something which is likely given the after-effects you experienced! And what about when they took you for the first time?' Lola cried hysterically.

'How do you know that?'

'Your mother told us,' Lola replied, calming down a little, 'I'm sorry for bringing it up but I understand why you'd not tell us about it.'

'I don't remember any of it anyway.'

'Don't you see? They could have done something to you the first and they could have done something this time round!'

'When I was returned, I wasn't in pain or anything, apart from the headache. I would remember if they did something really bad, wouldn't I?'

'Not necessarily.'

'Lola,' Hannah said softly after a few moments' silence.

'What?'

'I believe you, OK? I believe you. I've said it before but not really meant it. Now I mean it. I believe what Assa's doing is real and, as much as I don't want to, I believe we should all be scared because those bloody aliens…I honestly don't think they did anything to me, but how can I be sure? They might have done something to me…I've been denying it. I'm scared they've done something to me.'

'I hope they haven't, Hannah.'

They had been standing a few metres apart on the sand. Hannah now approached Lola and hugged her.

'I'm sorry for shouting, I was just being impatient.'

'You, impatient?' Hannah replied sarcastically, laughing and breaking the tension somewhat.

Lola laughed a little, though not as much as she would usually have laughed.

'I don't want this to be the end,' she sighed into Hannah's shoulder.

'It won't be.'

'Assa has the orb. This is what people have been dreading for ages,' she whispered softly.

'We are still here, Lola. Look around you; this isn't some afterlife is it? It's the world!'

Lola let go of Hannah and wiped her eyes and felt her forehead a bit. The others were standing a little behind Hannah looking nonplussed and dumbstruck.

'I need to ring someone,' was all Lola could say; she got her phone out of her pocket and dialled someone who might be able to alleviate her negativity.

'Natella? It's Lola,' she paused, unable to believe this was finally happening, 'I'm on the beach and we've just seen Assa fly up out of the sea...with the orb.'

'Are you sure, Lola?'

'Positive. Was the orb hidden under the sea?'

'Yes, that was its new hiding-place after Dazzle's office.'

'What does this mean?'

'It means we still have time. Even with the orb, Assa can't wipe us out in one go. It's an elaborate plan that can be foiled. We still have plenty of time to act, and we will, I can promise.'

'What are our chances?'

'Chances of what?'

'Of our survival.'

There was a pause before Natella replied, 'very high.'

'Natella, don't mess with me! Be honest – I want to know the truth.'

'Lola, I need to go. I have to ring someone.'

And with that, Natella hung up.

'Is everything okay?' Darren asked. Lola noticed Thomas and Edward were having a whispered conversation with each other.

'Do you believe me now, Darren? Please believe me because it's real, it's so very real.'

'Lola, just calm down a bit.'

'I can't be bloody calm!'

'Look, if this really is happening, then I'm sure it won't be as bad as you're making it out to be.'

'You don't understand; you really don't. If you did, you'd be just as paranoid as I am right now.'

'How can I believe something so ridiculous when there's no proof?' replied Darren heatedly.

'What do you think that thing before was then?'

'I don't know. But if you're asking me to believe that what we've just seen is the creator of this universe, then I simply can't easily accept that.'

Lola was going to retaliate when her phone started ringing. Lola saw Edward and Thomas looking confused, Hannah looking astonished whereas Darren was looking impatient; Lola could understand his reluctance to belief, but she hoped her insistence would overcome his scepticism. The beach was quiet and calm, as was the sea, which was almost still. She answered her phone: it was Natella.

'Lola, it's me. I have some good news,'

'Good news? What can there *possibly* be that's good news?'

'I just phoned Susie and she told me the orb Assa has is a fake.'

Chapter 17 –
The Darkness of Light

'What do you mean, it's a fake?'
'I just got off the phone with Susie. She told me the orb that was dumped into the sea was actually a fake designed to hold Assa up.'

'Are you being serious?'

'Yes I am, Lola.'

Lola was reeling in relief. She looked at her friends and broke into a smile.

'So it's not happening yet?'

'Assa will have realised by now probably that the orb is a fake. We don't know how long it will take to find the real one.'

'Where is the real one?'

'I don't know, and if I did, Lola, I wouldn't tell you.'

'Thanks for trusting me!'

'I know what you're like, Lola. You would panic, thinking the hiding-place wasn't good enough and would try to hide it somewhere you thought better.'

'No I wouldn't,' Lola replied, though she knew that was a realistic assumption.

'I have to go, Lola.'

'When do you think Assa will find the real orb?'

'I don't know. It could be in a few days, or a few months. I really have to go now, Lola.'

And with that, Natella hung up.

'What's going on, Lola,' Thomas asked; he looked cautious and unsure.

'There's nothing to worry about, for now. The orb Assa found in the sea is a fake. The real one is still hidden out there somewhere.'

Darren still didn't look convinced; the others weren't reacting in the way Lola had expected them to. They were just standing there, not knowing how to react.

'Don't you see? This is brilliant news! We have more time! It could take Assa ages to find the real orb.'

A little voice in Lola's head reminded her of what Natella had just told her,

'Or a few days.'

The anti-climactic moment had passed, as had the brief moment of relief.

Now it was just a matter of waiting again.

Lola looked out to sea: it was so calm and tranquil and always had been and always would be to her. She could watch the sea for hours on end.

She told her friends she was going to go home; they all decided on the same, given it was quite late. She apologised to her friends for her rashness and impatience, but they forgave her. They didn't know what to believe any more. One minute, they were told the human race was close to getting wiped out, the next it turned out that might not actually happen for some time. Lola could understand their hesitation to believe, and realised again that they hadn't seen or heard as much as she had. She had experienced so much in the past few months that she never thought she'd ever experience.

As they made their way to the monorail station, it started heavily raining all of a sudden.

'I'm surprised that beach wasn't busier given the other one's closed,' Thomas remarked after some time of silence. No one replied to him, however, as everyone was lost in their own thoughts and speculation. The monorail was just as quiet. Lola looked about and saw that hardly anyone looked jovial or happy.

Before long, Lola was back at home. She didn't know what she should be doing. She'd apologised to her friends once more for her rash behaviour, which clearly seemed to have affected them. No one really understood, she thought to herself, because it's too much to believe.

There was one person who she knew could she talk to. She told her parents she was going there; they told her to be back soon because it was getting late and the rain was still pouring incessantly.

'Where has this rain come from?' Lola's mum exclaimed as she got Lola's coat for her, 'it seems to have come from nowhere. Remember your coat,' she said, offering her her coat.

'Thanks mum. I'll be back soon.'

Soon enough, she had arrived at her destination; she knocked at the door but had to wait for a few minutes before the door opened.

'Lola! You're drenched! What are you doing here?' asked Demzel.

'I had to see you. No one else will believe me. Have you heard what happened today?'

'Do you mean that creature that flew up out of the sea?'

'Yes, well, it was Assa, and it had the orb.'

'Are you sure it was Assa?'

'Something told me it was Assa. I just knew it was Assa.'

'Come in. Where are my manners?'

Lola was admitted in and she sat down on Demzel's front room settee. It felt good to be somewhere dry. She was shivering a little.

'Do you want something to drink?'

'What do you have?'

'I could get you a hot chocolate; you look freezing.'

'Thanks.'

'So you're telling me that Assa now has the orb?' asked Demzel from the kitchen.

'Well, not exactly. Natella told me that the orb is actually a fake and that the real orb is still out there somewhere.'

'Where?'

'She doesn't know and said she wouldn't tell me even if she did know.'

'Let's look this up online,' Demzel said excitedly. He bumbled over to his computer, handed Lola her drink and went on to an up-to-date local news website.

'Aha! Here we are,' he exclaimed. Lola looked at the web page: the main news item was that of the creature flying out of the sea and across Helmia.

Demzel quickly scanned the article, then said, 'very interesting indeed. It appears that this creature, Assa, flew out of the sea, hovered for a bit then started flying toward Etolin Island. Someone saw it fly across the sky in Puddlepond and another person saw it flying off towards the island. It's amazing how fast these things get on the Internet, absolutely astounding.'

'And very handy, too.'

'I thank all the people who take their time to post what they've seen online. Hmm, so does Assa know the orb is a fake?'

'There's no way to tell.'

'Obviously. A stupid question on my part.'

'But there's no doubt Assa will soon realise the orb is a fake, and then the search will start all over again.'

'Are you okay, Lola? You seem a bit, well, different.'

Lola looked into Demzel's eyes then looked into her lap and sighed.

'I don't know where to begin, I really don't. I am so very worried about Assa and the orb and I truly believe Assa could wipe us out with the orb. I know the 'proof' isn't concrete, I mean, I've heard the same thing from a few different sources who say the same thing, but does that mean it's true? Part of me is so worried, yet another part of me realises that I don't know it for certain. How can I be certain? People are reluctant to believe, and I understand that, but what if it is real? How do you convince people of something so unbelievable?'

'I believe you and always have. It is something that is so hard for people to believe, I understand that.'

'I want to warn the world but know it's practically pointless because no one would believe me and it might turn out that Assa doesn't get the real orb for ages and we all play the waiting game and then people would grow tired of waiting for something that might never happen.'

'There is no way to prove this Assa being is the creator of this universe. It's empirically impossible, I think. People have always debated this: it's one of the big questions. Did the universe come into being of its own accord or did it have some creator? If there is a creator, then did that creator come into being of its own accord or did it itself have a creator? I think about these big questions sometimes and it hurts my head. The fact that Assa created this universe is still something I struggle to fully comprehend, but I believe wholeheartedly. It all makes sense to me from what I've heard and everything you've told me. It's something so hard to believe, that our universe has a creator, but it's a perfectly possible supposition.'

'Do you think it stops at Assa?'

'What do you mean?'

'Suppose Assa is definitely the creator of this universe, do you think Assa has a creator? It's a question I've never considered before.'

'I can't say really. It could be that this, realm, that Assa's from might have nothing beyond it that it came from. Or it might be that Assa's realm was created and that creator was created. The question is: do you stop at one or do you keep going on forever?'

Lola tried to decide on an answer but realised she couldn't.

'It's impossible to find the answer.'

'There are many questions we will never be able to answer,' sighed Demzel, 'which leaves us all the more thirsty for knowledge.'

'And then there's Hannah as well.'

'You think they did something to her, don't you?'

'It's obvious they did. Everything's back to normal now with her, but what's eating away at me is not knowing what happened to her.'

'I'm sure she is and will be fine.'

Lola lost herself in her thoughts for a few moments while Demzel kept looking online for information.

'Look at this!' Demzel exclaimed, making Lola jump.

'What?'

Breaking news. There's been an explosion on Etolin Island.'

'What?'

'It happened about half an hour ago. It says here an entire building just burst into flames. Look: "the notoriously secretive building, which government sources insist is abandoned, despite it being speculated that workers have been seen entering it, burst into flames almost spontaneously."

'I hope no one got hurt.'

'I think it's likely a lot of people got hurt, I'm afraid. I wouldn't be surprised if some have died, given the size of the explosion.'

'Do they have any ideas why it happened?'

'Hmmm. No theories have been proposed so far. It seems like some sort of bomb went off – this wasn't something gradual like a fire spreading, it was the entire building going up in flames in one go.'

'Don't you think it's a bit of a coincidence that Assa is seen flying towards the island, then a short time later, this building goes up in flames?'

'It does sound very likely that Assa is involved in this somehow. I agree, it is too much of a coincidence.'

'I'm scared, Demzel.'

'I am a bit too, but being scared won't do any good. We need to be strong and hope for the best.'

'What good will hope do? We need to stop Assa getting the orb! Hoping's not going to do anything.'

'But what can we do? Really, what is there we can do?'

'That's just it; I don't know,' Lola confessed disappointingly, 'either kill Assa or keep hiding the orb forever.'

Lola resented herself for what she'd just said. Then she realised both were arduous tasks anyway, and both were practically impossible. She looked out the window: it was still raining heavily.

'I'm going to go home now,' she told Demzel.

'Thanks for everything,' she added.

'Look, Lola. I understand your frustration. I know you want to scream it out to the world and convince everyone of something you believe to be real and impending. But realistically, if you announced the human race is going to be wiped out, what will everyone do? Some will prepare defences, but most people would just panic, and they would do that on an unbelievably large scale. It's only natural to do so.'

'So you think it's better everyone didn't know?'

'Part of me would tell them in advance, but like I said before, they'd only panic. Another part of me would delay telling them for as long as possible, but we simply don't know when it's going to happen. Are you glad you know?'

'I'm not really sure, to be honest. Now that I think about it, I realise that knowing all this has made me more paranoid and impatient than before. All I want is for everything to be like it was before these aliens came and disrupted everything. I know that's not going to happen, so, realistically, what I want most is for Assa to be stopped.'

Lola paused for a second then said: 'do you want to go to the island and see that base?'

'It'd be interesting, certainly, but there wouldn't be too much to see.'

'I'm thinking of going there and asking what exactly happened, you know, find some eye-witnesses.'

'There'll be statements from eye-witnesses online pretty soon, I imagine.'

'I know, but they always get abridged or distorted.'

'True.'

'Do you want to go then?'

'When?'

'Well, there's no time like the present.'

'I'll check what time the last ferry is,' Demzel said excitedly as he went back to the computer.

Lola was feeling excited and adventurous. She knew this was a very impulsive decision and would probably be just as effective as waiting for a bit then checking the news online, but she couldn't resist the prospect of this little excursion.

'Yes! We might just make the last ferry over to Etolin

and back. You'll have to get permission from your parents, of course.'

'Do you think they'll let me?'

'They should. They know you're with me.'

Lola got out her phone and saw it was nearly half ten. She phoned home.

'Hello, dad. I was just wondering if Demzel and I could quickly go over to Etolin island and then come straight back.' She realised being straight to the point was perhaps the most effective way of putting it.

'What do you want to go there for at this time?'

'What do I say?' Lola whispered to Demzel, who couldn't think of any suitable reply.

'Erm, there's apparently been an alien sighting over there and we thought we'd go and check it out.'

'I'll just check with your mother.'

'They're not going to let me,' Lola whispered to Demzel.

'We really don't feel sure about letting you go, but yes, you can go, but you stay with Demzel all the time, understood? And we want you to have your phone on at all times and be back as soon as you can get back, OK?'

'Yes, Dad.'

'Be very safe.'

'Bye Dad, love you.'

'Love you too.'

Lola hung up the phone.

'Yes! I can go! I'm surprised they let me, to be honest, though I guess they haven't heard about the explosion on the island.'

'Let's go then.'

They soon got into Demzel's car and he drove quite fast to the marina, from where they managed to catch the last ferry over to the island, Demzel paying for Lola's ticket.

'Thanks, Demzel.'

'No worries. This ferry departs from Etolin at quarter to twelve, so we'll not have long to ask questions.'

They were now on the ferry, yet it was still pouring of rain. Demzel had brought his umbrella, yet they both ended up wet by the time they got on. The ferry was quite small, with only a small indoor cabin and a few outdoor seats, as the journey to Etolin didn't take that long. There were larger ferries for busier times of the year.

Lola and Demzel sat in the indoor cabin, which was quite chilly.

'I never thought I'd be doing this,' Lola said to Demzel, 'thank you for coming with me.'

'It's my pleasure. I'm just as curious as you to find out what exactly happened.'

'I'm surprised they're letting people go there, to be honest.'

Lola saw there was a third person in the cabin: a young man in a smart suit. Demzel noticed him too.

'Is that you, Maxwell?'

'Sure is, Mr. Harmelo.'

'Please, call me Demzel. Lola, this is a former student of mine. Maxwell, this is a current student of mine.'

'Nice to meet you, Lola.'

Maxwell smiled a charming and confident smile at Lola, who tried to do the same back.

'So what are you doing here at this time?' Maxwell asked.

'We might ask you the same question,' Demzel replied coyly.

'You first,' Maxwell proposed, his voice velvety and slick. He had an air of importance and grandeur about him, Lola thought. He was probably very successful in whatever he did given his attire.

'We're going over to Etolin to see what's going on first-hand. It was an impulsive yet brilliant decision of Lola's.'

'I see. What do you know about it so far?'

'Well, we know a creature flew up out of the sea and was seen heading in the direction of Etolin Island. Some time later, according to the news, that so-called 'abandoned' building just burst into flames. We reckon something's up and we thought being at the scene of the occurrence would provide us with more accurate information than if we'd simply read about it online.'

'I see,' Maxwell remarked calmly.

'Is that why you're going?'

'Yes, as it so happens. I work in the village, as it happens, but today was an off day – I mean, a day off for me and as soon as I heard what had happened, I immediately came here. I read it online, I meant to say.'

'Do you know whether people do actually work at the abandoned building on Etolin Island?'

Maxwell took a deep breath before replying rather hast-ily:

'No one works there, because as you quite rightly said, the building is *abandoned*. I myself work on the island and I also have friends who live in the island, whom I am on my way to see and they assure me that the building has been completely empty for years.'

'You work at the abandoned building, don't you?' Demzel inferred, his eyes squinted at his former pupil. Lola was shocked at Demzel implying this.

'No I don't actually, because as I have already said, the building is *abandoned*, but I have friends who live in the island and - I wish to see if they're okay.'

'You could have just phoned them,' Demzel fired back.

'I couldn't get through and was worried so I thought I'd come here and see for myself.'

'Demzel, can I have a word with you?' Lola asked.

'Excuse us for a moment, Maxwell.'

Lola got up and walked over to the far edge of the cabin, which wasn't that far from where they'd been sitting.

'Who is he?' she whispered hastily.

'If you're thinking what I'm thinking, you're probably right. He's acting too nervous to be telling the truth.'

'*Do* you know where he works?'

'I don't know, unfortunately. I don't believe he works in the village. Look, he's on the phone.'

Lola looked back at Maxwell, who was speaking calmly but quietly on the phone to someone, looking from left to right frantically.

'He was even like this back in school; he was really fidgety, twitchy and quite scared of everything really. He's putting on some sort of tough guy act, alright.'

'How can you be so sure?'

'I taught him for five years and, while other pupils changed over time, he became more and more frightened and reclusive. I'm most surprised that he's in a suit, to be honest.'

They both then resumed their seats. The rain was still ceaselessly pouring outside.

'Sorry about that,' Demzel said in a friendly manner.

'I was just feeling a bit nervous about going to Etolin. I guess I persuaded Demzel to come with me quite impulsively without fully realising what we'd possibly see.'

The atmosphere between the three was tense and awkward.

'We should be there soon,' Maxwell said as he looked outside at the downpour.

'Can you believe this weather? Demzel remarked after a few minutes' silence.

'It's ridiculous if you ask me,' replied Maxwell, 'absolutely ridiculous. Hopefully this won't continue on into tomorrow,' he was now messing with his hair.

'Is everything okay, Maxwell?'

'Yeah, I'm fine, thanks, Mr. Harmelo, I mean, do I call you Demzel now?'

'Yes, please do call me Demzel.'

Maxwell took another deep breath. Lola didn't quite know what to make of him. He looked to be in his late twenties, with combed-over light brown hair, a thin, tall frame and very small eyes. If they hadn't met yet Demzel had described him to her, Lola would have pictured someone exactly like the person unbuttoning the top button of his shirt in front of her.

'It's warm in here,' Maxwell said, eliciting nothing but curiosity from Lola. She found his temperament to be quite puzzling, and thought he was clearly a bag of nerves for some reason.

'It's almost like when the snow was falling really heavily,' Demzel commented as he watched the rain hit the windows and trickle down.

'I hope not,' Lola replied, 'last time we had extreme weather, people died in the blizzards. We don't need more extreme weather to be killing people off. Not to mention those snowmen!'

After a few moments, the rain had completely stopped, much to everyone's relief. Soon enough, the ferry stopped and they all disembarked at the marina. The ferryman told them the last ferry back to Helmia would be leaving in forty minutes.

'Plenty of time,' Demzel reassured Lola. They could see in the distance to the right the burning building, illuminated in the black of night. It was only a few hundred metres or so away, Lola estimated, and she knew from having been here before that the building was surrounded a dense forest on the right hand side of the island, while the left hand side of the island was where the small seaside village of Etolin was located. The plume of smoke issuing from the building was clearly visible, lighted by the raging fire it was emanating from.

'I didn't realise it was that bad,' Lola said to Demzel; it was quite an eerie sight to see the village sitting quiet and somewhat dormant, which heavily contrasted what was happening on the other side of the island.

They walked off the dock and on to a street lined with cafes, souvenir shops and the odd B&B. Although the darkness fragmented the full view of it, Lola thought it looked a bit rundown.

'We need to follow this road to the right and it will take us into the forest and another road will split off from this, which will take us to the building.'

'Where's Maxwell?' Lola asked; they'd seen him get off the ferry – he'd got off first, but they hadn't seen him since.

'I thought he'd at least say goodbye to us,' Demzel replied rather sullenly. Lola looked all around her to check, but couldn't see anyone, apart from a few drunken revellers. The street felt eerie and creepy.

'Let's go then.'

They started walking alongside the road and into the darkened forest, its trees all tightly packed together, swallowing up anything that entered it. True to its appearance, as soon as they entered it, the darkness seemed to increase tenfold, such that even the few stars previously visible in the sky above were no longer there, nor was much of the sky or the moon. The trees were old and very tall. Lola looked back and saw the road they'd come up, sparsely illuminated by the lights on either side of it. She could just about see the marina and the glassy water in the distance.

'Are you sure this is safe?' Lola asked Demzel as they started on a curve.

'Lola, you disregard the word 'safe'.'

Lola laughed a little, then replied, 'what if something happens?'

'If something happens, it happens and we deal with it. This forest is largely uninhabited and this island has an almost a crime-free village. It's a very sleepy village, as you know, so sleepy that the people who live here can't even be bothered to commit crimes.'

'That's slightly reassuring.'

'Oh look, there's the fork in the road!' Demzel exclaimed.

Lola saw the split in the road and knew that soon enough they'd be heading directly for the site of the explosion. She was starting to regret coming here.

They walked on and on; Lola got a fright when a fire engine came zooming by, a flash of light and a rush of sound that both faded away as quickly as they'd come.

They were on the road that led to the building. Lola could feel herself getting more and more apprehensive though she didn't know exactly why.

'Thanks for coming here with me,' she said to Demzel.

'You're welcome. I'm glad to know someone as crazily impulsive as I am.'

'Ditto.'

Those were the last words they spoke before they turned a corner and saw the massive building, which was still ablaze and burning wildly. Even though Lola and Demzel were about a hundred feet from it, they were still buffeted by the heat.

They'd both stopped in their tracks. There was the building, parts of which had crumbled to the ground, overcome by the burning, and some police cars, ambulances and fire engines, which seemed to be stationed around the perimeter of the building to tackle the inferno from all sides. There were only a few people being consoled by the medics. They were yelling and crying loudly, clearly distressed and panicked. Lola examined the scene more closely, yet could see no more survivors apart from the few she'd just seen, one of whom was being questioned by the police. All the vehicles were parked that were on a plain.

'Should we really be here?' she whispered to Demzel.

'I don't see why not.'

They approached the random assortment of vehicles. The fire-fighters were shouting commands to each other, some were operating hoses, which were shooting continuous jets of water into the fire, jets which were so powerful and concentrated they were louder than the crackling blaze.

The first people they came to were a paramedic attending to a woman in a suit who didn't seem injured in any way, but was clearly traumatised.

'Who are you?' another medic shouted over to Lola and Demzel.

'We live nearby. We just came to see what was going,' Demzel lied. The paramedic came over to them, a sturdy young man of a heavy build and frame.

'Well, everything's under control here, so if you'd be so kind as to let us get on.'

Then the medic left and went to attend to someone, a man this time, who didn't look hurt at all either.

It was then that Lola noticed something she hadn't discerned before: a few of the vehicles were press vans and there were reporters and their cameramen setting up to do reports on the explosion.

They went over to the journalists, the first of whom they came to was a man who was drinking a large cup of coffee and was snapping at his cameraman.

'Hurry up, Steve! Am I paying you to dawdle all the time?'

'I'm trying, I'm trying!'

'If this fire dies out before we can get the perfect shot of it, *you're* fired!'

'I'm almost done,' he replied as he fiddled about with the camera, which to Lola looked extremely expensive. She thought it best to speak to him once he was done. Soon enough, his cameraman had given the thumbs and the journalist positioned himself in front of the inferno. Lola looked through the camera and saw he looked much closer to the building than he actually was.

'Etolin has been sensationally rocked by a massive explosion which occurred just recently in the late hours of Saturday night at the abandoned building in the forest, which is one of many reasons for the island's notoriety. The building has long been rumoured to be the home of some top-secret government operation, though this has never been confirmed. However, the rumours persist and people claim to have seen people entering and leaving the building. Tonight, we have seen people who were *in the building* been tended to by paramedics. As we understand it, seven people were in the building and managed to get out, all of whom are in work attire. What were they doing there if the building is supposedly abandoned? The mystery thickens.'

The reporter had been glib and slick in his speech. Once the report was done, his demeanour changed: he was back to snapping at his cameraman.

'Was it perfect?'

'Yes, Mike, it was, I promise you,' Steve assured him as he tried to stifle a yawn.

'We'll have to interview some of the people from the building.'

Lola and Demzel wandered over to one of the other journalists, who was also doing a report.

'It remains thus far unknown how and why this explosion happened, though as soon as we know anything, we'll let you know. How was that, Rodney?'

'Good.'

'Thank you.'

'Excuse me?' she said to Lola after catching her eye.

'My name is Doreen Long and I am a reporter for the Helmia Daily. Do you know anything about what's happened here tonight?' she asked politely, shoving a microphone into Lola's personal space. She soon felt the glare of the camera.

'I don't really know anything. I live in Helmia and me and my teacher, Demzel here, we came to see what had happened for ourselves. All we know is that this building went up in flames, but we do think the creature that flew up out of the sea earlier may be responsible. That's all we know, I'm afraid.'

'An interesting theory. I hadn't thought of that myself, Lola. Hmmm. That does make sense now, doesn't it, Rodney? Yes, I remember hearing that it was last seen flying towards Etolin! Ah! You've put two and two together and probably got four. I like your way of thinking, Lola.'

'Thank you. What do you know about the explosion?'

'It appears the entire building went up in a flash, and when the emergency services got here, they found those seven people on the grass. They were panicking and scared, but relatively unhurt.'

'Have you interviewed any of them yet?'

'No, but we're going to.'

With that, Doreen and Rodney left and went over to one of the people been cared for. Lola and Demzel followed.

'What were you all doing in an abandoned building?'

Doreen asked, having thrust the microphone into the woman's face.

'No comment. I'm not speaking to anyone.'

'Don't pull that on me, Missie, because that basically confirms, along with your suit, that you were working there.'

'I have no idea what you're talking about,' she said stubbornly.

'I wasn't born yesterday, so don't talk to me like I was.'

'You're getting nothing out of me.'

'Do you know what caused the explosion?' Lola asked.

'I have no idea.'

'Come on, Rodney, we're not going to get anything out of this one.'

They moved on to a trembling young man who was wrapped in a thin blanket.

'What do you know about the explosion? Any ideas as to who could have wanted to blow this place up?' Doreen asked the startled man, the microphone in its usual place and the camera rolling.

'I – I really don't know anything,' he said, then he took a deep breath and seemed to be trying to steady himself.

'What do you and the others do here?' Doreen asked persistently, 'there's no point denying anything because the whole world now knows this place wasn't abandoned.'

The man remained silent, however.

'Are you going to answer me?'

'I don't know anything.'

'What happened immediately before the explosion?'

'I was busy and then they said something was coming and we left then it exploded.'

'Could you be more precise? What's your name by the way? Come on, tell us!'

'I – I'm Ryan. We were busy and then we were told we had to get out straight away. Most of us didn't make it.'

Ryan broke down into tears and started panicking.

'What was coming?' Lola asked; she thought she knew the answer already, but wanted confirmation.

'I don't know.'

'Yes you do, Ryan,' Doreen replied sternly.

'Something was flying towards us. We were told we had to get out straight away.'

'Who told you, Ryan?'

Ryan hesitated a little, overcome by the shock and suddenness of it all.

'Come on, Ryan, these questions aren't going to answer themselves. People have a right to know.'

Ryan was hesitant once more.

'You might as well tell us because everyone knows about this place and what you're doing here will soon come to light anyway because the government won't be able to deny it.'

'OK, fine! You're not going to believe this anyway.'

'I don't care, just tell the camera,' Lola could tell Doreen was getting more and more impatient and flustered.

'We had a creature in there, an alien creature, who we were examining and it told us to run.'

'You had an alien creature in there? Was it one of the aliens who have been sighted in Helmia recently?'

Doreen's questions came thick and fast.

'It was a different one, a shape-shifter. We've had it there for a few months.'

'I see. So I'm assuming this alien saw this something approaching and warned you?'

'One of the workers saw the creature fly up out of the sea and watched as it started heading our way and told Hyuul, who then told us to escape. Only a few of us made it.'

'Hyuul? Is that the name of the alien?'

'Yes.'

Lola was flabbergasted. She didn't know what to think; she could only listen.

'And where is this Hyuul now?'

'It flew off saying it couldn't wait around to save us.'

'It can fly? Wow. So why didn't this alien want to hang around and save you if it had bothered to tell you the thing approaching was so dangerous?'

'It said…'

'What did it say?'

'All it said was that we were not to divulge the location of the orb, not that that means anything to you.'

Lola looked at Demzel, her eyes wide and her mind abuzz with wonder and adrenaline.

'I'm going to be fired for this, I can tell,' Ryan moaned to himself.

'I'm sorry to say this, Ryan, but grow up!' Doreen whinged to Ryan. 'That place is gone and I don't think you have a job to go back to anyway.'

'Who knows where this orb is?' Lola asked a disconcerted Ryan.

'We don't know where it is. All Hyuul told us was that it needed to be hidden.'

'Yes, but where?'

'Only a few of us knew. I wasn't one of them.'

'Yes you were,' Lola said, 'because earlier you said you were told not to tell anyone where it was, which means you know where it is.'

'Damn it!'

Lola felt proud of her cunning.

'Hyuul's gone for the orb and Assa's presumably giving chase,' she told Demzel, who nodded assent.

'Tell us where the orb is, Ryan.'

'We were sworn not to.'

'That thing that blew up the building is an alien called

Assa, who is after the orb. If you tell us where it's hidden, we might be able to stop Assa getting it.'

Ryan took another deep breath.

'I don't know exactly, but it was hidden somewhere in the Mariana Trench.'

'Damn!' Lola shouted. She knew this meant all they could do once more was wait – Hyuul had ensured no human could retrieve the orb.

'This is fascinating stuff, Ryan. Is there anything else you'd like to add?' Doreen asked, trying to get one last drop of information.

'No,' Ryan snapped. Lola and Demzel looked at each other once more. Lola could feel paranoia and anxiety creeping over her yet again. She was glad that she knew, but she was even more panicked that it was only a short while before Assa would inevitably find the orb, if its pursuit of Hyuul were successful.

She looked at Doreen and Rodney, who were just doing their jobs and, although Doreen was obviously very inquisitive, she was only so for the sake of her job. There wasn't any genuine interest there, Lola thought. To them it was just a story, to Lola and Demzel, it was all real.

'Are you very sure?' Doreen asked one more time.

'There's one more thing,' Ryan said, sounding defeated.

'Is it about the alien? The explosion? What you're doing here?'

'I heard something just after the explosion.'

'What?' Doreen snapped.

'A voice. I don't know whose but it wasn't someone I knew from work.'

'And what did they say?'

'The Darkness of Light will never stop me.'

Chapter 18 –
The Interruption

'The Darkness of Light will never stop me?' Lola repeated.

'Yes, I think that's what was said.'

'Do you have any idea who said it?'

'I have no idea.'

Ryan was clearly traumatised and seemed appalled at
himself for having spilt the secrets he'd been hiding.

'What is this Darkness of Light?' Doreen asked.

'I have no idea.'

'Hmm. Rodney, I think we're done here.'

Lola watched as Doreen thanked Ryan for his information and Rodney started putting his camera away. Ryan
meandered over to sit by one the ambulances. He sat down
and put his head in his hands.

'Well, he was easy to crack,' Doreen said to Lola as she
passed her.

'Are you done here now?'

'I think so. We've got the footage we need, so unless
something happens, we'll by on our way.'

'I hope he's okay,' Lola said, looking over to Ryan.

'He will be. He's overcome by what's happened and, well,

you have to be tough in this business to crack them. He's just survived an explosion which wiped out most of his colleagues and his work place, so he was naturally going to be very vulnerable and therefore easier to extract information from.'

'What do you make of what he says?'

'It's a load of hoo-hah if you ask me. I can't believe most of what he said.'

'So how are you going to report this then?'

'You'll have to wait and see. Come on, Rodney! We've got our scoop here,' and with that, the two got into their van after saying goodbye to Lola and Demzel.

'Wait!' Demzel shouted as they started driving off. They ran over to the van.

'Would you mind giving us a lift back to the marina?'

Doreen eyed him for a moment, then acquiesced.

'You'll have to get in the back mind.'

Rodney got out and opened the back door for them. Demzel and Lola climbed in and immediately started discussing what they'd just found out.

'But surely Hyuul wouldn't just lead Assa to the orb?'

'I don't think so. I'm guessing Hyuul fled so as to avoid the explosion.'

'So now only Hyuul knows the precise location of the orb?'

'It appears so.'

'But surely Hyuul wouldn't go to the Mariana Trench? That would just be leading Assa to the orb!'

'Let's hope not.'

Lola was worrying. To take her mind off things, she texted her parents and told them she was on her way back.

'At least this little trip's told us a lot,' Demzel remarked.

'Yeah,'

Lola could see Demzel looking at her.

'Are you okay?' he asked.

'Something's bugging me. It's what Assa said, according to Ryan.'

'The Darkness of Light will never stop me?'

'Yeah, that's it. I had a dream recently and in it I saw that phrase.'

'Maybe you've heard it before?'

'I don't think so. In my dream I was sitting some exam and all the questions were questions I'd been asking myself recently that I didn't know the answer to. One of them was about the Darkness of Light, which struck me as odd because I'd never heard of it before.'

'How very odd. Are you sure you haven't heard it somewhere before. Maybe you did but didn't realise it at the time.'

'I'm pretty sure. It stood out for some reason.'

They had stopped. The back door was opened and they got out and thanked Doreen and Rodney for the ride. They were back at the marina. Lola watched as the press van drove off into the night. She looked to the forest and saw the building was still blazing.

'I hope they manage to put it out,' she said.

'It's just a shame it wasn't raining here – that would have helped it a lot.'

They were soon on the last ferry of the night to Helmia. As they departed, Lola watched the island grow and smaller. She could see the blaze lighting up the night.

The rain soon came back thick and fast. The downpour was heavier than previously. It pelted the windows of the cabin furiously.

Lola was silent for most of the trip back; for once, she didn't want to voice her worries.

They arrived back at Helmia and Demzel drove Lola back home. Lola's parents had texted her saying they were going to bed and that she had to lock up and put the alarm. When she got home, she collapsed on to the settee and spent an unknown amount of time there. She curled up and put the TV on to take her mind off things.

She watched a few news reports about the explosion – it had made national news and was the top story. A rush of questions came to her, one of them pressing down on her more than the others. She went and turned on the family computer, then went on a search engine and typed in 'the Darkness of Light'.

The results that came up were random and seemed to have no relevance to anything. There was a play of that name, as well as a collection of poems and even a theme park ride. It was also a slang expression in a small part of some country she'd never heard of and there seemed to be a few TV episodes with that name.

'So what is the Darkness of Light?' Lola asked no one.

She was determined to find out why Assa had said this random phrase, which she'd dreamt only recently and what it all meant. As she searched on and on, finding nothing of real importance – at least, it seemed that way to her – she started getting sleepier and sleepier until she fell asleep at the computer desk.

Lola was in a world inside her head. She was in an alien ship soaring across some ocean, going higher and higher into the clouds. She was waving goodbye to Earth and her whole life. It was a dream she often had, yet never had she actually left Earth, for the dream always came to an end before they left the Earth's atmosphere. However, this time it was different: they were heading somewhere Lola knew not. She was full of excitement and eager for exploration. She asked one of the aliens, who she couldn't see, where it was that they were going.

'We are travelling into the Darkness of Light,' the alien replied mystically.

'Where is that?'

'We don't know, and neither do you.'

'But you must know where it is if you're flying me there.'

'We don't even know what it is.'

Before she could reply, she was abruptly woken up by her mother.

'Lola, come on, we have to go now!' she cried.

'What's going on?' Lola yawned, eyes still half-shut.

'Go and quickly pack some clothes and meet us down here in a minute,' her mum said before running upstairs.

Lola could tell something was wrong. Looking out of the living room window, she saw it was very early in the morning and the sun was only just rising.

'What's going on?' Lola asked her dad as he came downstairs rather hurriedly.

'Just go and get ready quickly, get a few clothes, then wait for us,' he said sternly. Lola did as she was told; once ready, she waited in the living room, looking out of the window. Her parents very soon came in from the kitchen.

'Do you have your phone with you?' her mum asked.

'Yeah,' Lola got it out and turned it on.

'Right, that's everything, let's go,' her dad said solemnly.

'Have you phoned your parents?' he asked Lola's mum, who replied that she had.

'Good.'

They were soon in the car. Lola's dad hadn't yet put the key in; he was just sitting there.

'Are you okay, dad?' Lola asked.

'We shouldn't be doing this, Ange; we should just stay put,' he said, looking at his wife.

'What's going on?' Lola asked more forcefully than before.

'Everyone has been ordered to go to the theme park right now. We have to go *now!*' Lola's mum shouted at her dad, who put the key in and pulled out of the drive.

'The theme park? Who's told us to go to there at this time?' Lola laughed.

'Never mind, Lola, there's nothing to worry about.'

'Tell me everything, damn it! I deserve to know!'

There was silence in the car. Lola could tell she's spoken out of terms but she didn't care.

'Those grey aliens told us to, OK! They've been going round to people's houses and have told everyone if they're not at the theme park by midnight, they'll be killed,' Lola's mum shrieked.

'Mum, calm down.'

'*How* can I calm down, Lola?' Lola's mum snapped.

'Sorry.'

'No, I should be the one saying sorry. I'm sorry, I'm just worried out of my head.'

'We weren't going to tell you. We thought you shouldn't have to deal with things like this.' Lola's dad added in a calmer manner than his wife.

'Well you should have told me straight away; I have a right to know these things.'

'Lola, you're fifteen! You're too young,' Lola's mum shouted.

'Too young to be told we have to go to the theme park or we'll get killed? Thanks.'

'Too young to be told that we're going to get killed anyway!' Lola's mum spat out before bursting into tears. Her husband comforted her as she broke down.

'And Andrew's not here,' she heard her mum sob.

So that was it: this was the beginning of the end; Assa

must have found the real orb at long last. Lola sat in silence and watched, unable to see anything properly for her mind was too abuzz with questions to take in anything else. There had to be some way to get the orb from Assa and hide it, or even destroy it completely. It had to be destructible, it just had to be.

The extremity of the situation hadn't yet hit her, such was her hope that something would happen to delay the extermination for even longer. She knew some resistance would be happening somewhere but was uncertain of whether it would be successful or not.

Before long, they were on their way. Lola looked out of the window and saw an almost empty street. She did see, however, the occasional group of people getting into a car. It was a family of four, parents and two young children in nightgowns. The father was snapping at his wife to get in the car; the children were in the back. Lola had had enough of this.

'So some Greys came up to the house, knocked on the door, then told us to drive to our deaths?' she demanded.

'They were on the T.V. as well. It just came on and there was this announcement telling us we had to go.'

'Who made the announcement?'

Lola saw her parents look at each other, then her dad said, 'The Prime Minister, Marvin Jacobson.'

'What!'

'We don't know why or how. But he was there telling us we had to vacate our homes and congregate at the theme park otherwise we'd get killed.'

'So you're doing this just because the Prime Minister told you to?'

'If the Prime Minister tells us to do something, I think we should be doing it. Anyway, it wasn't just him. Two of those grey aliens were there making sure he said everything they wanted him to.'

'You're joking?' Lola replied incredulously.

'That's why we believe it all.'

'Why would the Prime Minister advise us to do this?'

'We really don't know, Lola.'

'So what exactly happened during this announcement then?'

'He was at his desk with two of those grey aliens. He told us we all had to gather in the theme park and wait further instruction and that those who weren't there would be killed then I turned it off.'

'There were Greys there?'

'Yes. If it had been the Prime Minister by himself telling us to go to the theme park, I wouldn't have been convinced, but because the aliens were there – well, it just...'

'Makes it seem all the more real? Lola interjected.

Her dad nodded his head. Lola couldn't take it all in; she didn't know what to believe. So Assa had obtained the orb and had orchestrated this announcement to get everyone on the island into the theme park – but why? Surely Assa wanted to kill everyone in the world, not just those in Helmia? Or maybe Assa was taking it one place at a time – that was a preposterous idea, Lola thought to herself, though not entirely implausible.

'We can't go to the theme park!' Lola cried.

'Don't worry, we're not. We're getting off this island if it's the last thing we do.'

It had been Lola's dad that had done all the talking; Lola wondered what was going through her mum's mind.

'How are we going to get off the island?' Lola dared to ask, unsure of whether her parents had an idea.

'We'll get on the ferry to the mainland, then we're going to stay at your mum's parents'.'

'And what if the Greys won't let us?'

'Lola...'

'You have to be realistic, dad! These Greys clearly want us dead, and I guarantee you they're going to make sure none of us can get off the island.'

'Well, we're still trying.'

Lola wasn't sure whether the plan was a good one after all. She was certain all ways of getting off the island would be guarded, and, having once encountered the Greys, she wasn't sure she'd be able to survive another encounter with the sinister species.

On and on they drove along the quiet road. The tension in the car was such that no one talked any more. Lola's dad was full of confusion at the randomness of this happening, yet determined not to fall into the Greys' trap. Her mother, on the other hand, was being too quiet for herself; Lola guessed she was too frightened and befuddled to speak, which was understandable.

'The Greys didn't hurt you, did they?' asked Lola warily.

'No, they didn't. They just scared the hell out of me.'

'What did they do?'

'I woke up because there was a loud knocking at the door. I ignored it at first, thinking it was some drunks messing around, then I hear an even louder noise and go downstairs to see the door had been forced open and two Greys in the passageway.'

'You're joking?!'

'As soon as I saw them, I stopped on the stairs. I was petrified, Lola, honestly I was – I couldn't move I was that scared. I didn't know what on Earth they were or what they wanted.'

Lola remembered her own encounter with the Greys; she shuddered.

'Did they do anything to you?'

'They just told me that everyone had to be at the theme park by midnight and if we weren't there by then, we'd be killed, then I plucked up the courage to yell at them to get out. They then said we were all going to die anyway.'

There was a pause. Lola was overcome. Her dad carried on, 'they had these laser things in the hands, which was quite terrifying. I locked all the doors then saw the T.V. was on and that's when I saw the announcement; then I woke you two up.'

Lola yawned and then had an idea.

'Mum, give you me your phone, please.'

'What do you want it for?'

'The Internet.'

Lola's mum handed the phone over; Lola got on the Internet and searched for a recording of that announcement.

She'd found it. It was of a low quality, but she didn't mind, so long as she could hear what was being said. She quickly looked outside: they were tearing down a motorway into Puddlepond. The motorway was quite empty, but Lola could see a traffic jam up ahead.

She braced herself as she hit the play button.

The video had been shot in the Prime Minister's office only a few hours ago, according to the date stamp in the bottom right hand corner of the screen.

The Prime Minister was sitting at his desk, looking solemn and exhausted; it also looked as if he'd been crying.

'Citizens of Helmia, it is with the deepest regret that I have to address this message to you tonight.'

His speech was slow and paced. Four lights then came on, illuminating the space behind the desk, which had previously been pitch black. Two Greys appeared at either side of the premier.

'I have been informed by these aliens, who call themselves the Lormai, that the island of Helmia is, and always has been theirs, and that everyone on the island needs to gather at Puddlepond Theme Park and await further instruction. Anyone not at the park by midnight night, today being – I'm not doing this!'

'Say it, Marvin!' one of the Greys growled in its heavily-accented voice. Each of them placed a hand on the premier's shoulders. He shuddered, and took a deep breath.

'Now, Marvin!' the Grey yelled again.

'Anyone who isn't at the theme park by midnight tonight, will be...will be...killed.'

Just then, one of the Greys slapped the Prime Minister across the head. The screen started to go blurry, then the scene had changed completely: there were two people in a dark room; they were illuminated only by candles they were holding and the light coming from their camera.

'Are we live?' one asked the other; Lola then recognised the two people: her own headmaster, Harold Dazzle and the celebrity Mary Morton.

'Yes,' replied Harold.

'Everyone, this is Mary Morton and Harold Dazzle,' Mary said in a whisper; she was reading off a piece of paper she was illuminating with her candle.

'We have managed to intercept the transmission of the aliens' message in order to tell you not to gather at the theme park. The aliens, called Greys, will kill everyone who sets foot in the theme park. We are fighters and are determined not to see them win. As such, we have organised a meet-up point of our own, from where you will be transported to safety. Come to Puddlepond Stadium, where you will be safely transported to the mainland and the Greys won't be able to get you,' Mary said monotonously. She looked worried.

'The only way to guarantee your safety is if you're off this island. Don't bother going to any of the marinas or airports – they'll all have been closed by the aliens, but we've managed to secure enough transportation to get every single person off this island well before midnight.' Harold recited his part staring into the camera, unlike Mary.

'I repeat: come to the stadium where safe transportation awaits you.'

Then it ended.

'Dad, did you say you didn't see the entire announcement?'

'I stopped watching it when the Prime Minister started hesitating. I was too scared to see what might happen.'

'Well Harold Dazzle and Mary Morton interrupted the live transmission and told us secure transportation was being offered to everyone on the island.'

'Where?'

'In the stadium. They said the Greys are basically going to kill us all and that we need to get off the island.'

'We'll go to the stadium then.'

Lola's worry was slightly alleviated. She couldn't understand why those two had been the ones to offer Helmians a lifeline. It was too weird for her to fully comprehend. She handed her mum her phone back and told her to watch the full recording of the announcement, then she got out her own phone and dialled a number.

'Demzel! It's Lola.'

'Lola! Where are you?'

'We're on our way to the stadium. Did you see the announcement?'

'The one that got disrupted? Yes, I've seen but I'm not sure what to make of it.'

'We're going to the stadium now, but I'm not sure what to make of it all either.'

'I will see you at the stadium then.'

'I fear that this is it.'

'Me too,' Demzel said slowly; he hung up.

There was someone else Lola had to ring: Natella.

'Natella, it's Lola.'

'Lola, I'm glad you've called me. Did you see the announcement that Dazzle and Morton interrupted?'

'Yes, we're heading to the stadium right now.'

'No! Don't go to the stadium! It's a trick!'

'What?'

'Listen to me very carefully, OK? Mary and Harold were recruited by Assa fifteen years ago as sidekicks to help Assa. Mary was taken in by it all and wasn't strong enough to say no to Assa. We played on her weakness and got her to tell us everything Assa told her. She regrets ever having agreed to help Assa and is entirely on our side, but still is one of Assa's confidantes. And so, Assa has made her and Dazzle make this video.'

'Why though?'

'Morton and Dazzle appear like the good guys, offering us an escape route. People are going to go to the stadium for certain, whereas if they hadn't appeared in the video, there'd be no place people were guaranteed to go to, because realistically, very few will actually go to the theme park.'

'I see what you're getting at. So what should we do?' Lola demanded. She was impatient and the worry in her was rising by the second.

No reply came from Natella, however.

'Natella, what should we do?' Lola yelled. Her parents seemed to have not reacted to it, however; her mum was looking outside and her dad was concentrating on the road ahead.

'Lola, we believe Assa will visit both the theme park and the stadium to round up and kill people. The only thing you can do is leave the island.'

'And Assa definitely has the real orb?'

'Yes, Hyuul told Susie so.'

'How did Assa find it?'

'When the base exploded, Hyuul took off and flew away, but not in the direction of the orb. It turned out that when Hyuul got blasted by Assa and landed on the mainland a few months ago, Assa put an undetectable tracking device on Hyuul, who then fashioned the fake orb when under care at the base on Etolin Island as a decoy and had it placed in the sea to buy time. Assa gave chase to find Hyuul, managed to remove the tracking device and could see where Hyuul has been. The only place other than the base that came up was the Mariana Trench. Assa went there and, by using the tracker, was able to go to the exact place Hyuul had been to, thereby finding the orb.'

'How has this happened?'

'Lola, listen to me. Assa has the orb but defences are being mounted as we speak. The Blondies have come out of their ships and are preparing to fight, as is Hyuul.'

'What good is that going to do! Assa has the orb!'

'Lola, please calm down. We are trying our best to get the situation under control.'

'Well, that's not good enough,' Lola spat.

'Don't talk to me like that, Lola. I promise you we have been and are doing everything to stop this from happening. Now, I have to go. Get off the island as soon as possible and spread the message. No one, I repeat, no one is to set foot in either the theme park or the stadium.'

Natella hung up. Lola was reeling.

'Dad, pull over,' she said.

'Lola, we're almost there.'

'No, dad, we have to get off the island, please pull over.'

Her dad pulled over reluctantly.

'What is it, Lola?'

She looked at her parents and realised that now was the time to tell them everything; she could no longer hide everything she'd been through in the past few months.

'We need to get off this island, and this is the reason why.'

And so she told them; she told them about everything she knew about Assa, the Greys and the Blondies and even about when she encountered Greys at school and blatantly lied about it the next day.

'So that Assa you heard me mention is the creator of this universe and wants us all dead because we evolved by accident – we were never meant to even exist. It was meant to be the dinosaurs instead.'

Her mum was silent and sobbing; her dad looked quizzical. He then started driving again.

'We're going to the marina.'

'How could any of it be true?' her mother mumbled, the first time she'd spoken in a while, 'I mean, how could it even be possible?'

'I don't know all the ins and outs of it mum, but I promise you, what I know is true. What we need to do is tell everyone to leave the island straight away and not bother to go to either the theme park or the stadium. Get texting, mum.'

'Oh, right.'

Lola quickly composed a message and sent it to everyone in her phone book. Her mum seemed to be doing the same. Lola's dad asked her to send the same message to all of the contacts in his phone.

They were soon passing by the beach were the Blondies' landing site was. Lola watched with interest as the Blondies rushed about to and fro, some carrying large weapons, guns and sharp implements. She could still see the dome shielding them. One Blondie that was standing still seemed to be giving orders to the others.

'I hope they hurry up and do something,' Lola whispered to herself. She was pinning her hopes on these aliens who she knew hardly anything about. They had come here promising to help and so far they hadn't done anything. When would they satisfy their promise?

The car was starting to feel a little stuffy. Lola felt a bit warm in the forehead. Once aware of this, she neglected it.

They arrived at the marina to find a horde of other vehicles there too. They were all in a queue to get on a large ferry at the very end of the dock. It was the one that travelled between Helmia and the mainland and had space for over a hundred and ten cars. Lola quickly estimated there were only about thirty cars ahead of them.

'We'll get on alright,' she told her parents.

Up ahead, however, she saw that none of the cars at the very end of the dock were going on to the ferry, nor did any people appear to be doing the same. In fact, the ferry was very slowly moving away from the end of the dock.

Then she saw at the very end of the dock a silhouette of something. She couldn't quite make out what it was, for the blaring lights of the rising sun were obstructing her view.

Then she heard four very loud, distinctive noises, one right after the other, then there was a bang at the window Lola hadn't been looking out of; she turned round and saw a Grey staring back at her with its massive, glassy eyes. Lola let out a scream and could just about hear the sound of all the doors in the car being locked. She turned and saw there was an alien at each of the car's windows, as well as one standing directly in front of the car, a laser gun in its hand.

Her dad yelled for her and her mum to hold on as he put his foot down and attempted to run the Grey over, but the car didn't move.

'What the hell! Damn it!'

'Dad, why won't the car move?'

'The tyres must have been slashed.'

The Greys were pounding at the doors, all three people inside the car were screaming.

'Damn it!' Lola's dad yelled as he tried once more to move the car.

There was nothing they could do; they were surrounded by Greys.

'I'm going to get out of the car and distract them. I want you two to run,' Lola's dad said impulsively.

'You're not doing that! We're sticking together.'

The Greys were still incessantly banging at the windows. Everyone in the car was still screaming, unsure of what to do next.

Lola saw one of the Greys aim its laser gun at the side door and before she could react, there was a loud blast and the whole car seemed to have been shaken by it. Lola opened her eyes to see the door had been blasted open. She screamed as she clambered into the front of the car to avoid the Grey, which was climbing into the car, its small arm outstretched in a bid to get her.

'Mum! Dad! It's trying to get me!' she screamed, clinging to her parents with all the strength she could muster. Her parents grabbed hold of her very tightly and her dad was yelling at the Grey to let go of her. He pulled Lola forward and managed to lean over her and hit the alien; it let out a cry of pain and let go of Lola. She clambered over and sat on her mother's knee. Her dad tried driving again, but to no avail.

'We'll have to run for it,' he panted, once back in the front seat.

'They have guns, dad.'

'We have to do something!' he snapped back; Lola's mum was crying hysterically into her daughter's back.

Lola looked about her: all the Greys were still surrounding the car. They were looking at the humans inside with contempt and scorn. Lola decided then and there that she hated them.

The Greys then assembled and seemed to be discussing something. Lola's dad then ordered her and her mum to get out of the car and run for it. Both were now crying. Lola was just about to open the door, after being ordered several times by her increasingly impatient father, when she saw one of the Greys suddenly collapse. Then another one fell, then another and another. Pretty soon, they had all fallen to the floor.

'They've been shot!' her dad exclaimed.

He ordered Lola and her mum to stay inside while he went outside to investigate. Despite her mum's protests, Lola went outside too to see what happened.

Five Greys were lying there, each of them had indeed been shot, each of them was bleeding and looked very much incapacitated. One was even shaking.

They were exactly like the ones Lola had seen in school. They had the same massive, black eyes, the same shape head and were of roughly the same size. Two of these were a lighter shade of grey, one was a darker grey and the last two were varying shades of black. All had been wearing suits that seemed to shine in the morning sun.

'Get out of here!' a voice behind Lola and her dad sounded, making them both jump. They turned round to see two Blondies running towards them, each of whom had a large weapon of sorts in their hand.

Lola's dad told her to get back in the car, but Lola refused and insisted these aliens didn't mean any harm.

'Thank you so much,' Lola told them as they approached them.

'You need to get away from here and off this island,' one of the Blondies ordered.

'We were trying to till the Greys came.'

Lola could hear her mum banging on the car window.

She looked horrified. Lola went over to the window and reassured her mum that everything was alright.

'How do we get off the island?' she asked, 'the Greys are obviously making sure no one gets the ferry.'

The other Blondie was going to reply when something shot at it from somewhere Lola couldn't see and it clutched at its chest, its face contorted in agony, and it collapsed to the floor. The same happened to the other, but instead this one collapsed straight away after being shot at. It was then that Lola saw a trio of Greys running down the road towards them, all brandishing weapons.

'Out of the car, now!' Lola's dad shouted at her mum, banging on the window. She quickly clambered out of the car, still crying profusely. The rain was getting more and more sparse.

By the time her mum had got out of the car, however, it was too late. Lola felt something from behind grab hold of her: a Grey. They had also taken hold of each of her parents. Lola could even feel the Grey's saggy skin on its small hand and its cold breath on the back of her neck. She struggled and struggled but it was somehow managing to keep her restrained. She screamed out for her parents as more Greys arrived at the scene. Their weird, out-of-proportion bodies and their tight clothing made them look almost comical.

They were conversing in their own language, their voices raspy and guttural. Their large, glossy eyes were shining in the sun's rays.

One of them seemed to be the leader of this little group. It was a little shorter than the others, about a full head shorter than Lola, yet it looked the most menacing. When it looked at the two that were now holding Lola, Lola saw its eyes weren't as glossy as the others' and it had its full share of scratch marks and wounded on its black body. It snarled and shouted at the others, then it took out what looked to Lola like a syringe. Her parents were both furiously struggling, trying to kick, punch, break free. Lola was doing the same, but as she saw the alien approach her with the syringe in its hand, she stopped struggling and shouted to her parents that she loved them very much.

Her parents screamed as the Greys attempted to keep Lola still while the third injected her with something. Lola felt a tingling in her arm and suddenly lost all the will to shout out any more. Instead, all she wanted to do was sleep. She didn't want to put up a fight and get off the island. She wanted to let the Greys win and be at peace. She fell to the ground asleep, the screams and cries of her parents failing to wake her.

She awoke an unknown amount of time later. She had been placed in a seat so that when she woke, she felt a bit numb from sleeping in an uncomfortable position. She opened her eyes and saw, to her horror, that she was in Puddlepond Stadium. She looked around to see if her parents were nearby, or indeed any of her friends or anyone she knew, but everyone around her was a stranger. They were either asleep, just waking up, or looking around confused and panicking. The rain had pretty much stopped by now.

Lola felt constrained: she wanted to get up, get out of this place and find her parents, but something was preventing her from getting up. She saw that the stadium's seats, as well as the entire field, were packed to the brim with people.

She was just about to ask the people next to her what they knew about what exactly was going on when she saw a large being swoop down from the skies, miss the people down below by a few feet, and soar back up into the sky. It then flew back down more slowly and came to a halt, hovering directly above those standing in the middle of the field.

It was then that Lola felt that she should run, but the only thing keeping her in her seat was pure fascination.

Chapter 19 –
Res Horribilis

For the smallest instant, all the faces in the stadium had been fixed on the being hovering effortlessly above them; people couldn't help but wonder what it was, but just over a second after the being had appeared, that concentration broke, the wonder dissipated and the air was rent by screams from thousands of different people united in their fear of this being unknown.

It was the weirdest and most horrible thing Lola had ever seen. Its appearance was somewhat like an ice-cream cone: its head was large and spherical and its tail down from its bulging head, gradually getting thinner and thinner until it ended with a point. Its head had a black opening at the very top and many rings of artificial-looking eyes running round its head. It was a dazzling white and almost seemed to glitter. It must have been at least fifteen metres long; most of its length was taken up by its tail, which was pointing directly to the ground.

The screams continued as the whole stadium hurriedly made for the exits; the only thing that mattered to everyone was getting out, and nothing was going to stop them. Before long, people from the stands were flooding into the already-crowded field and streams of people were filling the corridors leading to the exit.

Lola was halfway down the stairs, being pushed and shoved in all directions by frantic strangers all determined to make it out alive, all not afraid to push their way in front of other people. It was every person for themselves. Lola looked round trying to see someone she knew but could only see strangers with faces contorted by fear and frenzy.

'There is no point in trying to escape; all exits are sealed,' the being said in a harsh, high voice that struck everyone in the stadium despite the din they themselves were creating. People were all the more spurred on to escape, such that the corridors leading to the exits were packed with people pushing harder and harder. The people closest to the exits were being squashed in all directions by the desperate crowd behind them stoked by the hope of escape, the fear of this being. The masses of people gathered around the exits kept getting bigger and bigger as more people hurriedly rushed to escape. The corridors were very soon packed to the brim of people, with everyone else left to pour out on to the field: these were the ones who were pushing and fighting the hardest.

Lola had now made her way into one of the conglomerations that had formed by one of the exits; she was on the field, strangers in every direction, pressing up against her. Up above the being was hovering eerily, watching intently as the tiny people below it attempted in vain to break free.

Then the being spoke again:

'You will all be let out of this stadium in due course. I have a great and wondrous plan, which involves this island.'

No one was paying attention to the being's words, despite them persistently ringing in everyone's ears. The words were clear and blocked out the sonorous noise of people vying to be closer to the exits.

'Now, you will all listen to me,' the being said, at which point Lola, oppressed by the power of the frenzied crowd, found herself instantly back in one of the stadium seats looking out to the field, above which the being was hovering. All the other seats were full of people and some people were sitting on the field itself. Lola was watching the being, her eyes were fixated on it; she could hear only its words, yet she felt as if some external force were making her do this. She couldn't take her off the being, no matter how hard, nor could she move. She was constricted by something unknown, trapped in her own body, unable to perform the simple of movements. The fear she had felt mere seconds ago was escalating to new heights.

Before she had time to wonder what had just happened, the being spoke once more:

'You are inhabiting a temporary island which I, Assa, so marvellously created. Chaos brought you into existence and it is thanks to chaos that my universe has fallen into disarray. I feel it's right to inform you that you have failed the test, which I ran to give you a chance of survival. It is not often that I run the test, given my determination to set this universe exactly right, so you were lucky to have been given that chance. I feel obliged to tell you that, therefore, I was considering keeping you, until the select few failed the test. However, I can rectify all errors that have been borne out of chaos and will strive to do so. You all have until midnight tonight to have completely vacated this island. My assistants and I will conduct a thorough search and anyone found on this island after midnight tomorrow will be killed with no exceptions made. You were all never meant to be. If you leave the island as instructed, you will have earned for yourselves a longer amount of time alive on this planet than if you should decide to disobey my order. That is all.'

And with that, Lola felt a tingle and she was free. Her

movements were no longer restricted. She looked round and saw everyone nearby having similar reactions to her: they'd all been released from the constrictive state she'd been in. There came again a cacophony of screams from all sides; voices had been bursting to break out. It was happening again: people were once more rushing to leave. In one fluid motion, everyone was up on their feet and was rapidly making for an exit, searching for loved ones on the way.

'NOW!' came a man's cry that sounded as if it were coming from a megaphone; the cry was louder than the being's voice and sounded urgent and desperate; it seemed to echo around the whole stadium. In an instant, there was a very quick succession of loud bangs, one of which came from somewhere near Lola; they were almost like gunshots. The being seemed to have been hit, as it let out a frightened roar, a roar that was so loud and so full of pain, as if its whole corporeal mass were being torn apart. The scream got louder and more intense and the gunshots carried on. Lola had to cover her ears because the cries coming from the being were so painfully loud. It was writhing about in the air; it seemed to have been seriously wounded, though Lola was too far away to see any damage to its body.

Then, once the gunfire ceased, the being started spinning round rapidly, faster and fast on the spot. It was very soon a dazzling white blur, an oddity to marvel at. Something fell from the swirling mass that was the being: it was flung about ten metres away and landed on the grass. Lola looked and saw it was the orb.

However, the being kept on spinning and screaming for what reason Lola did not know. She looked down and saw a woman running up the stairs, a frenzied-looking woman with a large, metallic and somewhat futuristic-looking gun of sorts in her hand. There was also someone running to where the orb had fallen: it was a man, a stout, burly man, who picked up the orb and started sprinting up some stairs. He, too, had one of those guns in his hand. No one dared get in his way.

There was a faint humming noise coming from somewhere. Within a few seconds it was apparent it was the noise of a helicopter, which Lola saw approaching the stadium from somewhere distant. She turned her head back and saw the woman reach the very top of the stadium and run round to a point where two other people were standing. The being was still rapidly spinning. After a few minutes, Lola looked back again and saw there were about ten people gathered together at the top, each one with an identical gun, including the man who had gone to get the orb, whose platinum-blonde hair made him stand out from the others. The helicopter soon flew down to meet them; once it was level with the top rim of the stadium, Lola saw most of them get in it before it started rising and flew gracefully to the middle of the stadium; it flew directly over the being and as it did so, Lola saw people's arms sticking out of the sides of the helicopter: there were a few more loud bangs, coming from guns all pointed at the revolving being, which by now was spinning so fast it was almost invisible. The people in the stadium seemed to collectively shudder.

It all seemed to happen in a flash: the helicopter was very soon flying off into the distance, gathering speed and altitude as it did so. All eyes were fixed on the bizarre sight in the middle of the stadium: some were attempting to flee and were running down stairs, whilst others, the vast majority of those in the stadium, were staying in their seats, not being able to discern whether attempting to leave was safe, despite how much they wanted to do so.

The being had slowed down entirely and was no longer spinning madly. Its plethora of eyes seemed to be jerkily looking all about for something: Lola could just about still see the helicopter high up in the distance, then she guessed what was going to happen. She looked at the being and saw a tiny red beam suddenly shoot out from its tail, which was pointing in the direction of the helicopter. As soon as Lola saw this, there was a deafening bang as the helicopter in the distance exploded, creating a massive fireball in the sky, which seemed to come into its fiery existence in slow motion. It seemed to slowly swell, flames of the being's fury spitting out of the swollen mass of incineration.

Lola turned back to the middle of the stadium and saw that the being had now gone, to her immense relief. Most of the fear in her had dissipated. She screamed out for people she knew. She thought she'd seen a few familiar faces in the bustling crowd and shouted out their names, but they turned out to be only strangers who were themselves searching for people.

With no one she knew about, Lola decided to make for an exit; she was pushed by the person who'd been next to her. An elderly woman, frantically shouting in a croaky manner, was pushing Lola with unexpected vigour. Lola started across the aisle, constantly being badgered by this frightened woman, screaming with confusion and anxiety. Lola was pushed into the person who'd been sitting on the other side of her, but this person didn't seem to care. Before she knew it, she was being shoved down the stairs, falling into the people before her. The air was abuzz with the sound of despair.

The pushing and shoving were getting more and harder. Lola felt herself being jostled by unknown people, strangers with unfamiliar faces and stories who nevertheless were all in the same dire situation. Another fall was broken by a stranger's back, a stranger who wailed in pain when Lola was pushed and fell down a few stairs, crashing into his seemingly brittle back with force. Lola hastily apologised, though she couldn't see who she was saying this to, as the people around her seemed to be constantly changing, all of them being merged into a blur.

She soon managed to make it down to the bottom of the stairs, still surrounded by people closing in on all sides. There were screams and cries from people all around her. Someone could be heard lashing out, hitting people and fighting to get through, having a panic attack of sorts, creating even more chaos. Lola could just see that person, about fifty feet or so away, a small ring of space around him. He looked to be in some sort of frenzied state, had just hit another person and was pointing at the people encircling him. He seemed to be shouting something to them, though his words were indiscernible. Lola was busy watching him when she was pushed again and the man disappeared from view.

The crowd started gathering speed: Lola could very soon see the exit up ahead, people bursting out of it into freedom. There were cheers and screams of relief as people realised they were now free.

Before long, Lola was out of the stadium and in the car park. There were people everywhere running in all directions. Lola shouted out for her parents, but knew deep down they were unlikely to be anywhere nearby. Just then, her phone started ringing.

'Mum!'

'Lola are you okay? Where are you?'

'I'm in the car park, right near the south exit of the stadium.'

'OK. Stay exactly where you are. We're coming to get you.'

Lola hung up and felt relieved to know her parents were on their way. She stood near a lamppost and remained there watching everyone running about; some determined to find loved ones, others simply wanting to be as far away as possible. She sat down and took a few deep breaths. She felt her forehead was a bit warm. Her mind was buzzing with questions, fears and wonder after all that had just happened. However, what was at the forefront of everything was the hope that everyone was okay. She typed out a quick text and sent it to everyone; she stared at her phone, her attention entirely focussed on it. She blocked out everything else that was going on: the screams and cries gradually faded and the people rushing by became a blurry stream. Her forehead was growing cooler.

Texts poured in: everyone was saying they were okay and were somewhere near the stadium or in the theme park. Lola decided she'd find people once her parents had found her, figuring they'd be furious if she wandered off. She looked up and saw the same scene she was now growing accustomed to: that of people running away in fear, not knowing what was going on, longing for the security they had in their lives previously. Then she saw something in the distance: a body on the ground. People running blocked her view for a few moments, but once she saw it a second time, she saw it was a Blondie. Looking around, she saw more Blondie bodies scattered about; people were hastily avoiding them. Lola felt disgusted; she hoped for their sake only a few of them had come to help and that the rest were in their ships. The sight of the bodies fuelled Lola's rage even further: she didn't care about anything else other than crushing Assa and the Greys. She concentrated the satisfaction she'd feel if she got revenge on them for what they'd done and were intending to do.

It all seemed to be slotting into place. So now Lola knew that this being, Assa, wanted to eradicate all humans because they weren't meant to be and because some had failed some sort of test, which would have allowed humans to live had it been passed. The calmness with which Assa spoke as it delivered the news of humanity's fate had shaken Lola to the core: it seemed twisted and sinister, almost macabre to speak of such a horrific act with apparent ease and glee. Lola didn't want to take it all in but knew she had to embrace it and try to deal with it. It was still something she couldn't quite grasp all the ins and outs of, and was still something she thought lacked solid, concrete proof. In all, Lola thought words weren't nearly enough to convince her; not even the appearance of a strange, horrific being could convince that this tale being real: that the universe had been created and that its creator was going round rectifying all mistakes that had arisen. Then again, Lola wasn't sure if there could ever be irrefutable proof for these claims being made. It was certainly a perplexing matter to consider. Lola still couldn't make her mind up whether she believed it all or not. Yet again part of her was more inclined to believe, given Assa's appearance, yet the other part thought Assa's appearance didn't lend any proof to any argument at all.

And apparently everyone had to vacate the island...but for what purpose? Lola wondered why Assa hadn't just killed them all in the stadium when there was the perfect opportunity to do so; Assa had, after all, seemingly effortlessly moved everyone back to the seats in an instant. Lola was wondering whether this horrific being's stated intentions would be fulfilled or not when she caught a glimpse of an alien ship up ahead, soaring across the sky away from her. She was now accustomed to spaceships flying overhead, such that the sight didn't strike fear or apprehension in her.

Her phone went off: someone was ringing her, someone who Lola had least of all been expecting to ring her.

'Natella!' was all she could say.

'Lola, are you okay?' Natella asked, her voice quivering.

'Never mind about me, what about you? Where have you been? Where are you now?'

'I'm okay. I was in the stadium too and what that thing, Assa, said was all sincere, just like I told you. You have to promise me you and your family will leave Helmia as soon as possible and will definitely have done so before time's up.'

'I want answers, Natella. I want the truth, do you understand? I want to know exactly what the hell is going on. You clearly know but you're not telling me everything! Why do we have to leave the island? Why didn't Assa just kill us all then and there?' Lola felt impatient and determined.

'Lola, this certainly isn't the time for this. Please, just make sure you get off this island, please,' Natella was now sounding hysterical, clearly crying away.

'I'm sorry, but I want answers, Natella. You can't just tell me some things and not tell me other things.'

'For crying out loud, Lola, it's not all about you and your curiosity!' Natella shouted, 'answering your questions is not the most important thing for me to do right now. In case you didn't see, Assa just killed those people in the helicopter, who will not be the first victims. We haven't got long left, Lola, not long at all. Just get off the island, stay calm and be with your family.'

Natella's final sentences were almost incomprehensible; her crying was so much. Lola wanted desperately to have her questions answered, but thought it best not to agitate Natella any further.

'I'll get off the island, of course I will.'

She wanted to know what exactly was going to happen, why they had all been ordered off the island, who those people with the guns were and whether they'd succeeded in getting the orb away from Assa. She sat there, having forgotten that her parents were on their way, and concentrated on trying to work out the answers for herself. The only thing she was sure of was that Assa was an extremely capable and powerful being, given the ease with which it caused the helicopter to explode. She hoped everyone would see sense and flee from the island. She looked all around her to make sure Assa wasn't anywhere; luckily, Assa was nowhere to be seen. Lola was really starting to panic now: she was all alone, watching people franticly rushing by; if Assa came back, she could be killed without ever seeing her loved ones for the last time. The thought terrified her: Assa could appear just as quickly as it had disappeared and do anything.

Lola felt entirely alone. She was without anyone to comfort her at this dreadful time, without anyone to comfort in turn. She would give anything to simply have someone else here with her, someone to ride out this dire situation with. Looking about, she could see no sign of her parents or of any friends at all. She didn't want to sit around and wait any longer; she was bored of that.

Then something in the distance caught her eye. Walking towards her, about a hundred or so feet away, were two Greys. They seemed to be walking slowly. Lola sat and stared; she watched as people seeing the Greys screamed and ran away from them, how the Greys were unperturbed by this and carried on their slow march towards her. One of them mercilessly kicked a lifeless Blondie body. Lola got up and turned to run, but bumped into someone who had been standing right beside her.

'Sorry,' Lola said, having not seen the person before her.

'Come with me, now,' the other said; Lola saw it was none other than Mary Morton.

'Mary Morton?!'

'Lola, those Greys are running this way. Come on, I have a car over there.'

Mary helped a stunned Lola up, then said, 'do you trust me, Lola?'

'Yes, I guess,' Lola replied, thinking the scenario bizarre. Mary grabbed Lola's hand and the two ran fast for a few minutes before arriving at Mary's car. Lola looked behind her and saw the Greys were now sprinting in their direction; the two from before were now accompanied by three more.

Once safely inside the car, Mary said, 'I don't know why they're chasing you, Lola. I was outside the stadium looking for my boyfriend when I saw you sitting there and then I saw the Greys coming for you.'

'Thank you so much,' Lola replied, slightly out of breath and taken aback.

'What were you doing there all by yourself, anyway? Why weren't you running like everyone else?' Mary inquired as she started up the car.

'I was…waiting for my parents! Oh no! I have to find them!'

'Don't worry, Lola, I'll take you home and you can meet them there. I don't think it's safe to remain here.'

Lola looked behind her, then to the sides of her.

'I can't see the Greys anywhere, Mary.'

She looked again: the Greys were definitely out of sight. She could only see people scattered everywhere.

'Mary, they're nowhere to be seen.'

'Lola, do you trust me?'

'What?'

They were now driving out of the massive car park.

'Do you trust me, Lola?'

'But I barely know you. I know all the stuff you've done, I mean, you're famous and I met you at that book signing a few weeks ago, but I wouldn't say I trust you.'

'That's a disappointment.'

'Well, I trust that you'll take me home.'

'But do you think you can really trust me, Lola? Do I come across as a trustworthy person?'

'I guess so. Why does this matter so much anyway?'

'We are in a very dire situation, Lola. There will come a time when people will need to trust others, even if they are complete strangers. Now, if I asked you to completely trust me right here and now, would you?'

'Yes, I guess.'

'You're hesitating.'

'OK, then, yes!' Lola said, feeling a little miffed.

'Good, because you can trust me entirely, Lola.'

They were now driving down a street lined with houses, which was almost deserted, save for a few people running to their homes. Lola sat pensive for a few moments, then something came to her.

'You haven't asked me for my address,' she said to Mary; she looked at the famous, award-winning actress at next to her, who looked and lot more composed than she had done at the book signing, yet she was stony-faced and appeared not to be listening.

'Mary, you don't know where I live!' Lola reiterated, slightly more panicked.

Mary pulled over near a park.

'What's going on?' Lola demanded. She tried the door handle, but it was locked.

'Why have you locked the doors?'

Mary looked completely pacified, the opposite of Lola.

'My parents are still looking for me.'

Lola went to get her phone out of her pocket, but Mary grabbed her hand and withdrew something from her own pocket with the other hand: a cloth, which she forced across Lola's mouth with both hands, unaffected by Lola's lashing out. After a few moments, Lola stopped hitting Mary, stopped panicking, stopped almost altogether: she was still, eyes wide open.

Mary started driving again.

'Having a breakdown's given me the strength to do this.'

Chapter 20 –
The Computer Room

Everything was blurry. Lola felt a pain in her head. She couldn't make out where she was, or when it was. Her forehead was warm. She was lying down on a hard surface. Dizziness crept over her as she tried to get up. Once up, she found she was involuntarily swaying from side to side. There were other people lying down, some of them gently stirring, one or two of them trying to get up.

Lola felt as if all her energy were depleted; she wanted so badly to ask the other people where they were, but she couldn't quite manage it. She felt completely exhausted: even speaking would require energy she seemed to not have.

She saw they were in a room with a grey ceiling; after looking round, she ascertained it was quite a big room: it was about the size of one of the classrooms at school. She could see the one and only door, but there were no windows. There was only one light in the middle of the room, which was far too bright.

Panic overcame Lola: it shocked her body into finding the energy it was currently lacking. She suddenly felt very much alive, yet very much isolated. What came to the forefront of her mind was the fear she felt when she'd been stuck in the lift with her parents all those years ago. Then she'd had her parents to comfort her and tell her everything was going to be okay, but none of these strangers was one of her parents.

'Where the hell are we?' she shrieked, looking round at the strangers, some of whom were still unconscious.

'Where are we? If you know just tell me where we are!' she cried at the person next to her who looked flabbergasted.

'Who are you?' the elderly man replied in an agitated manner, 'and don't speak to me like that.'

Before Lola could reply, there came a piercing scream from nearby: a woman had woken up and was having a panic attack; people were trying to console her and calm her down, but she was backing into the corner of the room, yelling that she would hurt them if they didn't back down.

More and more people started waking. Some woke confused, others woke panicked and agitated, many of whom had similar initial reactions to the woman.

The atmosphere in the room was one of panic and ignorance. The woman in the corner eventually calmed down. Lola felt stressed, shut up in this strange room with all these strangers. She couldn't remember how she'd got here. She told herself to calm down: being afraid hadn't got her out of the lift and it certainly wouldn't get them all out of this situation. She remembered she was older and more mature than the little girl she'd been back then.

'EVERYONE BE QUIET!' roared a well-built man, who was standing in the centre of the room, looking all around him.

'Does anyone know where we are?' he asked again, assuming an authoritative position within the group. No one replied.

'Does anyone know why we're here?'

Again, there was no reply from anyone; Lola could hear a few people sobbing, a few breathing heavily.

The man went over to the door then, having seen it was locked from the outside, he spoke again, 'this door's locked from the outside. We need to try and break it down.'

Once the man had spoken he went back to the middle of the square room and Lola looked round to see a few people who were previously looking apprehensive now looked a little more hopeful. Still, the atmosphere was tense. There was a mixture of people in the room: of the twenty-five or so, there were a few elderly people, three teenagers aside from Lola and some adults.

She noticed someone she recognised.

'Maxwell?'

'Who are you? Oh, yeah, you're Lola, aren't you?'

'Yeah. Do you know why we're here?'

'If I did I would have said already.'

Just then, the door started slowly creaking open; most people retreated a little, but the man who seemed to have taken charge ran towards it and pulled it wide open: he blocked the view of what lay beyond the threshold; for a moment, Lola thought there would be Greys there, but there seemed to be nothing there.

He left the room, keeping one hand on the door and looked round, then gave the all clear. Slowly but surely, people started leaving the room, keen on discovering their whereabouts. Lola was one of the last to leave the room: when she did, it was only to enter and even bigger room, which was much bigger than the school hall. Its ceiling was about twenty feet high and it was filled with row upon row of computer desks. There seemed to be no natural light coming from anywhere.

'We have to get out of here! That thing's going to kill us all if we don't get off this island!' one of the teenagers cried out hysterically. The man in charge responded, 'everyone just needs to calm down, OK? Freaking out won't get us anywhere. Does anyone recognise this place?'

Again, no one replied.

'Does anyone remember what happened to them right before they woke up here?'

'I was running away from the theme park,' one person said, 'then I remember getting hit round the head, then I woke up here.'

'Anyone else?'

'I was in the stadium. I'd fallen trying to leave and was being helped up then I remember just waking up here.'

'Can anyone see a door anywhere?'

The party dispersed a bit, though with some reluctance. There were about thirty rows of computer desks, all of which looked identical. The group seemed to be at the halfway point of the room, as it seemed to be of the same length in both directions.

At someone's suggestion, the groups coalesced and set off exploring the room as one. They kept to the edge of the room, slowly inspecting everything as they went: the walls were a dull metallic shade of grey and the floor comprised of white tiles, whereas the ceiling was a light shade of turquoise. It seemed monotonous and somewhat eerie. As far as they could tell, it was completely empty apart from themselves: the computers weren't even on so there wasn't even the faint hum they produced. It was almost silent in that room. It was sparsely lit as only some of the lights were lit and there didn't seem to be switches anywhere.

'Does anyone know what time it is?' someone asked. Everyone fidgeted about in their pockets, but to find nothing.

'My phone's gone!'

'Who's taken my wallet?'

'Where's my stuff?'

'Wait, it's nearly quarter past ten at night, it says so over there,' a man said, pointing to a large digital clock on the wall.

'We need to get off the island by midnight!' someone shouted, 'we need to get out of here now!'

Lola was now worrying even more than before. They had just over an hour and forty-five minutes to get out of this place and leave. It might be that they were in fact already off the island, but Lola had a feeling they were still on it.

They kept on walking, eventually hitting the corner of the room. They turned and carried on, yet along this wall there was still no door.

'No one has a phone?' someone asked; it turned out everyone had been stripped of their possessions.

'I remember something,' Lola said, standing still, her head inclined, deep in thought. She was trying to remember something she knew she should be able to easily recall.

'Before I woke up here, the last thing I remember was seeing a woman. I was in her car. I don't know where we were. I knew who she was, but I didn't know her. Then I was here.'

'What did this woman look like?'

'I can't...she asked me if I trusted her.'

'Was she someone from your family?'

'She...she told me I could trust her,' Lola said, struggling to remember all the details.

'That happened to me too,' said a woman nearby, 'I remember there being a man who was asking me if I could trust him, then I woke up here.'

'Do you know who it was?' asked the man in charge.

'I knew who he was, but I didn't know him. I don't remember who it was, though.'

No one said anything: everyone was watching one of the younger ones, who had gone over to one of the computers and had switched it on. The screen that came up had a few unknown symbols on it.

'Can we just concentrate on getting out of here!?'

'I wonder who works at these computers?'

'Who cares? Let's just find a way out of here.'

The group carried on. Lola was intrigued by the computer stations. She thought they were definitely alien: they looked like normal computers, except each one had a few loose wires coming from the monitor, which ended with large soft pads, which looked almost like suction cups.

Restless and impatient, the group kept to the walls and kept moving on, never finding a door. Soon enough, they arrived back outside the room they'd woken up in.

'There must be a way out! There's got to be!' one woman screamed hysterically. Others rushed over to comfort her.

'We will find a way out; we just have to keep looking. If there's a way in, there'll be a way out.'

'Unless they sealed the exits,' someone said ominously.

'Don't say that!'

'It's obvious who's behind all this – it's those damn aliens.'

'But people have been saying it was people who brought them here.'

'Yeah,' Lola said, 'like I said before, the last thing I remember is being in a car with a woman. Wait, there were aliens. There were two Greys running towards me,' it was all coming back to Lola now, 'she saved me. They were running towards me, but she drove me away in her car then I woke up here.'

'Who was it? Try to remember. You said you knew who she was.'

'I can't remember, as hard as I try. All I know is that I definitely knew who she was. I'd met her once before, but she was different.'

Lola was frustrated with herself; she knew the memory was somewhere there, but for some reason recalling it was hard.

'Does anyone remember anything about anyone they saw before waking up here?'

'I was with a man. Like you, I knew who he was, but I can't remember who exactly it was. It was someone I hadn't met before but I knew who he was.'

Lola was blocking out everything that was happening, everything people were saying. She was desperately trying to remember what had happened not so long ago at all. She knew it was there, it definitely was attainable, but there was something preventing her from accessing this apparently crucial memory.

The woman had appeared when the Greys were running towards her. The woman appeared in her mind enshrouded by mist...the outline of her was there. Lola tried harder and harder to remember; it was almost painful to recall exactly what this woman looked like.

'I remember! She's someone famous. I remember I met her once at...it was Mary Morton! She told me I could trust and we were driving away from the stadium...the next thing that happened was me waking up here.'

Lola could see it all clearly in her mind now: the image was clear and sharp.

'Mary Morton? The actress?' Maxwell asked nervously.

'Yeah, it was her. I'm sure of it. I don't know why she was there, or why she was going on about trust, but it was definitely her.'

'So now we know she's in on it,' someone said.

'Can we focus on getting out of here first? Please!'

A few people had started running away, looking for an exit. They were panic-stricken.

'We have to stick together!'

Lola watched as people started dispersing, horrified by the fact the group had not found a single way out of this large room. She suspected their attempts would be futile, and that no exit would be found.

'Why would Mary Morton do that?' a young man of around thirty asked Lola, looking hesitant and doubtful.

'If I had any idea, I would tell you.'

'Maybe it wasn't her though. Maybe someone else brought you here but you don't remember it.'

'She's the last thing I remember though; I'm sure she brought me here. All that I do know is that we need to get off this island, as soon as possible, and we need to find out whether Assa has the orb.'

'Assa? Who's Assa?'

'Assa's the creature that was in the stadium, the one that got shot.'

'How do you know it has a name? You're one of them, aren't you?'

The young man looked horrified at the conclusion he'd jumped to.

'No, I'm definitely not! Why would I be here if I was?'

'What's going on?' the man in charge asked.

'She's one of them!' the young man declared, his arm outstretched and finger pointing at Lola.

'What's your name?'

'Lola Spears.'

'Lola, I'm Mark. And what's your name?'

'It's David, but does that really matter? All that matters is that Lola knows stuff.'

'What do you know, Lola?'

Lola didn't know what to say. The two people before her looked somewhat intimidating. She thought for a few moments, mouth agape, then spoke: 'look, I promise you I have nothing to do with this. I want to leave just as much as you all do. All I know is what my friend has told me, which is that Assa is going to get everyone off the island for some reason then…then rid this planet of humans and restore it to how it should have been, because apparently humans were never meant to be.'

'What on Earth are you talking about?' Mark said, looking stunned.

'I know it sounds like nonsense – I thought it was at first, but it's true. Assa's appearance and what Assa said has convinced me it's all true. I don't know why we've been detained here, nor do I know where we are, but I do know that everything Assa said in the stadium was true. We are all in serious danger.'

'What about this orb you mentioned?' Mark asked, looking somewhat convinced.

'I don't know who took it, but they're on our side. Assa needs that orb to do certain things – basically, Assa needs that orb to be able to get rid of humanity. We have to hope that Assa doesn't have the orb right now.'

'But it was blown up. Those people who shot this Assa creature fled in a helicopter but Assa exploded it.'

'According to my friend, the orb is indestructible,' Lola replied

'So we're screwed!' the young man shrieked, 'great! Why all this drivel about Assa? Why not just get to the point and say we're all doomed!'

'Listen to me,' Lola said, impatience rising in her, 'I hate pessimism. It never solves anything and right now, it's only gonna cause more problems. Stop freaking out and assuming the worst because it's just annoying.'

'Didn't you see what that thing did to the helicopter?'

'Yes, Assa killed those people; I saw it too!'

'And that will be us if we don't stop arguing!' Mark intervened, stepping in between a fuming Lola and a despondent David.

'Now calm down both of you! This is not the time to be arguing so immaturely.'

'I am telling the truth. Mary Morton is involved, despite what you might of seen when she and Dazzle interrupted the Prime Minister's announcement.'

'The man I saw last before waking up here was Harold Dazzle!' an elderly man claimed. Everyone who was still there turned to look at him.

'I'm damn sure of it too, now that my memory's come back. It was foggy at first, but now I remember it well. I was in the crowd trying to get out of that rotten stadium. I was in the corridor getting pushed and shoved by everyone and I saw the restroom so I went in to escape from the crowd. I was the only one in there. I decided I'd wait for a bit. Then he entered. He told me who he was, but I already knew who he was, and he asked me to trust him, then I woke up here.'

'So John Dazzle and Mary Morton appear to be some-how involved in our being taken and placed here,' Mark concluded.

'They've double-crossed us; no one should have gone to the theme park.' Lola replied.

Harold Dazzle, headmaster of Puddlepond High School and a renowned scholar and documentary maker. Mary Morton, famous actress and TV personality.

'I remember seeing Harold Dazzle too,' someone else piped up, 'I was outside the stadium looking for my family when I saw some of those grey aliens, then Harold...he just appeared right beside me, he gave me quite a fright, and he told me to trust him then I woke up here.'

Lola was still thinking: her very capacity to remember seemed to have been disturbed by whatever had happened to them before waking up. She was focusing entirely on trying to remember something she knew was there.

'That's it!' she shouted out, 'she was at the school! I remember now, she was at the school waiting to see Mr. Dazzle on a Monday...the Monday after Assa and Hyuul came to Helmia! I thought I recognised that woman!' Lola felt energised and invigorated. The recollection of the memory seemed to goad her on.

'If they were in on this back then, then why would she see him so soon after the orb went missing?' she asked herself, aware she was voicing her thoughts.

'Lola, could you tell us what's going on please?' Mark asked.

'That Friday night those two aliens came to Helmia, one of them was Assa, the other was an alien called Hyuul who'd stolen the orb I told you about. Hyuul managed to hide it in Dazzle's office before being blasted by Assa. And Mary had a meeting with Harold a few days later...It just doesn't add up. Were they even in on it back then? If they weren't, it might have just been a random meeting that had nothing to do with this, but what if they were in on it? I have a feeling they were.'

Lola had been rambling on to no one in particular. People were staring at her, not knowing what to make of what she was saying.

'They came on Friday and his office got broken into that weekend! Of course! It must have been hidden there on Friday, but then why did it take so long for Assa to find it? And why hide it right under Harold's nose?'

'What exactly are you talking about?' Mark asked.

'His office was broken into and searched but nothing was found. That's it!'

'Lola, you're not making much sense.'

'I am making sense. Dazzle's office was broken into, yet

only a few tenners were taken, not even all of them. So why go through all the trouble to break into an office just to take a few tenners? So the office would be searched and Dazzle would see the orb wasn't there. Only, the orb *was* put there, just after it got searched. But who put it there and why?'

Lola was desperately trying to piece it all together; she was trying to remember the first day back at school after that weekend.

'There was Mary Morton waiting outside Dazzle's office, and there was some man with a top hat. It must have been him who put the orb there.'

There was a noise in the distance, causing everyone to jump and Lola's train of thought to be disrupted.

'There's an opening!' someone cried excitedly. The whole group ran round to a door that had opened up in the wall. There was a long cave passage lying in front of them.

Almost immediately, people started pouring into the passage. Lola decided to stay close to Mark, who advanced warily near the back of the group. The passage was dank and dark. After a while, the path began to slope upwards. It seemed to go on for ages. The people who had started running eventually gave up and the whole group was almost as one walking for what they hoped was freedom. After turning a corner, they saw light ahead and started running. Some were cheering and manic with delight, others were a little more apprehensive.

They were outside in the fresh air. Lola looked all around her and instantly recognised where they were: Symmetry Peak.

'We were inside the mountain?' Lola said, perplexed.

'We must have been,' Mark replied. They looked out over the island and could see Puddlepond in the west, Leafdew in the east and Moistree down below. In the harbours, boats that appeared to be full of people were leaving. A plane was taking off from Puddlepond airport. Shortly afterwards, another took off, then another.

'It looks like everyone's leaving,' someone said. Lola saw a few other people were running over to the souvenir shop to see if anyone was there: there wasn't, nor were there any cars there. She thought this nighttime view was very pretty.

'We'll have to walk down the road.'

People had started walking down the road, fully aware it would take a good few hours to get to Moistree from it.

'You lot over there, wait!' Mark ordered.

'What is it?'

'There's a ship over there, look! It's flying right towards us!'

Everyone looked and saw the ship get closer and closer. Some people started running down the road screaming; only a few remained behind to see what would happen.

'We should be running,' Mark said.

'It's not a Grey ship though,' Lola replied confidently. Within a few moments, the winds were stirring wildly as the ship with dancing lights landed on a level bit of land nearby. Lola and the others had run back a little so as to avoid the full blast of wind. Nevertheless, clouds of dust had arisen and everyone was coughing and covering their eyes.

The ship was saucer-like in shape and had landed softly. Lola knew at once who it belonged to.

Once the winds died down, the last remaining people of the group, only six in number, stood transfixed on the sight before them: they could now see a metallic ramp coming down from the ship, and on it were seven tall Blondies.

Lola heard a few people behind her scream and run away. She, however, knew the Blondies were on their side and wouldn't harm them.

The Blondies were now stood only a few feet from Lola,

Mark, some other person whose name they didn't know who was rooted to the spot by fear and Maxwell.

'We have been told to get you,' the Blondie on the right said.

'Who told you to get us?' Mark asked defiantly, trembling somewhat.

'They're on our side, Mark,' Lola reassured him.

'Mary Morton,' replied one of the Blondies. Lola was taken aback.

'Mary Morton?' she asked of the aliens.

'Yes, Mary Morton. We are to collect you all.'

Lola saw something in the ship behind the Blondies: a person, an actual human being was running down the ramp.

'All of you need to get in the ship NOW! You three, go and round up the others. They won't be far away,' she said sternly, looking angst-stricken. It was Mary Morton.

'You?!' Lola exclaimed.

'I'll explain everything once we're in the ship. Are the others inside or have they started running down the road?'

'They've all gone down the road,' Mark replied.

'They're down the road,' Mary shouted over their heads to the Blondies behind them.

'Right, you four, in the ship now,' she commanded, yet none of them budged.

'I'm sorry about bringing you here, but I had to. But now, we're taking you all to the mainland.'

'What? But you work for Assa!'

'Yes and no, Lola. I promise you I will answer all questions once you all get inside this ship. You have to trust me.'

Mary looked into Lola's eyes. Lola was stunned: it was understandable that the Blondies would want to rescue them, but why was Mary Morton with them when she was partly responsible for the situation in the first place?

'You said these Blondies are on our side, Lola?' Mark asked.

'They are, but I'm not sure about Mary.'

'I'm not getting on that ship,' the third person exclaimed, staggering backwards.

Lola partly agreed; she could trust the Blondies based on what Natella had told her, but could this all be a plan to get them to Assa? Could Mary have recruited these particular Blondies and was she now using them to do her bidding? Lola didn't know what to believe. She knew they had to get off the island as soon as possible. She had to decide whether her distrust for Mary outweighed her trust for the Blondies.

'I'm going aboard,' Lola declared, 'but I want and will get answers.'

'Lola, wait!' shouted Maxwell. Lola stopped, turned round and looked at the young man who was looking out of his comfort zone.

'Lola, are you sure you want to do this?'

'Yes, I am.'

'You don't know what these aliens are like.'

'I know they mean us no harm.'

'Listen, Lola. There's something you should know,' Maxwell said, eyeing the Blondies as he did so.

'No alien can be trusted, no matter what.'

'Why do you say that?'

Maxwell had a serious look on his face; he was looking at Lola sternly.

'Take my word for it.'

'Why should I?'

'When you first met me, I was on my way to the burning building because that's where I work. I'm the director. I disappeared because I didn't want you following me.'

Lola simply looked at him, expecting more.

'I've spent most of my life researching aliens and over the past few months, we've had one in our building.'

'Hyuul?'

'Yes. My father was the one who saw Helmia rise out of the sea and founded the base as a place for alien research. Eventually, things got complicated and it officially no longer exists. He put me in charge a year or so ago but we don't see eye-to-eye on a number of things. I've learned from Hyuul that aliens simply can't be trusted.'

Lola wasn't convinced; her mind had already been made up. She strode past Mary, but hesitated once she was on the ramp. She turned back and saw Mark looking at her doubtfully and the other person running away. Maxwell was shaking his head.

'I don't trust her, but I trust the Blondies,' Lola told them, though she knew deep down she couldn't fully trust them.

Mark walked over to join Lola, looking serious.

'Thank you,' said Mary, looking sincere, 'you *can* trust me, you know. Now hurry up and get inside! You too, Maxwell.'

'If I had a gun right now, I'd shoot each and every one of you aliens dead.'

Lola didn't know what to say. Everyone was looking at Maxwell.

'That's right. No aliens can be trusted. None of them! I tried warning you.'

And with that, Maxwell turned and ran away down the road.

Lola hesitated for a moment then continued on. Once inside, she looked round and was overwhelmed by the simplicity of it all: she'd expected it to be a high-tech affair teeming with computers and other fancy bits of super-advanced technology, yet it looked quite normal: the five rows of four seats were in the middle of the ship looked like seats found on a normal place; there were two larger seats facing a large, thick window, beneath which was an array of controls. The walls were a deep sea blue, whereas the floor was a light turquoise colour. Lola sat down on one of the plush seats.

Mary sat down next to Lola.

'Thank you, Lola. All I ask is that you remain here while I go and help the Blondies round up the others and that Maxwell. Don't worry – the Blondies won't harm you. I'll be back soon,' and with that, Mary left the ship, leaving Lola alone in this alien vessel with Mark. She looked around once more and wondered where it had all come from: was the planet nearby or millions of light years away? Was it bigger or smaller than Earth? What was the planet like? She was overcome with curiosity: she wanted to learn about this alien race, find out what they were like and whether they were similar to or different from humans. She wanted to go an interstellar voyage; she wanted to follow the path this ship had taken and arrive at their planet. It was somewhere unknown, somewhere alien, somewhere never seen by any human. She was picturing a planet in her mind, but knew that it was very far from its real counterpart.

First came the aliens, weird and wonderful to behold, strange and terrible, questionable and unknown, beautiful and mysterious: they were proof of extra-terrestrial life. Now, there were the ships, physical and wholly real, proof of the technological advancements and intelligence of said extra-terrestrials. With every new thing alien seen came so many more questions, and the realisation that there was a whole new world out there with an alien way of life, not necessarily different, and alien technologies, stories, languages, buildings, cities – did they even have cities? Was the planet similar to Earth in that respect or did it differ somehow? Lola had just assumed that all planets with intelligent life would have countries, cities, buildings and the like, but what if that were not the case? What if there were no big cities on the

Blondies' planet? What if they had no buildings but simply lived outdoors? What if their way of life was the complete opposite of the human way of life? All these questions and many more were racing through Lola's mind. One would come to the forefront bringing with it many more, each one of them in turn leading to more unanswered questions.

She saw in the distance the rest of the group standing in a circle, with Mary standing on a rock nearby.

'I understand that you may be frightened and confused, but I want you all to know that you can trust me when I say that the Blondies will get you safely to the mainland.'

Most of the people looked appalled; the Blondies were standing nearby looking down at the humans.

'I ask you all to trust me and the Blondies. We will ensure you make it to the mainland safe and sound.'

One woman passed out; the group reacted instantly: people rushed to comfort her, whilst the Blondies backed off a little. Mary got down and went over to help.

'Take her on board,' she instructed the Blondies, two of whom came through the parting crowd, picked the woman up and brought her on to the ship. They gently placed her in a chair a few rows down from Lola. As they did so, she caught a brief glimpse of a Blondie face: this particular alien looked apologetic and concerned. It looked tenderly at the woman and stroked her cheek.

'Right, everyone else, we're running out of time. If you don't get in the ship, we'll have to get you in by force,' Lola heard Mary say sternly.

'Don't get on that ship! They can't be trusted.' Lola heard Maxwell shout. She saw he was being restrained by one of the Blondies.

She then saw the two Blondies leave the ship, one of them carrying a large silver case. Lola's question was answered when a few moments later she saw the frightened crowd, still refusing to get on the ship, including Maxwell, who was staring directly at Lola sternly.

'Right, get them done,' Mary sighed.

'This won't hurt; it's for your safety,' she reassured the group. The Blondie with the case set it down on the ground by Mary and opened it. Inside was a black device with a few buttons on it. Mary reassured the group once again; they were surrounded by the Blondies, Maxwell having been let go. Mary ran back to the ship and up the ramp. Shouts and cries of fear and ignorance were coming from the group; a few were yelling at Mary to save them, others were yelling abuse at her and the Blondies. The wails were horrible to listen to.

There were a few noises from the small device and then a beep that lasted for a few seconds. Once it stopped, the frightened all started looking dizzy and swaying on the spot then, one by one, they softly fell to the ground: all seemed to be asleep.

'Are they asleep?' a worried Lola asked Mary.

'Yes. Don't worry. They'll wake up in about ten minutes. We only did this to get them on the ship.' Mary replied; despite her reassurance, Lola was uncertain what to make of this, however she appreciated the Blondies' humane approach to the situation.

Within a few minutes, the Blondies and Mary had collectively carried all the people on to the ship and had set them down either on chairs or, as there weren't enough chairs, on the floor.

'Lola, Mark, we're going to take off right now. It's going to be a very fast ride so you need to buckle up.' Mary told them, fastening the seatbelt of the sleeping person next to Lola.

'OK,' replied Lola; she looked out of one of the windows and saw they were indeed leaving the ground. Excitement bubbled in Lola: she felt tingly and nervous yet couldn't believe she was in an alien ship about to fly across to the mainland.

The ship continued to rise. Lola felt nothing out of the ordinary. Then it tilted to one side and started accelerating. As it did so, Lola felt slightly heavier, but then that ceased.

'Lola, are you okay' Mary asked; she came and sat down next to her.

'I'll be fine once I have some answers.'

'What do you want to know?' Mary said after a few moments' pause

'Can I *really* trust you? You keep asking me to yet up till now I thought you were working for Assa.'

'I do work for Assa, but what Assa doesn't know is that I am against everything Assa is doing. That is why I am really in allegiance with the Blondies. I had to take part in that fake interruption during the Prime Minister's speech to persuade people to go to the stadium and I had to kidnap you and others and take you to the mountain, as did Harold, because we were told to by Assa; if we disobey Assa, we are killed; it's as simple as that and someone else takes over from us. Assa is currently searching for the orb and will eventually find out that the Blondies managed to find you all and take you back to the mainland; the Blondies will, very kindly, not mention my participation so hopefully Harold and Assa won't find out,' Mary looked anxious.

'Who has the orb? Who were those people who shot Assa?'

'I don't know. None of us does. They're a third party. All we know is that they appear to be on our side and seem intent on destroying Assa, which is very good.'

'So you don't know where the orb is?'

'If the orb really was on that helicopter, Assa will have immediately found it: the orb is indestructible so will have simply fallen to the ground without a scratch on it. However, if the orb was *not* on the helicopter, which I suspect it wasn't, Assa will still be looking for it. I have confidence that that third party will have had the sense to ensure the orb was not on that helicopter.'

'So you think the helicopter was a diversion?'

'I can't say for sure because I don't know for definite. I hope so though and think it very likely; you don't know how much I hope so, Lola. I thought all this would never happen but then when Assa and Hyuul came to Earth I knew it was going to start all over again. I even had a breakdown but I was persuaded to throw myself back into work,' Mary stopped speaking and looked down into her lap.

'You have to trust me, OK? Once all the others are here, we'll get going and you'll be on the mainland soon.

'Why do you keep asking me to trust you?'

'Lola, everything is going to be okay. You're going to be okay, do you understand?' Mary iterated, though Lola saw the slightest hint of doubt in her face.

'Wait a minute. Your real name is Maude, isn't it? Mary's just your stage name?'

'Yes, why.'

'You know Natella. You're the one who met up with Natella!'

'How do you know that?'

'I was curious enough to follow her one day and overheard you both.'

'Well, yes, that's me. Most people don't know I'm actually called Maude Valentine.'

'So you're really on our side.'

'Of course. I was stupid to get taken in by Assa's promises and Susie's making sure I pay for my stupidity.'

'Who's Susie?'

'She is our boss. She tells us all what to do, especially me. She even had me keep the orb at mine before I dropped it off in Dazzle's office then she made me dump it in the sea, thinking it was the real one, when Assa could have been watching!'

Mary had been ranting, forgetting Lola was there.

'What happened to the real orb then?' Lola asked.

'I just recently found out that a man who works at the base on Etolin took the orb to Hyuul, who was being cared for. Hyuul made a duplicate and the man brought that back to Helmia while Hyuul hid the real one.'

'The night the Blondies came I checked Dazzle's office and saw the orb was gone. Had it already been taken by then?'

'Yes and I'd soon been made to drop a fake into the sea.'

'So why didn't Natella say anything?'

'Blimey, you do know a lot, Lola. I guess Natella didn't want you freaking out over the orb's location. She doesn't tell me much either. Because of my apparent betrayal to humanity I'm not kept in the loop much. We're nearly there,' Mary added after getting a sign from the Blondies.

Lola fell silent for once. Before she knew it, they had landed on the beach and the sleepers were being carried out and laid down gently on to the warm sand. She was led out of the ship afterwards by Mary. Quite a distance away was Old Merrington and its harbour, which was full of boats and ships, people leaving them in crowds.

'They'll be waking up soon. They'll be fine,' Mary reassured Lola, who looked down at the people and felt a pang of pity: she didn't agree with the way they were put to sleep, for they had no choice in the matter.

One of them started stirring: it was Maxwell. Within a few moments, he'd awoken and was on his feet scanning his surroundings.

'See, Maxwell, we're fine,' Lola told him.

'They've done something to us!' Maxwell insinuated, stepping back and pointing at the ship.

'No they haven't. I've been awake the whole time and nothing happened. They brought us here like they said they would.'

'I don't believe you.'

Just then a question came to Lola:

'If you don't trust aliens, then why did you follow Hyuul's orders? Why did you send that man in the top hat to retrieve the orb?'

'Because I was scared, alright! We had this alien shipped into the building and I had no idea how to deal with it. When it came to and started telling us what to do, we just obeyed because I was too afraid to not follow its orders.'

'Do you know who shot Assa?' Mary asked, 'because it wasn't anyone I know and your lot seem to know a lot about this.'

'It was Hyuul's idea. So I went along with it and sent some of my people to shoot Assa and retrieve the orb.'

'Where is the orb now?' Mary asked frantically.

'Hyuul will have it now. But don't worry, Assa won't have it anytime soon. Do you see why I don't trust aliens?'

'You'd start trusting them if you weren't so scared of them all the time,' Lola replied.

'Can you blame me?'

Mary spoke: 'we need to be leaving now. Maxwell, I hope this time Hyuul manages to hide it better than last time. I hope for all our sakes.'

And with that, Mary returned to the ship, which, after a few moments, started gracefully rising up into the air, a faint humming resounding everywhere along with its dazzling lights. Lola watched it intently as it rose higher and higher than tilted and started soaring over to Helmia.

There were few murmurs and groans coming from

nearby, but Lola drove them out of her mind. She sat down on the sand and looked out at her island home. She wondered whether she'd ever go back there again. There was something deep within her stirring: anger towards Assa and the Greys. She wanted to crush them all for the people they'd already killed and the atrocious plans they were intending to see through. Enmity was at the forefront; Lola's fear was secondary. She would not let anything hurt her family or her friends and would do everything she could do to ensure Assa would never be able to see the plans through.

The sea was calm and the sun was aglow. The island seemed to sparkle in the distance, as did the sea. Lola thought it a beautiful image; she'd never really had the opportunity to observe the island from a distance like this before. It was soothing to think that her entire world was there in the distance on that tiny island full of so much.

A few more people started stirring. Maxwell was sitting down with his head in his hands.

The worst thing about this scenario was that Lola didn't even know for certain who had managed to get off the island.

She watched the Blondie ship as it soared back to the island. It was a tiny speck now yet it was just visible. She knew what was going to happen before it did: right then and there, without warning, it exploded.

Coming soon:

The Darkness of Light:
The Everlasting Egg